The Accursed Realm

The Blood Gem

Kevin Morrison

PublishAmerica
Baltimore

First printing

ISBN: 1-4241-6023-5
PUBLISHED BY PUBLISHAMERICA, LLLP
www.publishamerica.com
Baltimore

Printed in the United States of America

I hereby dedicate this book to my friends at the video store.
You know who you are.

Acknowledgments

I would like to take the time to thank my family first for encouraging me in everything that I do. Peggy and Holly for reading my stuff in its early stages and giving me insight on relationships. Sue for your opinions on my writing style and the encyclopedia you gave me. Mary for your quick proofing and inspiration to get this published. Mike and William for your interest and willingness to read my manuscript. Brian for your technical know-how and helping me out of a few binds I had along the way. Dave for your role-playing know-how and your reference material for story telling. I would like to thank also all those involved at PublishAmerica for making this book possible.

Contents

Introduction

In the world of fantasy or dreams there are many realms. Imagine a realm that exists where nightmarish creatures or creatures of darkness are born and thrive.

Welcome to the Accursed Realm where creatures of the night thrive when the sun is down. Darkness is their friend and for the humans living becomes survival. Some night creatures live in harmony with humans while others are constantly trying to tip the balance of power. Have no fear, for all of the dark brethren are weak, slumbering, or hiding when the sun rises. With the creatures of the night a constant threat to the humans, bounty hunters, slayers, and other vigilantes, whether lawful or not, hunt them from every corner.

In the beginning humans thrived in the world and practically conquered everything. Technology had advanced to the point of space travel and possible colonization of other habitable planets. At that time mankind decided to work for the benefit of all. Wars began to dwindle to the point of very small skirmishes that were dealt with so quickly that they were soon forgotten. It was a new age of excellence and complacency was spreading among them like a cancer. It seemed all challenges in the world to excel had been met. Every known disease had a cure and life spans had been expanded to the point that a person could live for two hundred years. Genetic defects had been virtually eliminated from the gene pool of humanity. Humans marveled at their scientific and medical accomplishments. They began to think of themselves as gods, the source of all the answers to problems. Their creator frowned upon such arrogance. Soon afterwards most of society relied on itself and had forsaken its creator.

Although most of the world had been civilized and charted at this time, there were still remote areas to explore. A very large island was discovered at this time. This uncharted island was virtually invisible to present technological scanning equipment for unexplainable reasons. Some theorized that it could have been Atlantis, the lost continent. This uncharted area of the world was named Genesha, a place untouched by the hand of man until now. Like any uncharted area, humans began to develop it and vast civilizations where spawned. Researchers of all kinds and fortune hunters flocked to the island to discover its many treasures. One of its treasures was a mysterious box of unknown origin. There were no designs or distinguishable markings except for an inscription on the lid of the box. The inscription was written in an ancient language, possibly from biblical times. The inscription was translated and read: *Misfortune awaits all who seek it.*

The founders contemplated on whether they should do a more in-depth study of the box or venture on opening it. Humans, being the arrogant creatures that they were at this point, decided to open it. Once the box was opened, the fate of the island's inhabitants was sealed. Thus, the change of the island began and the outside world will never know the horror that took place.

All of the scientists who were at the excavation site of the box were forever changed by the dark mysterious power that was unleashed. The land area surrounding the site was destroyed and an unexplainable chain reaction began. Earthquakes, volcanic eruptions, floods and violent storms manifested all over the island. The disasters happened too frequently for the inhabitants to react fast enough. All major metropolitan areas and surrounding cities were leveled like an arrangement of dominoes. Dark clouds filled the skies, creating a perpetual darkness over the island. Several sightings of strange beasts were reported attacking anyone they came into contact with and devouring their flesh. Corpses were coming out of their graves and the dead walked among the living. Crazed humans started attacking people and draining them of their blood. Fiery creatures appeared from out of the shadows terrorizing the innocent. War broke out for the first time in a millennium, but this time it was not a war between nations. It was a war between the humans and these dark creatures that appeared when the night fell and soon would not end. Perpetual darkness covered the island at this time of great despair. Many tried to leave the island, while others attempted to call for aid. It seemed the island would not let anyone come in or leave at this point. Violent storms at sea sunk ships, while thunderous clouds grounded aircraft. Mist surrounded the island as the island simply vanished from the outside world. Mankind was on the verge of being eradicated or enslaved by the night creatures, a wretched ending to the highest life form in the world. Many believed the island was cursed at this point, doomed to face darkness with the gates of hell wide open for demons of all kinds to roam free. The island was then considered a totally different place, a realm shut off from the rest of the world. Little did they know the island disappeared from the real world and became a world or realm of its own, a realm of nightmares or the Accursed Realm.

The inhabitants began to look again to a higher power. Prayers for deliverance from this nightmare sought after their creator. The creator felt pity on them and decided to give a helping hand. When all hope seemed lost, the balance of power started to shift as the oppressors, named creatures of the night, started to fight each other. Soon, the demons where cast out of the area little by little. The darkness over the realm receded and daylight was seen once more. Sunlight repelled all the creatures of the night and literally killed some directly. Some of the humans were then blessed with gifts that gave them an edge in fighting the forces of darkness. The gifted or destined ones fought back and reclaimed their freedom from the tyranny of the night creatures. Complacency and arrogance of the humankind was over. Survival was now a new priority, since they were not alone in the realm anymore.

It was a new dark age and the creatures of the night were driven back to a stand still. Civilization was utterly destroyed, since all technology was fragmented, reduced to ashes, or forgotten. The complexity of civilization would recover, but it was going to take centuries to start from scratch. In essence the realm was wiped clean like a slate. Since the balance of power was shifted again, the humans now outnumbered the creatures of the night. Most of the night-bred kept to themselves and had few encounters with the inhabitants.

As centuries passed technology slowly advanced, society gradually rebuilt itself, and the night-bred learned to coexist with the humans within the shadows of the day and only being active at night. With the change of time treaties with creatures of the night and people were signed, behind closed doors and unofficially.

The mysterious box that supposedly caused all these catastrophes was never found. Theories have been noted that the box could have been the infamous Pandora's Box. Others believe it could have been the Ark of the Covenant. Some would go so far as to say that aliens placed the box to be found. Regardless as to what the answer is vampiric, were-kind, demonic, and other night-bred now exist in this realm and not all of them will share the realm without a fight. Hopefully, mankind will avoid being arrogant, highly regard their creator, and maintain a sense of harmony with the night-bred. Only time will tell.

Three major areas help define the Accursed Realm; they are magic, technology and civilization.

Magic by definition is the use of a special object containing properties for casting of spells or casting specific spells under one's own power. A magic caster can cast spells under his own power without the use of a magical object. It is estimated that half of the humans and creatures of the night use magical items or have the ability to casts spells. Magic use is partially accepted, but still feared among ordinary humans and weaker creatures of the night.

Technology by definition consists of the complexity of humans and creatures of the night using machines to do everyday things. It is further broken down into three general areas: transportation, weapons, and medicine. Every household commonly has appliances and electrical power. Automobiles, planes, ships, and other related vehicles are widely used. Weapons consist of all kinds of metal blades, various batons, firearms, cannons, bombs and missiles. The firearms can fire bullets, grenades, stakes, and shot shells. Most blades and ammunition is silver based, since most creatures of the night have a weakness toward it. The practice of medicine is moderately advanced. Surgery is commonplace, but is limited to organ transplants, blood transfusions, and foreign-object extraction.

Civilization by definition is the complexity of how society in the realm lives together. It is further sectioned into three general areas: government, law enforcement, and military. Several major metropolises now exist, connected together with a vast network of subways, highways, railways and airplane routes. The government regulates everything. Every human has a living record registered with the government. Nocturnal activities are not something the government can regulate, since most of those activities happen in the shadows of society. An elected president governs the vast city areas.

The law is enforced by an elite multitask force. Since human law enforcement is beyond the scope of nocturnal activities, mercenaries, like bounty hunters and slayers, are hired to eradicate certain creatures of the night. Creatures of the night, who are involved in a crime against humans, are not brought to trial or imprisoned. They are exterminated. Suspected humans are brought to trial and cross-examined by a psychic. Lawyers are found to be obsolete in this type of system. The guilty are punished by a predetermined assignment to the crime committed. A human with a history of three offenses is sentenced to death. There are not appeals or exceptions, unless the president of the city area pardons them. The military is a specialized security force, consisting of soldiers and attack vehicles to defend the major city areas from outside invaders. Bounty hunters and others defend the inner part of the city. Bodyguards such as slayers, casters, and constructs or a combination of the three defend the inner core of the city.

Chapter 1
The Fortress of Light

Our story begins on the hour of midnight five hundred years in the past in the outskirts of the kingdom called Demicroft in a place known as the fortress of light. Demicroft was well known as the city of demons. Demons roamed more frequently here in this area than any other major civilized area, since they were more easily summoned here compared to other areas of the realm. If you were looking for a dark priest, demon knight, or a beast master, the practitioners of demonic manipulation, this was a good place to search for them. Many statues and fountains depicting demons or angels were common in the area.

Technology, five hundred years in the past, was at a very low level at this time. Life was simple and every person had a role to perform in his society. Every household had well water with no indoor plumbing, simple farming of crops with livestock, and simple tools for everyday tasks. People drove animal-pulled carriages, rode horses, paddled small canoes, sailed larger boats, or simply walked to satisfy their transportation needs. Weapons were simple and required low maintenance. Depending on the person or group, various blades, arrows, catapults, and one-shot pistols were used. Some swords, daggers, and ammunition were made of silver, since most creatures of the night have a weakness toward it; otherwise they were made of steel. Medicine was created by the use of refining herbs and animal extracts. Medical treatment was rendered by use of medicine, simple surgery, or healing magic.

The kingdom of Demicroft, five hundred years in the past, consisted of small villages surrounding a castle. Obviously a king and queen sat on a throne at this time to rule over the kingdom. The castle had three different types of guards at the king's disposal. One group was an elite set of guards to protect the king at all times within the castle grounds. Another set would keep the laws enforced and maintain order among the villagers. The third set was established to protect the kingdom from forces threatening the interior and the outside boundaries from invaders. At this time lawbreakers were brought before the king to settle disputes and pass judgment on the crime committed. Lawyers or representatives were used in this type of trial, but were not always effective. The fate of the lawbreaker was therefore firmly in the hands of the king.

The fortress of light was a rebel stronghold and had become a thorn in the king's side, since it housed many rebels as well as many powerful magical items. It was a fortress built and carved on top of a giant pillar-shaped rock formation that was immeasurably high and surrounded by water at the base. The tide was calm and did not cause a threat to the pillar, because the fortress was protected by magic. Only small boats could possibly dock at the base of the pillar. Road access to the fortress' main gate was a very thick and wide natural bridge that connected it to the mainland. The natural bridge on the mainland side was connected to a very steep cliff with no beach below to the water. From an area view the fortress was hexagonal in shape with three levels. Like a layered wedding cake, each level became smaller in size, except the height of the walls remained the same, as it progressed from the bottom up. Each corner, where the walls met, was a circular landing with walkways connecting all landings on that particular level. The circular landings had average-waist-level walls with three gaps in the top of the wall for the soldier firing positions. Each landing had three oil-burning torches spaced out between the gaps on the wall, a set of stairs leading down to the roof of that level, a wooden barrel full of oil, and a wooden crate full of crossbows with many arrows. A staircase, starting from the base of the first level and facing north to the sea, was cut into the pillar that spiraled all the way down to the sea level for access by boat, essentially connecting the fortress to the sea for small supply boats or a possible escape route.

The water level surrounding the pillar was shallow in comparison to the water level at sea, which made it impossible for a very large ship to dock at the base of the pillar. Because of this, an invasion by sea would be unheard of and very little protection was thought to be needed.

A very small guard station, made out of stone, was built into the rock formation, capable of housing two guards overlooking the small docking area. Access to the guard station was possible by a simple ladder cut into the rock, connecting the spiral steps to the back of the guard station. The roof of the guard station was made of wood and the windows, which spanned the only two walls overlooking the area, were only a foot high to allow for the guards to duck below the wall in case of enemy fire. Outside of the block-shaped guard post were two oil-burning torches, one on each corner to illuminate the dock area at night.

Two guards occupied the guard post all the time in case of a small band of robbers attempting to infiltrate the fortress from below. All of the guards of the fortress were armored from head to toe in steel, plated armor. They all wore round-shaped helmets with a slotted face shield that could be lifted when needed, breastplates with a cross symbol in the center, armor skirts, greaves, and gauntlets made of leather and steel on the top. Under their armor pieces were chain mail, cloth garments, and socks. All guards were armed with steel broadswords and daggers. Their broadswords were four feet long and three inches wide and their daggers were a foot long and two inches wide. The double-edged swords and daggers had leather-wrapped handles with a cross engraved into the base of the blades. Leather sheaths contained the broadswords on their backs and the daggers were sheathed on a leather belt that buckled around their waists.

The guard post was stocked with provisions of dried food and water as well as a few crossbows and many arrows neatly stacked in a wooden crate for easy access. At the base of the staircase the wooden dock spanned around the pillar for about ten feet lengthwise. The dock was five feet wide with four three-feet-high posts connecting to it evenly spaced on the edge spanning the dock. An oil-burning torch was mounted on the furthest post out on the end of the dock. A small wooden rowboat, no more than ten feet long and four feet wide, was tied at the same last post.

On this night thick fog engulfed the area at sea and on the land. The light from the torches outside of the guard post and on the dock were not nearly enough to illuminate the area in this thick fog. Because of the thick fog, the guards at the guard post could not see anything clearly ten feet out from the edge of the dock. Fifty feet from the dock a rowboat slowly approached carrying two people, a man and a woman.

The man, who stood five feet eight inches tall, was dressed like a priest in a charcoal-gray-colored robe and cloak. On his head he wore a rimless hat that looked like a layer of a cake and matched the color of his robe. His feet were covered by a set of black leather calf-length boots. The robe and cloak did an excellent job of hiding his thin-type build. Most priests wore white garments in comparison, but he was clearly not a light priest at all. Around his neck he wore a pentagram symbol connected by a small chain, made out of steel that hung down to the middle of his chest. This was no ordinary man with pale skin, brown eyes, short black hair, thick eyebrows and a long gouty, extending down to the base of his neck. Judging from his facial features and hands, he could have been possibly forty years old. He had no visible weapons to speak of, but he was indeed an evil man imbued with dark magic. The man was undoubtedly a dark priest, the most powerful practitioner of summoning and manipulating demons.

The woman with him, who stood six feet tall, was a servant of the dark priest. Compared to him, her skin was golden brown and more youthful looking. Her beauty was beyond comparison with long thick shimmering white hair that hung all the way down to her behind and an irregular saw-tooth hairline that complemented her facial features. Eyes; *clear as blue water on an icy lake during winter* described hers perfectly. Judging from her lovely facial features and youthful-looking body, her age could have possibly been twenty-five years. She could have easily passed for an Amazon, with her muscle-toned arms, legs, and a firm-looking waist. Her firm breasts were quite large for her physique, but did not hinder her in any way. The servant was dressed in a leather vest, skirt, boots, forearm bands and a cloak. All of her garments were the same black color, except her hooded cloak was dark brown. Her midriff was bare, since neither the vest nor the skirt covered it. The vest supported her breasts well and accented her cleavage. It was fine made with stitching starting from the bottom of her breasts to the bottom of the vest in the front. Her skirt had similar stitching like her vest, across the waist and down one side half of the length of the skirt; the rest of the skirt was open like a slit on that side. The woman's medium-heel boots were calf-length and fine made with stitching in the front down to the foot. Her forearm bands were simply made and covered her forearms. The hooded cloak she wore was held together by a golden broach with a red heart-shaped gem in the center. A pair of golden hoop earrings about three inches in diameter decorated her ears. Hanging off of her hip was a large belt holding a sheathed sword. The leather belt was dark brown in color with a golden buckle to fasten it to her waist. Her sword had a single-edged curved blade about three feet in length with a leather-wrapped handle.

She asked, "Master, what is the plan?"

He replied, "After you have taken care of the guards at the dock, I shall summon my soldiers to aid us."

She inquired, "How should I take care of them, master?"

The dark priest responded with a devilish grin, "You may feed on them if you like, but they must die. I know it has been a while since you fed last."

She slowly agreed, "It has, master."

The dark priest continued, "My oafs will climb the pillar, while we climb the steps to the top. The guards will be overwhelmed when they attack."

The servant inquired, "Are you sure they will not be alerted by their presence, master?"

He replied, "No, between the fog covering the area and the attack on the front gate, the element of surprise will be on our side."

"The rear of the fortress will be undefended for us to enter with ease," said she.

"Precisely, the fools will not know what hit them," remarked the dark priest.

As the boat slowly approached the dock the servant was lying down and pretending to be unconscious. The dark priest was hiding from view under a gray tarp. At this time one of the guards noticed the boat approaching.

"I see a boat is approaching," said the first dock guard.

The second dock guard replied, "Let's check it out."

Both of the guards left the guard post and met the boat coming in at the dock. The first dock guard grabbed the edge of the boat and tied it off at the second post on the dock.

The second dock guard took a closer look at the boat. "What's this?" He noticed the servant lying in the boat.

The first dock guard noticed his reaction and said, "What did you find?"

"A woman," replied the second dock guard.

The first dock guard came over to look for himself and said, "Let's get her out of the boat. She's either unconscious or dead." The second dock guard helped him lift her out of the boat.

The first dock guard commented, "She's a big one. I like a woman that has some meat on her bones."

They laughed as they set her down on the dock.

The second dock guard took off his helmet, set it down, and placed his head on her chest to listen for a heartbeat.

The first dock guard looked at her and inquired, "Well?"

The second dock guard lifted his head up, looked at him, and said, "She's breathing normally and her heartbeat is strong, but she seems to be unconscious."

The first dock guard said, "We should check her for injuries."

With lust in his eyes the second dock guard smiled and agreed, "Good idea. I'll start with the torso." He took his gloves off and dropped them.

The first dock guard turned away and looked around for anything else coming in the thick fog.

The second dock guard looked down on her chest as he unfastened her top. He pulled her vest open and exposed her breasts. He commented, "Very nice. Check out these puppies. I would love to bed this one."

The first dock guard responded, "This is not sport and I said check for injuries, not undress and molest the lady."

The second dock guard replied, "I meant when she wakes up."

"Sure you did," said the first dock guard.

"What's wrong with you?" asked the second dock guard.

The first dock guard responded, "I don't like this. We might be under attack."

The second dock guard said, "You have got to be kidding. No one has ever successfully attacked the Fortress of Light and succeeded."

"There is always a first time," said the first dock guard.

Immediately her eyes opened as she slashed the second dock guard's throat with her razor-sharp fingernails. Even with chain mail covering his throat, her inhuman fingernails cut through it like paper.

He hunched over from the shock and started to choke.

She quickly grabbed her sword handle, while the first dock guard was distracted by the other choking.

With concern the first dock guard looked at him and said, "What's wrong?"

The servant drew her sword from her sheath and violently thrust her blade through the first dock guard's thick armor, permeating his gut. Without hesitation she pulled the blade out of his gut.

He automatically fell backward after being freed from the blade.

The servant pushed the second dock guard off of her like a soon-to-be-dead carcass slowly bleeding to death. Immediately she refastened her vest and tied off the leather lace. She scowled, "That pig would have tried to mount me if the other guard had not said anything." She crawled over to where the first dock guard lay and straddled his gut, as she looked him in the eyes.

He responded in a weak voice, "Who are you?"

The servant answered as she removed his helmet and tossed it aside, "That does not matter now. Your concern for me was touching even though in vain. Sorry, I was only following orders. Relax and I'll ease your pain." She gently placed her hand on his chin and brought her lips to his as to kiss him.

For a brief moment he felt no pain and slowly drifted away, losing consciousness as she drained him of his remaining life energy. When she was finished, his body was a shriveled-up corpse. The servant was a high-level succubus, one of many kinds of demonic minions used by dark priests. She stood up as the dark priest came out from under the tarp in the boat.

He got on to the dock and said to her, "Well done."

She responded as she wiped the blood off of her sword with a dark rag from the boat, "I am finished, master."

The dark priest drew closer to her as he noticed the blood that was splashed on her chest from one of the guards. "Good. Stand still," ordered the dark priest.

The servant had a look of disgust on her face as she stood there and let him lick the blood off of her chest.

When he was done he said, "That's better."

"You're disgusting, master," retorted the woman.

The dark priest grabbed her chin and responded, "Your body does not interest me at all. Do not forget, Kescha, it was I who summoned you. Your abilities are my only interest and they belong to me."

Kescha defiantly responded, "Master, if you wish to scold me, now is not a wise time to do so."

Although she was right, he did not agree, but smiled and said, "Your intelligence does seem to outweigh your insolence at times. Let's proceed. Shall we?"

She nodded as he pulled from his garments a couple of orbs, the size of a baseball. Both of them were dark in color and had the appearance of glass. He held them out in front of him and said, "Come to my aid, my soldier demons."

The two orbs began to glow a bright purple color as four very large demonic creatures emerged from each orb and landed on the dock. Soldier demons were called oafs, which stood about seven feet tall and had red-colored skin.

Fearsome in appearance, they had a solid muscular build like a professional weight lifter. They had small horns protruding from the top of their heads pointing to the rear of them. Their thick three fingers and thumb-like hands had four-inch-long razor-sharp claws, as did their three-toed feet, which were only two inches in length. Both their claws and horns were dark in color with a glossy look. At the base of their spine was a thick three-foot-long tail that tapered to a point and touched the ground when they would squat. Three yellow narrow-pupil eyes forming a triangle were seen on their hideous faces. A flat nose, slightly pointed ears, and jagged teeth finished off the face. With a large chin to house such a big mouth, two bicuspids protruded from their lower jaws. Oafs were expendable soldier demons to their master. They were fearless, followed orders of their master without question, vicious in battle, felt no pain, and not very intelligent.

"Go, my minions, kill the guards. Leave only the maidens alive," ordered the dark priest.

All eight oafs began to spread out and started to climb the pillar. With their long and sharp claws, the task was easy and effortless to scale the rock.

At this time the dark priest's three henchmen arrived on horses thirty feet from the gate, leading to the natural bridge connecting the mainland to the Fortress of Light. The gate, which faced south, was a very tall rock formation, shaped similar to a trapezoid. At the base of the gate it measured around thirty to forty feet across and ten feet wide with a ten-foot-square hole cut into the bottom center. Over the outside of the hole were two ten-foot-tall and five-foot-wide heavy wooden doors to serve as the gate. The six-inch-thick doors were dark brown in color with a large cross carved on each. On top of the rock formation was a guard post, similar to the guard post overlooking the dock below. The main difference was this guard post could hold three guards. Behind the guard post was a ladder cut into the rock formation on both sides. Outside of the guard post in the front and above the gate were four oil-burning torches that the guards could easily reach to light when needed. Both guard posts also had an alarm, which was nothing more than a large horn that made a noise loud enough to be heard at the top of the pillar from either the front gate or the dock area. The horn was made from some kind of animal tusk, which was hollowed out. Inside the guard post the horn was mounted and curled up until it extended past the window and faced the sky, measuring at least three feet in length. Three guards were sitting in the guard post overlooking the area for any possible threat coming their way. These henchmen were no ordinary men for they could see through the darkness and fog without any trouble. They were creatures of the night, vampires. Unless they allow their vampiric side to come out, they can easily look like humans. Even thirty feet away, the fog was too thick to see the henchmen approaching. All three henchmen were riding their own horse, dressed in dark brown cloaks and various outfits.

With all three riding beside each other, the one leading the group was Flusken in the center. Drake on his right was second in command and Sinco on his left was following the both of them.

Flusken rode a black horse with no markings and a black mane. He stood about six feet tall with a thin-type build. His arm, leg, chest, and abdominal muscles were developed, but not as bulky. He had average looks with high cheekbones, a clean-shaven strong chin, short-length dark hair combed straight back, and brown eyes. His skin was pale. The only jewelry he wore was a small golden ring on the ring finger of his right hand. It was a square-shaped ring with a molded skull having fangs on the top of it. On the forehead of the skull was a letter D engraved. Most vampires receive a medallion or ring to symbolize their affiliation with the clan they are a part of. Under his hooded cloak he wore a dark brown leather coat, a loose-fitting collarless stitched shirt, a snug-fitting pair of pants that draped over his calf-length boots with stitches in the front of them. Around his waist he wore a black leather belt that fastened with a steel buckle. As far as weapons go Flusken carried a steel long sword in a sheath on another belt below his waist belt and a dagger sheathed on the same belt, fastened with a large steel buckle. His long sword was double-edged, five feet long, and three inches wide tapering down to a point with a leather-wrapped handle. The dagger, he carried, was double-edged, a foot long and two inches wide with a leather-wrapped handle. On the hilt of the sword was the fierce image of a skull.

Drake rode a white horse with no markings and a gray mane. He stood about six feet five inches tall with a macho-type build. His arm, leg, chest, and abdominal muscles were well developed, but not too bulky to slow him down. He was a handsome fellow, clean-shaven, with wild neck-length dark brown hair and saw-tooth bangs over his forehead, and brown eyes. His skin was fair. The only jewelry he wore was a small dangling golden earring in his left ear and a round golden medallion, hung by a chain around his neck. His medallion, the size of a fifty-cent piece, also had a skull molded on it, but a letter C was engraved in the forehead of it instead. Under his hooded cloak he wore a red long-sleeve collared buttoned shirt, a vest that draped all the way to his crotch, snug-fitting pants, and boots that were calf length with four buckles on the outside part. His vest was fastened together with four small evenly spaced steel buckles. Around his waist and over the vest he wore a brown leather belt that fastened with a steel buckle. As far as weapons go Drake carried only a steel broadsword in a sheath on his back that fastened in front over his vest diagonally with a large steel buckle. His broadsword was double-edged, almost as tall as him, and six inches wide tapering down to a point with a leather-wrapped handle. On the hilt of the sword was a flaming image of a skull.

Sinco rode a brown horse with no markings and had a dark brown mane. He stood about five feet ten inches tall with a solid-type build. His arm, leg, chest, and abdominal muscles were very developed, but he was very agile despite his bulkiness. He was an ugly man, with a neatly trimmed mustache, neck-length brown hair and even bangs over his forehead, and blue eyes. His skin was pale. The only jewelry he wore was a small golden ring, just like Flusken's, on the ring finger of his right hand. Under his hooded cloak he wore a brown sleeveless and collarless shirt with stitching up the sides and down the middle of the front, a loose-fitting pair of pants with similar stitching like his shirt, and calf-length boots with stitches in the front of them. As far as weapons go Sinco carried two steel sickles sheathed on the same waist belt with a large steel buckle and a few steel throwing daggers on either side of it. The throwing daggers had three-inch-long handles with four-inch-long double-edged blades. His sickles were single-edged, three feet long, three inches wide, and crescent shaped that tapered down to a point with leather-wrapped handles.

At thirty feet away the henchmen stopped in front of the gate, while still on their horses.

"The guards cannot see us," commented Drake.

"But we can see all three of them," replied Sinco.

"Sinco, take out the guards," ordered Flusken.

"Okay ," answered Sinco. He grabbed three of his throwing daggers and quickly threw them in a row, one after the other at the unsuspecting guards. The daggers flew straight through the fog with no resistance.

The first dagger hit the first gate guard in the throat as he fell backward from the shock and started choking as the blood began to slowly leak out of the wound.

The second dagger hit the second gate guard in his right eye as the shock killed him instantly.

The third dagger hit the third gate guard in his breastplate. He was the fortunate one for his armor was thick enough to stop the throwing dagger from harming him. Surprised by the sight of the dagger, he pulled the dagger out. He turned to the others beside him and noticed the first gate guard was lying down and the second gate guard was sitting still. At first he didn't notice the second gate guard was bleeding when he touched his shoulder. "What are you doing? Ready the weapons! I'll sound the alarm," said he.

Instantly, he fell backwards as the third gate guard looked in disbelief.

"What's wrong?" asked the third gate guard as he noticed blood on the floor and where it was coming from. "This can't be happening!" screamed he as he dropped the dagger. He crawled over their dead bodies as he went over to sound the alarm. Within seconds the horn alarm was sounded and everyone within a three-hundred-yard radius could hear it.

Where the natural bridge connected to the fortress was a main gate with a guard lookout above it. The main gate consisted of two ten-foot-tall and five-foot-wide heavy steel doors. The three-inch-thick doors were dark in color with a large cross engraved on each. The guard lookout was wide enough for three to four guards with five two-foot squares evenly spaced above the gate.

At the look out of the main gate the three guards took notice of the horn sounding and responded promptly.

"Ready the weapons!" ordered the first lookout guard. Immediately, the second and third lookout guards grabbed a crossbow and positioned themselves by a window, while the first one looked upon the outside gate. Of course in the presently thick fog a mere human could have seen nothing.

In the barracks of the fortress on the first level the commander, the commander of the guard, was found relaxing in his chambers. The barracks of the fortress consisted of four rooms, twenty wooden bunk beds in each, to accommodate forty guards. At the end of the barracks was the commander's room, which was simple as far as layout. Inside was a bed in the one corner of the room with a four-legged wooden nightstand beside it. On the top of the nightstand was a simple round candleholder. At the opposite side of the room was a small wooden desk with a wooden chair. On the desk were an ink holder and quill for writing letters and another candleholder. Both candles in the room were lit at the time.

Currently, the commander was in the sitting at the desk writing a letter. His brawny looks were obvious with a few battle scars on his arms as proof of his experience in battle. He stood five feet ten inches tall with a macho-type build. His brown hair was scruffy looking with a thick mustache and eyebrows to match. The man's rough exterior had a strong presence, but his brown eyes had a sort of softness to them. He was wearing a cloth shirt, leather trousers and calf-length boots. The letter read, "My dear beloved, I miss you so much. So far we have been able to fend off the enemy and have held strong in the fortress of light. However, the enemy is cunning and I wonder now if it was wise to bring the item in question here. This accursed bordering kingdom of Demicroft is plagued with evil, an evil I cannot put into words. We must move the item soon for I fear the enemy is planning to strike at us when we least expect it. Currently, this ghastly fog, which has lasted for six days and nights, hinders our pathway and until it lifts, we are trapped here. I fear this moment in time will be the best opportunity for the enemy to attack. This feeling of what is to come makes me so restless that I cannot sleep. For it is not the day I am concerned with being attacked by the enemy, it is the night. When the fog lifts, I shall be on my way to see you soon. Until then, I send my love and long for your warmth."

He was about to sign it, when he heard the horn sound from outside. Without hesitation he put down the ink quill and got up from the desk.

Meanwhile back at the front gate of the fortress, Flusken turned to Sinco and said, "You idiot. You missed one of the guards and our presence has been alerted."

"So much for the silent approach, Flusken, I guess it won't matter now if we really make some noise," replied Drake.

Sinco answered, "That's okay . I have more to use." Sinco took another dagger and threw it at the last guard. The dagger hit him in the side of the neck. He was stunned and fell over as the blood leaked out of the wound.

Drake got off of his horse and walked a few feet away from the group and straight toward the gate. With his right arm extended and palm facing out toward the gate he uttered these words, "Stream of running flame, burn a path through any obstacle!"

Instantly, a stream of fire, four feet in diameter, formed from his right hand and quickly flew toward the gate. Upon impact, the stream of fire burned all the way through the thick wooded doors, like a hot knife through butter. The stream of fire continued through the front gate and hit the main gate of the fortress, where the flames dispersed.

Drake returned to his horse and mounted it. He turned to Flusken and said, "It appears the main gate is made out of metal. I like a challenge."

"Let's go," ordered Flusken. The three of them on their horses galloped toward the front gate.

At the main gate the commander arrived in full armor like the other guards. The only difference was he had a tail of horsehair coming out of the top of his helmet. "What's going on?" inquired the commander.

"We are under attack, commander," answered the first lookout guard.

"Explain," replied the commander.

The first lookout guard looked at him and said, "We don't know who the enemy is, but they used fire that ran like a stream to burn through the front gate. The fire was so powerful that it continued on until the main gate stopped it. What kind of catapult could be that powerful, commander?"

"That was no catapult. They have a magic caster among them," answered the commander. He shook his head. He put his hand on the shoulder of the first lookout guard and said, "The true enemy has arrived. I am leaving you in charge of the main gate. I must alert the priestess and see to her safety. Hold them off as long as you can."

The first lookout guard questioned, "But, commander, you speak as if you shall not return."

"I fear this is a battle we may not win. In that case I selfishly ask for your oath to be fulfilled this night and prepare to die if necessary to protect the priestess. My place is by the priestess's side and to defend her to thy death. Is that understood?"

"Yes, commander, we shall honor that oath and defend the fortress of light until death befalls us all," answered the first lookout guard.

The commander turned to leave, but stopped, faced the first lookout guard again, and said, "May God be with us all."

"Amen," replied the first lookout guard. The commander quickly went on his way to where the priestess was.

Drake and the others left their horses behind at the front gate and continued on foot across the natural bridge toward the main gate. When they were within ten feet of the main gate the guards in the guard post spotted them.

"There's only three of them," commented the second lookout guard as they all aimed their crossbows.

"Fire!" ordered the first lookout guard. The three guards fired their crossbows at Flusken, Drake, and Sinco. Flusken, Drake, and Sinco stopped at the same time, while catching an arrow shot at each of them.

Flusken turned to Drake and Sinco and said, "Sinco, take care of those guards. Drake, take out the main gate."

"Okay ," said Sinco as he took the arrows from Drake and Flusken.

"I have just the thing," replied Drake. Drake pulled a black orb out of his pocket, just like one that the dark priest used, and commanded, "Hell bull, come forth!"

Instantly, a demonic creature magically emerged from the purple glowing sphere. The demonic creature was a low-class demon beast called a hell bull. Drake was a demon knight, another practitioner of the demonic arts. Unlike the dark priest who could cast many kinds of spells and control most demon class types, Drake could only cast certain spells and control medium-class and lower-class demons.

A hell bull was about the same size as a regular bull with a hellish make-over. Its overall body was the same size as a bull, but it had thicker legs and a wider jaw. Instead of two eyes it had four altogether, two on each side of its head. It had a flat nose and a very wide mouth with large razor-sharp teeth. Its horns were twice as long and thick as a normal bull's. It had a tail, which was twice as long and thick. Considering its size, it was faster and more maneuverable than you would think.

"Ram the gate," ordered Drake.

Without hesitation the hell bull charged at the gate and struck it with its head.

At the same time Sinco jumped ten feet in the air and threw all three arrows at the guards above them. The first arrow hit the first lookout guard in the eye, which killed him instantly and he fell backward. A second arrow hit the second lookout guard in the Adam's apple, which stunned him as he fell forward. The first lookout guard was lucky for the second lookout guard was still alive and suffered a slower and more painful death. A third arrow hit the third lookout guard's shoulder as he ducked for cover.

Surprised by all that happened to the first and second lookout guard, the third lookout guard quickly left the guard post and entered the main room where the main gate was below.

Behind the guard post and the main gate was a circular room, the main lobby of the fortress of light. Stone steps led from either side of a platform, connecting to the guard post, against the walls all the way down to the rock floor of the main lobby. Three oil-burning torches were mounted on each of the walls with stairs to light the room. The room was very spacious and the stone ceiling was about twenty feet high. On the other side of the room was an eight-foot-tall doorway with three-inch-thick wooden doors that formed a point at the top. In front of the closed door were three guards standing in ready with their broadswords unsheathed. On both sides of the stairs were four guards with crossbows evenly spaced standing in ready for what might breach the gate. Behind the main gate doors, three wooden boards were placed on three different levels of the doors to brace them.

Upon entering the main room and standing on the landing, the third lookout guard shouted, "They're coming!"

The hell bull began to ram the gate with its large thick head.

The guards held their positions, even though the sense of fear began to seep into the room.

Repeatedly, the hell bull rammed the doors as cracks and splinters formed on the bracing boards. The tension began to build in the room as the boards began to splinter and break. Finally, the wooden boards gave way and the heavy gate swung open as the hell bull ran inside the room.

Fear had its grasp on a few guards holding crossbows as they hesitated to attack the hellish beast.

"Have courage, men, and send that creature back to hell!" yelled the third lookout guard.

The four lobby guards on the right side of the stairs fired their crossbows at it.

The hell bull saw the arrows coming and charged up the steps after the guards that shot at it. The beast was so quick that the guards could not react in time to draw their swords or reload their crossbows. The first lobby guard was speared in the belly by one of its horns as it tossed him off of its horn and onto the floor below. The hell bull continued up the stairs as it grabbed a hold of the second lobby guard's arm and bit it off.

He screamed in pain as he fell off the stairs.

The third lobby guard dodged to no avail as the hell bull speared him through his throat. Without hesitation he was tossed off the stairs like a rag doll as the blood sprayed over the floor.

The fourth lobby guard was frozen with fear as the hell bull came toward him and speared him with one its horns on his inner thigh. He lost his balance as he writhed in pain and fell off the stairs landing on top of one of the other guards lying on the floor.

As the hell bull approached the landing the third lookout guard shouted, "Shoot it! Shoot it now!"

The hell bull stopped within a few feet of him and looked at him.

The four lobby guards on the left side of the room fired their crossbows at the beast. All of the arrows hit it, but none of the wounds were fatal.

At this point the hell bull lashed out its immeasurable tongue and ensnared the neck of the third lookout guard. He struggled as the hell bull picked him up and tossed him on to the floor below. Unfortunately, he landed on the top of his head, which crushed his skull instantly.

Drake and the others entered the room as the guards, still standing, scrabbled to reload their weapons. Drake held out his left hand, holding a black orb, and said, "That's a good boy. We'll take it from here."

Instantly, the hell bull magically turned into smoke and returned to the purple glowing orb.

The fifth lobby guard shouted, "Fire!"

The four guards on the left side fired their crossbows at the others.

Drake quickly drew his sword and deflected three of the arrows.

Sinco caught one and threw it back. The arrow flew back and struck the eighth guard in the eye. He went into shock and fell off the stairs.

The five guards in front of the door were the door guards. They looked different in appearance from the guards in the lobby and outside, since they all wore blue capes. All of the door guards approached Drake and the others. "Who are you?" questioned the first door guard.

"You may not live long enough to find out," answered Drake. "You two go ahead I'll take care of these guards," ordered Flusken.

Drake looked at Flusken and said, "Suit yourself. I don't think these guards could give me much a challenge any way."

"I want the top level," replied Sinco.

The first door guard spoke up, "No one will get past this level as long as we are alive."

Drake smiled, put his sword away, and jumped over top of the five door guards.

Before they could react, Sinco ran in between the second and third door guard and slashed their throats with his large sickles.

The first door guard was surprised, but boldly said, "Come back here, coward, and face me."

Drake landed, turned around, and drew his sword. Instead of facing him, he threw his sword directly at him. The sword went flying through the air spinning and speared him in the chest through his armor. Drake held out his hand and mentally retracted his sword. His sword flew back to him as he caught it in the air. He whisked the blood off his sword, put it away and said, "You're not worth it."

"Why didn't you taste the blood?" questioned Sinco.

Drake shook his head as they were walking toward the door and responded, "I don't lick my weapons like you do." Sinco laughed fiendishly as he followed Drake out of the room.

Flusken stood in the middle of the room and motioned with his hand for the all of the guards to encircle him. With Flusken facing the doorway the fourth and fifth door guards approached him from his left side.

The three remaining lobby guards dropped their crossbows, descended the stairs, and approached Flusken from his right side.

"You are a foolish man to be taking on all of us at once," voiced the fifth lobby guard.

"I am not a man like yourselves," remarked Flusken.

All of the guards encircled Flusken from a few feet away, the fifth lobby guard faced him, the sixth on Flusken's right, the seventh behind Flusken and beside the sixth, the fourth door guard on Flusken's left, and the fifth behind Flusken and beside the fourth door guard. At the same time all of the guards drew their swords from their backs. In response Flusken drew his sword as well. There was a slight pause as no one moved a muscle, while the tension began to fill the room.

The fifth and sixth lobby guard broke the stillness and rushed in first to attack Flusken.

Flusken ducked below the fifth lobby guard's attack, tripped him, and parried the sixth's side attack. Instantly, Flusken kicked the sixth lobby guard in the gut, which drove him back a few feet.

The fifth door guard then saw an opening and rushed in from behind to attack Flusken.

Flusken sensed his approach, turned in his direction and stabbed him through his breastplate and into his chest. Without hesitation Flusken retracted his sword effortlessly as the fifth door guard dropped to his knees and fell forward dead on the floor.

The fourth door guard took a chance and attacked Flusken from the side. In a continuous move Flusken parried his attack and swung back and cut his head off. The lifeless carcass fell backward, hitting the floor like a chopped-down or uprooted tree.

With Flusken's back turned to the seventh lobby guard, he tried to attack Flusken with a forward thrust attack.

Flusken anticipated a rear attack and sidestepped as he charged in. While sidestepping, Flusken countered and stabbed the seventh lobby guard's throat. He fell over dead on his side as Flusken retracted the blade.

At this time the fifth and sixth lobby guards were up and decided to attack Flusken simultaneously from opposite sides. As they charged in Flusken ducked under the fifth lobby guard's attack and countered by cutting his right arm off. He lost his footing as he fell and writhed in pain from the severing of his arm. While still on his knees, Flusken countered the sixth lobby guard's attack and cut his left leg off. Automatically he fell forward as he screamed from the intense pain. Shock had set in as he was slowly bleeding to death, while the fifth lobby guard helplessly held his wounded shoulder and waited to die.

Flusken stood up, ignored the sixth lobby guard, and walked over to the fifth one.

The fifth lobby guard looked up at Flusken and said, "What are you?"

At that moment Flusken's upper bicuspids grew into fangs as he removed his helmet. "A means to your end," replied Flusken. A look of horror had shown on his face as Flusken grabbed his head and violently bit him on the neck. A horrible scream echoed from the first level as Flusken fed upon the man.

Vampires over five hundred years old appear to be faster than humans, however, they usually aren't any faster. Most of them at that age have mastered the skill of dilated perception. They have learned to speed up their sight awareness to the point that the movement of objects appears to be in slow motion. This ability comes in very handy when facing multiple enemies at once. The downside to using this ability is that a vampire will tire quicker, considering how much mental energy it takes to use it. Flusken, Drake, and Sinco possessed this ability. Compared to humans, darkness or fog does not hinder their eyesight in any way.

Aside from a vampire's visual abilities their strength is vastly higher than humans.

At this time Victor, the dark priest, and Kescha, the succubus, had reached the top of the steps leading up to the first level of the fortress outside. At the top of the steps was a stone landing about ten feet in diameter. A large wooden door, facing north, was closed with an oil-burning torch on either side. The door was eight feet tall, four feet wide, and four inches thick. Two guards stood on the landing to stop any possible intruders that possibly climbed the staircase.

At this moment Victor and Kescha came into view of the guards on post.

"Intruders!" yelled the first guard as he and his partner drew their swords.

Victor smiled and said, "Kescha, deal with them."

Without hesitation Kescha answered, "Yes, master." Kescha stepped in front of Victor, raised her hands with her palms facing upward and concentrated by closing her eyes. A ball of flame, the size of a grapefruit, appeared in each hand instantly as the guards approached. In no time at all Kescha opened her eyes and released the fireballs from her hands. Each fireball targeted a guard and knocked both of them clear off the landing. With no hope of recovery they both fell to their deaths below, for if the fall did not kill them the weight of the armor would cause them to drown.

"Excellent. Quick and effective, I was wondering when you were going to use your powers, Kescha," commented Victor.

"The footing was limited, master," responded Kescha.

Victor laughed at her response as he pulled out two other black orbs from his garments. He held out one orb in his right hand, like before, and commanded, "Awaken, my eyes of destruction, and do my biding."

The orb began to glow a bright purple as five demonic irises appeared from it. Demonic irises, the size of a basketball, were medium-level demons and basically a floating eyeball. Irises were dark in color with a closable eyelid and two arms, one on each side, with bat-like wings. Their cornea was bright yellow with a narrow slit like pupil. Even though their wings were small, they did not need them for they could easily float in the air.

As the demonic irises floated away Victor held out his left hand with the other orb and commanded, "Come to my aid, my generals of soldier demons." The two male demons emerged from the orb and landed on the platform. Bruts were very large like oafs, but more intelligent and agile, making them very formidable in combat. Their musculature was very similar to oafs, but they had a more human-looking face, two eerie yellow eyes, a nose, and a broad chin. Unlike the oafs, they had larger black horns on their heads above their ears and pointing out like a steer. They had a longer tail and black finger claws, like the oafs. Their other main distinguishing feature was their legs had large hooves, like a horse instead of feet.

Victor looked at them, pointed to the top of the fortress, and instructed, "Go and aid your brethren to the top of the fortress. Destroy any guards in your path."

Both bruts nodded and leaped to the top of the first-level North Wall. With the same orb his summoning continued, "Dragon of darkness, come forth and serve me well."

A gigantic winged black dragon emerged from the orb and awaited his master's instructions. The dark dragon was the most powerful demonic beast of hell. Like most dragons, it had the body of a large dinosaur with wings to match and horns starting on its head and going all the way down to its tail. It had four yellow eyes, two on each side of its broad head, and many long and sharp teeth.

Victor was enjoying this very much as he ordered, "Destroy the bridge and help your brethren."

In an instant the demonic dragon took off flying to its first target.

"Isn't this a little overkill, master?" questioned Kescha.

Victor looked at her and answered, "There are one hundred sixty possible guards in this fortress, Kescha. They have us outnumbered. Your point is taken. Now let's go."

"As you wish, master," responded Kescha as Victor opened the door and proceeded inside the fortress.

The dragon wasted no time as it flew over to the other side of the fortress and hovered over the natural bridge. It opened its mouth and breathed a fire so hot it melted the rock as if it were butter. The melted rock broke off from the mainland and the pillar and fell into the sea below. With that task completed it turned around and flew back toward the fortress to aid in the onslaught.

On the first level outside the demonic oafs, irises, and bruts began to wreak havoc on the unsuspecting guards.

The first iris floated near South Landing Number One and struck it with a massive electrical bolt that ignited a barrel of oil and fried the three guards posted there. They all writhed in pain, as they died a slow and agonizing death.

On the Northwest Wall the first oaf reached the top and knocked a guard off the wall. He screamed as he fell off the outside of the wall and to his death.

Another guard rushed the oaf from behind as it whipped its tail and knocked him off the outside of the wall. He screamed in vain as he fell to his doom.

The oaf charged ahead, speared another guard in the chest, and shook him off its claws as it moved forward.

"It's some kind of hideous monster!" panicked the last two guards on the wall as they jumped off the wall to their impending death below.

The dragon swooped down and hovered in front of the South Wall above the main gate.

"It's a dragon, prepare to fire!" ordered the first guard to see it. Five guards on the wall fired a volley of arrows as they saw the beast come into range.

The dragon reacted and breathed fire on the incoming arrows, burning them up instantly. It then retaliated by breathing a frost breath on them all, freezing all five of them solid as large blocks of ice in seconds.

The fifth iris descended upon South Landing Number Two and encountered three guards. As one of the guards fired an arrow it fired a massive electrical bolt. The massive electrical bolt hit the tip of the arrow in midair and split it into three smaller bolts that struck all three guards at once. They were instantly electrocuted and died where they stood.

The first brut landed on the North Wall, while the second brut moved on and leaped to the second level wall.

The first brut met no immediate opposition as he moved toward North Landing Number One. Three guards, posted there, spotted him and aimed their crossbows toward him.

"Shoot that monster and send him back to hell!" ordered one of the guards.

As the brut approached closer the guards fired a volley of arrows at him. He faced the oncoming arrows with no fear as he opened his mouth and spewed a long stream of fire. The fire stream incinerated the arrows before they hit him. He quickly turned his head back and forth in order to burn all three guards on the landing. With no time to react the guards were caught in the path of the waving fire stream and screamed in terror, while they all burned where they stood.

The fourth iris proceeded to North Landing Number Two as five guards scrambled for crossbows to fire upon it. "What the hell is that thing?" asked one of them.

The iris wasted no time and fired a massive electrical bolt, which went straight through all of them as the electricity arced between the suits of armor, killing them all instantly.

The second oaf reached the East Landing and surprised the three guards posted there. It quickly grabbed the face of one of the guards and threw him over the side. He screamed as he pummeled to his death below.

As the oaf got his footing on the landing the second guard drew his sword and said, "Get that thing!"

The third guard responded by drawing his sword.

The second guard attacked as the oaf blocked his sword and grabbed it. While trying to free his sword, it grabbed him by the throat and lifted him off the ground.

"Let him go, you monster!" yelled the third guard as he moved in and stabbed it in the belly.

The oaf felt no pain from the steel blade as he looked at the third guard.

"What kind of creature is this?" babbled the third guard as he was surprised by the demon's expression.

While he paused, the oaf head-butted him in the face. The demon's attack was so strong that it fractured his skull. The third guard dropped dead at its feet. By this time the oaf had choked the second guard to death and threw him over the side of the wall. It grabbed the handle of the sword and pulled it out of its gut, dropped it, and moved on.

The second iris arrived at the Southwest Wall, while looking upon the guards standing there. The five guards were evenly spaced apart from each other along the wall with no chance of a continuous arc attack.

"Draw your swords, men, and face this foul demon," ordered the guard in charge. The unsuspecting guards responded to the order and drew their swords in hopes of attacking it.

The iris kept its distance as it shot an electrical bolt at each guard one at a time.

All five guards hopelessly dropped one by one like flies hitting a bug zapping light.

The dragon flew down to the Northeast Wall and hovered for a second, while it faced the five guards on the wall. "It's a dragon! Take cover, men!" exclaimed one of the guards.

The guards scrambled for cover as the dragon breathed fire upon them and flew away. The fire was so hot that it melted their armor and cooked their flesh where they stood, leaving behind figure-like statues frozen in movement.

The second iris floated to the West Landing and met a volley of arrows from three guards posted there. With no chance to dodge the arrows it took an arrow in the center of its pupil. Instantly, the second iris turned to ashes as the guards were amazed by what they had done.

"We did it! They can be killed," proclaimed one of the guards as he raised his crossbow above his head. Because their attention was focused on the demonic iris, they did not see the first oaf approach from behind.

It quickly grabbed the helmet of the closest guard and snapped his neck like a twig. As the oaf let go of him, another guard turned in its direction.

"There's another one!" reacted the other guard.

It quickly speared him in the throat as the other guard drew his sword.

"Die, you demon scum!" yelled the sword-wielding guard. He attacked in a slashing motion as the oaf backhanded him and knocked him over the wall.

The first brut wasted no time jumping around on the first-level wall and landing at the Southeast Wall where he met five guards.

"What kind of demon is that?" questioned one of the guards.

"A demon that is going to be dead before this night is over," answered the next guard. All of the guards staggered themselves on top of the wide wall as they faced and approached him with sword in hand.

The brut stomped the wall with his large hoof, causing a massive crack to form and fracturing the top of the wall. The top of the wall began to crumble causing them all to fall off the inside and outside of the wall. Three guards fell off the outside of the wall as they fell to their deaths below and screamed on the way down. Two guards fell to the inside of the wall, landed on the roof of the first level, and cracked their skulls open.

Inside the fortress beyond the door leading from the main lobby, Drake and Sinco ascended a spiral staircase to the second level. The staircase was made of stone steps, very wide and thick.

On the second level were four corridors branching out from the spiral staircase leading to many rooms. The room with the staircase in the middle of it had a radius of about twenty feet. In the corridors oil-burning torches were mounted between the wooden doors of the rooms. The ten-foot-wide floors and twenty-foot-tall ceilings of the corridors were made of stone and marble.

Upon reaching the second level, Drake and Sinco were spotted by a guard.

"Intruders!" shouted the guard. The twelve guards were in groups of four covering three of the corridors, while facing Drake from their direction. Like the door guards, they also had capes, colored red.

Drake raised his hand to hold back Sinco and said, "Go ahead to the top level. I'll handle these pathetic guards."

"Yes. The top," replied Sinco as he continued up the steps to the top level.

"Take him down, men!" ordered the guard in charge as all twelve of them prepared to attack Drake.

Drake nonchalantly grinned and said, "You all are a waste of my blade. I'll let you play with my pets instead."

"What are you talking about?" questioned the guard in charge.

"You'll see," replied Drake as he pulled a couple of orbs from his pockets. "Hell bats, come to my aid," commanded Drake. The orb in his right hand began to glow purple as twenty crimson-colored bats emerged. These bats were very large, hideous looking, and had a two-foot wingspan.

Fear overcame the guard in charge and a few others as the bats filled the area like a colony of bats usually do when they attack.

"It can't be! A practitioner of the demonic arts! A demon knight!" shouted the guard in charge. He backed away as the other guards prepared to fight.

Two bats targeted the second guard as he drew his sword. He swung with his sword to fend off the bats to no avail. The one bat caught the sword in its mouth and bit through it as if it was candy, while the other bat bit him in the neck.

The third guard swung at two hovering bats as he inadvertently stabbed the fourth guard in the back of the neck. Distracted by the shock at what he had done, he was unable to see another bat fly in and bite him in the face and through his helmet visor.

The fifth guard showed promise as he managed to slash the wing of a bat close to him. It fell to the ground, since it could not continue to fly. Without warning it bit through his greave, causing him to fall to the floor. Another bat joined in and bit the guard in the throat, while he lay there.

The sixth guard was blinded when a bat draped his body over the visor. Because of this he panicked and started to swing his sword frantically. Unable to shake the bat off of him, he accidentally cut off the arm of the seventh guard.

At the same time a bat flew between the sixth and seventh guard and slashed their throats with its wings. Both guards fell over as they choked.

Two bats flew by the eighth guard and slashed through his armored shoulders. He dropped to his knees from the pain and waited to be finished off.

The ninth guard managed to stab another bat in the torso. To his amazement it turned to ashes as he retracted his sword. Two other bats viciously attacked him by biting his arms.

The tenth guard fought bravely and cut off the head of a bat. Within no time it turned to ashes as the guard was distracted and slashed in the face by another bat.

The eleventh guard swung his sword recklessly and missed a bat as it flew by and slashed his gut wide open.

The twelfth guard was so taken by grief by all the blood spilled, that he dropped his sword and said, "I surrender."

Drake looked at him and said, "Who said I was taking any prisoners?" At that moment a bat flew in and bit the guard on the back of his neck.

The guard in charge backed further away and made a run for it down a corridor. Two bats flew after him. When the two caught up to him, they picked him up by his shoulders and flew him back to where Drake was. The two bats dropped the guard in charge right in front of Drake.

He got on his knees and begged, "Please, don't kill me."

Drake held out his orb and said, "Good job, boys, that's all for now." Immediately all of the hell bats became smoke and returned to the orb.

"Thank you, my lord, how may I serve you?" asked the guard in charge.

Drake smiled and kicked him in the head. The force from the kick caused him to fly a few feet back. "You disgust me. You are nothing more than a traitorous coward looking to only save your own skin. And I thought the guards of this fortress were willing to die to protect its treasures and people. You deserve to be eaten by dogs and my boys are very hungry." Drake walked down the corridor and left him lying on the floor. As he looked around he took off his helmet and got up. At that moment he saw a black orb rolling toward him.

"Why did he leave this orb behind?" His eyes got big as he said, "Oh no!" He knew that something nasty was about to emerge from the orb as he drew back from it.

As if on cue the black orb took on a purple glow as three dog-like creatures emerged from it. They were hell pinschers, lower-level demonic beasts; black-colored dogs the size of a Doberman with razor-sharp teeth like the hell bats.

The three hell pinschers looked at him with their yellow glowing eyes as they all started to growl at him.

As soon as his eyes met their gaze the guard was paralyzed with fear and remained still.

At the other end of the corridor Drake smiled as he heard screams of terror, meaning the guard was soon at his end.

On the second level outside havoc continued as the demonic minion forces engaged in battle.

The third iris appeared above the Southeast Landing as three guards prepared to fire upon it. It fired a massive electrical bolt at the guards, but the bolt missed them and was drawn to a metal sword that happened to be thrust into the side of the wall in front of them.

"It's another one of those floating things. Fire!" ordered one of the guards. With the distraction of the bolt drawn away from them, they fired their arrows and shot it in the middle of its pupil. It turned to ashes instantly as the guards looked with surprise.

"They can be killed," said one of the guards.

The third oaf climbed to the top of the landing and attacked. Its claws speared the closest guard from behind as it lifted him off the ground and threw him off. As the other two guards turned to face it, the oaf rushed in with its arms extended and knocked both of them off the landing to join their friend below. Both of them screamed, as they would soon meet their end.

The second oaf scaled the East Wall and reached the top to be met by five guards.

"Take this, demon scum!" yelled the first guard as he moved in and attacked it from behind as it got to the top. It turned in his direction, grabbed him, and threw him at another guard. The other guard could not get out of the way in time and was knocked off the outside of the wall as the two fell together to the depths below. Both yelled to no avail as they plummeted down. The oaf turned back the other way and faced the third guard. He was frozen in fear as it charged him like a bull and knocked him off the outside of the wall.

"You'll pay for that!" exclaimed the fourth guard as he charged, while the oaf was distracted, and stabbed it in the back.

It turned and speared the fourth guard in the eyes, causing massive trauma to the brain. The oaf moved toward the last guard as it ignored the sword stuck in its back. As he moved in for the attack, the oaf blocked his attack and grabbed the guard's arm and opposite leg. Before he could break free, it pulled him in and stabbed him in the chest with the sword sticking through its gut. The last guard was in agony and became lifeless as the oaf pulled him off the sword and dropped him like a piece of garbage.

It continued on to the Northeast Landing with the sword still in its body. The oaf did not get far, since the sword did slow it down a little and it could not get it out. Three guards saw its approach and took aim with their cross bows.

"Get ready to fire, men, and send this demon back to the abyss," ordered one of the guards. All of the guards fired their weapons at the same time as it approached. Fortune was on their side as the first arrow struck it in the eye and the second arrow pierced its heart. With death swiftly dealt the oaf turned to ashes instantly, while the sword and arrows dropped and landed on the top of the wall.

Without warning the dragon swooped down and snatched all three guards in its claws as it flew away from the fortress. Within seconds the dragon let go of them and watched as they helplessly screamed and fell to their death.

The first iris approached the South Landing and engaged three guards. It struck the middle of the landing with a massive electrical bolt and split it in two. All three guards fell off the landing as it gave way and crumbled.

"Die, you floating abomination!" yelled one of the guards as he grabbed his dagger, threw it directly at the iris, and fell from the crumbling landing. The dagger pierced its pupil as it froze and turned to ashes instantly.

The third oaf made it to the top of the Southeast Wall as it climbed from below. Five guards faced the oaf as it prepared to engage them.

"Attack it from both sides. It can't kill us all," ordered one of the guards.

Two guards charged it from the front as two charged it from the rear.

It caught the swords of the front two guards as the other two stabbed it in the back. While the front two guards held on to their swords, the oaf retaliated by throwing the one front guard off the outside of the wall and throwing the other front guard off the inside of the wall. One of the back guards was whisked off his feet by its tail as he screamed and fell to his death on the outside of the wall. The oaf quickly turned around and speared the other back guard in the face as the last guard charged in for the kill.

"Good will always triumph over evil!" proclaimed the last guard as he pierced its heart with his sword. It uncontrollably slashed with both hands as the last guard fell down after his throat was slashed, while the oaf turned to ashes.

The second brut entered the battle as he landed on the Northeast Wall and met five guards. Five guards stood on the wall almost in a straight line as they prepared to attack him.

"He is only one. We can take him, men," said the guard in front. The brut held his fist out and formed a fiery whip, with a variable length. They all charged as he snapped his fiery whip at them from the outside. With smooth and continuous motions he sliced the guards to pieces, like a hot wire going through a piece of wood. All of the guards literally came to pieces after the whip went through them and fell off the outside of the wall.

The fourth iris floated over to the North Landing and surprised three guards.

"It's one of those things!" exclaimed one of the guards.

Without hesitation it shot a massive electrical bolt that went through all three guards like a laser through metal. They all dropped like flies, since their hearts were burned to a crisp.

The iris floated to the Northwest Landing and struck the base of it with a massive electrical bolt. Three guards fell to their deaths and screamed in terror as the landing crumbled. In an unsuspecting turn of events the crumbling landing fell and crushed the first oaf as it began to climb to the second level.

The fourth oaf appeared on the Northwest Wall and prepared to fight five guards.

"Attack!" ordered one guard as he charged it from behind when it got its footing.

The oaf reacted as it placed its hands on the wall and back-kicked the guard with its feet.

He was sent back a few feet as he knocked over two other guards. One guard lost his footing and fell off the outside of the wall.

As the oaf got up another guard slashed its one arm off. It felt no pain as it grabbed the guard's throat and threw him at the last guard. The thrown guard landed on the edge of the last guard's sword and knocked him over the inside of the wall. The thrown guard's impalement was lethal as the momentum forced the last guard hard to the roof of level two and broke his neck.

By this time the first two guards got up and prepared to attack again.

"We are not finished yet!" yelled the guard as he and his partner rushed the oaf, while it turned their way.

The fourth iris passed by at that instant and shocked them both with a massive electrical bolt.

The oaf watched as they fried in their armor like tin cans on a campfire. The iris moved on as the oaf picked up its arm and reattached it.

A demon's resilience and healing was simply amazing and almost instantaneous. As the bone, muscle, nerves, and skin grew back together, the oaf found a curved stairwell leading down to the second-level floor of the fortress. It proceeded down the stairwell and entered the fortress.

The dragon flew over to the West Wall as five guards scrambled for cover.

"It's a black dragon of hell!" yelled one of the guards as the other guards scrambled.

The dragon flapped its huge wings, which caused all of them to fall over from the force of the wind created. With no time to spare the dragon breathed a frost breath, freezing all of the guards still lying on the top of the wall.

The first brut took to the Southwest Wall and engaged five guards standing there.

"Get him!" ordered the first guard. Before they could rush him, the brut opened his mouth and spewed a long fire stream that engulfed them all. With no hope of escape they all burned where they stood as the fire stream consumed them like a flamethrower.

The sixth oaf reached the top of the Southwest Landing and startled the three guards standing there.

"Kill it!" ordered the one guard as they all fired their crossbows without trying to aim it first. One arrow flew by it as another hit it in the arm and the other hit it in the chest. The arrows did nothing to slow it down as it went to attack the guards.

Since it would take too long to reload, they all dropped their crossbows and drew their swords. Two of the guards attacked the oaf at the same time.

The oaf caught their swords and threw them off the landing as their screams faded away and fell to their death below.

While it was distracted, the remaining guard stabbed it in the gut. Without batting an eye it ripped his helmet off and bit half his head off. With the last guard dead the oaf chewed on his flesh, dropped his body, and moved on to look for another fight.

Meanwhile inside the fortress, Sinco had reached the third level at this time. This was the final level in the fortress, not counting the roof. On the third level beyond the spiral staircase was a large spacious and empty room. Only two corridors with a few rooms in each were perpendicular to the staircase exit and extended from the room surrounding the staircase. Most of the surroundings were the same as the second level. The room with the staircase in the middle of it had a radius of about twenty feet. The two corridors had stone walls with oil-burning torches between the wooden doors of the rooms. The ten-foot-wide floors and twenty-foot-tall ceilings of the corridors were made of stone.

Upon reaching the third level Sinco was met by the first guard.

"An intruder!" shouted the first guard. The ten guards were in two groups covering both sides leading to the corridors, while facing Sinco from their direction. Upon the first guard's response to Sinco's entrance, all of the guards unsheathed their swords to attack. Sinco smiled fiendishly as he pulled out his sickles to attack.

The first guard charged in to attack Sinco from his right while the second charged in to attack Sinco from his left.

Sinco dropped to his right knee and slashed with his sickles. The first guard's left leg was severed at the knee while the other guard's right leg was severed at the knee. Instantly both guards fell to their sides away from him, while writhing in pain. Sinco turned to his right and charged towards the third guard and cut his head off. His body dropped to the floor, like a puppet having its strings cut.

The fourth guard rushed in and attacked Sinco from his left side.

Without hesitation Sinco countered and cut off his arm. Sinco turned around as the fifth guard approached and quickly stabbed him in the head. He retracted his blade as the sixth guard attacked. Sinco parried with his one sickle and stabbed him in the chest with the other.

While pulling the blade out of his chest, Sinco was attacked by the seventh guard.

Sinco parried with his free sickle and slashed him in the throat. With Sinco's other blade free the sixth guard fell to the floor. The seventh guard began to choke and fell backward from the cut.

The eighth and ninth guard faced Sinco and attacked him head-on.

Sinco sidestepped them, parried, and slashed both of their throats before they could attack again. Both of them fell in opposite directions as the blood poured out of their throats.

The last guard feared for his life as he saw Sinco lick the blood from his blade and turned to him. He decided to make a run for it and took off before Sinco attacked him. Sinco smiled as he ran down the corridor after him.

The last guard luckily made it to the end of the corridor. At the end of the corridor was a staircase that led up to the roof in a curved pattern. The stone-made stairs were long and thick, like the staircase.

As he reached the roof he yelled, "We're under attack! The gate has been breached!"

"What could possibly get through this fog-covered night?" responded the guard on the roof.

From behind a sickle was thrust through the back of the panicking guard and emerged from his chest. He died instantly as the sickle was retracted and Sinco appeared out of the shadows.

"You will see soon enough," remarked Sinco as he licked the blood off his blade.

Meanwhile, Victor and Kescha arrived on the third level of the fortress from the spiral staircase.

"My servants have done well. We have met no resistance, since we entered the fortress," remarked Victor.

Kescha turned to him and said, "We have been lucky, master." Victor and Kescha were surrounded at this point in time. Kescha was standing by Victor's right as a guard was facing her right. Another guard was facing Victor's left and standing next to a third guard, who was in the middle by the first.

"Your luck has just run out," responded the guard on the right as he and two other guards unsheathed their swords.

Victor fiendishly smiled and said, "Take care of them, Kescha."

"Yes, master," answered Kescha as she drew her blade from her sheath.

The first guard viciously attacked Kescha as she parried. Upon his second attack, Kescha parried and countered with a slash to his throat. He fell to the floor instantly as he choked in agony.

The third guard immediately rushed in to attack as Kescha ducked below his sword and slashed his left leg. At that moment he lost his balance and fell while he writhed in pain.

Kescha followed up and stabbed him in the chest through his breastplate. Within seconds he died from the trauma to his heart.

The last guard saw an opening and decided to charge against Kescha.

Kescha stood up as she pulled her sword free and turned in his direction. Kescha dodged his downward slash, but the tip of his sword managed to cut the lacing on her top. Kescha was distracted by her breasts being exposed and didn't see his next attack.

The guard blind-sided her with a punch to the face as the force of it knocked her down. He laughed as he said, "No woman has ever bested me in combat." His gaze was fixed on her exposed flesh as he remarked, "Very nice indeed. I think I'll make you my concubine when this is over."

Kescha licked the blood from her lip as she looked at him in the eyes. Her eyes began to glow an eerie yellow as she remarked, "How dare you consider me nothing more than a wench?" Her whole body caught on fire as her skin turned a crimson color and her clothes burned away like paper. Kescha's hair turned to a jet-black color as did her razor-sharp nails, while they grew to a length of three inches. She got to her feet as large black bat-like wings sprouted from her back and curved foot-long horns grew out of her head.

The guard backed away from her as his fear of her presence overtook him. "A demon!" exclaimed the guard.

Kescha crossed her arms and said, "What's the matter? Am I too much woman for you to handle?"

He dropped his sword and ran away in terror down the one corridor.

Kescha smiled as she created two fireballs in her hands like before. Only this time she brought the two fireballs together and let them form a larger one. She kissed the ball of flame as she sent it hurling down the corridor after him. The huge fireball caught up to him in no time and burned him to a crisp instantly, leaving behind an empty suit of armor and ashes on the floor. Kescha transformed back to her human form with all of her clothes still intact from before. She clinched her fist and said, "I was going to be easy on you. Arrogant humans disgust me the most. Greed and lust will be your downfall."

Victor clapped his hands and said, "Excellent. Check on the others ahead. I will handle any other opposition in my path."

Kescha walked towards the staircase and responded, "Yes, master."

Meanwhile the battle raged on outside as the surviving demonic minions made their way to the third level. The seventh oaf scaled the Southeast Wall and grabbed the leg of a guard as he climbed up.

"What the?" responded the surprised guard as it threw him over the outside of the wall. He hopelessly screamed as he fell to his doom and the other guards reacted. While getting up the oaf did an uppercut motion with his claws and stuck another guard in the gut. He writhed in agony as it threw him off his claws and dropped him over the outside of the wall.

"Kill that foul beast!" yelled the third guard as he went in to attack it from behind.

The oaf turned his head and whipped him off his feet. With nothing to stop him he fell off the outside of the wall to his impending death below.

The last two guards stood there in disbelief that a demon could dispatch three guards so easily.

"Die, you foul demon!" yelled the fourth guard as he charged at the front of it.

The oaf faced him head-on and caught his helmet as he stabbed it in the gut. It began to squeeze the guard's helmet, like an empty can of soda, until it slowly crushed his skull. When he was no longer moving, it tossed him over the outside of the wall. The oaf looked upon the fifth guard as it pulled the sword out of its gut.

Fear had consumed him as he jumped off the outside of the wall and said, "You won't get me like the others!" As he screamed while falling, the oaf watched the guard fall, scratched his head, and moved on.

The fifth iris ascended to South Landing Number Four as it struck a barrel of oil with a massive electrical bolt. Three guards caught on fire as they tried to avoid the flame that ran as the oil spilled out of the broken barrel. They burned alive as it moved toward the center of the fortress.

The second brut landed on the West Landing, surprising three guards posted there. He wasted no time as he punched the first guard, backhanded the second, and whipped his tail at the third. The first guard was knocked off the platform and landed on the top of his head, crushing his skull from the force of the impact. The second guard was knocked off the outside of the platform and landed on the wall below, while breaking his neck. The third guard was whipped near the outside of the wall and fell to his death below.

The dragon swooped down to North Landing Number Three, ready to attack the three defenseless guards. All three guards fired a volley to no avail as the dragon spewed a fiery blast at them, burning them all to a crisp in no time.

The first brut landed on South Landing Number Three and met up with three guards.

The first guard drew his sword and attacked him.

The brut caught his sword with one hand, broke a large piece off, and stabbed him in the neck. As he fell down the second guard rushed in as the brut grabbed his throat and head-butted him. He was stunned as he fell off the landing to his death.

The third guard slashed downward on the brut and broke the sword on his forehead.

The brut punched him so hard in the helmet that his fist went through it and crushed his skull. He fell over dead as the brut moved on.

The fourth iris floated up to North Landing Number Four as three guards prepared to attack it. As soon as it was in range all three fired their arrows. The iris was purely ambushed as all three arrows hit it in its pupil. It turned to ashes as they all cheered.

The fifth iris hovered beside the East Landing as three guards prepared to fire. It was too quick for them as it zapped all three guards with a massive electrical bolt. As they fell from being fried from the inside out the last guard, unexplainably, drew his sword and leaped into the air to attack it. He succeeded as his sword cleaved it in two pieces, while he fell from the wall. The iris instantly turned to ashes as the last guard met his fate awaiting him below.

The seventh oaf appeared on the Northeast Wall as five guards strategically retreated to the center of the fortress roof.

The first brut closed in between the seventh and eighth oaf as the other guards bunched together.

The eighth oaf appeared on the Southwest Wall, as five more guards strategically retreated to the center of the fortress roof.

The fifth oaf appeared on the Northwest Wall, as five more guards strategically retreated to the center of the fortress roof.

The second brut closed in between the eighth and fifth oaf as the other guards bunched together.

The dragon decided to perch on North Landing Number Three and watch as the battle continued.

"Have courage, men. If all we can do is die to protect the priestess and this fortress, then so be it!" shouted the last guard. All of the remaining guards accepted their fate as they drew their swords in hopes to take some of the demonic minions with them.

Meanwhile inside on the second level of the fortress, Drake was looking around the corridors for any more opposition. "They didn't even last ten minutes. How boring," remarked Drake. As Drake walked past the dead bodies on the floor he heard a scream from a far room down one of the corridors.

In a room not far from Drake was a girl being attacked by a couple of oafs. The room was very spacious, compared to the commander's, with four three-foot-high two-inch-wide slits, windows, that were a foot apart from each other. Near the doorway was a wooden handcrafted closet with double doors. The maple-colored closet was eight feet tall, ten feet wide and had a depth of about three feet. In the center of the room was a large round bed with colorful sheets, blankets, and many pillows. On one side of the bed was a wooden nightstand, measuring about three feet by three feet, with a candle and holder on it. On the other side of the bed, facing the window slits, was a wooden dresser desk with a padded wooden chair. The dresser had drawers and was three feet wide and four feet long. Mounted on the wall in front of the dresser was a thin piece of metal, used as a mirror. The room was well lit with candles in holders that were mounted on the walls opposite to the window slits facing to the outside. Like the corridors, the ceiling was twenty feet high.

At this time Drake had entered the room and found two oafs attacking a poor defenseless girl.

The nineteen-year-old girl was quite pretty with brown eyes, shoulder-length blonde hair, and standing at about five feet tall. Her body was quite slender with larger than average breasts. She wore a white-colored bikini-like outfit with a pale green piece of fabric that was draped around her waist and held on by a single broach. The fabric served as a skirt even though her legs were partially exposed. She also wore a hooded cloak that matched her skirt, tied together with another broach. Golden oval-shaped earrings with a blue jewel decorated her ears, while a matching pendant hung from her neck. On her right arm was a matching armband to complete the outfit. Sandals covered the bottom of her feet, since most of the floors were made of cold stone.

As Drake entered the room he found one oaf holding her arms as the other was looking at her. The girl screamed in terror as Drake approached them.

Drake boldly stated to the oaf holding her, "Let her go, stupid oaf."

Both oafs looked at Drake and did nothing. Without hesitation Drake drew his sword to attack. The oaf with his hands free snarled and lunged in the air to attack Drake. Drake sidestepped and dodged its lunging attack. Before it could turn around and attack again, Drake stabbed it in the chest with his sword. Instantly, the oaf turned to ashes as Drake pulled his sword from its chest.

The other oaf threw the girl onto her bed as it charged toward Drake.

Drake extended his hand with his palm facing toward it and said, "Be gone with you, demon. I relieve you of your contract." The oaf was stopped dead in its tracks as a red glowing pentagram appeared below its feet and sucked its spirit through a portal. Its body remained and turned to ashes. Drake sheathed his sword as he approached the frightened girl.

Without hesitation she hugged him and said, "Thank you so much! I thought I was going to die."

"Are you all right?" asked Drake.

"I think so," answered the girl as she pulled away and looked at him.

"What's your name?" asked Drake.

With a shy response she answered, "Daphne."

As Drake took his sword off of his back he said, "Those stupid oafs. They can't even follow simple orders. They were to kill only the guards and leave anyone else, who posed no threat, alive."

His comment surprised her as she backed up and responded, "You're one of them." "Oops. I blew it now. You're right and I am so lucky to find you," responded Drake.

Her heart rate picked up as she said, "What do you want?"

Drake smiled as he responded, "Well, my commander wants this blood gem, but all I want is you right now." He looked into her eyes as she fell under his charming and mesmerizing gaze. Under his spell, she was in a trance and did nothing as he began to caress her. While he began to kiss her, Drake took the liberty of undoing her cloak and pulling her straps down past her shoulders. As her breasts were exposed he began to fondle them gently, while kissing her neck. She was in a mild state of ecstasy as he continued to arouse her. In an instant Drake heard a noise at the door and looked in that direction.

In the doorway was Kescha standing with her hands on her hips as she said, "What are you doing? This is no time for feeding, Drake."

Drake smiled and responded, "Who said anything about feeding? I have other needs too. Want to make it a friendly threesome, Kescha? I'll have my way with her and then you can feed on her too."

Kescha shook her head as she replied, "You are supposed to clear the area and meet up with the dark priest in the ceremonial chamber."

Drake snarled back at her and said, "Why aren't you at your master's heel?"

As she crossed her arms she answered with authority, "Because he told me to check on the others, which includes you, Drake. Bring the girl."

With regret Drake yielded and said, "You are no fun, Kescha."

Meanwhile, the commander reached the ceremonial room to alert the priestess. The priestess was wearing a full-length long-sleeve light-colored dress, a matching cloak, and a gold cross necklace. She had very short dark hair with jagged bangs above her eyes. Her ears were decorated with long golden earrings. This very large room was in the third level of the fortress. The ceiling was twenty feet high with a circular skylight in the middle. An open skylight, that measured ten feet in diameter, allowed moonlight to show on the floor below. Narrow one-foot-wide windows reaching twelve feet high helped light the dark room on either side. Many candles were mounted on all of the walls to further illuminate the room. The floor was made of stone tile in a checkerboard design. In the center of the room was a stone pedestal with a unique-looking jewel in the middle of it, surrounded by an invisible magical protective barrier. The red jewel was the size of a baseball with a hexagonal base, which formed a point at the top. Its bottom was mounted into a golden metal base with four legs, having claws at the ends. Four guards, wearing black capes, were in the room with the priestess near the barrier surrounding the blood gem.

As he entered the room he wasted no time in telling her, "Priestess, the fortress is lost. I must get you to safety."

She turned his way and responded, "All right, but I must get the blood gem first. I fear my barrier will not be enough to protect it." The priestess began to walk over to the center of the room as the commander followed her.

As soon as the priestess was within five feet of the barrier three oafs dropped down to the floor from the open skylight. The priestess froze as the three oafs surprised the guards and attacked them.

The fifth oaf thrust his right hand and speared the helmet of the first guard. He fell to the floor lifeless as the oaf retracted his hand from the helmet.

The seventh oaf whisked his tail at the second guard as it landed, knocking him off balance. It followed him down and speared the guard in the chest. Blood spurted out as it retracted its claws from the wound.

The eighth oaf grabbed the helmet of the third guard and twisted his head so fast you could hear the bones snapping in his neck. It let go of his helmet as it tossed him away like a rag doll. The fourth guard was lucky enough to have time to draw his sword as he backed away.

With the eighth oaf still distracted the fourth guard attacked and severed its head from its body. The body instantly turned to ashes.

During all this action the commander drew his sword and said, "Don't worry, Priestess, I will give my life to protect you if necessary."

The fifth oaf saw the commander and lunged in for an attack. He sidestepped it and stabbed it in the throat. As the oaf backed off of the sword it turned to ashes in seconds.

The fourth guard got careless as he went to attack the seventh oaf. It caught his sword in its mouth and bit it into pieces. The sight of his sword broken caused the guard to freeze up as the oaf squashed his head like a melon.

The commander saw an opening and slashed with his sword, cutting the seventh oaf vertically in half. Its body turned to ashes before both halves hit the floor. The commander turned to the priestess and said, "Foul demons. They were no match for my sword." At this time the commander heard a fiendish laughter and turned around to see who it was.

Sinco appeared in the doorway and remarked, "You can't escape, Priestess. No you can't." Without warning Sinco drew his sickles, rushed in, and attacked the commander.

The commander parried Sinco's attack and held his ground. Sinco continued to attack as the he parried. On his next attack Sinco was too quick and slashed the right arm of the commander.

The commander held his ground even though the slash was very deep. Sinco slashed again as the commander tried to sidestep him for a counter. The commander's counter failed as Sinco slashed his left leg, forcing him to fall to one knee. Sinco pressed on and struck downward as the commander raised his sword to parry and possibly counterattack. His parry was to no avail as his sword broke from the downward force struck upon it. Sinco's double downward slash cut off both of the commander's arms at the shoulders. Blood spewed from his shoulders as the commander fell backward on to the floor. Sinco licked his sickle as he watched the commander go into shock and bleed to death.

The priestess placed her hands on her cheeks as she watched in horror and screamed, "Commander!"

Sinco put his sickles away as he turned to her and said, "We have you now, Priestess. Yes, we do."

It was a dark hour at this time, for the fortress of light had been seized by the enemy. At this time Victor, Flusken, and three oafs entered the room.

Victor saw the priestess on her knees beside Sinco as he ordered, "Seize her, my minions."

Sinco grabbed the priestess and picked her up as he said, "It's time to get up, Priestess, our leader is here." The first and second oaf each held an arm of the priestess, even though escape was pointless at this time. Soon after Drake, Kescha, and Daphne arrived to witness the situation.

The priestess noticed their arrival and screamed, "Daphne!" Kescha held on to Daphne so that she could not go anywhere as they watched. The young woman was the priestess's sister, Daphne.

"At last the blood gem is mine," commented Victor as he approached the blood gem and extended his hand to grasp it. Without warning his hand was shocked by an invisible barrier that surrounded the blood gem.

Immediately, Victor retracted his hand as he said, "Clever. I should have expected this from one of the most powerful priestesses in the area."

While extending his hands outward toward the blood gem, Victor evoked a spell, "Powers of darkness, I call upon your power. Break this physical barrier that impedes my path." Bolts of lightning left his hands and zapped the barrier around the blood gem. His shield-breaking spell was cast to no avail. Victor was impressed by the strength of the barrier spell. He then turned away from the blood gem and slowly approached the priestess. She looked into his red eyes and knew that he was a vampire as well as a dark priest. She frowned and did her best to hide her fear. The dark priest smiled fiendishly at her.

"There is no escape. Release the barrier spell on the blood gem," he said.

She replied with contempt, "Why? So you can resurrect your blood queen? Never! I would rather die than help you."

"Defiant to the end, I need you alive to cancel the spell," he said.

Thinking she had him in a corner, she spouted, "Then I guess you lose, dark priest."

He lifted up her chin with his finger and said, "You have underestimated me, my pretty." Victor turned to Flusken and ordered, "Flusken, place your sword at the girl's throat." Flusken went over to Daphne as he drew his sword.

The priestess was very surprised and feared for her sister's life. She cried out, "Daphne!"

The dark priest smirked and said, "I know you don't care what happens to yourself, priestess, but what about your dear sister?" Flusken placed the tip of his sword at the throat of Daphne. The priestess tried distracting the dark priest.

"You wouldn't," was all she could think of to say.

"Are you willing to take that chance?" replied the dark priest.

Daphne spoke up, "Don't do it, Sis! You have to protect the blood gem!"

The dark priest was becoming impatient. His red eyes began to glow as he said, "For the last time release the shield on the gem or your sister will be carved like a suckling pig."

Drake moved the sword away from her throat, stepped in front of Flusken, and said, "Victor, I will not allow the shedding of innocent blood. She is unarmed."

While gritting his teeth, Victor inquired, "You dare to defy me, Drake?"

Defiantly, Drake replied, "Is your mind control that weak, dark priest?"

"Your insolence will not be tolerated, Drake," responded Victor.

The priestess held her head down and said, "All right. You win. I will do what you say. Just don't harm my sister."

The dark priest gave the word to his minions, "Release her so she can chant the spell." The two oafs released the priestess so she could do it.

The priestess extended her arms toward the blood gem. She concentrated by closing her eyes and the now glowing barrier surrounding the blood gem disappeared.

At this time a black orb had finished rolling in the direction of where Drake was standing. Before Drake could take notice, the orb glowed a bright purple and a demonic serpent emerged and entrapped Drake in its coils.

Bound by the tight coils Drake retorted, "How dare you use one of your minions on me, Victor?"

Victor smiled as he said, "Excellent. I will deal with you later, Drake. Retrieve the gem and kill them both."

The priestess was shocked by his response and said, "You fiend! You have what you want. Killing us now won't matter."

"I am just covering my tracks, my dear," replied the dark priest.

"Then I shall do the same," retorted the priestess as she grabbed the blood gem. Daphne nodded to her sister, as she knew what had to be done.

"You can't get away. What are you doing?" asked Victor.

She held on to the blood gem as she said, "If I can't protect the blood gem, then I will send it to a place where it will never be found." The priestess closed her eyes quickly to cast a light spell, "Light that penetrates all darkness blind my enemies with such fury!"

"No!" shouted the dark priest. In an instant a light so intense blinded and stunned every dark creature in the room that had their eyes open.

The priestess opened her eyes as she threw the blood gem to Daphne across the room. "Run, Daphne!" shouted the priestess as Daphne caught it. Daphne quickly ran out of the room as her sister told her to do so, hoping to escape with the blood gem. Unknown to anyone, Kescha opened her eyes, stepped out of the room, and followed her. By this time everyone was slowly recovering from the light spell cast.

As fast as she could Daphne ran down the spiral staircase to the first level of the fortress. Kescha knew Daphne had a good head start and stopped before approaching the staircase.

In an instant Kescha transformed into the form of a shadow. All that could be seen of her in this form was a dark naked female silhouette of herself. Her shadow form gave her many advantages, like hiding in shadows or passing through things. Kescha then passed through the floor and commented as she slipped away, "She's a fast one."

On the first floor of the fortress Daphne left the staircase running and continued on at the same pace, while entering the kitchen. The kitchen was very spacious with a large rectangular wooden table, a long counter with many wooden cupboards and a large iron wood-burning stove. A large chandelier full of candles lit the entire kitchen with ease. Above the counter were many pots and pans hanging along with plenty of knives on a rack.

The kitchen was empty at this time as Daphne ran all the way through the kitchen and stopped at the wine cellar door. She grabbed a lit candle nearby on the table as she went for the handle on the wine cellar door. Daphne quickly opened the door to the wine cellar, went inside, and closed it tightly.

The wine cellar was full of bottles on many racks covering most of the walls. Since the wine cellar was dark, only Daphne's candle was lighting her path. Daphne began looking at the floor in search for a trap door. At last she found it as she squatted down to open it.

A voice broke the silence as she grabbed the handle on the large wooden trap door, "Going somewhere?" The voice startled Daphne as she let go of the handle and fell backward on her rear.

"Who's there?" asked Daphne. Kescha stepped out of the shadows in her human form and into the light. Daphne recognized her and responded, "You were the one holding me in the ceremonial room. You're one of them."

"Relax, I am not here to capture you," answered Kescha.

"Is this some kind of trick?"

Kescha toyed with her and said, "You are so cute. I could eat you up."

Daphne quickly pulled a dagger from behind her back and stated, "I won't go easily."

Kescha squatted down to her level and remarked, "If I wanted to catch you, you would have been knocked out by now. Listen, we haven't much time.

The others will be looking for you very soon." Kescha looked at the trap door and asked, "Where does this lead?"

"Down to the dock below," answered Daphne.

"Good," said Kescha as she grabbed the handle and opened the trap door.

Both of them stepped down a few stairs to a stone ledge overlooking a very large shaft leading all the way down to the bottom of the pillar. The shaft was dark, since no light made its way into the shaft.

Daphne brought her candle as she closed the trap door and looked around for a way down from the ledge. As Daphne looked around, while standing on the ledge, she saw nothing to grab onto or climb down from with her candle lighting her way. "Oh no. They never built the hoist to go down the shaft," responded Daphne as Kescha looked around more.

Kescha went over to Daphne and said, "Don't worry. I can see in the dark and I have a plan."

"What is your plan?" asked Daphne.

"I don't have time to explain. Just trust me," replied Kescha as she grabbed Daphne from behind and placed one arm around her waist and the opposite hand over her mouth. Kescha immediately stepped off the ledge with Daphne and freefell all the way down the shaft. Within seconds of reaching the dry bottom of the shaft, wings sprouted from Kescha's back and spread open to slow their fall. As soon as they landed Kescha let go of Daphne and her wings retracted into her back.

Daphne turned around looking at Kescha and said, "What in the realm are you?"

Kescha smiled and answered, "A very naughty girl."

At the dock area where the Kescha first arrived, the place was deserted. Instantly, the rock wall under the guard post busted open as Kescha and Daphne stepped out of the hole created.

Kescha led Daphne to a boat tied off and ordered, "Quick. Get in the boat. The fog will cover your escape by the time they look for you." Without hesitation or argument Daphne listened and stepped into the boat.

As she sat in the boat Daphne turned to Kescha and said, "Wait, my sister is back there."

Kescha responded as she untied the boat, "There is no time to save her. The fortress is lost and so is she. You must go on without her."

"But," retorted Daphne.

"Don't let her sacrifice be in vain," responded Kescha.

Not satisfied with the answers given, Daphne continued, "Why are you helping me? You are one of them."

Kescha pushed the boat away from the dock and with regret said, "I'm sorry this is all I can do. It is true. I am one of them, a succubus bound to a dark priest that summoned me. I am a slave that serves a master with no chance of freedom, unless he wills it. I envy the freedom that humans take so lightly. And until I am free, I will defy him every chance I get. Live on and protect the blood gem. Hide it where no one will find it."

Chapter 2
The Target

Our story continues five hundred years later in the present city area called Vampiro City. The Vampiro City area was another evolved kingdom that bordered the same villages of Demicroft in the past.

Vampiro City was well known as the vampiric metropolis or the city of vampires. All of the creatures of the night could be found here, but the vampiric breed, vampires, vampeels, and ghouls were the most frequent. Among the three types, vampires were the dominant breed and controlled most of the action in the underground nightlife of the city. The most powerful vampires lived like kings as they watched over their territories. Ghouls served their vampire masters, while vampeels were very rare and outcasts for the most part. Any significant action going on in the nightlife of the city was known by at least one of the vampire clans. Fear not, for slayers and bounty hunters did play their part to keep them in check constantly.

This major metropolitan area was divided into three sectors. The rich or high-roller sector covered about fifty percent of the city. The middle or workingman sector took up about forty percent of the city. The poor or slum sector housed the remaining ten percent of the city.

Vampiro City had terrain that was irregular with many hills and valleys, along with one major river that flowed through the center of it. The woodlands were few in the center of the city and most of the land bordering the river was developed. Throughout the city, many statues and fountains, depicting bats or wolves, were found all over. The downtown area of the city had a vast transportation network, including highways, subways, elevated rail, and regular city streets.

Technology in the present day was at a medium level. Life was more complicated and everyone had a job or owned a business. Every household had many useful appliances and electrical power was common. People drove automobiles, flew planes of all sorts, and sailed ships of all kinds, or simply rode public vehicles, like buses, rail cars, and trains to satisfy their transportation needs. Weapons were more advanced and required a medium level of maintenance. Depending on the person or group, various throwing weapons, bullet-firing guns, cannons, bombs, and missiles were used. Some swords, daggers, and ammunition were made of silver, since most creatures of the night have a weakness toward it; otherwise they were made of steel. Medicine was more refined by the use of medical facilities and well-educated doctors to treat wounded and sick people. Medical treatment was more advanced and surgery was commonplace, but limited to organ transplants on the highest level.

Vampiro City had a healthy population, exceeding two hundred thousand people. The city area had a government that worked like an independent country. Everything public was regulated and all citizens had a complete record registered with the government from birth to death. The city was governed and ruled by a president that was elected by the citizens and advised by a committee.

The law was enforced by an elite multitask police force. Suspected law breakers were brought to trial and cross-examined by a psychic to determine if the suspect was guilty. Lawyers were found to be obsolete in this type of system, because of bribery or underhanded swaying. The fate of the offender was predetermined; depending on what punishment was assigned to the crime committed. If the suspect was found guilty and had a history of three offenses, then the suspect was sentenced to death. Only the city president could pardon an offender.

A specialized security force consisting of soldiers, other than the police, and attack vehicles defended the city from outside invaders. Bounty hunters and slayers defended the inner part of the city. Government bodyguards protected the president and the advisory committee from any foes within the core of the city.

The Grand Hotel was the largest and most popular hotel in the wealthy sector of Vampiro City. Only celebrities, government advisors, wealthy businessmen, or members of powerful families met and did business here. It was a very large establishment, which housed eight hundred guest rooms, fifty deluxe suites, and twelve penthouses. With that many rooms it had a right wing, a left wing, and a main wing to house them all. From an area view the three wings were attached to each other like spokes on a wheel. At the end of each wing was a large round landing area. The right and left landing area wing on the ground level had an entrance of its own and a sidewalk connecting it to the main entrance outside. The main wing housed the lobby, the meeting rooms, the ballrooms, three restaurants, and two bars. Each room had a sliding glass door that led to a balcony, which allowed a guest to have a view of the outside no matter what side of the wing his room was on. Shrubbery decorated all the fronts of the wings in between the windows. At the main entrance was a large revolving door with a red carpet that extended all the way out to the driveway. A red canopy with brass poles covered the red carpet from the door to the driveway. In front of the main entrance was a large fountain. Around the fountain was a circular drive for taxis, limousines, and any other cars to arrive at the main entrance. The base of the fountain was circular and made out of stone. In the center of the fountain was a large statue of a bat with its wings wrapped around its body. Water spilled out of its mouth constantly and filled the base of the fountain. Around the perimeter of the hotel grounds was a very tall brick wall. The wall was about a foot thick with security cameras on top. The cameras were mounted on the wall every ten feet and pointed to monitor any activities on the outside of the wall. The morning was still clinging on to the darkness of night, as the action within the hotel was about to unfold.

Inside the bar of the hotel lobby was a quiet scene of people sitting, enjoying their drinks, and socializing. It was Saturday and the clock on the wall read 4:00 a.m. The bar was open twenty-four hours with no windows to the outside to indicate night or day. The dim lighting of the bar helped to enhance the romantic atmosphere of couples or helped others to hide from prying eyes. A three-foot-wide round counter, shaped like the quarter of a circle segment, made up the bar and took up a fourth of the floor space. Five bar stools were placed and evenly spaced on the outside of the counter. To the left of the bar were three large round tables with four chairs around them. The dark brown paneled walls were decorated with elegant candleholders to help illuminate the room lightly. Fancy white marble tile covered the floor, while the eight feet ceiling was made of wood that matched the paneling. The bar, stools, chairs, and tables were made of finely crafted mahogany wood. Each stool and chair had a red velvet seat that also matched the color of the tablecloths. Small elegant candleholders, made of glass, lit the tables a little to add to the atmosphere. Behind the bar was a shelf, full of many different kinds of liquor in various bottles. Near the far end of the counter was a dispenser for draft beer. Many different kinds of glasses hung from above the counter for the bartender to use in serving customers. On the opposite side of the bar was the exit to the main lobby of the hotel.

A bartender, standing about six feet tall with a macho-type build, was washing a glass at the time. He looked about forty-five years old with chiseled facial features, dark hair and a mustache. His hair was short and slicked back, while his mustache was thick and curled at the ends. He wore a white long-sleeve shirt, dark slacks, a dark vest and a black bow tie. His blue eyes were serious looking and it appeared he liked his job.

A woman with the height of five feet ten inches was sitting at the far end of the bar, near the beer dispenser. She looked about twenty-five years old with average-sized breasts and an athletic build. The toned look of her arms and legs was obvious with the outfit she was wearing. Her shoulder-length hair was dark brown with red highlights, which had a wild part on the side, a little spiky, and saw-tooth bangs partly hiding her eyes. Red was the color of her eyes with narrow pupils like a cat. She had a natural beauty about her face, which was only enhanced more by the makeup she wore on her eyelids, under her eyebrows, and lips. The only jewelry she wore was a set of long silver dangly earrings. For some reason her right earring was missing a piece and did not exactly match the left one. Her skin was a creamy pale color that had a lovely glow in this dim light. The polish on her fingernails and toenails matched her lipstick perfectly. She wore a black dress with thin straps that was quite conservative in showing cleavage, but had a slit that showed a generous amount of leg to the alert eye. When she stood, the dress draped all the way down to her ankles. The dress fit her like a glove, but the material was not too thin for her nipples to make an impression. On her feet she wore a set of open-toe high-heel shoes that matched her dress. On her shoulder was a matching black leather purse to complete the outfit. To some she looked like a vampire, while others might think she needed a little bit more sun. Her name was Katrina.

Katrina sat at her stool with her legs crossed as she enjoyed a fancy mixed drink with a little umbrella in it. While she was sipping her drink a couple came in the bar. The couple was a well-dressed man and a sleazy-dressed woman holding on his arm.

The man stood about six feet four inches tall with a macho-type build. He had average looks with short hair and a mustache that went all the way down to his chin. His hair was jet black and slicked back, showing his forehead. Fair skin and brown-colored eyes described his complexion. He wore a buttoned shirt, jacket, dress slacks, and slip-on shoes. His blue shirt was unbuttoned halfway down his chest, where his medallion hung from his neck and close to his skin. It was a medallion, the size of a fifty-cent piece, with the same skull symbol of Flusken's ring in the past. The jacket and trousers where a dark color with an expensive feel to them. His shoes were dark brown and very classy. This guy had expensive taste, when it came to clothing. He could have been possibly age thirty by his appearance.

The woman stood six feet tall with an athletic build and very large breasts. Her firm breasts were quite large for her physique, but she carried them well. Her skin was golden brown with long thick shimmering white hair that hung all the way down to her behind. An irregular saw-tooth hairline complemented her facial features, like her clear blue eyes. The bulk of her hair was tied back in a ponytail that hung more to one side of her head. Judging from her lovely facial features and youthful skin, her age could have possibly been twenty-five years. She wore a crimson-colored dress with half-inch-wide straps that met behind her neck in the back. When she stood, the dress draped all the way down to her calves. The dress had a sleazy look, since it had a very low V cut in the front and showed a generous about of cleavage. Her matching high-heel shoes finished the outfit as well as her matching leather purse. Although her dress was sleazy, her makeup was conservative and only highlighted her good features. The dangling diamond earrings, necklace, and bracelet finished off her outfit like icing on a cake. If she was a paid escort or prostitute, it didn't matter. She carried herself as a high-class woman all the way.

The couple sat down at the table closest to the exit on the other side of the bar. As the couple was getting comfortable the woman pulled a small metal case out of her purse. Out of the metal case she pulled a cigarette, which she held out for him to light it. She snapped the metal case shut as she smiled at him and put it away. The man pulled out his fancy metal lighter, lit her cigarette and whisked it shut, like any cool guy would. She held the cigarette in her hand, like any classy lady would, and took little puffs off of it.

Katrina was watching the whole seen of the couple subtly as she sipped her drink. The other tables were full of regulars she had seen before. Customers occupied the rest of the bar stools as well, but only the couple in the farthest table interested her. She carefully watched as the man got up from the table to order some drinks at the counter. She paid no mind to the woman, but continued to watch the man. Actually, she wasn't interested in the man at all, even though it could have looked that way.

Just after the woman had her cigarette lit, the man got up, walked over to the counter to order some drinks. As he walked over to the counter Katrina noticed the golden medallion hanging from his neck. She watched as the man made idle conversation with the bartender.

"What will it be, sir?" asked the bartender.

"Two glasses of red wine," answered the man.

"An excellent choice, sir. The lady shall approve," commented the bartender. The bartender opened a dark-colored wine bottle, using a corkscrew to remove the cork.

"Good. I hope she likes it," said the man.

"You are a lucky man, sir," stated the bartender as he gracefully poured the wine in two elegant wine goblets.

The man asked, "What do you mean?"

"You are in company with a very beautiful woman. If I were you, sir, I would show her all that Vampiro City has to offer, especially at night."

The man grinned as he replied, "The only thing I am going to show her is the inside of my penthouse suite and how many times I can make her scream with pleasure."

The bartender was unaffected by his remark as he grinned and said, "Very good, sir. The room is stocked with stamina drinks." He laughed at the bartender's remark as the bartender placed the wine goblets near him. The man proceeded to pull out a thick wad of notes, held together with a golden money clip, to pay with. He pulled it off the wad as he prepared to pay for the drinks. The money clip had an engraving of a skull with fangs on it. He pulled out a few notes and handed them to the bartender as he put the rest back on the clip.

"Keep the change," said the man as the bartender took the notes.

"Thank you, sir. Enjoy your evening," replied the bartender as the man put the rest of his money back in his pocket.

Katrina recognized the medallion the man was wearing around his neck. She smiled, like she was about to do something naughty, and continued to blend in with the crowd. The man picked up the goblets as he noticed Katrina smiling at him, so he smiled back and raised his glass to her. She played along and raised her glass back at him as he began to step away with the drinks. Katrina thought to herself, “What a pig.”

Minutes went by as the couple got up and left the bar. Katrina finished her drink and set it down on the counter. She reached into her purse and pulled out her cell phone. Her hand pressed a button on the side, which caused the phone to flip open. She dialed a number on the number pad and held the phone to her ear.

A man answered, “Yeah, Katrina?”

Katrina answered, “It’s on. Where are you?”

“I’m in room 201,” said the man on the phone.

“I’ll be there in a few minutes to join you, sweetie,” responded Katrina.

“I’ll be waiting,” answered the man on the phone.

Katrina closed her phone and put it away. She got up off the stool and said, “Time to go to work,” as she left the bar. Katrina was always careful when she was doing a job. She did her best to think of every possible scenario. Working alone was the way she preferred doing things. Although she wouldn’t admit it, she wasn’t too proud to seek help when a job became complicated. She was one of the best in her line of work. Her only fear was her target getting away or getting the best of her. She loved the hunt. It was in her blood.

In the right-wing hallway a woman, dressed in a maid outfit, was walking along when her cell phone rang. The right wing and left wing were identical in design and had the same amount of rooms on each floor. Each hallway of a wing measured ten feet wide with plain ten-foot-tall ceilings. Red carpet blanketed the floor, while the color of pearl covered the walls. Each inset room door had fancy numbers with color to match the walls. All of the walls of the hotel wings had simple rectangular trim designs to help give the walls some definition. Fancy brass-mounted lights were mounted throughout the right wing in between the room doors on both sides of the hallway. Only small round emergency lights were in the ceiling.

The maid stood about five feet three inches tall and had a slender build. Her legs and arms were a healthy thickness with very little muscle definition and her breasts were quite large. Light brown was the color of her hair, which had a shoulder length and her skin was fair. Her hair was parted at the very top of her head with neatly trimmed bangs partially covering her forehead. Her eyes were a lovely shade of green, like a jade stone. By her cute looks she was about twenty-three years old. The knee-length maid dress she was wearing was very conservative. It had short sleeves with cuffs and a rounded collar that opened to a V. At the base of the V buttons went all the way down to the bottom of dress. Around the waist was an apron with a couple of pockets for carrying small things. She also wore pantyhose with sneakers. The whole outfit was a combination of light blue and white. Her name was Emma.

Emma grabbed her ringing cell phone from her pocket. Her cell phone was the same design as Katrina's and she opened it the same way. She held it to her ear as she answered, "Hello."

"We're on. Bring the stuff," said the voice on the phone.

"Okay," answered Emma. She smiled as she immediately got off the phone.

Meanwhile in room 201 a man was holding a cell phone. The room was very spacious with a bathroom, two beds, a dresser, a table with a couple of chairs, a snack bar, and a cabinet holding a TV. The walls were plain except for a few mounted abstract paintings throughout the room. Fancy lamps throughout the room lit the room evenly. The floor had matching carpet, like the hallway. A cart about four feet long and two feet wide was sitting in the room. The metal cart had a white cloth that concealed anything on the bottom two shelves. On top of the cart were a few metal covered dishes and a bucket with a wine bottle. None of the dishes had been touched nor the wine bottle uncorked as it sat in the ice.

The man in the room stood about five feet five inches with a solid-type build. His green eyes and fair skin was the only thing gentle about him. From his rugged looks he was about forty years old. His dark buzz-cut hair and neatly trimmed mustache was a trademark of ex-military or ex-law-enforcement. The man was wearing some dark coveralls and working boots, a hotel maintenance uniform. His name was Mak.

The man was sitting in a chair, while waiting for someone as the clock on the nightstand read 4:45 a.m. In an instant there was a knock at the door. The man got up and looked through the peephole of the room door. He stepped away from the door as he opened it. Katrina entered the room and shut the door behind her.

Mak greeted her with a compliment, "Nice dress, Katrina."

Katrina smiled and said, "Thanks, Mak."

In a serious tone Mak got right to the point, "You are all set, Katrina. I just brought the basics as far as weaponry." He stepped over to the cart and lifted the cloth covering the lower shelves and said, "It's all on the lower level of the cart. I suggest you don't use any firearms unless it is absolutely necessary, otherwise the police might show up."

On the lower level of the cart were a sword, a few silver stakes, and a couple of handguns. The steel sword was about four feet long with a single-edged straight blade. The handle was overlaid with a hard plastic that had indentations in the molding for a better grip. The stakes were a half-inch in diameter, a foot long, and ground down to a point on the one end. The handguns were nine-millimeter Glocks, loaded with silver bullets.

"Good. Thanks for bringing my Glocks. I may not have to use them," said Katrina as she smiled.

Mak asked, "Are you sure it's him?"

With confidence she said, "It's him all right. The one I have been tracking for the past few days."

Mak asked, "Does he suspect anything?"

Katrina replaced the cloth to cover the weapons as she answered, "I doubt it. He seems to be preoccupied with some whore at the moment. Remember, vampires have enhanced sight not hearing."

Mak continued, "The sun will be up soon."

Katrina nodded in agreement, "I know. That will work to my advantage. What room is he staying in?"

"The penthouse suite number 2," responded Mak.

She crossed her arms as she commented, "Perfect. He is either brave or stupid. He has nowhere to go, but down in the building."

With concern Mak said, "Be careful, Katrina."

"Don't worry, Mak. He is dead meat. It's only a matter of time," responded Katrina as she heard a knock at the door. Katrina went over to the door and looked through the peephole. "Emma is here," said Katrina as she turned to Mak. She opened the door and let Emma inside the room. Immediately, she shut the door behind her and went over to Emma.

Emma had with her a hotel hostess uniform on a hanger. The uniform consisted of a long-sleeve blouse and a skirt. The blouse was basically a beige dress shirt, while the knee-length skirt was dark brown.

With enthusiasm Emma handed it over to Katrina and said, "I got you a uniform, Katrina, and a bra too. I hope all of it fits." Emma took a bra from her pocket and handed it to her as well. The white strap bra was lacy with a fastener in the back.

"Thanks, Emma. I am sure it will. You know my size after all," said Katrina as she took the clothes on the hanger from Emma. Katrina placed all the clothes on the bed closest to her and said, "You know I hate to wear bras."

Emma retorted, "But you need it, Katrina. It completes the outfit and it is one of your own."

Katrina agreed, "You're right, Emma. I just feel so constricted wearing them."

Emma remarked, "You're lucky you don't have breasts like mine, Katrina. Unlike you, I really do need the support."

Katrina smiled as she turned to Mak and said, "Mak, could you turn around while I change?"

"Sure," said Mak as he turned and faced the closed curtains of the window.

Katrina kicked her shoes off, while Emma unzipped her dress in the back. Katrina pulled the straps of the dress down and let it fall to the floor. She took the bra and put it on, like any woman would do. Katrina slipped into the skirt and put on the blouse. She liked to show a little skin so she left a couple buttons at the top of the blouse undone. After tucking the blouse into the skirt, Katrina zipped up the skirt on the side and fastened it shut. "Okay, Mak. I'm decent," said Katrina as she slipped on some low heel shoes that matched the skirt.

"How do I look?" asked Katrina, when Mak turned around and saw her dressed.

"You would look good in anything, Katrina," answered Mak.

Katrina smiled as she responded, "Always the charmer, Mak."

"Uh, Katrina, I think you look too good," said Emma after looking at her face.

Mak went over to Katrina and handed her a pair of glasses. "She's right, Katrina. Here, wear these, lose the makeup, and tone down the hairdo."

Katrina took the glasses and agreed, "You have a point there, Emma, Mak. He might recognize me from the bar in the lobby."

"Allow me," said Emma as she took a moist towelette and wiped her makeup off. Katrina pulled her hair back into a ponytail and tied it off.

Mak asked, "What about the earrings?"

Katrina answered firmly as she put on the glasses, "They stay."

"Whatever you say, Katrina," said Mak as he knew not to argue with her.

"Let's go, Emma, the sun is going to rise soon," ordered Katrina.

Mak commented, "When you are done, I'll meet you in the service area, Katrina."

Katrina responded with a wink, "You got it, Mak." Emma followed Katrina out of the room, while pushing the cart.

Emma pulled out a special card key, resembling a credit card with a magnetic strip and having the hotel name on it. She inserted it into a slot on the panel next to a service elevator, one that only employees could use. The doors slid open as Katrina and Emma entered with the cart. The security of the hotel was top-of-the-line, since only special card keys would allow employees access to the service elevators that went to any floor of the hotel. The service elevator was not very fancy with metal doors, plain walls, a floor, and a ceiling with an overhead light. To the right of the doors was the control panel with round numbered buttons for every floor. Below the panel was a portable phone in case of an emergency.

As the elevator went up the shaft to the penthouse Katrina and Emma were talking.

"I can get you inside the suite, Katrina," remarked Emma. Since she was a maid at the hotel, she had full-access card keys to enter any kind of guest room.

Katrina countered with, "That won't be necessary, Emma. I only need you to get me to the level."

With feelings of disappointment Emma inquired, "Why can't I come with you, Katrina?"

"I don't want you to be in danger," answered Katrina.

Emma continued to plead, "You won't even know I'm there."

In a firmer voice Katrina said, "This is not open for discussion, Emma."

Like a persistent child wanting something, Emma went on, "I just want to watch."

"Come here," said Katrina as she extended her arms.

Emma smiled as she placed her arms around Katrina and hugged her. Katrina smiled as she warmly hugged her closely. There was an aura of stillness between them that seemed timeless, but it only lasted less than a minute when Katrina broke the silence and looked her in the eyes. "You mean the world to me, Emma. I almost lost you once and I would never forgive myself if something happened to you, because of letting you stay near me while hunting. Do you understand?"

Emma knew Katrina was right and answered, "Yes."

Katrina smiled and kissed her on the cheek as she said, "That's my girl." Katrina looked at her and said, "As soon as I get off the elevator you take it straight down to meet your Uncle Mak. Are we clear?"

Emma agreed, "Yes."

In the penthouse suite number 2 the time on the alarm clock read 5:00 a.m. The penthouse suite was twice the size of a special suite and three times the size of a regular guest room. It was divided into five rooms, the main room, two separate bedrooms, a deluxe bathroom, and a hot-tub room. In the main room was a circular king-size bed, located in the back near the window doors. A red-colored silk bedspread covered the bed with heart-shaped pillows on top of it. Beside the bed was a square four-legged nightstand, near the north wall. The wooden nightstand was simple and had a cherry-wood color. A red velvet couch was beside the bed, near the middle of the room and facing an entertainment center in the south direction. The entertainment center was a large wooden cabinet, like the nightstand, with a fifty-inch-screen TV and a theater system. It was very versatile for entertainment, since it could play movies, music, or link up to the data network. On the north and south side of the room were the two other bedrooms. The deluxe bathroom was on the north side of the room beside the one bedroom. On the south side of the room and beside the other bedroom was the hot-tub room. Near the center of the room was a long coffee table with two chairs, one facing north and one facing south. The chairs matched the couch in color and style. In front of the glass coffee table was the entrance to the room. Closets facing north and south were in the main room near the entrance. The floor was covered by thick red carpet that matched the heavy drapes hiding the window doors, except where the window door was open. Outside the window doors was a very large balcony. The balcony was so large that it had room for a round wooden table and two chairs. The brown-colored table and chairs had a light blue umbrella in the center of it. Dark red colored the otherwise plain ten-foot-tall walls of the room. On the nightstand and throughout the main room were fancy brass lamps with pink shades.

Some vampires, especially young ones that are less than one hundred years old, will indulge themselves in their old habits and activities they had when they were still human. Habits and activities like smoking, drinking, sexual intercourse, as well as others still fill a part of their needs and desires. Other than feelings, old habits are one of the few fragments of humanity vampires have left.

The couple from the bar earlier were getting more intimate on the king-sized bed. He had her locked in a deep kiss as they were sitting on the bed. While she was kissing him, she unbuttoned his shirt and removed it. He wasted no time as he slowly worked his way down her neck, kissing every inch of it. She enjoyed the pleasure of his touch as she threw down his shirt. The man went around her back and continued to kiss her neck as he undid her strap behind her neck. Slowly, the straps slid down her chest, off her breasts, and fell down to her waist. With her breasts exposed the man began to fondle them with his masculine hands. She was enraptured by his touch as she took off her necklace. He continued to caress her breasts as he kissed her neck and shoulder. His eyes turned bloody red with narrow pupils, like a cat. Fangs appeared on his upper jaw as he prepared to bite her exposed flesh. The man was indeed a vampire. With her eyes closed she turned her head as she gently guided his mouth to hers with her one hand.

Without warning there was a knock at the door. He stopped before he could do anything else as his eyes returned to being human like. He closed his mouth to hide his fangs and said, "Who is it?"

"Room service," answered Katrina from the other side of the door.

She looked at him and said, "It's okay. Go ahead and answer it. Maybe they made a mistake. I can wait."

The vampire, being annoyed from the intrusion, got off the bed to answer the door. The woman pulled her straps up and refastened them, while adjusting her breasts to look presentable. The vampire decided to play along, even though it was not wise to feed off the employees of the hotel. His fangs reverted back to normal human teeth before he opened the fancy wooden double doors and let Katrina come in.

Katrina pushed the cart in as she asked, "Where would you like it, sir?"

He looked at her and the cart as he said, "I don't remember ordering room service."

She played along and said, "Should I take it back, sir?"

He was puzzled by the possible mistake and pointed to his left and said, "No. It would be a shame to take all this lovely stuff back. Put it right there." Katrina moved the cart to where he pointed as he closed the door behind her. He turned to Katrina and said, "It is not wise for a vampire to show their eyes in a public place like this."

She covered his inquiry and said, "It is not wise for a vampire to stay in the penthouse with sunlight becoming a threat soon."

He complimented her response, "You're a smart one. I like that. Let me guess. You were just turned recently?"

"Yes," answered Katrina.

He grinned as he said, "I see. You haven't learned how to disguise your eyes yet."

"Right," answered Katrina.

He went on, "I didn't know the hotel has vampires working this early. As you said the sun will be up soon."

She continued to play along, "My shift is almost over, sir."

"Well in that case would you like to join us?" offered the vampire.

She smiled as she saw those lustful eyes gazing upon her. If she were human, his mesmerizing gaze would have had her under his power by now. She decided to exploit his weakness for pretty women and replied, "I'm sorry, sir. I can't stay. I have other work to do."

He continued to flirt with her as the woman on the bed watched patiently. She lay there on the bed on her side with her right elbow propping her torso up as she stroked her sensuous lips. "Nonsense, your job is to satisfy customers. If you stay, I'll make it worth your while," he said as he reached in his pocket and pulled out a wad of money. He handed her a large money note from the wad.

She slowly grabbed the note as the vampire quickly grabbed her hand. Katrina knew what he was doing and let him hold her hand.

"Please, I insist," he said as he bent down to kiss it.

Little did he know she had a silver stake stuck in her skirt behind her back. She hid it quite well from him, even though he closed the door behind her. While his head was still down to kiss her hand, she quickly pulled out the stake and got ready to stab him.

Much to her surprise he caught her hand holding the stake at the wrist before it even touched him. He had a death grip on her wrist as he looked up to her. His eyes turned blood red and glowed as he looked up to her. With a fiendish grin he showed his fangs and said, "Was it something I said?"

"I told you, sir. I have other things to do," answered Katrina. Katrina's strength was unmatched by his own as he squeezed her wrist and forced her to drop the stake.

"Wait a minute. Vampires cannot touch silver without being burned by it. How can you have vampiric eyes and fangs and still handle silver?" inquired the vampire.

Katrina knew she was found out so she began to taunt him, "I'm blessed and highly favored."

He looked her over some more, as he said, "No. It can't be. I have heard of your kind. Your kind is very rare, vampeel."

Instantly, Katrina lunged forward and head-butted him between the eyes. The shock from the impact caused him to let go of her as he backed up a couple feet. Immediately, she spun around and kicked him in the gut, which drove him back a few more feet, almost knocking him off his feet. He shook his head as he got his bearings and looked at her with delight. She took off the glasses and threw them down as she said, "You're smarter than you look, fang boy."

His fingernails extended a few inches as he said, "I will enjoy sucking every drop of blood from your veins, half breed."

Hoping for a quick kill, she knew she was going to have to fight this one. He obviously had a higher intelligence than she could have predicted, but slaying targets was never a clear-cut job. The unpredictable always reared its ugly head when least expected. Katrina decided to measure his fighting ability and use his arrogance if possible against him. Being half vampire she had the same reaction time as a vampire that had grown a few levels. Her strength was the same as a vampire's, but he was larger than her, so it was obvious strength alone would not defeat him. She had no fear in fighting him, since she knew martial arts.

Katrina positioned herself in a fighting stance and replied, "Come and get me, you arrogant blood sucker." As she faced him, she turned her body sideways, clinched her fists near her face, and slightly bent her knees.

He lunged towards her, like a wild animal pouncing on its prey. She dodged his attack and landed a kick to his gut. The force of her kick caught him and the momentum caused him to flip over and land on his back. As he fell he landed on top of the glass coffee table and shattered it.

Realizing she could fight, he slowly got up and commented, "You're pretty good."

Katrina smiled and replied, "I'm just getting started."

He moved in to attack her with his claws as he slashed at her horizontally, while she ducked under. When he slashed with his other arm, Katrina countered by punching under his arm and hitting his kidney area. He paused for a second as he recovered from the stun of her punch.

The vampire charged her again as she prepared to counter. Unfortunately, she forgot there was a chair behind her, which distracted her long enough for him to land a devastating uppercut to her waist. The blow of his punch almost knocked her out as she gasped for air. Quickly he grabbed her in a bear hug and slammed her against the wall. The initial shock stunned her for a second as he attempted squeeze the life out of her. Being half human had its drawbacks, since she still had to breathe and suffocation would possibly kill her.

Katrina continued to gasp for air as she struggled to pull herself free of his grip. Instinctively, she hit his ears with the palms of her hands. The blow was devastating enough to force him to let go as she slipped out of his grasp. Within no time at all she grabbed his head and gave him a crushing knee bash. He instantly fell backward as his head violently whipped back and followed.

Katrina went for the cart, but he grabbed her ankle and tripped her. She kicked him in the face as she broke his grip and got up. He also got up and had a fiendish grin on his face as he placed a finger on his nose.

"I think you broke my nose," he said as he pressed on it and pushed it back into place.

Katrina could hear the bones crackling back together, like eggshells being knocked against each other. "It will take more than a nose job to fix your looks," replied Katrina as she prepared to continue fighting him.

The vampire wasted no time as he came at her from the side with his slashing attack. Katrina ducked under his attack and kicked the back of his knee. With him forced off balance, she swung around and kicked him in the face with the heel of her foot. The force of her kick plowed his face into the carpet. His resilience was amazing as he got up and was thirsty for more punishment. Katrina was not impressed as she liked a challenge and enjoyed giving her target a beating if necessary.

"I'm having more fun with you than with that two-bit whore over there. I think I'll slam you first and then I'll drink you," said the vampire as he got his bearings and licked his bloody lip.

With a look of disgust on her face she said, "You're a pig."

"Thank you, my dear," was his reply as he bowed and slashed at her again.

She dodged him some more as she tried to work her way back to the cart a few feet away. As she continued to dodge he drove in closer and ripped her shirt open with his claws.

He paused as he looked at her exposed flesh. Katrina wasted no time as she snapped him in the jaw with a kick, which stunned his attack for a moment. Her shirt was fully ripped open and her lacy bra was exposed. Luckily, her bra only had shallow claw marks, otherwise it would have ripped open as well.

Katrina quickly looked down as she said, "Emma is going to kill me. You'll pay for that!" She seized the opportunity and jumped in the air to deliver a powerful kick to his face.

He recovered quicker than she thought as he grabbed her leg and threw her against the wall. She hit the wall so hard that she went right through it and into the bedroom. He stepped into the room and picked her up by the throat, while she was still stunned. She struggled as she grabbed his wrists. He held her there in the air as her feet dangled a couple of feet off the ground. His squeeze on her throat tightened a little as he looked at her firm breasts and defined abdominal muscles. He began to trace her midline of her torso from the bottom up with his claw as he commented, "It would be a shame to kill you so quickly." He groped her breast and said, "The fun is just starting."

Katrina's eyes glowed red as she said, "I'll show you fun!" She immediately kicked him in the groin. He quickly loosened his grip on her throat as he writhed in pain. Katrina, while still holding on to his wrists, pulled him forward as she fell back, placed her foot in his gut, and flipped him overhead. He landed flat on his back, still stunned from her kick to his groin.

She raced for a weapon as he slowly got up. Katrina grabbed the stake on the floor as he got to his feet. She wasted no time as she threw it at him. He backed up as he saw the stake flying through the air towards him. Instead of dodging the stake he caught it before it reached his heart. Still feeling the shock of the pain in his groin, he didn't realize the stake was burning his hand. Within seconds he responded to the burning of his flesh by the stake and dropped it. Without realizing it he kept backing up and the momentum carried him outside to the balcony. Before he could stop himself he fell off the balcony when he hit the railing.

Knowing from past experience that vampires don't usually die from falls, she ran to the cart to grab her sword.

As the vampire was falling head first, he instantly transformed into a bat with a wingspan of four feet. The bat flew back into the room from the open glass door. The vampire bat was hideous with long ears, razor-sharp teeth, and two red glowing eyes.

By the time the bat returned to the widow Katrina was ready with another stake in her hand. The bat flew in as Katrina threw the stake at the bat. The bat surprisingly dodged the spinning stake thrown at it as it flew closer to attack her. Katrina faced it head-on with her sword behind her back as it flew in to attack her. When the bat was close enough, she lunged in and impaled it in the lower torso with her sword. The bat squirmed and squealed helplessly as she grabbed its neck with her other hand. She took it outside and thrust the sword with the bat still on it into the outside wall. To add insult to injury she pegged both of its wings with a silver stake to the wall. Katrina looked at the bat and said, "The sun will be up in a moment. This is where the fun ends. Game over."

The sun began to rise as the bat continued to struggle to no avail. As the sunlight touched the vampire bat's body it began to burn instantly. While the sun continued to rise, the flames consumed the bat entirely. When nothing was left but ashes, Katrina retrieved her sword and stakes and wiped them off.

As she reentered the room the whore smiled and clapped her hands. Katrina looked at her with surprise and forgot she had an audience, since she thought the whore was put in a trance by the vampire. The woman replaced her necklace around her neck and looked at Katrina.

She spoke up, "Well done, vampeel. You have ruined my plans for the night."

Katrina responded sarcastically, "Sorry, but he had it coming."

She sat up as she said, "The master will scold me for failing to acquire the information I was to obtain from him. Oh well, the Drenkel family is foiled again."

With curiosity Katrina inquired, "Who are you? What do you know about the Drenkel Clan?"

She sat up with her hands on the bed and slightly leaned forward as she replied, "I know you are on a quest to destroy the Drenkel Clan. Good luck."

Katrina asked, "How do you know me?"

Kescha took a cigarette from her purse and answered, "I am a spy for one of them. That is all I can say."

Not satisfied with the answer Katrina pulled a gun from the cart and aimed it at her. "You will tell me everything I want to know or I am going to stain the sheets you are sitting on, bitch," ordered Katrina.

She did not show the least bit of fear as she looked at Katrina in the eyes. The woman held the cigarette in her hand as she smiled and remarked, "I'll only tell you that you are way out of your league. You will need more allies if you are to stop the ones who would tip the balance of this realm."

"Suit yourself," responded Katrina as she fired her gun. As the three bullets flew towards the woman she instantly turned into a shadow. The bullets passed right through her, like rocks going through smoke. Katrina looked with disbelief as the shadow disappeared from her sight.

The woman re-formed in the flesh beside Katrina's shadow and grabbed her by the throat with one hand. In the initial shock Katrina dropped her gun as the woman lifted her off the floor.

She smiled as she gloated, "I could easily snap your neck, but that would only aid my master." Katrina thought she was done for when unexpectedly the woman released her. As she fell like a rock Katrina held her throat and caught her breath.

Katrina looked up to her and asked, "What are you?"

"I am a demon who was summoned by a dark priest. Vampires are not the only things that go bump in the night," answered the woman as she crossed her arms.

"I have heard of your kind. You're a succubus," responded Katrina.

"Impressive. Yes. We are both born from darkness, but there is a difference. You are free to fight the forces of darkness, while I must serve them," replied the woman.

Katrina was puzzled by the demon's answer and asked, "Why are you telling me this?"

She looked at Katrina and said with sincerity, "I envy you, Katrina, but you are not powerful enough to free me from my master."

At that moment as if by magic the woman's hair changed to a jet-black color as she undid her ponytail. Her dress also changed to a white color. The dress had thicker straps and a slit down the middle of the front. The dress was open in the front showing her breasts with a more loose cleavage down the middle. Like the other dress the straps attached behind her neck and showed off her back a good bit. Her shoes also matched the white dress.

Katrina looked on with surprise as the woman took her cigarette and lit it with a small flame from her hand.

The woman walked towards the door, turned around and said, "May be we'll bump into each other again. I enjoyed the show." She winked at Katrina as she put on a pair of dark round-shaped sunglasses.

"Will you at least give me your name the next time?" asked Katrina.

Kescha smiled as she took a puff off of her cigarette and answered, "Maybe." She left the room at this time and closed the door behind her.

Katrina got up and looked in the room for any of the vampire's belongings. She was in luck for she found a wallet, a money clip full of notes, and a medallion on the nightstand. It was definitely a medallion belonging to the Drenkel vampire clan. Katrina grabbed the wad of notes, the wallet, and the medallion and put on the vampire's coat he wore earlier. She thought for a second as she said, "I don't believe it. A demon that wants to fight the forces of darkness, but then again, that's cool. " She placed the medallion and the wallet in the coat pockets and left the room.

It was 7:00 a.m. by the time Katrina and Emma made it back to their place. They lived together in the uptown area of the workingman sector of Vampiro City, a good centralized location of the city region. There they resided in an old abandoned firehouse, a place used by firefighters until they built a new facility and left this one behind. Their place wasn't perfect, but it was home to them. The old firehouse was three stories tall, sitting on a quiet corner of town, and resembled a giant chimney of red brick and mortar. Time had elapsed as both of them had taken a shower and were getting ready for bed.

On the residential level of the firehouse Emma was in the kitchen pouring some shots of whiskey. She was wearing a pink-colored set of pajamas.

Katrina was in her bedroom sitting on her bed, while drying her hair with a towel. She felt somewhat refreshed after taking a relaxing shower. Katrina was wearing nothing more than a plain light blue nightshirt and a pink pair of panties.

Her room was a modest size with dark blue-colored walls and blue carpet. It consisted of a closet near the door, a bed, a nightstand, and a dresser. The wooden nightstand had a shaded lamp and a regular phone on it. The phone was a plastic black cat that Katrina found at a novelty shop. When the phone rang its eyes would glow and it meowed like a cat. The wooden dresser was composed of six small drawers and a desk to sit at with a wooden chair. Various stuffed cats decorated the top of the dresser. They were all cute and varied in size, color, and how they were posed. On the desk part of the dresser was a large circular mirror. On either side of the mirror were two shaded lamps. Near the edge of the desk was a picture of a woman standing in a park with her hands on the shoulders of a little girl. The ceiling was plain, except for a ceiling fan in the center with wooden blades. Her bed was double size with a couple of pillows, sheets, and a spread in different shades of blue. In the opposite corner of the room from the door was a door to a small bathroom.

Emma entered the room with a couple of shot glasses of whiskey.

Katrina smiled as she entered the room and said, "You're just in time." Emma sat down.

"Here you go," said Emma as she handed Katrina a shot glass.

"Thanks, Emma," said Katrina as she brought the glass to her mouth and remarked, "Bottoms up." Emma smiled as she took her shot of whisky and gulped it.

"One less vampire to worry about preying on the helpless," remarked Emma.

Katrina looked at the picture on the dresser and replied, "Yes… One less vampire."

Emma knew from the expression on Katrina's face that she said something that triggered a bad memory and apologized, "Oh, Katrina. I'm sorry. I didn't mean to bring up the past."

Katrina turned to Emma and placed her arm around her and said, "It's all right, Emma. We are celebrating."

Emma asked, "You still miss her a lot. Don't you?"

"Sometimes," answered Katrina as she clinched her fist and continued, "And because of it, that clan member and anyone else will suffer my wrath."

Emma inquired, "Tell me. How did it go, Katrina?"

Emma looked on with eagerness as Katrina explained, "He was tougher than I thought. However, the reward was well worth it." Katrina neglected to tell her about her unusual encounter with the succubus. After all, she did not want her to worry about her needlessly. Katrina reached for her bag and continued, "He had plenty of cash on him and this."

She pulled the Drenkel Clan medallion from her bag and showed it to Emma.

Emma took it from Katrina's hand and looked at it as she inquired, "What is it?"

Emma looked up at Katrina as she answered, "He was part of the Drenkel Clan. This medallion proves it. I will not rest until that entire clan is wiped out."

Emma looked at Katrina with concern and said, "Are you sure you are all right, Katrina? You look tired."

Katrina smiled and winked as she replied, "Nothing that a little blood and a good night's sleep won't cure."

With no pause Emma said, "Okay."

Katrina reprieved, "I was just joking about the blood part, Emma."

Emma slowly unbuttoned her pajama top as she said, "Really, Katrina, it's okay . You can have some."

Katrina looked into her innocent eyes and was at a loss for words to counter her willingness to help her. After unbuttoning her pajama top, she pulled it open to expose her neck, shoulder, and breast. Katrina's thirst for blood was awakened after looking upon Emma's exposed flesh. Her beautiful skin was so clear, delicate, and alluring, the way a predator fixes its eye on its prey.

Katrina smiled at her as she commented, "You make it so hard to say no, Emma." Emma smiled in response.

Katrina continued, "Your uncle would be mad at me if he knew we were doing this."

Emma had no feeling of guilt as she replied, "He doesn't have to know, Katrina."

"Well, I'm not going to tell him," remarked Katrina. With that last statement Katrina opened her mouth and exposed her small fangs as she drew closer to Emma's shoulder. Katrina gently sunk her fangs into Emma's shoulder as she closed her eyes and began to suck her blood. Emma closed her eyes as she went off into a trance. The sharp pain from Katrina's bite subsided and turned to pleasure as their thoughts merged as one for a short time. Emma reached her arms around Katrina and gave her a loving embrace as Katrina continued to feed.

Chapter 3
The Inquiry

It was Sunday and the clock in the lobby of the Grand Hotel read 1:00 a.m. The lobby of the hotel was very spacious in the main wing. Beyond the revolving doors of the main entrance, fancy blue carpeting covered the entire floor of that area. All of the walls on this level were done in mahogany-wood paneling. From the high ceiling hung several large crystal chandeliers, which illuminated the area quite well.

In the center of the floor was a large fountain with a sculpture. The stone sculpture was made up of three vampire sisters. All of them were wearing linen that revealed their legs a little and some cleavage. Their standing poses were all slightly varied. They all slightly varied in height, while all of them had a similar slender physique. One had short hair and average-sized breasts. The second had long hair and larger-than-average-sized breasts. And the third had shoulder-length hair and very large breasts in comparison. As they stood there water poured out of containers they were holding and spilled into the base of the round fountain.

Behind the sculpture fountain was an escalator that went up two more levels. The second level was a restaurant level, where three restaurants had allotted space. And the third level was the entertainment level, where the hotel housed a few ballrooms, a theater with stage, an arcade, and a casino with bar.

To the far right of the entrance was a set of public restrooms. Along the same wall were several meeting rooms. Past the public restrooms was the lobby bar.

To the far left of the entrance was the reception desk for people to check in and out as well as a limousine service counter. Along the same wall were a section of public phones, about eight stalls. Past the front desk were several more meeting rooms.

At the end of the main wing, where it met with the circular landing, four elevators were available to take guests to their rooms. In the circular landing was a massive circular staircase, which also connected the main wing with the other two wings.

At that time the lobby was full of the usual weekend crowd of people, who were having fun and in no hurry to go to their rooms. Regardless of the time of day or night the hotel staff were always busy with every day tasks at hand.

A man, standing about six feet tall, entered the lobby and headed straight for the reception counter. He was an ugly man with a macho-type build. His appearance was a bit wild with short spiked dark hair, thick eyebrows, a goatee, and brown eyes. His skin was pale. The only jewelry he wore were golden hoop earrings in both ears and a large gold chain around his neck with a Drenkel medallion on it. Every piece of clothing he wore was black. He wore a buttoned shirt, a full-length leather jacket, pants, a pair of fingerless gloves, and a pair of boots. Judging from his looks, he appeared to be thirty years old. This man did not fit the high-class crowd the hotel was accustomed to receiving. He was a vampire named Shawn.

People stayed clear of his way as he approached the reception counter. Behind the light-marbled counter stood an attendant. She stood about five feet five inches tall with a slender-type build and smaller-than-average breasts. The woman was very cute with short brown hair and neatly trimmed bangs. She had tanned skin and green eyes. Her outfit was basically a blue blazer, a matching skirt, a matching pair of heeled shoes, and a light-colored blouse. A red tie pulled the collar together and accented her blouse. Judging from her looks, she appeared to be twenty years old.

She greeted Shawn with a smile as he approached the counter, "Welcome to the Grand Hotel. May I help you?"

Shawn looked at her like she was a late-night snack as he asked, "Could you call the room that Basil Smith is staying in?"

"Just one moment, sir," answered the attendant as she looked at the computer in front of her for the registry. She hesitated as she looked at him and answered, "Uh, sir, he is no longer with us."

"You mean he checked out," asked Shawn.

She talked in a quieter tone of voice as she replied, "Sir, Basil Smith has been slain."

Shawn's eyes were full of fury as he reacted, "What?"

Charles, the hotel manager, stepped out of a nearby doorway behind the counter and faced Shawn. He placed his hand on her shoulder and said, "I'll handle this. Go take a break."

She acknowledged his order as she looked at him, "Yes, sir." The attendant immediately walked to the doorway and left behind the situation at the counter.

Charles stood about five feet eight inches tall with a thin-type build. His looks were average with high cheekbones and a narrow chin, a thick mustache, short-length brown hair combed straight back, and brown eyes. His skin was fair. Judging from his looks, he appeared to be forty-five years old. He wore a dark pinstriped suit with matching pants, a red tie, a white shirt, and black dress shoes. On his right ring finger he wore a ring like Drake's in the past.

He looked at Shawn with authority and said, "Come with me." Shawn followed Charles into a nearby vacant meeting room. Charles closed the door behind him.

The meeting room was large with four tables put together like a square picture frame. The tables were dark and shiny, like mica stone. Elegant brass chairs with cushions were neatly pushed in under the tables on the outside. The cushions were a blue color, which matched the carpeted floor. Four smaller-scale crystal chandeliers hung from the high ceiling and illuminated the room. Three of the walls were solid, but the wall adjacent to the other meeting room was modular and could be moved, like a curtain, to create a larger room. All of the walls were beige in color with a few lines of trim on them to give them dimension.

Shawn sat down on a chair and propped his feet up on the table. Charles pulled a chair out and sat next to him, while facing him.

Shawn looked at him and said, "What is going on here, Charles?"

He crossed his arms and replied, "Getting uncontrollably upset will not change the fact that your friend is dead."

Shawn ignored Charles's remark, as he demanded, "I want answers, Charles."

He continued, "Out of respect for the Drenkel Clan, I will tell you what I know. When the maid went in to clean the room, there was no trace of anyone. No belongings of any kind were found, except for a pair of lady's glasses. Oh, and some blood was found splattered on a wall."

"His blood?" asked Shawn.

"Most likely, other than that a strange set of holes were found outside in the wall of the balcony," answered Charles.

Shawn inquired, "What kind of holes?"

Charles replied, "The kind made by a sword or stakes, most likely."

Shawn asked, "What about fingerprints?"

"The whole room was searched. None were found," said Charles.

Shawn thought about what Charles said earlier and asked, "What about the glasses?"

"They had no prints and the lenses had no magnification," responded Charles.

Shawn curiously asked, "You mean glasses used for a disguise?"

Charles confirmed his train of thought, "Precisely. This slayer is very resourceful, a professional, no doubt. It is quite obvious the slayer is a woman. Her slaying was practically clean with very few clues to go on. She must be very thorough and possibly had some help in order to accomplish this under my nose."

Shawn frowned as he spoke. "You speak of her as if you're impressed."

Charles smiled as he replied, "I am indeed impressed. Her job to take out Basil was nearly flawless. She must have been wearing gloves or had her fingerprints removed. I would also say that she must be quite good, since none of the other guests noticed her."

Shawn was hungry for even more answers as he continued, "Do you know of any slayers that may have done this?"

Charles answered, "That information will cost you."

Shawn got up, stared down Charles, and said, "How dare you extort me for information?"

Charles was not the slightest intimidated by Shawn's behavior as he remarked, "I have a business to run and you are taking up my valuable time."

Shawn clinched his fist as he angrily stated, "If you were not in good relations with Flusken, I would rip your heart out for saying such things."

Charles's eyes glowed red as he mentally picked up Shawn and placed him against the wall, a few feet off the floor. Shawn was held against the wall and could not move a muscle as if he was glued to it. Charles exerted pressure upon

Shawn as he pinned him to the wall.

Shawn was foolish to pick a fight with a high level vampire like Charles. Charles's power was so great that he could use telekinesis to move objects mentally. Only very high-level vampires, who can act on their own without a master's consent, have mastered the power of telekinesis.

"Centuries before you were born, I was serving vampires of royalty. Killing a vampire like you would be too easy and not very entertaining. A young vampire like you, Shawn, has much to learn. For unless you can take out Flusken, a dog like you hasn't a chance in hell of hurting me," remarked Charles. Shawn was in pain as the force placed upon him was increasing to the point he gave in.

"All right, Charles. I yield for now," said Shawn as he admitted defeat.

Charles's eyes returned to normal as he released Shawn and watched him fall to the floor.

"Are you finished with the macho act, Shawn," asked Charles.

Shawn got up and said, "Yes. You made your point, Charles." He reached into his pocket and grabbed a few notes.

Charles took the money handed to him as he answered, "I have heard of one. Her name is Katrina."

"Where can I find her," asked Shawn.

"I don't know. But don't worry. I am sure she will find you," replied Charles.

"What are you saying?" asked Shawn.

Charles smiled as he responded, "She has a particular grudge against vampires of your clan. Watch yourself, Shawn, you maybe next."

Chapter 4
The Fortuneteller

It was Sunday and the wall clock of the parking garage read 6:00 p.m. as the daylight was slipping away and losing its hold over Vampiro City. The ten-level parking garage was located somewhere in the workingman sector of the city. During the time of the sun setting, creatures of the night slowly emerged from their hiding places, since the sunlight was no longer a threat to them. The parking garage was half full of cars as many commuters were leaving the city area and returning to their homes in the city or suburbs. It was springtime and the temperature outside was beginning to cool down, while the sky was clear.

On the sixth level of the parking garage the doors of an elevator opened on the far end. A woman stepped out of the elevator as she made her way across the concreted level to her vehicle parked nearby. The level was partly full of different vehicles, such as sports cars, pickup trucks, station wagons, minivans, sedans, and a few sport-utility vehicles. Long fluorescent lights on the steel-and-concrete ceiling began to turn on automatically as the daylight was slipping away into the dusk. Traffic sounds from the street below could be heard from the level, since it was open and no windows or doors closed off the noise of cars and trucks moving on the streets below.

The woman stood about five feet eight inches tall with a slender-type build and larger-than-average-sized breasts. She was a pretty woman with tan skin, dark hair, and green eyes. Her makeup and jewelry only enhanced her looks, while her age was about twenty-four years old. Her lovely hair went all the way down to her back and had a part on one side. She had saw-tooth bangs that covered her forehead, except where it parted. Her hair was also slightly spiky and had uneven jagged ends. She was wearing a light-colored sleeveless dress and matching sandals. Her dress had a U-shaped neckline that was low enough to show off a little cleavage. Dark buttons in the middle of the dress started at the base of the neckline and followed all the way down to the end of the dress. The dress complemented her figure and the length of it went down below her knees. The only jewelry she wore was a necklace, earrings, and a ring on her finger. Her necklace had a gold chain that hung down to the top of her cleavage with a pentacle symbol, the size of a fifty-cent piece. The golden earrings she wore were wide round hoops. On her right middle finger was a golden ring with a round smooth gem, a shade of green, in the center of it. On her shoulder she was carrying a leather handbag that matched her outfit. Her name was Telka.

She left the elevator behind as it closed its metal doors automatically. Telka was walking toward her van when she stopped, like she heard something unusual. She wasn't sure what her intuition was telling her as she looked around where she stood to see if someone was there. Even though there were traffic sounds on the streets below, it seemed awfully quiet on the level she was on. All she could hear on the level was the humming of the fluorescent lights, since no other cars were moving and no one else was walking on that level. Convinced that no one was there, she pulled her keys out of her bag as she headed for her van.

Telka's van was full size with a glossy black finish and chrome wheels on the tires. The van's rear was higher than the front, since the rear tires were larger than the front tires. The only windows on the van were the driver, the passenger, and the windshield. The windows had a purple tint, so the interior was invisible to the outside. The rear of the van had full-size doors and a simple spoiler on the roof.

Telka was within a few feet from her van when she turned around again. She saw nothing as she prepared to use the remote on her key chain to unlock the door. As she turned in the direction of the van a man stepped into view beside the van. The unexpected sight of a man startled her enough to drop her keys.

The man stood about five feet nine inches tall with a thin-type build. His looks were average with hollow cheeks and a narrow chin. He was clean-shaven with shoulder-length blonde hair and brown eyes. The man was dressed in a brown trench coat, a black shirt, gray pants, and black dress shoes. His presence projected an uneasy feeling, as he looked at her with hunger in his eyes.

He smiled as he said, "I'm sorry. I didn't mean to scare you like that. Are you all right?"

Telka held her chest as she replied, "I'm all right. You just startled me, that's all."

The man slowly stepped forward as he said, "Allow me." When he got close enough he squatted down and picked up her keys. He handed them to her as he stood up.

She took the keys from his hand and said, "Thank you."

"You're welcome. By any chance would you care to join me for dinner?" asked the man.

Telka grinned and said, "Do you always try to pick up girls in parking garages?"

He smiled and responded, "Only the pretty ones."

Telka smiled and replied, "Thank you."

"Well, is that a yes?" asked the man.

Telka pulled a business card from her purse and handed it to him. "I'm sorry, but I already have plans for the evening. Maybe we could do lunch?"

The man took the card and looked at it. He looked at her and said, "So, you are a fortuneteller?"

"Yes," answered Telka.

He placed the card in his pocket as he looked at her and said, "How about a quickie instead?"

She frowned as she backed up and replied, "That's not funny. You should be trying to pick up girls in a bar, not places like this. Vampiro City has plenty of them."

"Yes, but bars have too many witnesses," said the man.

She instinctively backed a step away from him as she said, "What do you want?"

The man had an evil grin on his face as he grabbed her by the arms. "To taste you, my dear," answered the man.

She struggled to break free to no avail as he held on to her tightly. "Let go of me!" she screamed. She saw his fangs emerge from his mouth as she continued fight him. His eyes turned blood red as he looked upon her neck. Her fear was arousing his hunger for blood even more as he drew closer to her neck.

Most vampires are mentored by their master who turned them, but this one seemed to be a stray or one who was forsaken by his master. Nevertheless, he did not yet learn how to mesmerize people with his gaze in order to hunt and feed discreetly.

She continued to make it difficult for him as she tried to push his face away. At the same time she dropped her keys and reached in her pocket with her other hand for something. Without warning she placed a golden cross, no more than six inches long, on his forehead.

The cross burned his skin like a searing hot iron used for branding. At that moment he let go of her as he backed up and writhed in pain.

His glowing red eyes looked at her as he held his head and screamed, "You will pay for that, bitch!"

Telka smiled as she pulled a tarot card from her bag. The card, which was twice the size of a regular playing card, had the picture of a fiery salamander creature on it.

He was still stunned by the branding of the cross as she held it out in front of her. With glowing red eyes he looked at her as he snarled.

Telka held him at bay knowing that a vampire is easily repelled by a holy item that just burned them. She boldly stood and replied, "I don't think so. You should have asked first." As his claws extended and he looked upon her she threw a card near him and spoke, "I summon Fire Salamander!"

Instantly, a red-colored salamander emerged from the card on fire. It had glowing yellow eyes and a fierce gaze. The fire salamander was a magical beast from the fire suite of the tarot deck. It looked like a salamander, but it was as large as a Komodo dragon lizard.

"Sic him," Telka commanded.

The vampire backed up as it approached him. He began to panic, as he said, "No! Stay away from me!" Fearing for his life he ran away in the opposite direction. The fire salamander took off running and caught up with him in no time.

He ran for an open side of the garage and jumped off. Not knowing how to land right he fell on his leg wrong and broke it. He writhed in pain as he tried to pop the bones back into place. The fire salamander jumped down from the garage and landed on the open street below. There were no cars coming at this time on this two-lane side street, so it seemed almost quiet. Still unable to stand, the vampire tried to crawl toward a manhole cover on the street. It drew closer to him and breathed fire upon him from ten feet away. With nowhere to go the vampire caught on fire instantly. As he succumbed to the flames he yelled, "My clan will avenge me!" He shrieked in terror as he continued to burn to ashes.

Telka smiled as she said, "Good boy." Instantly, the fire salamander turned to smoke and disappeared. Telka was a fortuneteller, but not just an ordinary one in carnivals and other shows. She had the power to wield the magical tarot card deck, a rival to be reckoned with. She walked back to her van as she thought out loud, "The forces of darkness are plotting something. But, what?"

Chapter 5
The Recurring Nightmare

It was Monday around 3:00 p.m. and Katrina was sleeping peacefully in her bed as her mind went into a dream state. Her room was dark as night, since the heavy drapes kept the sunlight out when shut. Emma was still sleeping in her room as the sun was lowering from the sky.

Katrina's dream took place in Vampiro City, forty-five years in the past. Technology was pretty much the same as the present, except for a few things in the past would be considered antiques now. In the workingman sector of the city a small crowd of people were being let out of a movie theater. It was 9:00 p.m. on the street clock overlooking the corner of the movie theater. It was a clear and warm summer night as the stars could be seen for miles.

The two-story theater building sat on a corner of a semi-busy city street. It was a single-screen theater with a main level and a balcony. In the middle of the front was a small ticket booth that could fit one person. Above the ticket booth in large lights the lettering of the movie being shown was displayed. On the right and left of the booth were glass doors to enter the theater. In the immediate area other various department-store buildings shared the street with the theater. Across the two-way four-lane street were other department stores as well as places to dine in. The round-shaped street lamps, mounted on metal poles, lit the sidewalks on both sides of the streets as people left the theater. Traffic was very quiet at this time of night, since most of the businesses in the immediate area were closed.

Katrina was a little girl at the time, about the age of five. She was walking with her mother as they left the theater and headed down the alley from the theater. She was small and had long brown hair and blue eyes. Her vampiric side was still dormant, so she appeared to look like a normal little girl. At the time she was wearing a pink dress with short sleeves and matching shoes. She was very cute back then as she held her mother's hand while she walked.

Katrina's mother stood about five feet five inches tall with a slender-type build and petite-sized breasts. Her brown hair was shoulder length with bangs hanging over her eyes. The end of her hair was tied with a red ribbon and rested over her shoulder in the front. Her eyes were a lovely shade of green, which went well with her fair skin. She was wearing a pink dress, similar to Katrina's, but larger with matching shoes. The only jewelry she wore was a set of dangling earrings. Judging from her looks she appeared to be twenty-five.

Katrina's mother led her along as they turned the corner and walked away from the theater. Her mother had parked her car nearby on a side street, a short walk from the theater. The side street became ever more quiet and still as they walked further away from the theater. Only a few dim-lit buildings and parallel-parked cars on either side occupied the two-lane side street.

As they approached the car a shady-looking man, standing about six feet tall, stepped out of the shadows. He was an ugly man with a macho-type build. His appearance was a bit wild with short spiked dark hair, thick eyebrows, a goatee, and brown eyes. Almost every piece of clothing he wore was black. He wore a buttoned shirt, a suit, pants, a pair of dress shoes, a fedora hat, and a red tie. Judging from his looks, he appeared to be thirty years old. The only jewelry he wore was a ring like Flusken's on his left hand.

The site of the man startled Katrina's mother as she stopped in her tracks. The man tipped his hat to her and said, "Good evening. Nice night for a walk. Isn't it?"

Her mother was kept her distance as she bravely responded, "Yes, it is. Excuse us."

The man would not budge as he replied, "I'm afraid I can't do that, miss."

There was an uneasy chill in the air as she asked, "What do you want?"

He looked upon her with lust in his eyes, like a predator watches its prey. She backed a couple steps back, like she was ready to run, when he smiled with a devilish grin, showing off his fangs, and responded, "Your blood." Without warning the vampire grabbed her and pinned her to her car nearby. Katrina was knocked a few feet back from the force of the impact.

The vampire wasted no time as he held her head back and sunk his fangs into the side of her neck. She fought him off to no avail as he continued to drink her blood from the bite marks he made.

Katrina watched hopelessly as her mother went into a trance while the vampire fed upon her. Even though her mother was being violently attacked, Katrina did notice a ring the vampire wore on his left hand.

The vampire stopped feeding as he turned to look upon Katrina with his bloody mouth. His evil grin scared her to the point that she screamed, "Mommy!"

At that moment Katrina woke up from her dream and sat straight up in bed. She was panting like she just ran a long marathon as she came to her senses. Realizing she just woke up from a nightmare, she began to slow down her breathing. Katrina ran her hands through her hair as she calmed herself down. Her heart was still racing as the cold sweat ran down her neck.

Emma heard Katrina's scream and rushed into her room with concern as she asked, "Are you all right, Katrina?" She was still wearing her pajamas from last night.

Katrina looked at Emma and said, "I'm fine."

Emma humored Katrina with the usual question, "Another nightmare?"

"Yes, when will they end?" asked Katrina as her fear turned to anger.

Emma sat down beside her and placed her arm around her back and said, "It's all right, Katrina. The nightmares will end when your mother is avenged."

Katrina turned to her and asked, "You really believe that?"

"I strongly believe it, Katrina," responded Emma.

Katrina began to cry as she hugged Emma lovingly. Emma returned her hug as she asked, "What would I do without you, Emma?"

Emma let go of her and looked her in the eyes as she said, "Perish the thought, Katrina. Blood sisters to the end."

Katrina felt better as she smiled and agreed, "Blood sisters to the end."

Chapter 6
Coincidence

Moments later, Katrina was alone in her room as she managed to make her bed. She stood up and stretched her arms out as she let out a yawn. Katrina grabbed the ends of her nightshirt and pulled it off as she walked toward a white plastic hamper near the bathroom door. With one hand she opened the lid and dropped the shirt in with the other. Delicately, she grabbed the top of her panties and pulled them down and off as she bent over. With her pink panties in the hamper she entered her bathroom.

As she entered she turned on the light from a switch beside the mirror. It was a simple layout of a bathroom with a white porcelain sink, bathtub, and toilet. The sink was practically clear, except for a bar of soap near the faucet. Above the sink was a standard-sized mirror, which opened to reveal a medicine cabinet behind it. Beside the mirror was a toothbrush holder, mounted into the wall and holding one toothbrush. Simple lighting fixtures were mounted on either side of the mirror. On the other side of the sink was the toilet, no decorations or accessories on it. Beside the toilet on the other side was the bathtub. It was a good size with a sliding glass door on it, instead of a shower curtain. Light blue covered the walls as it met the white-colored tile floor. The ceiling was plain, except for an overhead light with an exhaust fan duct built in. On the opposite wall from the sink and toilet was a metal towel bar, which could hold a few towels.

Katrina looked at herself in the mirror for a moment, like any woman would do after getting out of bed from sleeping. The bright light from the room made her pale skin and matted hair look very unattractive.

Full vampires did not cast a reflection in any mirror during night or day. Since Katrina was only half vampire, she would always cast a reflection. Only the vampiric eyes of a vampeel could ever be seen in a mirror.

Katrina turned on the faucet of the bathtub in order to get ready to take a shower. After adjusting the temperature, she went in and slid the glass door shut. She welcomed the warm water as it splashed upon her body and rinsed away the filth of her dream. Even though Katrina was a vampire slayer, she had no scars or marks to prove it. At times she appreciated her vampiric side for its miraculous regenerating powers. Of course her healing time was the same as a human, unless she fed upon fresh blood. As she lathered up she felt a mild sensual sense of pleasure, while rubbing her soft and smooth skin. It was a pleasure one enjoys for a brief time, when the pressures of life seem to be temporarily washed away as the soap and water refreshes the skin. Katrina closed her eyes as she took it all in and enjoyed the brief moment of stillness.

Moments later, the sound of a phone ringing disturbed Katrina's peace as she opened her eyes and looked in that direction. Emma entered Katrina's room and spoke up, "I'll get it." Katrina smiled as she continued her shower without needing to get out right away.

Emma was wearing only a white-strapped bra and matching panties as she answered the cat phone. She picked up the receiver and answered, "Hello?"

"Hi, Emma," spoke the voice on the phone.

Emma smiled as she responded, "Oh, hi, Tula. How are you?"

"I'm great, Emma. How are you doing?" asked Tula.

"Just fine," said Emma as she sat on the bed.

"I have good news," stated Tula.

With curiosity Emma asked, "What?"

"I'm coming to see you," answered Tula.

With enthusiasm Emma said, "Cool. When are you arriving?"

"Today," said Tula.

"That's great. What time?" asked Emma.

"Well, if the train I'm riding is on schedule, then I'll be there at the station by 8:00 p.m.," responded Tula.

Emma was concerned as she responded, "Oh no."

Tula asked, "What's wrong?"

"I'll be working at that time," answered Emma.

Tula nonchalantly replied, "That's okay. I'll take a taxi and meet you at your work place."

"Wait. Maybe I can have Katrina pick you up," said Emma.

Tula asked, "Are you sure it's all right?"

"Hold on, I'll ask her," said Emma.

Tula held on the line as Emma got off the bed to ask Katrina.

At that time Katrina was finished and stepped out of the shower onto a towel as the water dripped from her naked body. Katrina grabbed a towel from the rack to dry herself as Emma asked, "Katrina, could you do me a big favor?"

"What?" responded Katrina as she patted her face with the towel.

Emma looked at Katrina in the open doorway as she said, "Could you pick up my friend Tula at the train station tonight?"

"Sure. What time?" replied Katrina.

Emma smiled as she answered, "Around 8:00 p.m. Thanks." She took off and pounced on the bed. As she lay there with her knees bent and legs crossed she picked up the receiver and answered, "Tula, Katrina said yes. She'll be there to pick you up at 8:00 p.m."

"That's wonderful, Emma. I look forward to meeting her," said Tula.

"I'll see you when I get off work. Bye," said Emma as she hung up the phone.

Katrina finished drying and came out of the bathroom with a towel wrapped around her.

Emma hugged Katrina as she said, "Thanks for helping me out, Katrina."

"Anytime," said Katrina as she gently hugged her back.

Emma pulled back from her and said, "Oh. Katrina?"

Katrina looked at her in response, "Yes."

"Wear something nice," suggested Emma.

"Sure. I'll leave the slayer outfit at home," responded Katrina.

Emma smiled as she walked toward the door.

Katrina stopped her by gently grabbing her shoulders and said, "Emma?"

Emma stopped and replied, "Yes, Katrina?"

Katrina slid her hands down Emma's arms as she said, "You messed up my bed."

Emma's eyes got big as she responded, "I'm sorry."

Katrina's mouth drew closer to Emma's neck. She could feel Katrina's breath upon her exposed skin. Katrina smiled as she said, "Sorry doesn't always cut it, Emma. You must pay the penalty."

Emma was feeling like a dog about to be punished by her master, not knowing what Katrina was going to do next. Katrina instantly grabbed Emma's large breasts and gently squeezed them. Her breasts fit in Katrina's hands like a couple of large melons.

Emma blushed as she was surprised by Katrina's actions. She soon became angry with Katrina and broke away from her. Emma turned around and looked at Katrina as she said, "Katrina, you're bad. I thought you were going to bite me."

Katrina giggled as she replied, "Sorry, Emma."

Emma smiled as she responded, "I know. I'm just glad you're in a better mood."

As Emma left the bedroom Katrina went over to her closet to pick out an outfit to wear for the evening at hand. In her closet hung various kinds of feminine clothing ranging from dresses to skirts to jackets and pants. After putting on a white tube top and matching panties, she decided to wear a blue long-sleeve buttoned blouse and a light blue knee-length skirt. She took the blouse and slipped it on, but only buttoned it halfway. Katrina laid the skirt on her bed as she went over to her dresser. She pulled out the bottom drawer, revealing all sorts of weapons.

In the bottom drawer was a neat arrangement of various weapons. There were three handguns, boxes of ammunition, a few clips full of bullets, syringes, some daggers, and some weapon holsters. Two were nine-millimeter Glocks and the other was an HK brand. Holy water was contained in the syringes. Various types of ammunition were contained in the boxes, like regular, phosphorus, and silver. The small daggers were double-edged and easy to conceal. Even if she was not hunting a target, Katrina was always armed with some kind of weapon, just in case the situation presented itself.

Any slayer can become another victim himself if he is not armed in some way. Lucky for Katrina, vampires cannot enter her home without her invitation.

Katrina sat on her bed and strapped a brown leather thigh holster on her right and left leg. Her right holster was shaped to hold a handgun, while her left holster was shaped to hold a few daggers. She stood up and placed three daggers in her left holster. Katrina grabbed her HK handgun and slapped a clip full of silver ammunition in it. She cocked the gun and placed it in the holster. With her skirt on no one could see the weapons underneath.

While sitting down, Katrina slipped on a pair of boots. The black leather boots were calf length with zippers on the inside leg and medium heel.

In her top dresser drawer was a black leather choker, which hooked in the back. A silver cross, which fit in the palm of her hand, hung from a metal piece in the middle of it. Katrina picked it up and fastened it around her neck.

On the top of the dresser was the same pair of dangly earrings she wore the night before. She put them on, looked at her mother's picture, and said, "I will get him, Mother, and his whole clan. I swear it."

All out-of-town trains were routed to arrive at the Central Main Train Station of Vampiro City. Vampiro City was large enough to support the Central Main Train Station and three smaller ones spread across to other parts of the city. The Central Main Train Station was located in the center of the workingman sector of the city. Subways and elevated rail were on a separate system.

The Central Main Train Station was a two-story building with an outdoor patio and restaurant on the roof. A round clock on a pole read 8:00 p.m. on the corner of the street in front of the station. Katrina had arrived at that time and pulled her car into a parking garage next door to the station.

Katrina's car was reminiscent of the muscle-car era with a few modifications. Its exterior color was two toned with the upper half glossy black and the lower half silver. The interior was beige with black trim. Its tires were black walled, reinforced, and puncture resistant. Its heavy-duty wheels were shiny chrome steel. The windows were shatter proof and bullet resistant. Plated steel, like Kevlar armor, was installed in all parts of the body to make it more resistant to impacts and bullets. The grill was reinforced with a perforated steel plate behind it. To compensate for the extra weight added to the body a modified V8 engine was installed that had the capacity of 600 horsepower. In case of an emergency a nitro kit was installed as well. On the rear of the car was a license plate that read: *BITE ME*. The car resembled a 1960s Shelby GT Cobra Mustang. Katrina stepped out of the car as she headed for the station.

She crossed the adjacent street and went through one of the many glass doors of the entrance. Inside the station she went past the ticket counter and straight into the waiting area.

The waiting area was a large section of dark blue padded chairs. Many rows of the steel-framed chairs lined the blue-carpeted square. The surrounding floor was shiny and done in a black and white checkerboard pattern. The white-colored drop ceiling was even across the level and had many panel lights and overhead sprinklers installed. The place was very well managed, considering the area was well lit and clean. From where Katrina was standing she could see many people coming in from the arrival platform beyond the many automatic sliding glass doors.

It was the last arrival time for trains that day and Katrina could not see Tula among the crowd coming in. In a large group like this she was not concerned about people noticing her vampiric eyes as long as she kept moving around. She looked over to her left where the baggage claim area was and saw nothing. Katrina waited for the crowd to fan out and still didn't see her. She continued to look to her right at the restroom area and saw nothing. Katrina looked at the clock hanging from the ceiling in the center of the room and confirmed the time. It read 8:10 p.m.

Katrina was starting to be concerned as she said, "Where is she?" She walked over to the stairs leading up to the second floor as she said, "I don't mind picking up Emma's friend from out of town, but something tells me she is in trouble."

Katrina found an empty spot to stand in by the wide marble-like staircase with metal rails and closed her eyes. When she opened them her vision changed to an aura vision.

Certain level vampires and vampeels have the ability to alter their vision to an aura vision. In aura vision mode they can see people's auras and tell what kind of creature they are. It comes in very handy, since every creature of the night has a different kind of aura and aura vision penetrates walls and floors easily. Every creature has a specific color of the rainbow and walls and floors have a gray or bluish shade to them.

With her aura vision engaged she scanned the place for any vampires and found none on the first floor. Katrina raced up to the second floor and looked around. No vampires were seen, until she looked up at the ceiling. On the roof she saw a red aura and a green aura. Vampires had a red aura, where humans had a green aura. "A vampire," commented Katrina as she climbed the stairs to the roof. She closed her eyes and returned her vision to normal; otherwise the other auras in the area would possibly distract her. Katrina reached under her skirt and drew her gun, as she got ready to open the door.

Past the restaurant section on the roof was a concrete patio full of five wooden tables with chairs and red umbrellas. Shawn had a woman in his arms near the railing of the far side of the roof.

The woman stood about five feet six inches tall with an athletic-type build and very large breasts. She was a pretty woman with tan skin, dark hair, and green eyes. Her makeup and jewelry only enhanced her looks, while her age was about twenty-one years old. Her lovely hair went down to her neck with jagged ends, smoothly flowing down to her neck and above her shoulders. On top of her head the hair was parted perfectly in the middle. She was wearing a white dress, a matching set of high-heel shoes, and a small purse on her shoulder. Her dress was a good blend of conservativeness and sex appeal, while being strapless, sleeveless, moderately cut low, and ankle length. It had only one slit up the one side to ease in movement, since it was close fitting. All of the golden jewelry she wore went well with the outfit, a pair of large hoop earrings, a large chain around her waist, a smaller chain around her neck, an even smaller chain around her right ankle, and a few simple bracelets around her wrists.

She was charmed under his mesmerizing gaze. Shawn showed his fangs as he drew closer to her neck. He hesitated as he heard the door from the other end of the roof open.

Katrina stepped out with gun in hand as she said, "Let her go, leech."

He turned around as he responded, "What do we have here?"

Katrina drew closer, while aiming her gun, and repeated, "I said, let her go."

Shawn looked at her and inquired, "You must be a vampire hunter. Are you the one who slain Basil?"

With sarcasm Katrina answered, "Who wants to know?"

Shawn smiled as he replied, "My, aren't we cold? Let me guess. He did not give you a proper introduction."

"You're right. I did kill a vampire recently and not remember his name," said Katrina.

Shawn retorted, "How impersonal and professional at the same time, you are. No sense in knowing his name, since you're going to kill him any way, right?"

With contempt she responded, "Why? He meant nothing to me anyway other than the fact his clan was Drenkel."

Shawn clinched his fist as he said; "He was a close friend of mine in the Drenkel Clan."

Katrina rolled her eyes at him as she continued, "Oh, how touching. Vampires have feelings all of a sudden."

Shawn's eyes glowed red as he proclaimed, "Rest assured, slayer, the time will come when no one will be safe from our kind. In due time I will make you suffer and then you will die a slow and painful death."

Katrina smiled as she said, "Dream on, fang boy. I've killed vampires less arrogant than you."

"Unfortunately, I don't have time right now to teach you that lesson that you well deserve," said Shawn as he jumped on top of the wide railing, while carrying the woman.

Katrina put her gun down on a table nearby. She unbuttoned her blouse, took it off, and placed it on a chair. Katrina stepped a few feet away from the table and motioned him on and said, "Go ahead. Let her go and give me that lesson."

As the wind flapped his coat Shawn said, "We shall meet again, vampeel. Shawn is my name. Remember that, Katrina. But, let's see if this one means nothing to you." In an instant he dropped her, as Katrina yelled, "No!" Shawn instantly dove off the roof, transformed into a bat, and flew away.

Katrina made a mad dash toward the railing as another vampire floated up towards her. She backed up and said, "What the?" The vampire handed the woman to Katrina as he said, "Good evening, daughter. I have found you at last."

The vampire stood about six feet five inches tall with a macho-type build. He was a handsome fellow, with thick eyebrows, a mustache that went down to his chin, and neck-length dark brown hair that was parted in the middle. His brown eyes were compelling, but gentle considering his strong presence. He wore a long coat, a shirt, pants, and boots. His full-length leather coat was black and very stylish. His pants were black and draped over his expensive-looking black leather boots. A brown leather belt with a steel buckle made his pants look even tighter. His dark blue shirt was unbuttoned halfway down, revealing the definition of his well-developed chest. Around his neck was a golden chain with a medallion, which seemed to be missing part of it.

Katrina was shocked by all that was happening as she asked, "Who are you?"

The vampire said, "Take care of the girl, Katrina. We will meet again soon. I look forward to it." He vanished as soon as he was finished handing the woman over to Katrina.

Even though the other vampire appearing unexpectedly puzzled her, she did notice he was wearing the same Drenkel Clan ring.

Katrina gently let the woman lie against the railing sitting up as she pondered, "Daughter? My father is dead and this one carries the same family ring of my enemy. Still, he felt familiar to me for some reason." Katrina stood up and looked over the view from the roof to make sure the area was clear. She found no sign of either vampire. With herself assured of no immediate danger

Katrina turned her attention toward the woman lying there below her. She looked like she was in a peaceful state of sleep. Katrina looked at her neck and found no bite marks as she responded, "Thank God." She placed her head on the woman's chest as she listened to her heartbeat. Katrina was satisfied with her vital signs and felt relieved. She gently placed the woman's head in her lap as she stroked the sides of her face with her hands.

The woman opened her eyes as she said, "Where am I?"

Katrina smiled as she looked into the woman's eyes and said, "It's all right. You are on the roof of the Central Main Train Station." Katrina helped her up as she asked, "Are you all right, Tula?"

"I think so. I don't remember how I got here though," said Tula. At that moment she was surprised as she noticed Katrina's eyes and said, "Those eyes."

"Don't be afraid. You're safe now," said Katrina as she gently touched Tula's arms.

"You must be Katrina," commented Tula.

Katrina smiled as she placed her hands on her hips and said, "That's me. Your protector for the evening and a vampire's worst nightmare."

Tula continued, "Yes, Emma told me about you. I was waiting for you to pick me up, when this man approached me. Everything after that is a blur. He was a vampire?"

"Yes, vampire. They really do exist. In fact you almost got close and personal with one," said Katrina. She looked Tula over as she commented, "I can see why you were charmed by that vampire. He has good taste. You are prettier than your picture."

Tula smiled as she said, "Thanks. What do you mean by charmed?"

"You were under his spell. Some vampires can mesmerize or hypnotize the ones they feed upon. Unless you have a very strong willpower, a good look into their eyes is all it takes to make you go into a trance. I was lucky I got here when I did," explained Katrina.

Tula kissed Katrina on the cheek as she said, "Thanks for saving me, Katrina."

Katrina smiled and said, "You're welcome, Tula. So my appearance doesn't bother you?"

Tula smiled and said, "No. I am so glad to meet you, Katrina. In fact I think you're hot."

Katrina blushed by her comment and said, "Thanks."

Tula raised her arms and placed her elbows behind her head and said, "It feels so good to be back in Vampiro City. I can't wait to party with you two. Where's your car, Katrina?"

Katrina walked towards the table and picked up her blouse. She put it on as she answered, "It's not far from here." Tula followed her over as she watched Katrina pick up her gun.

Tula asked, "Why do you carry a gun?"

"In a big city like Vampiro City you can't afford not to," answered Katrina as she pulled up her skirt and placed her handgun in the holster.

Tula asked, "That's a cool blend of sexy and deadly."

Katrina smiled a she said, "In my line of work I am always armed with something."

Tula felt compelled to ask, "What is it you do?"

"I'm a vampire slayer," replied Katrina.

They started walking towards the door as Katrina said, "Did she tell you that Emma and I live together?"

Tula smiled as she replied, "She told me a lot of things, except about the part of you being a slayer. In some ways I feel like I know you already, Katrina. Any friend of Emma's is a friend of mine."

Katrina smiled as she said, "I am beginning to like you already, Tula."

Chapter 7
The Gathering

The clock read 10:00 p.m. in the meeting room of the Delchor Corporate Building, the current main headquarters of the Drenkel Clan. In the meeting room a group of vampires were about to conduct a business meeting.

The long room was composed of cherry-paneled walls, a white drop ceiling, and dark brown carpeting on the floor. In the center of the room was a very long rectangular table. The black-topped, metal-framed table had thirteen chairs around it. They were padded swivel chairs covered in black leather. Panel lights installed in the drop ceiling illuminated the room and gave the table a glossy look. On the right side of the table was a large fifty-inch-screen TV built into the wall. In the upper left corner of the room was a safe built into the wall, hidden behind a painting.

The painting was a portrait of a woman with long flowing bleached-blonde hair and creamy pale skin. In the portrait she was lying in a bed of roses with her arms bent and hands resting under her head with only a sheet to cover her naked body. The sheet she wore was a thin piece of canary-yellow linen wrapped around her body. Wrinkles of the fabric held to her figure like a glove and covered most of her very large breasts and her crotch. A rose stem was held between her red luscious lips. Her blue-eye-shadowed green eyes were mesmerizing and finished off her lovely face, like icing on a scrumptious cake.

At the far end of the room Flusken was sitting at the head of the table. To Flusken's right were three other vampires beside each other at the table, Morgan, Larrin, and Curton. All of the vampires at the table with Flusken were wearing a Drenkel Clan ring, like Flusken's.

Flusken was wearing a dark suit and dressy slip-on shoes. Under his jacket he wore a white turtleneck shirt. In his upper suit pocket he had a red handkerchief.

Morgan stood about six feet three inches tall with a macho-type build. His looks were average, clean-shaven, with neck-length dark brown hair and saw-tooth bangs over his forehead, and blue eyes. His skin was pale. Morgan was wearing a dark brown suit, and matching dressy slip-on shoes. Under his jacket he wore a yellow shirt with a black-colored necktie. The necktie had a golden pin in the center, the size of a dime, with a fancy letter M in the middle.

Larrin stood about six feet tall with a thin-type build. His looks were average with high cheekbones and a narrow chin, a mustache that curved past the mouth, a bald head with spiky hair around the ears, and green eyes. His skin was pale. Larrin was wearing a charcoal-gray suit, and black dressy slip-on shoes. Under his jacket he wore a gray shirt with a light-blue-colored necktie. In his left ear lobe he wore a diamond stud earring.

Curton stood about five feet eight inches tall with a solid-type build. He was a good-looking man, with a round face and a chin beard, completely bald, and brown eyes. His skin was pale. Curton was wearing a dark blue pinstriped suit, and brown dressy slip-on shoes. Under his jacket he wore a white shirt with a burgundy-colored necktie. In his right hand between his index finger and his middle finger he held a thick cigar.

Shawn opened the dark brown metal double doors of the meeting room and entered. He was wearing the same outfit as before. As he entered a secretary in the other room closed the door behind him. Shawn approached the table and sat down in a chair on Flusken's left.

Flusken looked at Shawn and asked, "What do you have to report, Shawn?"

"We are still searching for the blood gem," replied Shawn.

Flusken had a look of disappointment and asked, "I would hope so. If I find you are just attacking humans needlessly, I will punish you myself."

"Master, I only wish to serve the clan and recover the blood gem," said Shawn.

"Don't patronize me, Shawn. I know you went to the Grand Hotel and bothered Charles," replied Flusken.

"He is not one of us," commented Shawn.

Flusken stared down Shawn as he stated, "He is a valuable informant and I won't have you going around badgering someone we have a good business relationship with. Is that understood?"

Shawn looked down and answered, "Yes, master."

Flusken smiled as he said, "Good. Because if you get into serious trouble by your own recklessness, none of the members of the clan will help you." Flusken pressed a button on a black box intercom on the table and spoke, "Bring in the financial reports I requested." Flusken turned to Shawn and asked, "Anything else?"

As Shawn was collecting his thoughts the secretary entered the room holding a file folder. The woman stood about six feet tall with a slender-type build and very large breasts. She had long flowing bleached-blonde hair, which hung all the way down to her behind. It had a part on the one side and a sloping saw-tooth hairline that complemented her facial features. Her eyes were emerald green and her skin had a creamy pale tone. Judging from her lovely facial features, her age could have possibly been thirty years. The dark eye shadow and red lipstick only enhanced her mesmerizing beauty even more. She wore a canary-yellow blouse, a brown knee-length skirt, dark pantyhose, and high-heel shoes. Her long-sleeve blouse was unbuttoned down to her bra, showing off a good bit of her neck and cleavage. The skirt had a slit up both sides for easy movement. Everyone's attention was focused on her as she went over to Flusken.

"Yes. In my searching I have found a woman who could be a potential threat to us," said Shawn.

Flusken looked with disbelief and responded, "Oh really? What do you mean?"

"There is a vampire slayer by the name of Katrina who seeks to destroy our clan and she is a vampeel as well," stated Shawn.

At that moment the secretary smiled at Flusken and bent down in front of him to lay the file down on the table. As she got up to walk away, Flusken grabbed her. She was surprised as she fell back onto his lap. Before she could do anything, Flusken held her head back and sunk his fangs into her neck. At that point her mind went into a state of ecstasy. She closed her eyes and enjoyed the moment as he continued to suck her blood. After a couple of minutes, Flusken stopped and looked up at Shawn, while the blood dripped from his fangs.

"Yes, we have heard of her deeds before. So far she has managed to thin out the weakest in our clan. For a flower garden to thrive and remain beautiful, it must have any weeds choking it pulled out from time to time," commented Flusken.

Shawn stood up and angrily said, "Are you saying Basil was weak?"

"Sit down, Shawn," ordered Flusken. Shawn sat down, as Flusken continued, "No, I thought Basil had a lot of potential. Too bad he was reckless and stupid."

Shawn frowned as he said, "Master, let me take care of her."

Flusken licked the blood from the bite marks on her neck. As he let the secretary go he looked at Shawn and said, "No. The vampeel is of little consequence. Your personal vengeance will have to wait."

The secretary got up and wiped the remaining blood from Flusken's mouth.

Shawn pressed on, "But, master, she is a thorn in our side. Can't you see that?"

"All I can see is that you are too emotional to deal with her right now. When the blood gem is in our hands, you may take revenge on the vampeel. In the meantime check out the fortuneteller's shop in the lower district. She may have a lead on the location of the blood gem; if not, do as you wish with her," instructed Flusken.

With feelings of disappointment Shawn agreed, "Yes, master." At that moment Shawn stood up and left the room.

As the secretary stood up her puncture wounds on her neck closed up and healed.

Flusken looked at the secretary and said, "Sorry about that. I couldn't help myself. Remind me to give you some dictation later."

She smiled as Flusken said, "Leave us." As soon as she left the room the meeting continued.

Morgan waved out his hand and said, "Master, can you really trust Shawn with such a task?"

"I have faith in him," responded Flusken.

Larrin spoke up, "Master, Shawn is a loose cannon, a wild beast. He is dangerous to the well-being of the clan."

"That he is. But, with the right motivation he is a powerful asset to our cause," agreed Flusken.

Curton placed his hand flat on the table and said, "Master, the dark priest warned us about a slayer that could destroy us all."

Flusken was infuriated with all of the worry talk from his subordinates that he could stand no more. His eyes glowed red as he shouted, "Enough! To hell with the dark priest! I was with him centuries ago when he failed to obtain the blood gem and he has failed us ever since. It is our time to bring back the blood queen. We know now that it is somewhere in this city and we will find it. Is that clear?"

All the vampires bowed their heads in respect to Flusken and responded.

"Yes, master," said Morgan.

"Yes, master," said Larrin.

"Yes, master," said Curton. All of the vampires left the room soon after.

A shadowy figure emerged from a dark corner of the room. The figure materialized and Kescha appeared. With her hair down she was wearing a vest, pants, and high-heel boots, something a biker chick would wear. All of her clothing was made from black leather. The leather clothing fit her like a tight glove. The vest showed off some cleavage and some of her midriff. Around her waist was a brown leather belt with a belt buckle in the shape of a skull. Her boots had zippers up the sides and went up to her knees. On her hands were fingerless gloves to complete the outfit.

Kescha smiled, crossed her arms, and said, "Hmm. So, the Drenkel Clan is still in search of the blood gem. We'll have to see about that."

Meanwhile, Katrina was driving Tula back to her place.

Tula commented, "I like your car."

Katrina smiled and said, "Thanks, she's a real beauty now. It took a lot of work to fix her up. I am glad I had Mak to help me."

Tula inquired, "Who's Mak?"

"He's the guy that takes care of most of my weapons needs. On occasion he helps me with my targets," answered Katrina.

Tula was impressed and said, "Wow. It seems you have this city wired."

Katrina grinned and said, "Not quite. But, you can never have too many friends and connections." Katrina stopped the car at the red traffic light of the intersection by her place. She pointed to her right and said, "We're here."

Tula looked upon her right and said, "This is your place?"

"Yep," said Katrina.

The front part of the three-story firehouse had three large brown garage doors. To the left of the far left garage door was a single brown metal door. On the second and third floor three double windows were evenly spaced across the level. The right and left side of the building had no windows. A single matching garage door was on the right side of the building and faced a side street.

She touched a button on a remote device clipped to her sun visor. The left garage door in the front of her place rose up upon its tracks and began to open. When the traffic light turned green, she drove the car through the intersection and pulled it into the open doorway. As soon as the car was inside she pushed the button again and the door closed. Inside the garage area she pulled the car in further and steered it to face another garage door that faced the right side of the building.

The concrete floor of the garage area was very spacious and had a very high drop ceiling. Most of the cement block walls were plain and had very little on them. Near the back of the garage was a brown wooden staircase that started out as a few steps and then turned to the right and disappeared up into the next floor. In front of the staircase were three brass poles that were mounted into the concrete floor and went straight up to the next floor, poles formerly used by firefighters to get down to the fire truck quickly in an emergency. On the right wall was a large metal rack with a vast assortment of tools hanging on it. The rack was well organized and consisted of wrenches, ratchets, saws, hammers, screwdrivers, power tools, and others, a tool lover's dream. Since there were no windows in the garage, panel lights in the ceiling illuminated the room.

In front of the right garage door inside was a stretch limousine parked in front of the tool rack. The model of the car was very similar to a luxury car, like a Cadillac. It had a gloss black finish with gold trim and gold-colored wheels.

Tula got out of the car, looked around, and said, "This is quite a place you have here."

"Wait till you see the upstairs," said Katrina.

At that point in time she turned and saw the limousine. Her eyes lit up and she said, "Wow! You have a limo? Can we take a ride in it?"

Katrina smiled and answered, "Maybe some other time."

She looked at the limousine and asked, "Why do you have a limo anyway?"

"You never know when you are going to need one for a job," answered Katrina.

"Oh," said Tula.

Tula and Katrina walked over to the poles. She looked at Katrina with a childlike look in her eyes and asked, "Can I try the poles sometime?"

Katrina grinned and said, "Sure."

Katrina and Tula made it upstairs and sat on a couch in the living room. While they were relaxing, both had a drink in hand. The room was fairly spacious with the layout of furniture and an entertainment center. It had a brown couch with two matching chairs, which faced north. Perpendicular to the couch, one chair faced east, while the other faced west. A wooden coffee table was in between the chairs. In front of the couch and chairs was a large wooden entertainment center that housed a TV, stereo, VCR, and a DVD player. The black TV had a nineteen-inch screen and stereo sound. All of the entertainment equipment looked fairly new as well. Green carpet covered the floor of the room. An overhead lamp hung from the ceiling and illuminated the whole room.

Katrina asked, "What do you think?"

"I like it. It's very cozy," answered Tula.

"Thanks. You should have seen it before we got it fixed up and remodeled," responded Katrina.

"I bet that was fun. It's hard to believe this use to be a firehouse," said Tula.

Katrina commented, "I found it hard to believe that no one wanted it. By the way, we do have an extra room. You are welcome to stay here if you like."

Tula was pleased by the offer and asked, "Are you sure it's all right?"

"I don't see why not. Besides, Emma would love to have you around for the time being," answered Katrina.

Tula grinned and said, "I don't know what to say, Katrina."

Katrina grinned back and said, "Thanks are a good start."

Tula leaned into her and said, "I can do better than that." Tula gave Katrina a big hug. Katrina was a little surprised, but took it graciously. Tula let go of her and asked, "So, when does Emma get off work?"

Katrina looked at a clock on the wall and replied, "Oh, I would say around 4:00 a.m."

At that moment Tula was experiencing an intense pain in her head. She held her head with her palms in response to it. Katrina was concerned and asked, "Tula, what's wrong?"

The pain subsided and Tula looked at Katrina as she lowered her hands. "My sister is in trouble."

Katrina inquired, "What do you mean?"

With a serious look Tula explained, "I didn't want Emma to worry, but I mainly came back to Vampiro City because I have been having these dreams that my older sister, Telka, is in pain and suffering. Lately, the images have been coming to me while I am awake. I believe she is in some kind of danger. I wasn't sure how I was going to help her, but I had to come back and try."

Katrina gently placed her hands on Tula's shoulders and asked, "I'll go check on her. Where is she now?"

"She should be in her shop in the lower district. She is a fortuneteller. The place is called Telka's Readings," said Tula.

"Don't worry. I'll make sure she is all right," replied Katrina.

Tula pleaded, "Let me come with you."

Katrina shook her head and replied, "Oh, no. If there is trouble, I don't want you in the middle of it. Stay here where it is safe."

It was Tuesday morning and the clock inside the fortuneteller's shop read midnight. Outside the shop Shawn and two other men with him arrived. The two men were ghouls, servants of a vampire.

The one ghoul stood about six feet two inches tall with a solid-type build. His looks were average, clean-shaven, with a round face, a thick neck, and no hair. His skin was pale and dark, and round-shaped sunglasses covered his eyes. He was wearing a black trench coat, a dark pair of pants, and brown dressy slip-on shoes. His trench coat was buttoned all the way up to the collar. On his bald head was a black fedora hat.

The other ghoul stood about five feet ten inches tall with a thin-type build. His looks were average with high cheekbones and a narrow chin, a goatee around the mouth, a bald head with gold hoop earrings in both ears. His skin was pale and dark rectangular-shaped sunglasses covered his eyes. He was wearing a black leather full-length coat, black leather pants, and brown dressy slip-on shoes. His jacket was open showing a gray t-shirt with a black wavy line in the middle.

The front room was a lounge for receiving clients and a place for them to wait until the fortuneteller was ready for them. To the left of the entrance were a couch and a couple of chairs, facing each other. The red velvet couch and matching chairs looked very comfortable and practically new. To the right was a glass counter with a register on top of it at the one end. Under the glass counter were several items on display and for sale. Most of the items were things dealing with fortune telling, knickknacks for decoration, and various candles. Behind the counter was a shelf, holding various kinds of books for sale. Most of the titles on the books dealt with something related to the occult. Candles illuminated the room and were mounted on the walls in skull-shaped holders. Orange was the color of the walls and went well with the candlelight. Black carpet covered the floor of the small room. The ceiling was plain except for a ceiling fan that hung from the center of it. In the background non-vocal music could be heard that promoted a tranquil atmosphere.

A woman greeted the men as they entered the shop. The woman stood about five feet four inches tall with a slender-type build and average-sized breasts. She was a pretty woman with tan skin, dark hair, and green eyes. Makeup and jewelry only enhanced her looks, while her age was about eighteen years old. Her lovely hair went all the way down to her ankles. She had saw-tooth bangs that draped over her forehead and almost covered her eyes. Her hair also had uneven, jagged ends. Since her hair was so long, she kept it in a ponytail with the tie near the high end of the back of her head. She wore a white blouse, a black skirt, and black boots. Her ponytail was tied with a black velvet ribbon. The blouse had short sleeves, which hugged her slim arms. Its top part was elastic and left her sensual shoulders exposed as it hugged the top part of her chest and arms. Her cotton blouse overlapped her velvet skirt with a close fit, which complemented her figure. Around her waist was a thick black leather belt with a golden buckle. The skirt draped over her calf-length leather boots. Her boots were fancy with high heels and zippers up the sides. Around her neck she wore a black leather choker with a golden pentacle symbol, the size of a fifty-cent piece. Her ears were decorated with large golden hoop earrings. Several plain golden bracelets encircled her thin wrists. Every one of her lovely fingers was wearing some golden ring with various symbols pertaining to white magic. Her name was Teresa.

Teresa smiled at Shawn and his ghouls and said, "Welcome. How may we help you?"

Shawn looked at Teresa and replied, "I'm here to see the fortuneteller."

Teresa stepped past them towards the double doors and said, "Right this way," as she led the men into the next room.

Beyond the cherry wooden double doors was a spacious middle room. To the right of the room was a small bathroom with a commode and a sink. To the left was a door to a storage room. In the center of the wooden floor was a large pentacle symbol, painted on with white paint. Hanging from the plain eight-foot ceiling was a large chandelier with many candles lit, which did a decent job in lighting the room. The chandelier was made of metal with a similar skull design, like the candleholders out front. Like the front, the walls were a shade of orange.

Teresa smiled as she approached Telka and said, "We have guests, Sis."

At the back of the middle room was an archway with hanging red beads, which worked like a see-through curtain. In the center of the room was a round table with a red velvet cloth covering it. Three velvet-padded wooden chairs were placed around the table. Like the front, a ceiling fan hung from the center of the room. Behind the table was a large window with black curtains over it. The back room had black carpeting just like the front. To the right of the room was a door leading to the upstairs of the place. Like the front, candles were mounted on the walls with skull-shaped candleholders.

Telka sat in the one chair that faced the doorway with beads. She was wearing a sleeveless burgundy dress, a long-sleeve red blouse, and brown leather boots. Her velvet dress had thin straps and a low cut in the front, while it hung below her knees. Her cotton blouse was worn open with the sleeves rolled up and her collar sticking up. Over her blouse and around her waist was a thick black leather belt with a golden buckle. Her high-heel boots went above her ankles and had zippers in the front. The only jewelry she wore was a necklace, earrings, and a ring on her finger. Her necklace had a gold chain that hung down to the top of her cleavage with a pentacle symbol, the size of a fifty-cent piece. The golden earrings she wore were wide round hoops. On her right middle finger was a golden ring with a round smooth gem a shade of green in the center of it.

Telka smiled as she said, "Welcome. How can I help you?"

Teresa stood close to the doorway as Shawn approached closer to Telka. The tall ghoul fanned out toward Telka and the short ghoul stayed close to Teresa.

"I need some information," said Shawn.

Telka looked at Shawn and inquired, "Would you like me to give you a reading on love, money, or maybe your health?"

Shawn laughed as he remarked, "Let's cut the crap. I am not here for that. Either you can tell me what I want to know or you can't."

Telka looked at him as she took a Devil card from a tarot deck on the table in front of her. She placed it face up, looked at it, and said, "I sense that you are an evil man." She picked up a Death card from the deck, placed it by the other one, looked at it, and said, "You are on a conquest of empowerment." She picked up a Tower card from the deck, placed it by the last card, looked at it, and said, "And you will kill all who hinder you, including your own kind."

Shawn glared at her with his vampiric eyes as he asked, "Where is the blood gem?"

"I don't know what you are talking about," said Telka.

Shawn was impressed by the fact that he could not charm her so easily. He scratched his chin and said, "Hmm. Your willpower is strong. Either you don't know or you won't tell me." Shawn snapped his fingers and the tall ghoul grabbed Telka from behind as the short ghoul grabbed Teresa from behind.

Teresa struggled as she said, "What are you doing?"

Telka pleaded, "I swear I'm telling the truth."

Shawn went over to Teresa. The short ghoul was holding her arms as Shawn lifted her chin and looked into her eyes with his mesmerizing glare. Teresa was charmed by his mesmerizing glare and did not resist. Shawn turned to Telka and said, "There is only one way to be sure at this point."

With concern Telka said, "Please, don't harm my sister."

"Silence!" ordered Shawn. He had a devilish grin as he turned his attention toward Teresa and said, "Teresa, be a good girl and show us some skin."

Telka watched helplessly as Teresa was compelled to heed his order. The short ghoul let go of her arms and she slowly unbuttoned her top. With her blouse unbuttoned down to her belt, she pulled it open and exposed her firm breasts.

Shawn pulled a two-inch-wide dagger from underneath his coat. He held it by the foot-long double-edged blade and handed it to her. She grasped the black leather-wrapped handle and held it as she waited for the next order from Shawn. Teresa held it upright as Shawn ordered, "Teresa, if I snap my fingers again, take the dagger and stab yourself in the gut."

Shawn turned away from her and walked over to Telka. He pulled a chair out and sat right in front of her.

Telka frowned as she said, "You're a vampire."

"Very good. Then you know what I am capable of. Your dear sister's life is in my hands."

Telka was horrified by his hold on her sister's mind, but she held her ground and said, "All right. I'll do anything you ask. Please, don't harm her."

"Then tell me what I want to know," remarked Shawn.

"I have told you already. I don't know," answered Telka.

"Perhaps it is buried in your subconscious? I guess I am going to have to read your mind. If you fight me, your sister dies," said Shawn. Telka nodded that she understood. Shawn drew closer to her and reached around her hair. In no time he untied her bandana and placed it over her eyes. He drew closer to her ear and remarked, "I am going to enjoy toying with your mind."

The tall ghoul took his hands off of Telka and backed away from her, when Shawn nodded at him. Shawn grabbed the ends of her blouse and pulled them down past her shoulders. He continued to undress her by pulling on the straps of her dress until her breasts were fully exposed.

Telka was embarrassed and felt so powerless, since she had no control over what was possibly going to happen next.

Shawn looked upon her exposed flesh and said, "Very nice. Maybe I'll make you and your sister my servants."

His remark angered her and she said, "You pig."

Shawn extended his fingernails as he said, "Careful. You don't want to upset me. My claws might slip." He started to trace his one fingernail down her chest as he felt her firm breast. Telka trembled with fear as her heart rate began to climb.

He drew closer to her neck and said, "I can smell your fear and I know your heart is beating fast. What a turn-on." Shawn spoke close to her ear and remarked, "So much hair in the way and too much jewelry." He caressed her neck and said, "I'll just bite you a little lower."

Telka opened her mouth in shock by his remark as his fangs came out. As Shawn prepared to bite her, a small dagger flew through the air and hit him in the left shoulder blade. He immediately backed away from her and screamed, "Pull it out!"

The tall ghoul pulled the dagger out of Shawn's shoulder blade as he looked upon a dark figure in the other room. The short ghoul walked past Teresa and looked at him as well.

The dark figure stood about six feet one inch tall with a macho-type build. His shadowy appearance looked mysterious and frightening in the candlelight. He wore a long coat, pants, boots, gloves, a mask, and a bulletproof vest. Most of his clothing was black and his coat, pants, and boots were military issue. His trench coat was open with the collar sticking up. The cargo pants fit him loosely and were tucked into his boots. His leather boots were dull with no shine and laced in the front. A fedora hat with a very wide brim covered his head. Underneath his coat was a police-issue bulletproof vest with a few pockets on it. Leather fingerless gloves covered his hands. Over his face was a modified gas mask with some steel plating painted black over it. The round goggle eyes of the mask had red lenses, which added to the eerie look of the outfit.

Shawn turned around and faced the dark figure from where he stood.

The dark figure remarked, "Is this a private party? If so, I'm crashing it."

Shawn gritted his teeth and asked, "Who are you?"

"You first, Drenkel Clan scum," responded the dark figure.

Shawn yelled, "Kill him!"

Teresa awoke from her trance and noticed the dagger in her hand. She held on to it as she covered her breasts and headed over to where Telka was sitting. She placed the dagger on the table and sat in the chair facing Telka. Teresa reached around her, untied the bandana covering her eyes, and said, "It's me, Telka.

Telka hugged her and said, "Thank God you're safe." She looked at Teresa and said, "What's going on?"

"I don't know. The strange men are fighting someone else in the shop," answered Teresa. She looked at Telka and asked, "Why are your breasts and my breasts exposed?"

Telka pulled her straps up over her breasts and covered them and replied, "I'll explain later."

Teresa nodded and buttoned up her blouse to cover her breasts.

The two ghouls raced out of the room and headed toward the dark figure. The short ghoul extended his fingernails and lunged at him. He grabbed the short ghoul's arm and threw him over his shoulder. The short ghoul was sent flying into one of the double doors, hit it head first, and fell hard to the floor.

The tall ghoul with his fingernails extended attacked him next. He dodged under the tall ghoul's attack and kicked his knee on the side. The tall ghoul fell to one knee as he punched the ghoul in the face. The tall ghoul's head hit the wall and fell to the floor.

The dark figure pulled a large bowie knife from his outfit as the short ghoul got up. The short ghoul attacked him again and he kicked the short ghoul back. With no time to recover he threw the bowie knife into the short ghoul's chest. The short ghoul backed up and fell forward on the handle of the knife as he hit the floor.

The dark figure grabbed another blade, a machete. At this time the tall ghoul got up and attacked him. He dodged his attack and slashed the tall ghoul's throat. The tall ghoul bent over choking in agony. The dark figure said, "Shut up and die," as he chopped the tall ghoul's head off with one stroke.

Shawn crossed his arms and remarked, "I am impressed."

The dark figure stood there as he wiped off the blade and said, "Relying on ghouls to do your dirty work? It will take more than a couple of degenerate ghouls to kill me, vermin."

Shawn's eyes glowed and said, "I have more than that."

The dark figure dropped the machete, positioned his body in a fighting stance, and said, "Come and get me."

Telka and Teresa were close to each other as they watched all the action that took place. Telka turned to her, pointed at Shawn, and whispered, "Teresa, he's the one who made you and me undress."

Teresa frowned, picked up the dagger, and threw it at Shawn. The dagger flew through the air and stuck Shawn in the back of his left hand.

Shawn turned away from the man and looked at Teresa as he grabbed the handle of the blade. He looked at her fiercely as his eyes glowed, and said, "Why, you little bitch. I'm going to rip your heart out, after I take care of this one." He pulled the blade out as the pain intensely bothered him.

At that moment Katrina had arrived at the front of the shop. She was wearing a long coat, a tank top, pants, boots, and gloves. Her black leather coat was full length, open, and the sleeves were cuffed up, exposing her forearms. Leather gloves covered half of her forearms and matched her coat. Her gray tank hop hugged her torso like a glove and was tucked into her tight charcoal leather pants. Around her waist was a black leather belt with a steel round buckle. Below her belt was a charcoal belt, with small containers that held bullets. On the back of the ammo belt were two holsters that held her Glocks. A small charcoal backpack was on her back and under her coat with a charcoal sword sheath over it. A strap came around to her front and buckled above her waist. Her black high-heel boots came up to her calves with zippers on the sides. Around her right boot was a small knife strapped to it. Around her left leg was a charcoal two-strap knife sheath, which could hold a foot-long blade. Around her neck was the same cross choker she wore before. Her ears were decorated with the same earrings and her hair draped over her shoulders. The hilt of her sword could be seen behind her left shoulder and pointed at an angle. All of her blades looked like oriental blades and had black hard molded-plastic handles with grooves for easy handling. Glasses with round red lenses covered her eyes.

Katrina quietly entered the shop and drew her Glocks.

Shawn dropped the dagger and focused his attention on the dark figure, when he noticed Katrina entering the room. He looked at her as she pointed her guns at both of them and said, "Hello again, Katrina."

"There you are. It looks like I made it just in time. Not only do I have to save the one girl, but you and your friend have to go after her sisters as well."

The dark figure looked at her and remarked, "What a babe."

Katrina turned her attention to the dark figure and said, "Don't try that charm with me, vampire."

While Katrina was distracted, Shawn backed away toward the back room and said, "This isn't over." As Katrina looked upon Shawn he ran and jumped through the glass window in the back. Shawn transformed into a wolf while still in the air and ran as soon as his feet hit the ground.

Katrina ran to the window and looked to see which way he ran. Since she lost sight of him, she frowned and said, "That is the second time that coward has eluded me. He is up to something and my fate seems to be drawn to him for some strange reason." At that moment she forgot about the other man and turned around. She pointed her Glocks at him and said, "Thanks to you he got away. Were you arguing on who had first dibs at feeding on these two?"

"If I wanted to I could have attacked you when you chased after him," said the dark figure.

"Well, that's true, but I still don't trust you," remarked Katrina.

"I could have also ran the other way, while you were distracted," commented the dark figure.

"You do have a point there, but that does not prove anything," retorted Katrina.

"Let me put it this way. I was the one who killed his ghouls on the way in," stated the dark figure.

Katrina looked him over and asked, "Well, if you are not another one of the Drenkel family's flunkies, who are you?"

"Give me yours and I'll give you mine," said the man.

Telka got up and asked, "Who are you people?"

Katrina turned to her and asked, "Are you two all right?"

"Yes. I think so, thanks to that man over there," answered Telka.

Katrina put her guns way and said, "Well, I guess I won't be needing these now. Who are you, anyway?"

"That is not important now. We are on the same side," said the man.

Katrina crossed her arms and said, "You're a vampire. I hunt vampires. How could we possibly be on the same side?"

"We have a common enemy, the Drenkel family to be precise," said the man.

Katrina asked, "What are you talking about?"

He asked, "Why do you hunt them?"

Katrina answered, "A member of the Drenkel family killed my mother. I will not rest until every member of that family is dead. Why do you ask?"

"A vampire of the same clan killed the only one I ever loved. I too will not rest until that fiend is wiped off from this plane of existence," replied the man.

Katrina coldly retorted, "Are you serious? A vampire in love with a human? Ridiculous."

His eyes glowed as he angrily stated, "You know nothing! All vampires were human at one time. The body has changed, but the feelings remain the same."

Katrina loosened her crossed arms and said, "I am sorry. My thirst for vengeance can cloud my thinking at times."

"It's okay. She has been dead for a long time," replied the man.

She looked at his mask and said, "Tell me something."

He replied, "What?"

Katrina curiously asked, "What's with the mask?"

"It's all part of the look. I'm a bounty hunter and identity is one thing I like to keep secret. But in your case, I'll make an exception," explained the man. When he was finished, he took off his hat, dropped it, and undid the fasteners in back on the mask. With his hands in front of his face he pulled the mask off. He had a handsome face, a clean-shaven broad chin, and long golden-blonde hair covered his head. His hair was parted in the middle with jagged edges hanging from the sides, while the back was pulled back in a ponytail and hung down his back. His eyes were a sparkly blue.

Teresa spoke up and said, "Whoa, what a stud. He is so hot."

Telka looked at Teresa and said, "Teresa, calm yourself."

Teresa stopped and said, "Sorry."

Katrina laughed. She grinned and said, "I see. I usually work alone, but maybe we can help each other.

"I would like that very much," replied Nick.

"And unless you tell me your name, I am going to start calling you Mr. Hot," commented Katrina.

Nick laughed and said, "My name is actually Nicholas. But, you can call me Nick."

Katrina shook his hand and said, "It's nice to meet you, Nick. My name is Katrina. Just remember that if you cross me, I won't hesitate to kill you."

"I understand," said Nick.

The two walked over to Telka and Teresa. Telka pulled a Wheel of Fortune card from the tarot deck. She looked at the card and said, "I believe fate has brought us together here tonight for a reason. My name is Telka and this is my sister, Teresa."

"It is nice to meet both of you. I am not sure I believe in all of that fate stuff, but let's talk about why we are here," stated Katrina.

Nick looked at Telka and said, "You have a point there. Why did they attack you?"

"They are after something called a blood gem. They thought I knew something, so they decided to interrogate us. I don't know what it is, but I do have a question about what you said earlier," replied Telka.

Katrina asked, "What?"

Telka looked at her with curiosity, "You spoke of saving a girl earlier and making it here in time to save us. What did you mean by that?"

"Oh, well. That's easy. Your sister Tula sent me. I happened to be the one who saved her from that same vile vampire earlier."

Telka and Tula walked over to Katrina. Telka smiled and hugged Katrina as she said, "Thank you, Katrina." She kissed Katrina on the cheek and smiled.

Teresa hugged Katrina and kissed her on the cheek. She smiled and said, "Thank you, Katrina, for saving our dear sister, Tula." Katrina was overwhelmed with their affection that she blushed.

Telka asked, "Where is she?"

Katrina answered, "Don't worry. She is safe over at my place."

Telka and Teresa smiled at Katrina, as Telka asked, "Is there any way we could possibly repay you, Katrina?"

Teresa spoke up, "We'll do anything."

Katrina blushed, smiled, and replied, "I'll think of something." She looked at Nick and asked, "This blood gem you speak of. Does it ring any bells, Nick?"

"Never heard of it," responded Nick.

Telka offered, "If it would help, I have a chest in the storage room that has been in my family for generations. It contains a few rare items. You may look if you like."

Katrina agreed, "It's worth a try. Show us where it is."

Telka turned to Teresa and said, "Teresa, be a good girl and lock up the front."

Teresa smiled and replied, "Okay," and left the room.

Telka opened the door to the storage room. The storage room was filled with all sorts of junk and quite smaller than the other rooms. Telka pulled a gray tarp off and revealed an old chest.

The chest was old and had an antique feel to it. It was dark brown with a glossy varnish look to it. It was fairly large and had a rounded lid, like the canopy of an old wagon. The front had two fasteners on either side with a latch in the center for a padlock to go.

Telka turned to Teresa and asked, "Teresa, could you help me pull this chest out?"

Teresa nodded as she reentered the room and said, "Yep." Teresa helped Telka pull the chest out that didn't seem that heavy.

Katrina watched as they pulled the chest out in the middle room. She was feeling dizzy and started to shake her head a little.

Nick looked at her and asked with concern, "Are you all right?"

"I'll be fine. I just need some blood. I haven't fed in a while," replied Katrina.

Nick inquired, "Vampires don't get dizzy when they get thirsty. What do you mean?"

Katrina explained, "The truth is I am a vampeel, not a vampire. My father was a vampire and my mother was human. Vampeels are more human than vampires, but they still need to feed."

Telka asked, "You mean you drink blood?"

"Yes, but I usually don't kill the ones that I drink from," replied Katrina.

Teresa looked at her and asked, "Do you eat food?"

"Yes," answered Katrina.

Teresa inquired further, "Do you prefer drinking a man's blood or a woman's blood?"

Nick laughed.

Katrina grinned and replied, "It doesn't matter if it's a man or woman I feed on."

Telka asked, "Do you ever drink vampire blood?"

"Occasionally, but I prefer human blood," remarked Katrina.

"Oh, I see," replied Telka.

Katrina walked between both of the women, looked at Telka, and then turned and looked at Teresa.

Telka looked at Katrina awkwardly and asked, "What is it, Katrina?"

Teresa spoke up, "Why are you looking at us like that?"

Katrina asked, "You two are both virgins. Aren't you?"

Telka blushed and replied, "Well, yes."

Teresa blushed, placed her hands on her cheeks, and replied, "I am so embarrassed you would ask us that."

Katrina smiled and said, "Perfect. I know how you can pay me back. May I have some of yours, Teresa?"

Teresa looked at Katrina with surprise and asked, "You want to drink some of my blood?"

"Yes," answered Katrina.

"That sounds kinky," commented Teresa.

Telka inquired, "Why hers, Katrina, and not mine or Nick's?"

"Because your blood and your sister's is pure and it is rare for me to have such a delicacy. The reason I want to drink Teresa's blood is because I sense her willpower is lower than yours. I could help increase her willpower, while I am feeding on her. The only thing is she might pass out when I am done, but she will sleep peacefully," explained Katrina.

Teresa asked, "You mean vampires will not be able to charm me if you do this?"

"I can't totally guarantee it, but at least your willpower will be stronger like Telka's and it will be more difficult to be charmed by one," answered Katrina.

Telka responded, "Being her elder sister, I will allow it. Just this once, since I am thanking you for saving my life and hers."

Katrina commented, "The decision is still hers."

Teresa blushed as she said, "Okay. You can do me, Katrina."

"Good," answered Katrina.

Katrina led Teresa by the hand over to the back room. She had Teresa sit in a chair by the table. Katrina got behind her as she waited for Katrina's next instruction. She pulled her sword out of its sheath and placed it on the table. With her sword out she took her coat off and draped it over the other chair. To make herself even more comfortable she took off her backpack and placed it on the floor. Katrina took her gloves off and laid them on the table. She carefully undid Teresa's choker, placed it on the table, and commented, "You have lovely skin, Teresa."

"Thanks," said Teresa as she blushed a little. Her heart began to beat faster as Katrina gently placed her hands on her shoulders.

Katrina gently massaged her shoulders and said, "Just relax. It only hurts for a moment. After that you will begin to feel a pleasurable sensation. Embrace it and let yourself go, while it lasts."

"Okay," answered Teresa.

Katrina opened her mouth and her fangs emerged. She closed her eyes and gently sunk her fangs into the side of Teresa's neck.

Teresa slightly jerked by the prick of her fangs, but soon after that she felt herself drift away. Ecstasy was expressed over her face as if she was having pleasurable sex. Teresa enjoyed the moment as Katrina continued to gently suck her blood. The sensation she felt was incredible as her breathing became heavier. Teresa closed her eyes and started to caress her breasts as she moaned softly.

Telka looked on in surprise as she watched Katrina continue to feed. Telka was so engrossed in the erotic scene that she placed her hand on her heart and felt her heart beating faster.

Teresa was falling deeper into the trance and the pleasure she felt increased. The sensation she felt reached a point that caressing her blouse-covered breasts was not enough to satisfy her sensuality. In that instant she pulled the top of her blouse down to above her waist. Her hands caressed her bare breasts even more sensually as she squeezed them and moved them in circular patterns.

Telka was blushing as she looked on with her gaping mouth. The scene had almost hypnotized her as she was captivated by Teresa's actions. Telka felt compelled to know and asked, "Why is she doing that?"

"Teresa is in a sensual trance," replied Nick.

Telka was puzzled by his remark and asked, "Sensual?"

"It's like her mind is in a dream state. A pleasurable one at that," explained Nick.

Telka further asked, "Why is she feeling herself? Doesn't she know what she's doing?"

"Since she is experiencing some pleasurable event in her trance, her body is acting on instinct or reflex. If she knew what she was doing consciously, she would stop doing it out of embarrassment," answered Nick.

Telka inquired, "Will she remember any of this?"

"Highly unlikely. Most people don't remember their dreams totally from their sleep the night before. She will probably only remember that she felt good or better after the experience," replied Nick.

"I thought vampires just bit people and sucked their blood," commented Telka.

"Only inexperienced vampires do that. A vampire who has fed several times will eventually discover the blood link," said Nick.

Telka asked, "What is the blood link?"

Nick answered, "Vampires share a temporary mental link with the person they are feeding on. The experience can be pleasurable or painful, depending on the motive of the vampire. In Teresa's case she is experiencing a very pleasurable and relaxing episode, like having a sensual massage."

Katrina drew her fangs away and licked the bite marks on Teresa's neck. Within seconds the bite marks disappeared. Katrina got up and licked the blood off of her lips. She had noticed from behind Teresa's breasts were exposed, grabbed the top of her blouse, and pulled it up to cover them. Katrina then faced her, gently caressed her face, and said, "Wake up, Teresa."

Teresa shortly came out of her trance and remarked, "Wow. I have never felt like that before."

Katrina smiled and said to her, "Rest now, Teresa."

Teresa agreed, "Okay." As she stood up and said, "Good night, everyone."

Teresa walked into the other room and went up the stairs to the living quarters.

Telka commented, "That was intense. Is she going to be all right?"

"She'll be fine. She just got a little too worked up in it. If I feed on her again, the process will be less of a strain on her."

Nick looked at Telka and asked, "So, Telka, do you want to know what it feels like firsthand, instead of just watching?"

Katrina pulled out her one-foot blade and pressed it on Nick's throat. "No, we need her alert right now. Aside from that you're not bad-looking for a vampire. Don't make me cut you," remarked Katrina.

Nick backed off, smiled, and said, "Sorry I asked."

Telka grinned as she opened the chest. All three of them looked inside of it.

Katrina pulled a book out of the chest and asked, "What's this?" The thick leather-bound book read, "Ancient Treasures of Mysterious Power."

"Just like the title says. It's a book of ancient treasures of mysterious power, commented Telka.

Katrina opened the book and whisked through the pages until she stopped at a certain page.

Nick looked on with interest and asked, "Find something?"

"Yes, here it is. It says here that the blood gem possessed dark power and was used to cancel white magic," answered Katrina. She looked at Nick and continued, "What would they possibly need it for? Any ideas, Nick?"

"I have no clue," replied Nick.

Katrina commented, "Well, at least we know what it is used for. It must be pretty important for the Drenkel Clan to want to acquire it so badly."

"If it will help, you may take what ever you like from the chest," said Telka.

"Really? Cool deal. I'll take this," said Nick as he pulled out a pouch full of daggers. The brown leather pouch was full of small throwing daggers. He looked at the finely crafted blades and closed up the pouch where it buckled.

"You can have them on one condition," stated Telka.

Katrina inquired, "You want something in return?"

"Yes. I want to help you defeat this great evil that you are going to fight," answered Telka.

Nick placed the strap of the pouch over his shoulder, crossed his arms, and said, "Lady, you couldn't even hold your own against those two ghouls and a vampire. We saved you and your sister, remember?"

"I was only in trouble because I could not reach my tarot cards and Teresa was under that vampire's control. I was trapped by his tactics."

Katrina was curious and inquired, "Tarot cards? What are you talking about?"

Nick laughed and said sarcastically, "What are you going to do? Predict them to death?"

Telka grabbed her black pouch of magical tarot cards from the other room. She faced Nick as she pulled a Sun card from the deck and commanded, "Light, come forth!" A light as bright as the sun was cast from the card. Nick was weakened from the light and brought to his knees.

Nick struggled and said, "Okay. You have made your point. Turn it off, please."

Telka smiled as she put the card away.

"I'm impressed. You may join us," stated Katrina.

Nick had recovered and stood up at that point. He turned to Katrina and asked, "Why didn't the card affect you?"

Katrina smiled and responded, "I'm immune to sunlight, silly."

Nick looked at the book and said, "Let me have a look at that page you turned to in the book."

Katrina showed him the page, which had a drawn picture of the blood gem and the description of it on the next page beside it.

As Nick looked he commented, "Wait a minute. I've seen this before."

Katrina inquired, "Where?"

"At the Vampiro City Monarch Museum," answered Nick.

"We'll have to go after it tomorrow then," suggested Katrina.

"Good idea. It will be dawn soon," commented Nick.

Telka said, "We should meet back here at dusk."

Katrina spoke up, "I have a better idea. Meet me over at my place at dusk."

Nick inquired, "Sounds good. So where is your place?"

"I live in a remodeled firehouse on the corner of Delos and Gryne," answered Katrina. Katrina walked over to Nick and said, "Oh, by the way, Nick, you are invited to enter my home."

"Thanks, I would hate to have to wait outside," said Nick.

Telka brought her right hand to her mouth and laughed at his remark.

Katrina looked at Telka and asked, "What is so funny?"

Telka explained, "Katrina, don't you see the irony? You are a vampire slayer and you just invited a vampire into your home. You must really like him."

Katrina blushed, looked at Telka and firmly said, "Not another word, Telka."

Meanwhile, at the Delchor Corporate Building, the clock on wall of the alchemist room read 2:00 a.m.

The room was very spacious with a cauldron in the northeast corner, a large bookcase with books in the northwest corner, a set of shelves full of various liquid containers, and a rectangular work bench in the southeast corner. The iron black cauldron measured about two feet across and stood on a base. The stone base was made up of four large bonelike fingers. Below the cauldron and in between the base was a large gas burner, which kept the liquid in the cauldron heated. The large four-level bookcase was full of various books on alchemy, anatomy, and chemistry. It was made out of hickory wood and had a dark brown finish. Various round glass containers, large and small, occupied the set of shelves. On the workbench was a vast chemistry set with all kinds of apparatus. Various colored liquids were all over the bench in their respective containers.

The room was dim, since a control switch on the wall turned down the panel lights in the drop ceiling. The glowing bubbling liquid in the cauldron in the corner was lighting most of the room. The eight-foot walls were a blank white and there were no windows anywhere in the room. The floor was made of plain black tile, nothing fancy. Flusken and a woman were in the room at that time.

The woman stood about five feet six inches tall with an athletic-type build and very large breasts. She was a pretty woman with creamy pale skin, dark red hair, and brown eyes. Her makeup and jewelry only enhanced her looks, while her age was about twenty-seven years old. The metal-framed glasses with round lenses gave her a sophisticated look and added to her sexiness. Her lovely hair went all the way down to her behind. On top of her head the hair was parted perfectly in the middle as jagged ends tapered out from her face and down to her neck. Her hair was pulled into the back and braided, starting at the base of her neck. Between each braid was a silver ring, going all the way down to the end. She also wore silver jewelry on her ears, arms, hands, and her left ankle. Round disk-like earrings decorated her ears and rings decorated her thumbs. She wore a wide bracelet on her left wrist and a thinner one on her right arm. A dark green close-fitting dress covered her sexy body. Her silk dress was sleeveless and had a collar, like a Chinese dress. The flapless collar had fasteners that went all the way down one side and stopped at the slit. The ends of the dress were bordered in gold. In the middle of the chest area of the dress was an open circle that showed off a generous, but tasteful, amount of cleavage. Her matching high-heel shoes went well with the dress and completed the outfit. Her name was Carrie.

In front of the cauldron Flusken and Carrie were watching a magical image appearing in the liquid. The image was a scene of Katrina talking with Nick and Telka in the Fortuneteller Shop.

Carrie looked at the image and commented, "It turned out to be a good idea to place a tracking spell on that medallion after all."

Flusken had his arms crossed as he commented, "Excellent. Now we know where the blood gem is."

"Yes. And we will let the fools get it for us," stated Carrie. The image faded away and the pink bubbling liquid remained.

"A good idea. But…" agreed Flusken.

Carrie looked at him with curiosity, "What is it, Flusken?"

"I feel like I have crossed paths with that bounty hunter before," replied Flusken. He looked at Carrie and continued, "I just don't remember knowing any vampire bounty hunters that looked like him."

Back at Katrina's place around 3:00 a.m. Emma was driving her car and pulling into the garage. She parked it next to the limousine and hit the remote to close the garage door.

Her car was less breathtaking than Katrina's car, with the look of a family car or a four-door sedan. The wheels were factory stock and the exterior was midnight blue. Emma got out of the gray interior as she headed for the stairs.

Emma was wearing her hotel uniform, since she just got off work from there. As she headed toward the stairs she saw someone sliding down one of the poles. She was a little startled, but knew it was Tula sliding down the pole as she came closer.

Tula got off the pole and turned to Emma with a big smile and said, "Emma!"

Emma smiled, went over to her, and responded, "Tula!" Emma hugged her immediately as she said, "I'm so glad you're back."

Tula agreed, "Me too." Tula let go of Emma, but gently held on to her forearms and commented, "You're early."

Emma smiled and confessed, "My boss let me go home early, when I told her a friend from out of town was waiting for me."

"I like your boss. She must be cool to work for," commented Tula. She looked at Emma's outfit and said, "You're so cute in that maid outfit."

Emma blushed and said, "Thanks." She cleared her throat and asked, "So what do you think of the place?"

With enthusiasm Tula replied, "This place is great! I think I'll take Katrina's offer and stay here a while."

"You can stay here as long as you want as far as I am concerned. In fact I can put a good word in at the hotel if you want to work there," said Emma.

Tula smiled as she said, "Thanks, girlfriend. We are going to have so much fun together. I can't wait."

Emma smiled and said, "Come I'll give you the grand tour," as she led her up the stairs.

Chapter 8
Choices

It was 2:00 p.m. according to the clock in Katrina's room. She was sleeping peacefully in her bed as her mind went into a dream state. Her room was dark as night as usual, while Emma was still sleeping in her room and Tula was sleeping in the guest room.

Katrina's dream took place in Vampiro City, fifty years in the past. On the roof of the Grand Hotel a woman was standing near a ledge looking over the city. It was around 10:00 at night as she climbed up and stood on a stone ledge overlooking the front of the hotel. The gray flat roof was very plain except for a few ventilation ducts, rain gutters and drains, and the stair access.

She stood about five feet five inches tall with a slender-type build and petite-sized breasts. Her brown hair was shoulder length with bangs hanging over her eyes and gently flowed in the wind as she had it free to. Her eyes were a lovely shade of green, which went well with her fair skin. Judging from her looks she appeared to be twenty. She was wearing a black dress that went down to her knees. It was sleeveless and had thin shoulder straps that held it up. High-heel dress shoes were on her feet and matched her dress. The only jewelry she wore was a set of dangling earrings

A man mysteriously appeared on the roof and walked toward her. The man stood about six feet five inches tall with a macho-type build. He was a handsome fellow, with thick eyebrows, a mustache that went down to his chin, and neck-length dark brown hair that was parted in the middle. His brown eyes were compelling, but gentle considering his strong presence. He wore a long coat, a suit, and shoes. His full-length trench coat was black and very stylish. His jacket and pants were black and tailor made. Under his jacket his white shirt was unbuttoned halfway down, revealing the definition of his well-developed chest. His brown dressy slip-on shoes were nicely made and very expensive. Around his neck was a golden chain with a medallion, which seemed to be missing part of it. He had a red rose in his lapel pocket outside his jacket.

The woman noticed him approaching her closer and replied, "Don't try to stop me. I'm going to jump."

"Why would I want to stop you? I don't even know you," commented the man as he sat down on the ledge near her.

Shocked by his response she turned to him and said, "Because most people care. That's why."

He smiled and stated, "I am not like most people."

She inquired, "You mean you're not going to try to talk me out of it?"

"No. It is a shame though," he commented.

She asked, "What is?"

"Such a beautiful woman would want to throw her life away," answered the man.

She was surprised by his compliment, turned around to face him, and asked, "What?"

He said, "Life is so precious, because it can end at any time."

She commented, "Life is not worth living. It's full of pain and suffering."

He looked at her and asked, "I am curious, though. Would you mind telling me why you want to end your life?"

The woman was intrigued by his interest and stepped down from the ledge. "My lover left me for another woman," said she.

He asked, "Is that all?"

She looked him in the eyes and answered, "He left me for my best friend."

He was puzzled by her response and asked, "And you call this woman your friend?"

She looked down and replied, "Not anymore. She robbed me of my happiness and I can't bear the hurt she caused me anymore. I must end it."

The man drew closer to her and placed his hand on hers. "My dear, you don't have to die in order for the pain to go away."

She looked at him with curiosity and asked, "What do you mean?"

"I can make your pain go away forever," said the man.

She noticed his fangs and said, "You're a vampire."

He looked into her sad eyes and answered, "Yes. You are not afraid of me?"

"No, and I don't want to become one either," said she.

He commented, "For a woman that wants to end her life, you sure have a lot of spirit."

She drew closer to him and turned her head away with her neck exposed and her hair pulled back. She boldly said, "Go ahead. Drink the life out of me."

He looked upon her lovely neck and hesitated.

She looked at him and asked, "What are you waiting for?"

"I do not kill people that I feed on," commented he.

She was surprised by his comment and said, "I thought all vampires were the same in taking pleasure in killing people."

"You are wrong, my dear. Not all vampires kill for pleasure. I have done that in the past and regret it now. I only kill now if it is absolutely necessary," replied the man.

The woman got up and asked, "Tell me something. Can a vampire love someone?"

He stood up and answered, "Yes. One who is not totally possessed by the darkness."

With tears in her eyes she asked, "Did you mean it when you said that I was beautiful?"

He wiped the tears from her eyes and said, "Of course. The man who left you was a fool to do so. Why do you ask?"

She smiled and said, "Make love to me."

He inquired, "You want me to back up my words and love you tonight?"

She stated, "Yes. A night of love would keep me from jumping off this roof."

He asked, "You're serious?"

The woman climbed back on the ledge and said, "You can watch me die or stay with me tonight. My life rests in your hands."

The man extended his hand to her and said, "Wait. Please. Please, come down."

She followed his lead and looked into his eyes.

He caressed her face and said, "I do not wish to see your beauty splattered on the streets below."

She placed her hands upon his chest and said, "Tonight let's just be lovers."

In one of the hotel rooms the man was sitting on the king-sized bed, waiting for her to come out of the bathroom. The room was lit by a couple of dim lamps on either side of the bed.

She left the bathroom and approached him wearing a yellow full-length towel around her naked body. Her hair was still wet from taking a shower and her delicate skin was still slightly wet with the aroma of shampoo and perfume.

He looked into her eyes as he kissed her gently as he embraced her. While he was kissing her neck, he undid his shirt and took it off slowly. He subtly smelled the arousing combination of her hair shampoo and perfume as he nibbled her ear. She traced his chest as she continued to kiss him. She stopped and looked into his eyes as she undid her towel and let it fall to the floor.

He glanced at her exposed flesh as he kissed her shoulder. She closed her eyes as he caressed her gently and laid her down on the bed.

As the morning sunlight ended her peaceful sleep, she awoke and noticed she was alone in bed. She grasped the sheets to cover herself as she looked for any signs of him. She sat up and noticed on the pillow next to her was a red rose lying there, resembling the one in his jacket. She smelled the rose and smiled. A strange and wonderful feeling overcame her as she placed her hand on her abdomen and felt an energy welling up inside of her. At that moment she knew she was pregnant.

At that point in time Katrina woke up from her dream. She sat up and said, "Mother, I miss you."

Chapter 9
Collaboration

On the second floor of Katrina's place a workout room had been established. The room was spacious with very few things in it. On the south side of the room large windows were installed and allowed sunlight to directly show on the wooden floor. The plywood floor was light brown, seamless, and had a polished light brown appearance. A pearl color was used to cover the walls to help reflect the light from the windows and the panel lights in the drop ceiling. There were three fans with wooden blades that hung from the ceiling in order to circulate the air in the room. In the northwest corner of the room was a black leather heavy-duty punching bag that hung from a metal frame. It was 5:00 p.m. according to the clock on the wall.

Katrina and Emma were wearing white karate uniforms as they were finishing their sparring with wooden swords. Both of them had their hair pulled back in a ponytail.

Katrina and Emma were mirroring each other in fighting stances as they kept eye contact with each other. Both of them were breathing heavily as the sweat was dripping from their faces.

Katrina lowered her sword and said, "That's all for today, Emma. Your technique has improved."

Emma lowered her sword as well and said, "I have you for a good teacher."

"Well, thanks, Emma, but that's not what I meant," stated Katrina.

Emma asked, "What do you mean, Katrina?"

"You have become more of a challenge, ever since my blood was mixed with yours. In fact, I think your reflexes have sped up as well," commented Katrina.

Emma smiled and asked, "Strange. Isn't it?"

"I think it's cool," said Katrina.

Emma inquired, "Why do you say that?"

Katrina grinned, placed her one hand on her hip, and said, "Because now I don't have to be so easy on you. That's why."

Emma smiled and suggested, "Want to join me in the bath?"

Katrina replied, "Sure, I'll wash your back."

Moments later around 7:00 p.m. Telka's van arrived in front of Katrina's place. Katrina was in the den on the second floor of her place sitting in front of a computer. The den was a fairly spacious room with a wooden computer desk that took up one corner, a small wooden bookcase, and a wooden table in the center of the room. The dark brown computer desk was shaped like a V with the computer monitor in the middle and cabinets on either side of it. A black leather-padded chair on wheels was in front of it. The bookcase matched the computer desk and had a few shelves full of various books. The table in the center of the room also matched the other furniture and had a glass top with a screen underneath facing the ceiling. Blue carpet covered the entire floor. Panel lights illuminated the room from the drop ceiling above. The walls were a light shade of blue with no windows to speak of. Classical music could be heard in the background, while Katrina was working.

Katrina was wearing only a white tank top and a light blue pair of short shorts.

At that moment she heard the front door buzzer, stopped what she was looking at, clicked the mouse and brought up a camera window on the monitor. On the screen was a hidden camera view of the front door. She saw Telka and Teresa on the monitor and commented, "They're here." Katrina got up from the chair and rushed down the hallway. She quickly jumped on a pole and gracefully slid down to the garage area. Katrina answered the door and let Telka and Teresa in.

Teresa had her hair pulled back in a ponytail as usual, with the same jewelry as before. She was wearing a white short-sleeve blouse, an orange tube top, a light blue denim miniskirt, white socks, and sneakers. Her cotton blouse was open and the ends were tied into a knot above her waist. The miniskirt showed off her midriff and had a black belt with a round steel buckle.

Telka was wearing a light blue long-sleeve blouse, a light blue denim knee-length skirt, white socks and white sneakers. Her cotton blouse overlapped her skirt, was unbuttoned to show off some cleavage, had the sleeves rolled up a little, and had the collar raised up. She was wearing the same jewelry as before.

Katrina opened the door and said, "Hi. Come in." The two ladies came into the garage and Katrina closed the door behind them.

Teresa gave Katrina a big hug, a kiss on the cheek, and said, "Hi, Katrina."

Katrina asked, "How are you feeling, Teresa?"

Teresa smiled, pulled away from her, and replied, "I feel great."

"I'm glad to hear it," said Katrina.

Telka hugged Katrina as well, gave her a kiss on the cheek, and said, "Hello, Katrina." She pulled away and asked, "How are you?"

"I'm fine, thanks," responded Katrina.

Teresa spoke up, "Uh, Katrina?"

Katrina turned her attention to Teresa and replied, "Yes?"

Teresa had a naughty look on her face and asked, "Could we do it again some time?"

Telka blushed and turned to Teresa and said, "Teresa? What's gotten into you?"

Katrina laughed as Teresa smiled and said nothing.

Telka inquired, "I was told she would not remember anything. Why is she asking you, Katrina?"

Katrina grinned and explained, "She won't remember much, but the feeling she experienced. Sometimes the feeling can be so intense that no other feeling could possibly replace it. It can be addictive like a certain kind of drug."

Telka was a little irritated by her answer and asked, "Are you saying she liked it that much?"

Katrina responded, "No, I am saying that she loved it. In actuality it is better you found out now, than if some other vampire bit her. If she wishes I'd feed on her occasionally, so her blood count doesn't reduce to a dangerous level. Otherwise, she could turn into a blood junkie and seek out any vampire to feed on her. I don't think I have to explain what will happen next."

Teresa gave Telka a hug and said, "It's all right, Telka. We are so lucky to have Katrina as a friend. Right?"

Telka smiled, nodded, and said, "Yes."

Teresa let go of Telka and saw the cars parked in the garage. She looked with amazement and said, "Wow. You have a sports car and a limo? That is so cool. Can we have a ride in them some time?"

Telka spoke up, "Teresa, calm yourself."

Katrina laughed as she responded, "Sure. You are just like your sister, Tula."

Telka inquired, "Where is she?"

"She's out with Emma shopping. I am sure she will be back some time later," answered Katrina.

Teresa asked, "Katrina, where is that gorgeous guy from last night?"

"Oh, you mean Nick? I haven't seen him. You were the first to arrive," answered Katrina.

At that moment mist entered the garage from under the door. Telka and Teresa were surprised as Katrina turned around, drew her gun from the back of her shorts, and aimed it in the direction of the mist. The mist accumulated in one area and formed into a body. Nick appeared soon after.

Nick had his hair back in a ponytail with red oval glasses covering his eyes. He was wearing a purple long-sleeve cotton shirt, dark slacks, and brown leather shoes with laces. Around his waist was a brown leather belt with a steel buckle. On his right hand was a golden ring. The ring had a molded skull with a C on the forehead.

Teresa commented, "Wow, he looks hotter than last night."

Telka grinned at her comment.

Nick looked at Telka and Teresa and said, "Hello, ladies. How was that for an entrance?"

Katrina placed her gun at his temple and remarked, "Very stupid."

Nick put his hands up in the air and said, "Sorry. I got carried away."

Katrina lowered her gun and put it away. She frowned at Nick and said, "You know the rules of inviting. Still, I could have shot you anyway. Don't do that again."

Nick smiled and said, "You're right. I was just showing off. I'm sorry I tried to impress you."

Teresa spoke up, "Ah, Katrina, have a heart. He did say he was sorry."

Telka said, "It's all right, Katrina. No harm was done."

Katrina's cold exterior warmed up a little as she said, "Forget it. Just follow me upstairs and we'll discuss what we are going to do tonight."

Nick and the others followed Katrina upstairs and into the den.

Katrina ordered, "Gather around the table and I'll show you the layout of this place." She clicked a button on her computer mouse and the screen on the table lit up. Immediately a blueprint of the museum appeared on the screen.

Nick commented, "This is a nice piece of hardware. Where did you get it?"

Katrina looked at him and said, "This is not a time to talk about acquiring stuff. I don't quite trust you, Nick."

Telka asked, "This is amazing, Katrina. Public records are locked up pretty tight. Could you tell me how you got a hold of these blueprints?"

"That I can tell you. I just simply went into the Vampiro City Hall of Records, charmed an employee, and he burned me a copy on disk," answered Katrina.

Teresa inquired, "Won't he remember what you did?"

"No. Under the influence of the vampiric charm, a person will forget everything he did as if he was intoxicated during that time," explained Katrina.

Nick decided to tease Katrina and asked, "You sure you didn't try to use any of your feminine charms instead?"

Katrina blushed and just glared at him.

Teresa commented, "Here he goes again."

Telka laughed in response.

Nick smiled and said, "My bad. I mean a hot-looking babe like you would have no problem persuading someone to do something."

Katrina grinned and said, "Nice recovery, Nick. I'll let that one go." Katrina noticed his ring and asked, "Say, Nick, what vampire family does that ring belong to?"

"The Catholom Vampire Clan," answered Nick.

"Interesting," commented Katrina.

Nick inquired, "So, what's the plan?"

Katrina pointed at the screen and stated, "As I was saying, here is the layout of the museum."

Teresa looked on as Telka said, "Cool."

Katrina continued, "Okay. This will be a two-person operation. Nick, I will need your vampiric abilities to help me accomplish this task."

Nick inquired, "What did you have in mind?"

Katrina explained as she pointed on the map, "First, you are going to sneak into the building at the service entrance and knock out any patrolling guards. After the guards are knocked out, you will then let me in. Once I have bypassed the alarm system, we will make our way up to the main exhibit hall."

Nick asked, "What about the rest of security?"

Telka spoke up, "I have an idea."

Katrina asked, "What?"

Telka replied, "I have a tarot card that can put them to sleep. Don't worry. It will only affect the guards."

Katrina agreed, "Hmm. Magic to put the guards to sleep. I like that. It will be untraceable and by the time the guards are asleep we will be in the main exhibit hall. If everything runs smoothly, the blood gem will be in our hands in no time."

Teresa asked, "What do you want us to do, Katrina?"

"I want you two to stay outside in the van and talk us through the map, just in case we need some help," replied Katrina. Katrina handed all three of them headset phones as she said, "We'll keep in close communication with these."

Telka said, "We'll keep an eye out for the police as well and alert you of any trouble."

Katrina agreed, "Sounds good."

Nick turned to Katrina and asked, "Shouldn't we have a back-up plan?"

Katrina answered, "There is no back-up plan. If the alarm goes off, then we will disperse and meet back here. We must get the blood gem at all costs." She looked at everyone and asked, "Any other questions?"

Nick suggested, "Shouldn't we go in separate vehicles just in case we need to disperse?"

"That's not a bad idea, Nick. I'll take you in my car and we'll meet those two at the site," answered Katrina."

Telka inquired, "So, when should we meet up there?"

Katrina responded, "Midnight."

Nick smiled and said, "Cool. What do you say we break the ice and go have some fun first before the job?"

Katrina was surprised by Nick's forwardness and asked, "Are you asking me out on a date?"

Nick smiled again and said, "You could call it that."

Katrina grinned, turned to Nick, and placed her hands on her hips. She replied, "You are bolder than I thought you were, Nick. Let's get something straight. We are only working together because of mutual interest, nothing more. And I don't date vampires."

Nick said with a straight face, "Fine. If that is the way you want it. I'll meet you over at the museum at midnight." Nick walked out of the room and headed down the hallway.

Telka said, "That was cold, Katrina. He was only trying to be nice." Telka turned to Teresa and said, "Let's go, Teresa."

Teresa looked at Katrina with sad eyes and said, "I thought you were nice, Katrina. Are you always this serious? You are a woman after all. A girl has to have some fun in her life. Otherwise, what's the point in just living to work?" Teresa walked out of the room, as Katrina had nothing to say in response.

Nick was about to leave the garage with Telka and Teresa a few feet behind him. Katrina quickly slid down a pole and said, "Wait!"

Everyone stopped and turned around. Katrina ran up to the door and turned to Nick. "All right, Nick, I'll give you a chance to earn some brownie points with me. It's not every day I get invited on a date even under these circumstances."

Nick smiled and said, "Okay."

Teresa and Telka smiled at Katrina as she said, "You're right, Teresa. A girl has to have some fun some time." Katrina winked at her as she finished.

Teresa winked back in response.

Katrina turned to Nick and asked, "So, what did you have in mind, Nick?"

"Meet me at the Fright Club around 9:00 p.m.," said Nick.

"Fine. You have yourself a date," responded Katrina.

Nick smiled and said, "I'm looking forward to it."

Teresa and Telka were smiling at Katrina as Nick left the garage and the door closed.

Katrina looked at them and asked, "What?"

Teresa and Telka each grabbed an arm of Katrina's. "Let's go, Katrina," said Teresa.

Telka joined in, "It's time to make you look pretty for your date tonight."

Katrina objected, "Really, you don't have to help me. I can do it myself."

Teresa smiled and continued, "You are outvoted two to one, Katrina. You have no choice."

Telka asked, "Well, how long has it been since you've been on a date, Katrina?"

Katrina answered, "I can't remember."

"That is why we are going to help you. Think of it as returning the favor for the night before. I knew you were a nice girl after all," commented Teresa.

Katrina felt trapped as she commented, "Why did I give in?"

Meanwhile at the alchemist room of the Delchor Corporate Building the clock read 8:00 p.m. Flusken and Carrie were looking at a magical window from the cauldron. As before the room was dark except for the light coming from the cauldron.

Carrie was wearing her same jewelry as before. She was wearing a sleeveless dress with matching high-heel shoes. The silky dress was a dark blue with wide straps. The dress had a low U cut in the front that showed a fair amount of cleavage.

Flusken turned to Carrie and asked, "What is the plan?"

"We will wait until they retrieve the blood gem and then my minions will attack. They will be totally surprised and the blood gem will be ours," answered Carrie.

Flusken approved, "Yes. It is all a matter of time. Soon our blood queen will be revived."

Shawn entered the room and interrupted, "Master, let me lead the attack on the vampeel."

Flusken turned to him and responded, "No. I am most displeased with your recent efforts. We only know because of Carrie's talents and not by your reckless methods."

"But, master," said Shawn.

"You have failed me once already, because you have underestimated your enemy. Leave us," ordered Flusken.

Shawn commented, "Master, you need me on this. The blood gem is too important to be left in the hands of her minions."

Flusken's eyes glowed red as he shouted, "Silence!" He mentally lifted Shawn by the throat off the floor. "You sniveling worm. Be grateful I don't kill you," said Flusken.

Carrie spoke up, "Wait, Flusken. Why not have Shawn watch the perimeter?"

Flusken dropped Shawn as his eyes turned to normal. He turned to Carrie and said, "You have a point there, Carrie." He turned to Shawn and inquired, "Do you think you can handle guarding the perimeter of the museum, Shawn?"

"Yes, master," answered Shawn as he got up off the floor.

Flusken continued, "Excellent. You are not to engage the slayer or set foot in the museum. Is that understood?"

"Perfectly, master," said Shawn.

"Now get out of my sight before I change my mind," ordered Flusken.

Shawn turned and left the room.

Chapter 10
The Fright Club

The Fright Club was a popular dancing club and bar in the workingman sector of the city. It was the kind of club that attracted all kinds of people. The outside of the two-story building was pretty normal looking with brown brick and no windows. The entrance was a set of glass double doors with black covering the windows. A red neon sign above the doors read Fright Club. Some of the letters had sharp pointy ends, resembling fangs more or less. Since the time was 9:00 p.m., all the other businesses in that area were closed and the streets were practically quiet, except for a few cars driving by. Round lights on poles illuminated the empty sidewalks, as it appeared no one was standing around outside.

At that moment Katrina's car went past the place and pulled into the adjacent parking lot. She managed to find an empty space and parked the car. Katrina stepped out of the car and looked like she was dressed to kill, but in this case it really meant she was dressed to party.

Katrina was wearing a black halter top, a black knee-length skirt, and black boots. The back of her hair was pulled back and braided, while the rest of it was hanging in the front as usual. With her hair pulled back her sensual shoulders were exposed to the dim light. Around her neck she was wearing a small silver cross with chain that hung down to her chest. Her velvet halter top covered and hugged her firm breasts closely, while only the top, middle, and bottom straps touched her lovely bare back. The cotton skirt was roomy and showed off her midriff a little, while her leather boots were calf length, high heel, and had zippers up the sides. Her creamy pale skin looked like it glowed in the dim light and was only accented by the colorful makeup on her beautiful face. Purple and lavender covered her eyes, while burgundy accented her lips. She held a small leather black purse that matched the outfit on her one shoulder. As always she wore the same silver earrings without fail.

Katrina opened the door and entered the club. Beyond the glass doors was a small rectangular room with a counter. The wooden counter was long and rectangular, about two feet wide and five feet long. On top of the counter were a small cash register and a phone. The phone was in the shape of a skull with eyes that glowed red when it rang. Behind the counter was a woman sitting and facing the entrance. Small round yellow lights in the drop ceiling dimly lit the room. To the right of the counter was a set of violet velvet curtains with two men in front of them. Black carpet covered the floor and matched the ceiling. The walls were green and seemed to glow with the lights shining on them.

The woman behind the counter stood about five feet two inches tall and had a slender-type build. Her legs and arms were a healthy thickness with very little muscle definition and her breasts were average size. Red was the color of her hair, which had a short length with neatly trimmed bangs. Her eyes were a lovely shade of blue and her skin was creamy white. By her youthful looks she appeared to be twenty years old, but in actuality she was about forty years old. She wore a black sleeveless dress with wide shoulder straps. The velvet dress had a V cut from the neckline and showed off some cleavage. Around her neck hung a bat necklace with the bat's wings spread open. The earrings she wore were bats hanging upside down with their wings covering them. Her makeup was dark in color and gave her an eerie look. Her name was Michelle.

The two men standing by the curtain were both about six feet tall and had macho-type builds. Both were dressed from top to bottom in black leather. Their outfits consisted of a vest, a pair of pants and boots. On their pants were belts with a skull buckle. Both had bald heads with a dark mustache curving down to their rugged chins. Their skin was dark and dark sunglasses covered their eyes. They were in fact twins. Both stood there with their arms crossed and looked tough.

At that moment Michelle said, "Welcome to Fright Club."

Katrina walked up to her and said, "Hi. How much is the cover fee?"

Michelle asked, "You're Katrina, right?"

"Yes," answered Katrina.

"Since you are a guest of Nick, the cover fee is on me. I'm the owner, Michelle," stated Michelle.

"It's nice to meet you, Michelle. I like your outfit," said Katrina as she shook her hand.

Michelle smiled and responded, "Thank you, sweetie. You must be pretty special to Nick."

Katrina inquired, "What do you mean?"

"Nick made sure I knew you were coming. He even offered to pay your cover, but I said no. He never tells me about any girls he's meeting or bringing over. Don't let go of him, sweetie. He's a really sweet guy."

Katrina smiled as she turned away and walked toward the two men. The man on the right pulled the curtain open, which revealed a gate with black bars. The man on the left pulled a switch that raised the gate. Katrina watched as the gate rose up. "Hmm. Customers go in this way, but don't come out this way," commented Katrina. She walked on through the gate and followed a narrow dark hallway that led to the main floor of the club.

The main floor had a bar, booths, a set of restrooms and a staircase that went up to a second floor with rooms. The bar was shaped like a U with twenty stools around it. Behind the counter were plenty of bottles of liquor, wine, beer on the draft, and other drink fixings. On the edges of the main floor were square booths with tables. The counter top of the bar and the tables were made of wood with a shiny dark brown finish. Black padded leather covered the round bar stools and the booth seats. The middle of the floor was tiled in beige for dancing. In the back the restrooms were located below the light brown wooden staircase. Floor lights outlined the bar and booths and made it easier to see where the main floor ended. Only a few round lights from the high ceiling shown below and made the place semi dark like a movie theater. The second floor was made up of five back rooms and the DJ booth. From above the bar the DJ booth could be seen overlooking the main floor. The music heard was usually a combination of rock, hard rock or pop rock music, mainly the dancing variety.

The place was packed full of people as Nick was sitting at the bar and enjoying a drink.

Kescha sat down at the bar beside a stool that Nick was sitting on. She was wearing a black sleeveless dress that went down to her ankles. The dress had a V cut in the chest with three straps on each side that converged behind her neck where they fastened together. The V cut showed a generous amount of cleavage. While her sides were covered a generous portion of her sexy back could be seen. Slits went up both sides of the dress from the bottom to her thighs. On her feet she wore matching high-heel dressy shoes. Her jewelry was the same as before.

Kescha looked at Nick and said, "Hello, pretty boy. Want some company?"

Nick looked at her and said, "Thanks, but I have a date. She's just not here yet."

"Well, if she doesn't show, my offer still stands," offered Kescha as she smiled.

Nick smiled and replied, "I'll keep that in mind, but she will show."

Kescha then saw Katrina walk through the door. She smiled and said, "You are so sure of yourself. I like that." She placed her hand on her chin and asked, "Your date wouldn't be five feet ten inches tall, dark brown hair, athletic, and a light complexion?"

Nick turned to her and asked, "How did you know?"

Kescha smiled, pointed at the entrance, and said, "Because she just walked in. You better snatch her up, before she leaves."

"Thanks," replied Nick. Immediately, Nick put his drink down on the counter, got up, and walked over to her.

"Anytime, pretty boy," replied Kescha. She lit a cigarette with the tip of her finger and said, "This evening is getting more interesting by the minute."

Katrina walked in slowly and stood there like she was waiting for her blind date to meet her. Nick approached her and said, "Hi."

"Hi," said Katrina.

"You look great," commented Nick.

"Thanks, you look pretty good yourself, Nick," responded Katrina.

Nick offered, "Would you like a drink?"

"No," answered Katrina.

Nick asked, "Would you like to get a booth and chill?"

"I don't know," said Katrina. She looked at Nick and said, "Nick, I don't know what I am doing here." She placed her hands on her neck and continued, "I don't know even why I changed my mind about this."

Nick took his glasses off and asked, "What's wrong, Katrina?"

"Like I said earlier, in my line of work I don't get a chance to date too many guys and I usually go out with Emma, when I go out at all. I'm sorry. This was a mistake," explained Katrina.

Nick gently placed his hands on her bare arms and looked into her eyes. He said, "All right. Don't worry about me having a good time. Let me worry about that." He pulled her hands down, gently held on to them, and continued, "Let's make a deal. While we are on a date, I'm in charge. When we are at the museum, you are in charge. Does that sound fair?"

Katrina nodded and said, "Oh, all right. You have a deal, Nick. Just don't get any funny ideas about this. And don't leave my side. This place may have enemy vampires looking for a chance to attack me."

Nick responded, "Vampires usually don't attack in places this public. Don't worry. Nothing will happen as long as you stick close to me."

"That's not what I meant, Nick. I just feel a little vulnerable, that's all," said Katrina.

Nick drew a little closer to her ear and commented, "It's okay. You know as well as I do that creatures of the night won't risk exposing themselves in a public place like this. Too many witnesses."

"You're right," said Katrina.

Nick kissed her quickly on the lips before she could break away, since he was holding her hands firmly.

Katrina surrendered and allowed him to kiss her, since she did not want to attract too much attention. She knew that in the back of her mind the scene would establish to the crowd that they were together as a couple.

Nick backed away and smiled at her.

Katrina asked, "What was that for?"

"I was just sealing the deal with a kiss," said Nick.

Katrina looked at him sternly as she said, "You are lucky I don't slap you across the room."

Nick inquired, "You didn't like it?"

Katrina admitted, "Well, I did, but that is not the point. You are supposed to shake hands when closing a deal. Don't do that again."

Nick smiled and said, "Okay. Unless you want me to. I'm in charge now. Follow me." He took her by the hand and led her through the crowd of people to the staircase.

Without warning a young girl stepped in front of Nick and stopped him from going any further. The woman stood about five feet seven inches tall with an athletic-type build and very large breasts. She was pretty with creamy white skin, blonde hair, and brown eyes. Her makeup and jewelry only enhanced her looks, while her age was about eighteen years old. On top of her head the hair was parted perfectly in the middle as the even ends went down the sides of her face and touched her shoulders. She wore golden hoop earrings, which were mostly covered by her hair. Around her neck was a golden chain and cross. She was wearing a vest, a tube top, shorts, and boots. Her small vest and ankle-high laced boots were made of black leather. The vest was open and too small to be buttoned shut. The elastic tube top was white and hugged her breasts, allowing for some cleavage shown. Her black denim shorts were short and showed off her sexy thighs. Golden rings decorated her pinky fingers and her thumbs. Around her waist was a small black pouch to hold money. Her name was Sheryl.

Sheryl looked at him, while holding a round wooden tray, and said, "Where do you think you are going, Nicky?"

Nick replied, "She's my date, Sheryl." He turned to Katrina and continued, "I would like for you to meet Katrina."

Katrina shook her hand and said, "It's nice to meet you."

Sheryl turned to Katrina and said, "Hi. Excuse us." Sheryl grabbed Nick away from Katrina as she watched, "Nicky, I saw you over there kissing her. You didn't tell me you had a date tonight. I was hoping we could dance later too. You don't like me anymore. Is that it?"

Nick smiled as he replied, "You know that's not true, Sheryl. There will always be a place in my heart for you and your mother."

Sheryl gave Nick a hug and said, "Oh, Nicky, you're breaking my heart."

Nick hugged her back and said, "I'm sorry, Sheryl, I forgot to tell you. I'll make it up to you."

Sheryl looked at Nick and asked, "You promise?"

"I promise," replied Nick.

Sheryl let him go and went back to work.

Katrina grinned and went over to Nick and asked, "Who was that girl?"

Nick replied, "She's the daughter of the owner and she has a mad crush on me."

Katrina smiled and said, "Oh, the jealous type. How cute. I have some competition and she's just a kid. Nicky?"

"I'll explain. Follow me," instructed Nick as he held her hand and led her back to the staircase. From the base of the staircase he led her up the stairs and hung a left.

At the next door on the right he pulled a key out of his pocket and opened a glass door with metal framing. The windows and the door had blinds, like an office with all of them turned shut. As soon as the door was open, Nick flipped a switch and the lights turned on in the room. Katrina followed Nick inside and shut the door.

The room was basically a spacious office with a couch, coffee table, a couple of chairs, and a desk with chair. Panel lights in the white drop ceiling illuminated the room quite well. Brown carpet covered the floor, while the walls were covered in a maple-colored paneling. The brown wooden desk faced the door with two chairs in front of it. On top of the desk a computer monitor could be seen as well as other office things like a phone and papers, neatly stacked. To the left of the desk and chairs was a very long and comfortable couch with a glass coffee table in front of it. The couch was dark brown, leather, and matched the chairs in front of the desk. Behind the desk was a matching-color swivel chair. On the other side of the couch was a closed wooden door.

As soon as the door was closed only vibrations of the music could be heard. Nick led her to the couch and said, "Have a seat."

Katrina sat down, crossed her legs, and asked, "So, why did you bring me up here, Nick?"

Nick sat down on the other end of the couch and replied, "Since the music is so loud, I thought we could talk a little in a place more private. Would you care for a drink?"

Katrina was a little tense, placed her hands on her knees, and said, "Maybe later."

Nick inquired, "What's wrong?"

"Nothing. I just feel so awkward. I can't believe I'm talking to a vampire on a date," replied Katrina.

Nick crossed his arms and said, "I'm going to let that one go."

"Oh. Sorry. I just thought I would feel better if I got that off my chest, Nick. I tend to be honest and upfront with my feelings," said Katrina.

"It's all right. It's nice to know I'm not the only one who has a slip of the tongue," responded Nick.

"Don't misunderstand me, Nick. I don't have a grudge against all vampires. I just have one against the Drenkel Clan in regards to my past. And since that is the case, it makes it so much easier to talk to you," stated Katrina.

"I'm glad to hear it. After all, a clan does not make a vampire good or evil. What is in his heart is what matters most," commented Nick.

Katrina smiled and said, "You should consider yourself lucky, Nick."

Nick inquired, "How so?"

"You are the first guy who has ever kissed me and didn't get clobbered after doing so," stated Katrina.

Nick asked, "So, you have only dated men until now?"

"Yes, only human men. They were all the same though," said Katrina.

Nick asked, "What do you mean?"

Katrina frowned as she answered, "They all treated me like some exotic pet or some kind of freak. Most of them would ask the same stupid questions, pertaining to how human or vampiric I was. Some would get so vulgar with references to feeding and sex, that I would knock them out." She looked at Nick and continued, "I can't help how I was born. It's in my nature to drink blood. I'm sorry, Nick, I didn't mean to rattle on like that."

He responded, "It's okay. I don't mind listening. I know what it's like to have trouble fitting in."

She smiled, looked around and commented, "You must be doing quite well. This office is nice and cozy. I bet you have entertained plenty of women up here."

"I'm glad you like it. Actually, you are the first I have ever brought up here," replied Nick.

Katrina was in disbelief and said, "You're kidding."

"No. I'm being honest. You can ask the owner herself if you want," responded Nick.

Katrina grinned and said, "I am tempted to do just that." She inquired, "So, how did you come across a place this?"

"I did a favor for the owner and she gave me the room free of charge," answered Nick.

She further asked, "Oh, really? Would you care to expand on that?"

"I rescued her daughter, Sheryl. Ever since then, she is very protective of me and who I date," explained Nick.

"I see. How sweet. I'm beginning to like her," commented Katrina.

Nick stated, "She did offer herself as well, but I turned her down."

Katrina inquired, "How come?"

"The safe haven she granted me was more than enough payment for rescuing her daughter. It didn't seem fair to use her for blood and sex as well," answered Nick.

"Wow. You're starting to impress me, Nick," said Katrina.

Nick asked, "Starting?"

She smiled and replied, "If you help me successfully acquire the blood gem, then I'll be really impressed. Charm isn't everything, but it is a nice touch."

She asked, "So, do you live here too?"

"Yes, downstairs," answered Nick. He inquired, "Could you tell me more about your parents?"

"Sure, my late mother was human and my father is a vampire," explained Katrina.

Nick asked, "How old were you when you lost your mother?"

She looked away as she answered, "I was five years old."

"I'm sorry, I didn't mean to bring up painful memories," said Nick with concern.

"It's all right," said Katrina.

Nick asked, "Did your father raise you then?"

A smile came to her face, as she answered, "No. Actually, a human man adopted me after he saved me from the vampire who killed my mother. I owe everything to him. He raised me and mentored me in the ways of the slayer."

Nick commented as he asked, "He sounds like a good man. Is he still around?"

Katrina looked down as she answered, "I lost track of him many years ago."

Nick sympathetically said, "I'm sorry."

"It's all right. I don't want to believe he is dead," said Katrina. She placed her hand on her chest and said, "He will always be in my heart."

Nick asked, "So, you never met your father?"

Katrina looked at him as she said, "Well, yes, but only recently. It's strange how it happened."

Nick inquired, "How so?"

"He ran into me when I was saving a friend and took off. Then he appeared in a dream I had," explained Katrina.

Nick asked, "What kind of a dream?"

Tears welled up inside her, until she couldn't hold them any longer. They came running out in no time as Katrina turned away and said, "He gave me a memory of when he met my mother."

"You miss her. I can tell. All of my family has been dead for quite a while. I didn't mean to make you cry, Katrina," said Nick.

She looked at him as she wiped the tears from her eyes and said, "That's something we have in common then."

Nick extended his arm out gently and placed his hand on her shoulder.

Without thinking she gave in and let him hold her. She continued, "He saved her life and in doing so she gave birth to me." She smiled as she commented, "Some tough girl I turned out to be. I just met you and here I'm baring my soul without even thinking about it," said Katrina as she rested her head on his chest and shoulder. "You must think I'm weird," commented Katrina.

Nick gently stroked her arm as she leaned on him and said, "Not at all. I think you're strong, because you can express your emotions. I like a woman who is transparent."

Katrina looked at him and asked, "Really? You aren't just saying that to keep me interested?"

"Really. It pleases me to see this side of you. Actually, I was hoping to see this vulnerable side of you from the start. You seemed a bit rough around the edges when I first met you."

Katrina looked into his eyes and could tell his words were sincere. She said, "Here I am spilling my guts and I was interested in knowing more about who I am going to be working with."

Nick asked, "All right. So what else do you want to know about me?"

Katrina's eyes dried as she asked, "Oh, let's see. How long have you been a vampire?"

"I would say about two hundred years," replied Nick.

"You don't look bad for a two-hundred-year-old man," commented Katrina.

"You should know vampires don't age, since you are a vampire slayer," commented Nick. He asked, "May I ask how old you are?"

"Okay, I'll tell you. I would say about fifty years old, believe it or not," answered Katrina.

"No way," responded Nick.

"I'm not lying," stated Katrina.

Nick ran his fingers down her one arm as he commented, "Your skin is so soft and smooth to be that old." The feel of his touch sent chills up her spine. He stated, "A hot babe like you doesn't look a day over twenty five."

Katrina blushed as she said, "Thanks, but I am half vampire after all." She turned her body towards him and propped her head on her left hand. She smiled and said, "Careful, Nick. I'm starting to like you a little more."

With sarcasm he asked, "The ice queen is thawing?"

She waved her finger at him and said, "Any more lines like that and I might just clobber you."

Nick agreed, "Enough said." He looked at her exposed skin and said, "It's hard to believe from looking at your body that you are a vampire slayer."

Katrina asked, "Why do you say that?"

Nick replied, "Because I don't see any visible scars. How come?"

"I can thank my vampiric side for that too. I heal as fast as a human, but I heal perfectly," explained Katrina.

"I wish I could say that. If I get splashed with holy water or come in contact with blessed or silver objects, it will leave a scar," said Nick.

She was intrigued by his answer and said, "Interesting. I didn't know that. Of course vampires don't last long around me if they are a target."

Nick agreed, "Hmm. We both learned something."

Katrina asked, "Do you mind if I ask you something more intimate, Nick?"

Nick shook his head. "No. I don't mind."

She inquired, "Why did you become a vampire, anyway?"

He explained, "As you know my lover was killed by a vampire. I was too late to save her and her killer wounded me before he left me for dead. By chance another vampire arrived on the scene. She took pity on me and gave me a chance to exact my revenge. I crossed over that night and swore that I would not rest until I had avenged her death."

Katrina asked, "Don't you realize that you have condemned yourself to the darkness?"

"What is in my heart is what matters most. Love makes people do the unexplainable," answered Nick.

"Boy, that's deep," responded Katrina. She asked, "I see. Is your master a part of the Drenkel family?"

"No, she is the head of the Catholom Clan," stated Nick.

Katrina inquired, "Do you know how many vampire clans exist in the realm?"

"There are three that I know of," answered Nick.

With sarcasm she asked, "So how do you sleep during the day, Nick? In a coffin or upside down like a bat?"

He grinned as he answered, "I guess I deserve that for my sarcastic remark earlier. I sleep in a bed like any normal person would."

"I see. And here I thought all vampires slept like that," commented Katrina.

"I did try it once—not enough room," commented Nick.

Katrina curiously asked, "What do you mean?"

Nick nonchalantly stated, "It's hard to have sex with someone in a coffin even with the lid open."

Katrina blushed and asked, "Well, obviously my father had sex with my mother. What I don't know is if the activity is worth doing for a vampire."

"Oh yeah. As long as the blood flows," said Nick.

Katrina blushed even more.

Nick looked at her expression and laughed.

Katrina looked at him and said, "It's not that funny."

"I'm sorry, but my mind went south and that is all I could say in return," answered Nick.

Katrina grinned and said, "Well, it is partly my fault for asking. I guess my curiosity got the best of me."

Nick grinned and asked, "So you live with Emma?"

"That's right. She's my one link to humanity. I don't know what I would do without her. We're like sisters," answered Katrina.

"That's how I feel about Michelle and Sheryl. Without them, I fear the darkness would almost consume me. They help remind me that I have some humanity left," said Nick.

Katrina inquired, "So how long have you been in Vampiro City?"

Nick replied, "Well, I have been living in this place for five years."

With surprise Katrina said, "Really? It's been five years since I have been living at my place."

"We have more in common than you thought, Katrina," commented Nick.

Katrina smiled and added, "Now that is scary. You know this doesn't seem like a typical date."

Nick asked, "What do you mean?"

"People normally talk about their hobbies, professions, likes and dislikes, interests, and family," stated Katrina.

"We're not exactly normal. I was more interested in what is in your heart. I can find out about your other information later," said Nick.

"How sweet," said Katrina.

Nick said, "I'm really glad we had a chance to talk tonight, Katrina."

Katrina agreed, "Me too. Maybe I can trust you after all."

Nick smiled and said, "Let's go out to the main floor and dance for a while. What do you say?"

Katrina shook her head and said, "Oh no. I can't do that."

Nick got up and said, "Sure you can. Remember, I'm in charge right now."

Katrina agreed, "You're right. Let's go."

Nick reached out for her hands while she was still on the couch. She grasped his hands as he helped her up. Katrina held on to his hand and left the room with him.

On the main floor Katrina got nervous and stopped. Katrina said, "Nick, I can't do this."

Nick dragged her hand out to the dance floor. He said, "Yes, you can. Do you know how to fight?"

"Of course," answered Katrina.

"It's all about rhythm, just like fighting. Relax. It's a slow dance. Just follow my lead."

Katrina said, "Okay," as she stood there anxiously.

"Just move with me and let it flow," said Nick as he stepped behind her.

Katrina felt awkward, but followed his lead. He gently placed his hands on hers and embraced her from behind at the waist. Katrina also felt nervous, but hid it well even though her heart rate climbed. Her physical attraction for him was growing, although she wouldn't admit it. They continued to rock back and forth with the beat of the music. As time went on Katrina felt almost intoxicated by the music as she relaxed and let her nervousness fade away.

The music changed and Katrina took the lead and faced Nick. She smiled as she placed her hands around his neck. Nick smiled and placed his hands on her sides. They moved with the music naturally, like they were really a couple at this point. She looked into his beautiful blue eyes and continued to dance with him. Katrina held him closer as the feel of the music and his touch mesmerized her. Her attraction for him took over at that point and she closed her eyes and gently kissed him. The moment seemed like an eternity as she realized what she had done and backed away. She looked at him and said, "I'm sorry."

Nick replied, "Don't be."

"I need to freshen up. Watch my back," said Katrina.

"Okay," said Nick.

Katrina made her way though the crowd and went into the ladies' room. Beyond the wooden door marked "Ladies," she entered. At that time the place was empty and quiet, compared to the noise from the music playing outside. The restroom was laid out with six stalls on the left and four sinks in a counter on the right. White covered the tiled floor and reflected the panel lights in the matching drop ceiling. The walls were plain with a light shade of pink, except for the large metal-framed mirrors behind the porcelain sinks. The wooden counter that housed the sinks was not too fancy; beige colored, and matched the stalls.

Katrina went up to the first sink and turned on the brass faucet. She placed her hands under the running water and rubbed the cool water on her neck.

The water felt refreshing as she closed her eyes and said, "What am I doing? I just met him last night and yet I feel like I have known him for ages. I can't believe I just kissed him." She looked up at the mirror and said, "Get it together, Katrina. Don't fall for him." She pulled a stick of lipstick from her purse and reapplied it to her lips.

As soon as Katrina finished her self-talk, Kescha walked in the restroom. Katrina ignored her as she leaned on the last stall near the door, crossed her arms, and said, "My, oh my. Katrina, you turn up in the most interesting places."

Katrina turned around and looked at her as she said, "It's you again."

Kescha smiled as she said, "Relax. I'm not here to fight or cause trouble. Not yet anyway."

Katrina's guard went up as she placed the lipstick in her purse and asked, "What do you want?"

Kescha placed her right finger on her chin and replied, "Oh, nothing in particular at the moment. I saw you dancing out there. You have good taste. Why did you stop? The scene was getting interesting. You two looked like the hottest couple on the dance floor."

Katrina clenched her right fist and remarked, "He's mine. Stay away from him."

Kescha laughed.

Katrina was not amused and asked sternly, "What's so funny?"

"Oh, nothing. He must really like you. You must be special to him. That's all," answered Kescha.

Katrina walked over to her and asked, "What do you mean by that?"

"If it will make you feel any better, I'll tell you. I offered him company earlier and he turned me down. It's okay. I'll get over it. He must really want you, Katrina," answered Kescha as she crossed her arms.

Katrina blushed as she relaxed and gazed at the floor.

Kescha smiled and said, "You look so cute when you blush, Katrina. And I like your outfit. Are you going to let him have it later or is it the other way around?"

Katrina continued to blush, looked at her, placed her hands on her hips, and replied, "If you are just going to pester me then you can leave right now. You still haven't told me your name. Or should I think of one on my own?"

"If you manage to acquire the blood gem tonight, then I will give you my name," answered Kescha.

Katrina inquired, "How did you know about that?"

Kescha replied, "The search for the blood gem has gone on for centuries. You just happen to be caught up in the family that is searching for it, Katrina. I know more than you could possibly imagine. I even know your father."

Katrina asked as she grabbed Kescha's arms, "What do you know about my father? Please, tell me."

Kescha rolled her eyes as she responded, "Uh-oh. I have said too much already. Don't worry. I am sure he will see you soon. Don't you have to be somewhere else tonight?"

Katrina let Kescha go and said, "Oh no. I almost forgot. What is your role in all of this?"

"I don't have time to explain it, Katrina, but I will tell you that we are on the same side," said Kescha.

"I am not sure I believe you," said Katrina.

Kescha went over to the shadow side of the stall, transformed into shadow, and replied, "It doesn't matter at this point. You know you don't want to keep a man waiting for too long." At that moment Kescha's shadowy form passed through the floor and disappeared.

She pondered as she asked herself, "Why am I defending him like he's my boyfriend?" She shook her head as she continued, "All right. May be I like him a little." Katrina pondered, "What is she up to?" She shook her head in frustration and said, "I don't have time for this. I have to get back to Nick." Katrina commented as she left the room, "She sure knows how to make an interesting exit." She entered the main floor and rejoined Nick near the dance floor.

Nick looked at her with concern and asked, "What's wrong?"

Katrina said, "Nothing. What time is it?"

Nick looked at his golden metal-banded watch with the round face. He replied, "Oh, about 11:45 p.m."

Katrina's eyes got big as she responded, "Oh no. We have to get moving."

"Okay, head over to the exit and I'll meet you there," responded Nick.

Katrina asked, "What are you talking about? We have to go now."

"There is no sense in you following me all the way up to the office and back. I'll be right back and then we will go," explained Nick.

Katrina gave in and agreed, "Okay, but hurry up."

Nick winked at her as he put on his glasses and hurried up the stairs.

Katrina headed through the crowd to the red neon sign marked "exit." She waited there patiently as she stood there with her arms crossed.

A couple minutes later Nick joined her and they headed out the door. The door led out to the street that ran by the parking lot in the back. Nick was carrying a couple of black leather coats under his one arm. Katrina didn't ask any questions as they headed for the car.

Katrina pulled a remote from her purse and pressed a button. The locks on her car unlatched as they approached it. Nick threw the coats in the back seat and sat down in the front. With them both buckled in, Katrina turned the key on the ignition and started the car. A powerful roaring sound was heard as the engine started. The pistons fired smoothly up and down inside the eight-cylinder engine block. Katrina shifted the black-leather-handled gearshift in reverse and backed the car out of its parking space. The round headlights came on as the car straightened up from turning. As soon as the car was out of the space she shifted the manual transmission into first gear. The street was clear as she peeled out of the parking lot and zoomed down the street. Smoke from the rubber was all that remained in the quiet parking lot.

"Nice car," commented Nick.

"Thanks," said, Katrina. Without thinking she asked, "Don't you have a car?"

"I never needed one," answered Nick.

"Oh," responded Katrina as she shook her head and said, "I should have brought a change of clothes."

Nick asked, "Why? You look fine."

Katrina answered, "Because I wasn't planning on wearing this on the heist."

He asked, "Do you have all the things you need for the heist?"

Katrina kept her eye on the road as she answered, "Well, I do have my tools and most of my weapons."

Nick smiled and replied, "Well, I guess you are going to arrive as you're dressed now. We don't want to keep the ladies waiting."

Katrina looked at him and said, "You're enjoying this."

"Maybe just a little," said Nick.

She turned back to the road and said, "You're in charge of this date. I'm blaming you for us running late."

Nick had a grin on his face and replied, "Okay. That's fair. It's amazing how a hot babe can distract a man and lose track of the time."

Katrina smiled and said, "I'll have to admit. That was a good line."

Chapter 11
The Museum

It was Wednesday around the stroke of midnight according to a clock on the front of the Vampiro City Monarch Museum. Below the large round clock was the museum name in big stone letters reading: Vampiro City Monarch Museum. The rectangular-shaped museum had a gray stone appearance with gaps in the stone on top, like walls of a castle. The front of the building had a moat with a stone bridge that led across it to the entrance. A short stone wall was built in front of the moat and connected to the bridge to ensure no one accidentally fell into the eight-foot-deep body of water. The only windows that could be seen were in the front around the entrance. Other commercial buildings in the area surrounded the building. It had three floors with a spacious concrete patio in front with a few trees, shrubbery, and park benches facing the street. A parking lot was conveniently located next to the building and connected to a side street that led to the service area in back.

Katrina was on her way to the museum as she conversed with Nick in the car. She asked, "How did you manage to see the blood gem in the museum, when it closes at night?"

"The museum closes at 9:00 p.m. and the sun goes down by 7:00 p.m., which gives me almost two hours to explore it," answered Nick.

"I didn't know history interested you so much," commented Katrina.

"Well, sometimes you want to see how things were recorded compared to how you were told things happened," said Nick.

"Not too many people can visit the past like you I guess," said Katrina.

"That about sums it up," replied Nick.

Katrina's car had arrived at the museum as she saw Telka's van parked on the street near the back of the museum. She passed Telka's van and parked on the street at the corner to avoid any suspicion with parked cars near a closed museum.

As she parked the car she asked, "What did you throw in the back seat anyway?"

Nick replied, "I thought it might get a little cooler, so I brought a couple of leather coats with me."

She smiled and said, "Oh, how thoughtful of you." Katrina parked the car and they both got out.

Nick handed her a coat as he said, "Here."

"Thanks," said Katrina as she took it. Katrina put it on as Nick put his on. She was wearing a black leather coat that went down to her knees. It had buttons and a belt in the middle that buckled.

Nick was wearing a black leather sport jacket that went down to his waist and zipped up. Nick looked at her and commented, "It looks good on you."

Katrina grinned and replied, "Nick, we aren't on a date now."

"Just because we are not on a date now, you still look hot," responded Nick.

Katrina crossed her arms and replied, "All right. Thanks for noticing. And for the record your coat makes you look cool."

Nick smiled and said, "Thanks, boss. It's your show now."

Katrina pressed a button on her remote and the trunk opened up. The trunk was decked out with all sorts of guns and blades in a custom gray molded rack for every weapon. It had two nine-millimeter Glock handguns, one nine-millimeter HK handgun, a couple of Uzi nine-millimeter submachine guns, a couple of twelve-gauge pump shotguns with the barrels sawed off, several foot-long knives, a dozen silver stakes, an oriental sword, boxes of various types of ammunition, a couple of small black handbags, and a black bag full of tools. All the metal parts of the guns were colored dull black with the handle parts colored charcoal gray. All of the handles on the blades were colored dull black. A full-size spare tire was located under the weapon rack.

Nick was surprised by the display of weapons and responded, "I'm in love."

Katrina grinned and said, "Keep your pants on, tough guy."

Nick stated, "Uh, Katrina, the museum is closed and the security is going to be minimum."

"I know that. A girl likes to be prepared," responded Katrina as she looked over her weapons.

"I would suggest you stick to easily concealed weapons, just in case," said Nick.

"Point taken," replied Katrina as she looked again at the trunk.

Nick inquired, "So what are you packing?"

"Well, if you must know," answered Katrina as she lifted her skirt up to show off her weapons. Katrina had the same HK handgun holstered to her right thigh and a matching holster with three small knives strapped to her left thigh.

Nick looked upon her weapons and commented, "Sexy and deadly. I like that combination. What kind of handgun is that?"

Katrina pulled it from the holster and handed to him. "It's an HK or Heckler and Koch nine-millimeter with almost the same stopping power of a Glock. I like how well it fits in a thigh holster, since it's smaller than a Glock and less bulky. It has one drawback though."

Nick asked as he looked at the gun through its site, "What's that?"

Katrina explained, "The only drawback is its clip only holds eight bullets, not counting the chamber."

Nick asked, "What kind of ammo?"

"Silver," answered Katrina.

"Not bad," said Nick as he handed her back the weapon.

She noticed Nick looking at her thighs as she proceeded to insert the handgun back in its holster. She commented, "Keep your mind on the job, Nick."

Nick looked away as she pulled her skirt down.

"Of course I prefer Glocks over any other handgun, since they have some weight to them and carry fifteen bullets and one in the chamber," stated Katrina.

"I see," responded Nick.

Katrina added, "Not to mention there is no safety to worry about in tight situations." Katrina placed her hand on her hip and inquired, "While we are still on the subject of weapons, what are you packing?"

Nick pulled a larger black-colored handgun from his jacket and handed it to her.

Katrina asked as she was examining it, "Very nice. What is it?"

Nick answered, "It's a forty-four Magnum Desert Eagle. It packs a serious punch, so I'm not too concerned with its eight-bullet capacity."

Katrina asked, "What kind of ammo?"

"Silver," said Nick.

Katrina was a little surprised as she remarked, "Silver? But you can't touch that metal without being burned."

Nick explained, "I use gloves when I load my clips."

"I see," said Katrina as she handed the handgun back to Nick.

Nick put the gun away and suggested, "I think we are packing enough, Katrina. Why don't we leave the mother lode for another time?"

"Okay," said Katrina as she picked up the tool bag and hung it over her shoulder. With one continuous motion she closed the trunk of the car. Katrina turned to Nick and said, "Let's join the others."

Nick asked, "Okay. Can I make one more suggestion?"

Katrina responded with irritation in her voice, "Oh, all right. What is it?"

Nick suggested, "We should walk like a couple, instead of a couple of soldiers."

Katrina retorted, "There is no one around, Nick."

Nick said, "Maybe not, but the police do patrol this area from time to time."

"Fine, just watch where you place the hands," said Katrina as she placed her right hand around his back.

Nick smiled and replied, "As you wish."

At that point they walked closely together on the sidewalk, like a loving couple, as they approached the van. Right before they got to the van, a police car was approaching. Nick saw it coming and said, "It's a police car. Kiss me."

Katrina replied, "What?"

Nick pulled her into him and kissed her passionately on the lips as the squad car came into view.

Katrina let her guard down and kissed him back instinctively.

The squad car stopped beside the masquerading couple. It had a bar across the roof with alternating red, yellow, and white lights. Its exterior color was charcoal gray with the city emblem on the front doors. On the front doors was a shield with the letters: Vampiro City Police. The interior was gray with black trim. Its tires were black walled, reinforced, and puncture resistant with dull-gray heavy-duty wheels. The windows were shatter proof and bullet resistant. In the front of the car was a standard bumper with a special ramming bumper over it. It had a standard V6 engine with a turbo kit installed that had the capacity of 400 horsepower. The car resembled a 1990s Ford Taurus four-door sedan.

Simone looked and pointed as she commented, "Mike, they're necking on the sidewalk."

Mike turned to her and responded, "Relax, Simone, I'll handle this." He pulled out a heavy-duty black flashlight and turned to the couple, while shining it in their direction. He said, "Hey, there. This is public property."

Nick stopped and turned to Mike as he said, "Is there a problem, Officer?"

Mike stated, "Well, there is no loitering in this area. Could you please move along?"

"Sure, Officer, I just couldn't refuse kissing my girlfriend in the presence of a full moon," responded Nick.

Mike smiled and said, "All right, just be gone by the time we come around again."

Nick gave Mike and Simone a mesmerizing glare as he said, "You got it, Officer. You don't need to come back here again."

Mike was unmoved by his gaze and said, "I can't neglect my duties. After all, we are here to protect and serve." He turned off his flashlight and drove off.

Katrina tried to pull away from Nick and commented, "It's a good thing you said that a police car was approaching."

Nick commented, "You know I really liked your kiss that time. It had more feeling to it."

Katrina blushed in response. Nick looked away with concern as Katrina inquired, "What's the matter?"

"He'll be back. My charm had no effect on him. His willpower is pretty strong," replied Nick.

Inside the van Telka and Teresa were waiting for the others to show up. The interior of the van was simple with gray carpeting and charcoal-gray trim. All six of the bucket seats were gray and leather. In the back of the van was a place for a spare tire and a small fold-up table. On the table Telka had a laptop with the blueprints loaded on the screen.

Telka was dressed in black from head to toe. She was wearing a tank top, leather pants, boots, and a jacket. Her cotton tank top was low cut and her pants were tight fitting. Around her waist was a leather belt with a round silver buckle. A pentacle symbol was molded in the center of it. Her boots were high heel and calf length. She was wearing the same pentacle necklace and matching earrings as usual. A cotton bandana was in her hair as before and finished of the outfit.

Teresa was dressed like Telka in black from head to toe. She was wearing a long-sleeve blouse, a pair of denim jeans, and boots. Her cotton blouse was conservatively cut low and exposed her sensual shoulders, while her pants were tight fitting. She was wearing the same pentacle choker, rings and earrings as usual. Her leather boots were high heel and ankle length.

At that moment the van doors opened as Telka and Teresa saw them still holding on to each other.

Teresa placed her hands on her cheeks as she said, "Ah, how cute. They must have really hit it off at the club."

Katrina pulled herself away from Nick in response.

Telka held the door open and said, "They're still wearing their date clothes. I'm surprised you didn't change clothes on the way over. They must have had a really good time."

Katrina tried to justify, "It's not what you think, you two. There was a police car and we were acting out the part."

Teresa smiled and replied, "You don't have to explain, Katrina. It's nice that you are warming up to him. I wish I had a boyfriend."

Katrina blushed by her comment as Telka looked at Teresa and said, "That's enough, Teresa. What Nick and Katrina were doing is their own business."

"Thank you, Telka," said Katrina. She felt relieved that Telka was defending her.

Telka had a naughty grin on her face and commented, "You're welcome, Katrina. You can tell us about all the juicy tidbits of your date tomorrow."

Katrina was surprised by her comment and replied, "Telka, you are bad."

Telka smiled and agreed, "I know."

Nick intervened, "It's my fault. She just played along."

Teresa commented, "It's okay, Nick. You don't have to cover for her. Just get a room later."

Telka couldn't contain herself and started laughing.

Katrina was getting irritated with the two and ordered, "Everyone, get in the van right now."

With everyone in the van and the doors closed, Katrina ordered, "Okay, everyone put on your headsets."

Everyone put on his or her headsets. The headsets were black, small, and easily clipped on one ear as a small microphone piece curved down to the mouth.

Katrina reminded, "Telka, as we discussed earlier, stay here and use the blueprints to guide us through the museum."

"Okay," agreed Telka.

Katrina placed her hand on the door and said, "Let's do it."

Telka closed the door to the van as Nick and Katrina left.

The service entrance was a back lot with a loading dock. The concrete loading dock had one large brown door for a trailer to hook up to. To the side of the loading dock was a set of stairs and a brown man-sized door.

Katrina and Nick approached the service entrance. She looked at Nick and said, "Okay, Nick, do your stuff."

Nick nodded and changed into mist. The mist made its way through underneath the door. On the other side of the door he reformed in the receiving area.

The receiving area was very spacious and full of wooden crates, shelves and a desk. Many large crates were stacked neatly together awaiting a place to be stored. In one corner was a small yellow forklift for moving crates on pallets to wherever needed. Beyond the crates was a simple light-colored wooden desk and a brown swivel chair. A beige-colored phone and matching computer were on the desk. Past the wooden desk was a small storage area for newly received items and ones waiting to be shipped. Many rows of gray metal shelves lined the small storage area. The walls were plain gray cement block and the floor was concrete. A steel-girder ceiling, overlooking the place, had ceiling fans and long fluorescent lights hanging overhead. The place was empty of any people and very quiet. Since no one was working in the area, the place was completely dark to save on electricity.

Nick carefully looked around for any guards nearby. He noticed a guard approaching and quickly ducked behind a stack of crates.

The guard was dressed in a long-sleeve shirt, hat, a pair of black slacks, and a pair of shoes. His cotton shirt was gray with a black necktie. The shoes were slip-on and brown. On his head was a gray hat with a black shiny brim. Clipped on his brown leather belt was a ring of keys and a short-range radio.

The guard walked through with his black flashlight as he patrolled the area routinely.

Nick waited patiently as he walked by him in the darkness. As soon as the guard passed him, Nick grabbed him from behind and placed him in a sleeper hold. Within seconds the guard fell unconscious as his air was closed off from him to breath. Nick gently let down the guard to sleep peacefully by the crate. Nick went over to the door and let Katrina in.

Katrina sarcastically responded, "It's about time." She then noticed the guard on the floor.

"Sorry, I had to take care of a guard first," explained Nick.

Katrina inquired, "What did you do to him?"

"I put him in a sleeper hold and he fell unconscious."

"Good job," commented Katrina as she touched her headset and spoke, "Telka, we're in. Do your stuff."

Back in Telka's van, Telka pulled out the Hermit tarot card and commanded, "Card of the Hermit, release your sleeping dust and hinder my enemies."

An old man with a long white beard, wearing a dark green hooded cloak, magically appeared from the card. His eyes had an eerie yellow glow to them. The man was growing to full size as he floated in the air and passed through the door of the van.

Teresa looked on with amazement and said, "Wow."

Meanwhile Katrina and Nick were standing by in the museum for Telka's reply.

"I used the card, Katrina. The guards should be asleep in no time," said Telka.

"Good work, Telka," said Katrina as she asked, "Where's the security room?"

"You need to leave the service area and make your way through the room of the five kingdoms. It's a room full of five paintings. Beyond that room is the security room," answered Telka.

"Thanks, Telka," said Katrina.

The hermit passed through the service area and flew past them.

Katrina looked at Nick and said, "Let's go. By the time we get to the security room every guard should be asleep."

As they left the room, Nick asked, "How is your vision in the dark?"

"There are times I am grateful for my vampiric side, since I can see perfectly in the dark," explained Katrina.

"Cool," responded Nick.

In the security room a couple of guards were sitting in brown swivel chairs. The room was very plain with a white-tiled floor and matching drop ceiling. An off-white color covered the walls with a large glass window and gray metal door facing the hallway. Opposite to the window and door was a long table-height control panel with all kinds of buttons to control cameras and locks on all security doors. Above the control panel were several monitors built into the wall for monitoring the entire museum. On the wall by the door was a black phone mounted. Since the room was occupied, the panel lights above were turned on and served as the only source of light in the area other than small round lights in the ceilings of the hallways.

The fat guard looked at the monitor and noticed Katrina and Nick walking down a hallway. He said, "Hey, check it out. We have a couple of prowlers in the museum."

The thin guard turned and looked as he said, "How did they get in and get past Spanky?"

The fat guard continued to look at the monitor and replied, "I don't know. Maybe they surprised him? The chick is hot. Let's take out the guy and strip search the woman before we call the police."

The thin guard picked up his radio, pressed the talk button, and said, "Hey, Spanky." He let go of the button and there was no answer. He tried again, "Spanky, where are you?" Again there was no answer. He tried a third time, "Spanky, stop fooling around and answer me." Still there was no answer. The thin guard was frustrated as he put down his radio and said, "I don't like this. We should call the police now."

The fat guard responded, "We can handle this. This is our turf and there are only two of them."

The thin guard argued, "There might be more of them and we don't have any guns."

The fat guard said, "Yeah, right. We got tasers and these long heavy-duty flashlights, remember? We can handle them and without the police."

The thin guard was still worried and said, "Yeah, but they might have taken out Spanky."

The fat guard arrogantly said, "Oh, well. We know where they are and we know the layout of this place." He got off his chair and said, "Let's go ambush them. Then we will take care of business and then call the police."

At that moment the hermit appeared before the guards and surprised them.

"What the?" said the fat guard.

"It's a ghost," replied the thin guard.

The hermit quickly waved his hands as magical dust flew from his long sleeves and spread throughout the room. As they breathed in the magical dust they both passed out. The fat guard fell over on his belly and the thin guard fell asleep in his chair.

Katrina and Nick passed another storage area as they made their way through a dimly lit hallway.

Nick put on some black leather fingerless gloves as he asked, "Don't you need to wear gloves?"

Katrina responded, "No, I had my fingerprints burned off."

Nick smiled as he replied, "Mine were burned off as well."

Katrina grinned and said, "I like your style."

At that moment they entered the room of the five kingdoms. The room was simply laid out with pale blue walls and red carpet. Small round lights from the drop ceiling only lighted the room at the time. The walls were filled with paintings depicting the crests of the five kingdoms and there were portraits of every monarch that reigned during the era.

Katrina commented as she entered, "So this is the room of the five kingdoms."

Nick asked, "Haven't you been here before?"

She answered, "No, I guess you will have to be my tour guide as well."

Nick said, "Okay. This room represents the five kingdoms of the realm during the era of monarchy."

Katrina curiously asked as she walked by, "Who are these paintings of?"

He answered, "The rulers of the five kingdoms dating about eight centuries ago to the end of the era."

Many of the portraits did not interest her, until a particular portrait of a queen caught Katrina's eye, so she stopped to look at it closer.

The painting was a portrait of a young woman with long fiery red hair and creamy pale skin. She had jagged bangs in the front combed to the one side. In the portrait she was sitting on a chair with her hands on her lap. She was wearing a crimson-colored dress with long sleeves. The shoulders were puffy and the neckline was low cut and square, showing some cleavage. Around her neck was a sparkly necklace with rubies and diamonds alternating in a pattern. Her ears were decorated by matching dangling earrings. The velvet dress was close fighting and complemented her figure, while accenting her firm, larger-than-average breasts. On top of her head was a golden crown with a large ruby in the center surrounded by diamonds and more rubies. The bottom of the dress was shaped like a bell and hid her feet. Her lips were a luscious red and her blue eyes were mesmerizing. The expression on her face was a complex mixture of joy and sadness. For her smile expressed a sense of joy from victory, where her eyes expressed a sense of sorrow as if she had lost something dear to her. Below the portrait was the title that read: *Queen Brandilla Catholom.*

Katrina asked, "Who is this one? She's beautiful."

Nick answered, "Perhaps you will meet her someday."

Katrina inquired, "You mean she's a vampire?"

"You are actually looking upon my master," replied Nick.

She asked, "Your master is eight centuries old?"

"Yes," said, Nick.

"Cool," said Katrina.

Katrina and Nick made their way to the security room and entered. She noticed the guards were asleep and commented, "Hurray for Telka. The magic worked." She looked around and said, "I don't see the recorders here. They must be next door." She turned to Nick and asked, "Why don't you get the tapes out of the recorders, while I disable the alarm system?"

Nick agreed, "Okay."

Nick left the room as Katrina flipped some switches on the control console. All the alarm lights glowed red, meaning off. Katrina looked at the monitors and noticed something on the third floor. She commented, "There you are."

At this time, Nick found the audiovisual room and entered. The audiovisual room was very small and narrow. Small round lights dimly lit the room from the drop ceiling. On the right and left wall were gray metal racks with several recording devices on them. Nick made his way across the white-tiled floor and proceeded to remove all the tapes from the recorders. As soon as he was done he placed all of the magnetic tapes in a garbage bag. As he left the room he found a garbage bin around the corner. With no hesitation he dropped the bag in the gray bin.

While back in the security room, Katrina opened a gray metal junction box. She pulled a small metal device with a switch on top from her tool bag. With some pliers and a screwdriver she connected the device to the wiring. As soon as it was connected she flipped the switch on and a green light glowed. She closed the panel and put her tools away as Nick rejoined her.

Nick asked, "What are you doing?"

Katrina smiled and said, "Oh, just rigging my back-up plan."

"But you said there was no back-up plan," said Nick.

"It's more of an improvised idea than a back-up plan. I hope I don't have to use it," answered Katrina. Katrina ordered, "Let's go. The alarms are off now and I know where the blood gem is."

Nick inquired, "Where?"

Katrina answered, "The third floor."

Meanwhile the clock read 1:00 a.m. in the lobby of the Delchor Corporate Building. The lobby was very spacious with a high drop ceiling, an information counter and a small carpeted lounge. Panel lights in the drop ceiling illuminated the area as the shiny black marble floor reflected the light. The small blue-carpeted lounge had a glass coffee table in the center and two brown leather couches on either side of it. Perpendicular to the couches was a matching chair on both sides. A dark cherry panel covered the walls. The information counter was round like a donut and its base matched the walls, while the counter itself matched the floor. Within the middle of the counter were a black leather swivel chair, a dark computer terminal, and a matching phone. Behind the information counter were three elevator doors with a silver metallic look to them and a door leading to a staircase.

Carrie was in the lobby with three of her minions. Her lovely hair was flowing free in the back, instead of being braided, like before, with the same jewelry still worn everywhere else. She was wearing a sleeveless silky dress and matching high-heel shoes. The red dress had many folds and creases vertically as it wrapped around and hugged her sexy body like a glove. It crossed over and fastened at the waist as it showed off a generous amount of cleavage and fastened also behind her neck. On her arms she wore a matching set of gloves that attached at the middle finger and thumb and went all the way up past her elbow.

The minions had a human silhouette, but they were not human at all. Their faces were formless with a glowing red jewel where an eye would be. They made no sound and their skin had a sandy appearance. Dressed in gray trench coats and matching fedora hats they looked at her as she spoke.

Carrie said, "It is time, my children. Go and bring me the blood gem."

Carrie's minions nodded, turned, and left the lobby.

On the floor of Flusken's office the secretary was sitting behind her desk.

The back of her hair was actually pulled back in a golden broach and hanging over the back of her chair this time around, while her sloping saw tooth hairline hung freely. She was wearing a long-sleeve navy blue dress, dark pantyhose, and matching high-heel shoes. The silky dress had a low-cut V in the front, showing off a fair amount of cleavage, and clung to her figure from the waist up. Since the bottom of the dress was more open, it did not have any slits up the sides and went down to her knees. The sleeves only went a little past her elbows showing off a couple of bracelets, which accented her lovely wrists. Dangling gold earrings decorated her ears as they were easily seen with her hair pulled back. Her mesmerizing beauty was further enhanced with the dark eye-shadow and pink lipstick she wore.

The secretary's office was small and consisted of a desk, chair and a plant, right next to Flusken's office. Her open-air office had beige walls with vertical black lines every few feet and matched the hallway connected to it. Brown carpet covered the floor and matched the drop ceiling. Panel lights in the ceiling illuminated the area, since it was nighttime and the windows had the blinds shut. In one corner on the floor was a large plant in a brown pot. The desk was dark brown with a black computer terminal and matching phone. A hallway connected Flusken's office to the secretary's office as well as other rooms, a staircase, and three elevators.

At that moment one of the metallic silver elevator doors opened as two men left the elevator.

The first man stood about six feet three inches tall with a solid-type build. His looks were average with a round face, a strong chin, clean-shaven, long white hair combed straight back and showing his forehead, thick eyebrows, and brown eyes. His skin was golden brown. With his looks his age appeared to be twenty-nine years old. He wore a coat, a shirt, a pair of pants, gloves, and boots. His dark brown leather coat matched his calf-length buckled-up boots. On his hands he wore fingerless black leather gloves. Under his coat he wore a loose-fitting cotton black shirt. As for his nylon pants they were snug fitting, charcoal gray, and tucked into his boots. Around his waist he wore a black leather belt that fastened with a steel buckle. As far as weapons go he carried a steel broadsword in a sheath on his back with a strap that went across his chest and shoulder, which fastened in the front with a large steel buckle. His broadsword was double-edged, five feet long, and three inches wide, tapering down to a point with a leather-wrapped handle. On the end of the handle was a black glass-like sphere, the size of a golf ball. He was a beast master.

The second man stood about seven feet tall with a thin-type build. He was an ugly man, clean-shaven, bald, with dark eyebrows and blue eyes. His skin was pale. Judging from his looks he appeared to be thirty-five. He was dressed in a black trench coat, a matching round-brimmed hat, gray pants, black slip-on shoes, and dark sunglasses. No weapons to speak of were on him. His name was James.

They approached the secretary as she was applying pink-colored polish to her fingernails. She looked up as the men stood in front of her desk and replied, "May I help you?"

The first man said, "We are here to see Flusken."

She pressed the intercom button on her phone and said, "Flusken, the mercenaries from Demicroft are here to see you."

Flusken said over the intercom, "Show them in."

The secretary turned and looked at them and said, "He will see you now."

The second man commented, "Flusken is lucky to have such a beautiful secretary working for him."

She smiled and pointed at the door as she said, "His office is through that door."

The two men entered the room as the secretary got up and closed the door behind them.

Flusken was sitting in his office behind his desk waiting. It was a very spacious office with a couch, coffee table, a couple of chairs, a deluxe bar, and a desk with chair. Panel lights in the brown drop ceiling illuminated the room quite well and matched the brown carpet. The walls were covered in a charcoal-gray color. A black wooden desk faced the door with two chairs in front of it. On top of the desk a gray computer monitor could be seen as well as other office things, like a matching phone and neatly arranged papers. To the left of the desk and chairs was a very long and comfortable couch with a glass coffee table in front of it. The couch was black leather, and matched the chairs in front of the desk. Behind the desk was a matching color swivel chair. On the other side of the desk was the deluxe bar. The bar counter was glossy black, like the desk, and the under part was black. Four round stools with seats matching the color of the chairs were neatly spaced out in front of the bar. Behind the counter was a series of black wooden cabinets.

The two men approached Flusken's desk.

The beast master said, "You sent for us."

Flusken agreed, "Yes, I have a job for you two. In the event Carrie's minions fail, I will need you to retrieve the blood gem in their place."

James inquired, "How many are there?"

"Your main opposition will be a vampire bounty hunter and a vampeel slayer. Deal with them any way you chose as long as you return with the blood gem," stated Flusken as he placed manila colored envelopes in front of both of them.

They both took the money as Flusken said, "I will pay you half now and the other half after you bring back the blood gem. Are there any questions?"

The beast master asked, "When do we leave?"

"Immediately," answered Flusken.

Katrina and Nick were making their way up the staircase of the museum as she contacted Telka on her headset.

The staircase was dark with only a few small round lights in the ceiling to illuminate it. White covered the walls and matched the smooth ceiling. Red carpet covered the very wide steps to all the floors. In the middle of the staircase was a steel railing, which bisected the stairs perfectly for two-way traffic.

Katrina activated her headset and spoke, "Telka, the alarm system has been deactivated. Is everything okay out there?"

"Everything is fine. It's just a little too quiet out here," answered Telka.

Katrina stated, "We're on our way to the main exhibit hall. Stay alert."

"Good luck," replied Telka.

Outside in Telka's van Teresa's watch read 1:15 a.m. Telka was listening as Katrina spoke to her, "Thanks. I'll call you back if I have any problems."

Telka heard a noise from outside and said, "What was that?"

Teresa responded, "I didn't hear anything."

Telka moved over to the van door as she said, "I'm going to check to see if the police have returned." Telka pulled out her nine-millimeter Beretta handgun from a black leather holster on the back of her belt. She unlocked the door as Teresa watched.

Teresa said, "Careful, Telka. You don't know what's out there."

"It's okay, Teresa, remember, I'm the older sister," responded Telka as she opened the door. She peered outside the van and saw nothing but an empty and quiet street. She stepped out of the van while the door was still open. Telka turned the corner of the van and saw nothing. As she turned away, Shawn quickly appeared from behind and grabbed her mouth with his left hand as his right hand grabbed her hand holding the gun. He said, "Scream or fight me and I'll snap your lovely neck. Do you understand?"

Telka nodded in agreement.

"Good," said Shawn. With the same hand he took her gun from her and placed the barrel by the side of her head. Shawn moved Telka in front of the doorway, where Teresa could see them.

Teresa was surprised by the site of Telka held by Shawn and said, "Telka!"

Shawn smiled and said, "Hush, Teresa. We don't want to wake the neighbors."

Teresa kept quiet as she watched helplessly.

Shawn said, "Did you miss me, Teresa? I surely missed the both of you. I was deprived of some blood, but I'll make it up to you, especially for throwing a dagger at me." Shawn gave Teresa a mesmerizing gaze as he said, "Teresa, be a good girl and remove her neck jewelry."

Teresa came over to Telka and removed her necklace. Telka watched helplessly as Teresa obeyed his command.

Shawn ordered, "Teresa, be still and watch as I have some fun with your sister."

Teresa was mesmerized by his gaze and backed away as she remained still to watch what was to happen next.

Shawn pulled her hair away from the one side of her neck. He drew closer to her neck and sunk his fangs into it.

Telka jerked for a second as she slowly went into a trance.

Shawn dropped the gun as he kept his left hand cupped over her mouth. He took his right hand and slid it under her top. As he continued to suck her blood he squeezed her breast. Telka was in a state of torture rather than ecstasy as he mentally raped her, while tasting her blood.

Teresa watched helplessly as her heart rate began to increase. Her breathing became heavier as she continued to watch. Teresa's eyes closed as her breathing and heart rate escalated. At that moment she opened her eyes and was free of Shawn's charm. While remaining fairly still she subtly grabbed a small vial of liquid from her purse on the floor.

The glass vial was the size of a small bottle of perfume with a small spray mechanism on top.

She held the vial in her hand and said, "Get away from her."

Shawn stopped feeding as he faintly heard Teresa's voice. He looked up at her as he asked, "How did you break my hold on you?"

The anger she felt welled up inside her as she let it all out when she threw the vial at him and screamed, "I said let her go! You creep!" With no time to react, the vial made contact with Shawn and shattered like a glass Christmas tree ornament. Holy water splashed over half of his face as he let go of Telka and fell backwards on the pavement below. He writhed in pain as the holy water burned his skin like sulfuric acid.

Shawn held his face and stood up. He looked at Teresa and screamed, "You little bitch!"

Marcus suddenly appeared in between Shawn and the van. He mentally threw Shawn a few feet away from himself, like a gust of wind blowing a garbage can across the street.

At this point the right side of his face looked like melted wax. He got up and saw Marcus in front of him.

He angrily asked, "Who are you?"

Marcus said, "Go back to your master, like the dog you are."

Shawn was overwhelmed by the presence he felt by Marcus. He knew then that Marcus was vastly stronger than him as he transformed into a bat and flew away.

Teresa witnessed the whole seen with amazement. "Wow," said Teresa as Marcus approached her.

"Don't be afraid," said Marcus.

Teresa looked up to him and asked, "Who are you?"

Marcus smiled and replied, "I'm Katrina's father."

"Cool, I see where she gets her looks from," responded Teresa.

He looked upon Telka, who had fallen to the ground unconscious. Marcus turned to Teresa and affirmed, "Don't worry. She didn't lose much blood, thanks to you." He picked Telka up and said, "Come. It is not safe here."

"Okay," said Teresa as she stepped out of the van and followed him.

Nearby the police squad car from before returned to the scene and stopped in front of Telka's van. Mike looked upon the van being parked and saw the doors open as he said, "That's strange."

Simone asked, "What?"

Mike commented, "That van was here before, but parked in a different place."

Simone inquired, "Maybe they wanted a better space?"

Mike said, "It wouldn't matter at this time of night. Besides that, the back doors are wide open."

Simone asked, "You want to check it out?"

"That's right. Let's go," said Mike as he got out of the car. He turned on his flashlight as he drew his handgun.

Simone also got out of the car and drew her handgun as she readied her flashlight. She followed behind Mike as he slowly approached the back of the van.

Mike slowly peered around the door with his handgun ready to fire. As he faced the van he said, "That's strange."

Simone inquired, "What did you find?"

He turned to Simone as she approached and said, "There's nothing here but a laptop."

Simone suggested, "Maybe they went to get help because of car trouble."

Mike stated, "It doesn't make any sense."

Simone asked, "What should we do then?"

He went inside the van and examined the laptop more closely. Mike said, "I'm beginning to think someone is pulling a job on the museum."

Simone replied, "Tonight?"

"There's a map of the museum displayed on the laptop. Let's go," ordered Mike.

"Okay," said Simone as she followed him over to the main entrance.

They headed across the patio to the bridge leading up to the main entrance.

Simone stood about five feet five inches tall with an athletic-type build and average-sized breasts. She had fair skin, blonde hair, and green eyes. Even though she wore no makeup or jewelry in uniform, she was naturally cute with her round eyeglasses. Despite her cute looks, her age was about twenty-two years old. Her lovely hair went all the way down to her back. She had saw-tooth bangs that parted in the middle at the top, while the rest of her hair was pulled back in a ponytail.

She was wearing a total black outfit consisting of a shirt, a necktie, a pair of pants, and shoes. On the shoulder of both sleeves was the same police emblem as on the car door decal in the form of an embroidered patch. Her long-sleeve shirt and loose-fitting pants were made of cotton. Around her waist were a regular leather belt and a police-issue weapons belt. The weapons belt consisted of a small flashlight, a short-range radio, a pair of handcuffs, a handgun holster, and a nightstick. Her shoes were basically dark running shoes. In her holster she carried a police issue Beretta M9 nine-millimeter handgun, capable of carrying fifteen rounds in the clip and one in the chamber.

Mike stood about six feet two inches tall with a macho-type build. He was a handsome fellow, clean-shaven, with neck-length brown hair, which was parted on the side as the saw-tooth bangs draped over his forehead. His eyes were brown and his skin was fair. Mike was very mature for his age, but he was indeed twenty years old. Mike was wearing the same police uniform only a different size.

The main entrance had a set of steps from the bridge leading up to a set of three glass double doors. Beside each set of double doors was an electronic lock for access with a card key.

Mike approached the card key lock and said, "Cover me," as he holstered his gun and held on to his flashlight.

"Okay," responded Simone as she aimed her gun at the entrance.

Mike pulled out a card key from his pocket and swiped it through the lock. The light on the lock turned green and the door opened. Mike said, "Go."

Simone nodded as she walked in cautiously ahead of him.

Mike followed her in, put his key away, and drew his handgun. The door automatically closed and locked behind them.

Katrina and Nick managed to reach the third floor and drew closer to the exhibit room, where the blood gem was kept.

Nick inquired, "So what are you going to do, once you get the blood gem?"

Katrina answered, "I don't know. Probably the next logical step would be to find out why our enemy wants it so badly."

Nick agreed, "That's sounds fair."

Katrina and Nick found the room and looked at it from the hallway.

The treasure exhibit room had two doorways in from the hallway and was filled with many jewels under glass cases on pedestals. All the square wooden pedestals matched the white drop ceiling and the walls. Each wall had several glass cases in front of it and one glass case was in the center of the room. In the center of the high drop ceiling was a large rectangular skylight. The blue-tiled floor had a few running lights that illuminated the dim room a little. Invisible lasers emitted from the walls and also had connecting beams to the pedestals in parallel and perpendicular patterns.

Nick commented, "This is going to be simpler than I thought."

He stepped forward, when Katrina placed her hand in front of him and said, "Wait."

Nick looked at her and asked, "What?"

Katrina closed her eyes and shifted into aura vision. She opened her eyes and spotted the lasers in the room. Katrina said, "The room is full of lasers."

"I thought you took care of security," replied Nick.

"I took out the alarm system, not the defenses," explained Katrina.

Nick inquired, "What shall we do?"

She commented, "I bet they installed lasers to avoid installing floor sensors."

Nick asked, "How can you see them and I can't?"

"Because I have aura vision. I can see through walls in tones of gray and every living thing or emitting energy gives off an aura," answered Katrina.

"That's cool," commented Nick.

Katrina looked away, turned on her headset, and spoke, "Telka, I need some help with the treasure exhibit room." There was no answer. She continued, "Telka, do you read?" Still, there was no response. She tried again, "Telka, come in please." Only silence filled the void. Katrina became frustrated and yanked the headset off her ear as she said, "Damn!"

Nick inquired, "What's wrong?"

Katrina said, "I can't get a hold of Telka. I guess we're on our own with this one."

Nick asked, "Any ideas?"

Katrina suggested, "There must be a local control panel nearby for those lasers. We just have to find it and turn them off."

Nick offered, "I could carry you above the lasers."

Katrina agreed, "That's not a bad idea. Okay. Let's do it." She removed her coat and left it on the red carpet floor of the hallway. Katrina placed her hand around his neck as he supported her back with his left arm and picked up her legs under the knees with his right arm. Katrina smiled as she looked at him and said, "Just watch your hands, bud. I'm not blind, while my eyes are in aura vision."

"Yes, my queen," replied Nick. She shook her head as he lifted her up in the air. They floated inside and across the room, while avoiding the lasers.

Katrina noticed the control box and said, "That must be it," as she pointed to it. The two floated over to the gray metal panel. She opened it and flipped the laser marked switches. Within seconds all of the lasers turned off. When she knew they were off she said, "You can put me down now."

Nick replied, "Oh, sorry." He gently put her back on her feet.

Katrina closed her eyes and reset her vision to normal. She commented, "You were enjoying that, I bet."

Nick smiled and said, "I would be lying if I said no. Besides, you have firm thighs."

Katrina grinned as she said, "Thanks. Enough with the charm, Romeo." She pointed to the glass case in the center of the room and said, "Let's get that gem and get out of here."

Nick walked over to the display case as he extended his fingernails. Within seconds he cut a circular hole into the side of the display case. After knocking the glass out of the hole, he grabbed the blood gem and pulled it out.

Carrie's minions arrived at this time and gathered outside of the room.

"Not bad," said Katrina as Nick handed her the blood gem. She took hold of it and placed it in the tool bag.

Nick said, "Let's get out of here."

Katrina placed her hand on her hip and waved her other hand as she said, "That's my line."

Mike approached the room from the other direction with Simone behind him. Mike entered the room, aimed his gun at the two of them, and said, "Hold it right there. You're both under arrest."

They turned around and looked at Mike. Simone followed in and covered Mike.

"Ah great. We don't have time for this," responded Katrina.

Nick asked, "Who let him in?"

Carrie's three minions entered the room from the other doorway.

Mike was surprised and said, "What the…?"

Katrina and Nick ignored Mike and Simone for a second and faced the minions.

The first minion spoke, "Give us the blood gem."

Mike was puzzled by their order and said, "Blood gem? I don't know who you are, but you are all under arrest. Simone, call for backup. I'll handle this."

"Okay," replied Simone as she took off to radio for backup.

The minions drew closer to them. They started to change form by growing taller and their fingers became longer as they shed their hats and coats.

Katrina faced Mike and said, "Are you that dense? You can't arrest these things. Don't you know monsters fall outside the law?"

Mike said in disbelief, "This is unreal," as he fired his gun. The bullets went right through them and didn't even slow them down as they crept along closer.

While the minions distracted Mike, Katrina gave a wink to Nick as she tilted her head toward the panel. She did a crescent kick and knocked Mike's gun out of his hands. Before Mike could react she spun around and kicked him out of the room. Katrina ran out of the room as Nick leaped into the air. He grabbed a dagger from his jacket and threw it at the control panel. The lasers instantly turned on. Within seconds the lasers hit the minions and turned their sand-composed bodies into glass statues.

Katrina helped Mike up as she said, "Sorry about that. It was the only way."

Mike inquired, "Who are you people?"

"No time to explain. We got to get out of here fast," answered Katrina as she put her coat back on.

Nick left the room floating and landed on the floor of the hallway.

"That was too easy," commented Nick.

"Careful. There could be more," said Katrina.

Mike was confused by the entire calamity, so he went along with them for the time being, since his handgun was lost. They all proceeded to go to the second floor.

When they descended to the second floor, the beast master was waiting for them.

Katrina saw him and replied, "What the…?

Nick commented, "It's a beast master."

"There is no escape. Give us the blood gem and I'll be easy on you," said the beast master.

Nick asked, "Could we have a conference first?"

"Yes, but be quick about it," replied the beast master.

Katrina and the others gathered around in a group.

Mike inquired, "What is going on here?"

"If we get through this, I'll explain later," answered Katrina.

Nick asked, "Any ideas?"

Katrina asked, "What do you know about beast masters?"

Nick relied, "They control demonic beasts. They're immune to fire. And they're usually good with a sword."

Katrina stated, "He may be a beast master, but he is still a vampire. Can he be killed in a normal way?"

"I'm not sure, but I'm going to find out," said Nick.

Mike said, "I don't know what is going on here, but I'm with you guys."

Katrina said, "Okay. Here's the plan. Nick, when I give the signal, I want you to create a big cloud of mist. That should confuse him for a bit. I'll take the cop with me down this hallway. When I'm about halfway down the hall, I'll set off the security system. He won't be able to follow us and you can stay here and take the beast master down. Any questions?"

Mike agreed, "I'll go with it."

Nick stated, "It will be a pleasure taking out this arrogant windbag."

She looked at Nick and said, "We'll meet up sometime later," as she handed him a business card with her number on it. Katrina commented, "Oh, and one more thing, Nick, I am impressed. Call me."

Nick replied, "I hope you had a good time tonight."

Katrina smiled, "Except for the cheap moves, I had a great time."

Nick inquired, "Aren't you going to give me a goodnight kiss?"

Katrina grinned, as she said, "No, you'll have to earn the next one."

"I like a challenge," said Nick.

Katrina said, "Don't get killed, tough guy," as she winked.

Nick replied, "Don't worry. You'll see me again," as he winked back.

Katrina and the others turned around and faced the beast master. She stated, "Okay. We've decided," as she subtly grabbed her handgun.

The beast master assumed, "So, you've decided to give me the blood gem without any trouble. Right?"

Katrina winked at Nick again as she said, "Wrong!" She immediately aimed and shot at the beast master.

He instantly dodged for cover behind a very wide and round pole. Nick immediately turned into a thick cloud of mist. Katrina grabbed Mike's hand and ran.

In all the confusion the beast master stepped out from behind the pole. He commented, "The thick mist was a nice trick."

They continued to run down the hall as she pulled a small black remote out of her coat. She pulled the antenna out with her teeth and proceeded to press the button on the remote. The alarm sounded within seconds. They managed to make it down the stairs to the first floor as the Plexiglas doors came slamming down every twenty feet in the hallways.

Nick reformed as the beast master waited for the mist to clear.

The beast master said, "Fools. You cannot escape."

Nick replied, "Who said anything about escaping? I am your opponent now."

"Very well. My pet can go after your friends," commented the beast master.

"I just bought them some time," stated Nick.

The beast master pulled out a demon orb. He ordered, "Hellhound, come forth." The orb began to glow a purple color as a hellhound emerged from it

The hellhound was smaller than a hell bull and larger than a hell pinscher. It had long pointy ears and a long snout, just like a wolf. Like its brethren, it had large razor-sharp teeth and three eerie yellow eyes that glowed. The legs were powerful and the muscular definition could be seen easily from its dark exterior. Instead of one tail, it had two tails, slightly longer than a wolf's.

"Go, my pet. Bring me the blood gem from their corpses," instructed the beast master.

The hellhound obeyed its master and took off running.

Nick sarcastically said, "Aren't we cocky?"

"It makes no difference. I will feed your liver to my pet," proclaimed the beast master.

"Talk is cheap. Let's do it," said Nick as he took his jacket off.

They assumed fighting stances as they faced each other.

Nick initiated the fight in the hallway as he jumped in the air and spun into a kick at him. The beast master grabbed Nick's leg and flung him a few feet into the air. Nick flipped back before hitting a wall and landed on his feet.

He drove in and instantly attacked Nick with a series of punches. Nick blocked every punch and ducked under the last one before spinning around and foot-sweeping him. He fell backward as Nick rushed in to attack.

While lying on his back, the beast master kicked Nick in the gut and drove him back. The beast master quickly got up as Nick recovered. He saw an opening and rushed Nick.

Nick sidestepped him and kicked him in the gut causing him to flip over. He got up as Nick jumped in the air to kick him straight on. The beast master dodged the kick, grabbed his chest, and slammed him to the floor. Nick got up as the beast master unsheathed a sword.

The beast master commented, "I haven't had a fight this good in ages. Let's see how you are with a sword."

"That's fine by me," said Nick as he broke a glass case in a nearby room and pulled a long broadsword out of it. Nick backed into a large room full of weapons in glass cases as he motioned with his hand for him to follow.

The beast master followed him into the room. They faced each other, while walking in a circular direction. They immediately clashed swords, relentlessly attacking and parrying several times.

Nick finally dodged his strike and cut him on the arm.

The beast master commented, "Not bad."

"I'm just getting started," replied Nick as he attacked. Nick's attack was easily dodged as the beast master cut his hand. Nick licked his bloody hand and said, "Bring it on."

The beast master lunged in with his sword as Nick parried and countered with a punch to the face. He fell backward and shattered a glass case behind him. Nick gave him little time to recover, as he struck downward.

The beast master parried his attack and kicked Nick in the gut. Nick was driven a few feet back from the force of the kick. The beast master got up and viciously attacked Nick and knocked Nick's sword out of his hands. The beast master commented, "You've put up a fight longer than I expected. You may pray for a quick death now." He thrust the sword directly at Nick's heart as he faced him without flinching.

At the last second Nick dodged the sword and the sword went into the pit of his shoulder. Nick grabbed the blade with one hand as the beast master tried to free it. "It is you who should be praying for a quick death," said Nick as he hit the blade with his other hand and broke it off. The force of the break knocked the beast master back and off balance. Nick quickly lunged in and stuck his extended fingernails into his eyes.

The beast master dropped his sword as he writhed in pain from his punctured bloody eyes. Nick quickly grabbed the sword before it hit the floor and thrust it under his chin. The sword went through the beast master's throat and out through the back of his head.

The beast master backed up staggering and fell backward as he shattered another glass case on the way to the floor. Blood poured out of the back of his head as Nick watched for any signs of regenerating. The body did not move as the blood continued to pour out and covered the floor. Seconds later the body caught on fire from within and turned to ashes. Nick was satisfied with the beast master being dead and left the swords as is in the room.

Mike and Katrina made it to the first floor from the staircase. The area was very spacious with a high ceiling, red carpeting, and display windows in the distance. In the center of the room was a giant stone statue of a bat and on its left was a statue of a wolf.

Mike asked, “Did we lose them?”

“I’m not sure. I doubt it,” answered Katrina.

She heard another set of footsteps, stopped and said, “We got company.”

James stepped in the open area of the hallway.

Mike inquired, “Who is this guy?”

Katrina replied, “I don’t know. He is not quite human.”

James tipped his hat and said, “Hello, Katrina. I have heard so much about you.”

She crossed her arms and replied, “I didn’t know I was famous. Who are you?”

“Allow me to introduce myself. My name is James,” remarked James.

Katrina asked, “I pretty much know the answer, but I’ll ask anyway. What do you want?”

James extended his hand towards her and replied, “The blood gem if you please?”

Katrina commented, “This is unreal, a bad guy with manners.”

James explained, “Flusken sent me just in case there would be any complications. However, it would wound me deeply to kill you in order to retrieve it.”

She inquired, “And why is that? Might I ask?”

James said, “I detest killing women, my dear.”

Katrina laughed as blades emerged from his hands.

Mike drew his gun at the same time Katrina drew hers.

Blades came out of James’ shoes as they unloaded several bullets into his head, torso, arms, and legs. James fell backward as the blood poured from his body.

Katrina lowered her gun and said, “Well, that’s that.”

James got up as they looked on with surprise. James laughed as the bullets were coming out of his body and dropping on the floor.

"You win that round, Katrina, but my curse won't let me die by conventional means. Now it is my turn," said James.

She asked, "What in the realm are you?"

"You will see," remarked James as he removed his hat and trench coat. Blood continued to spew from his wounds as it floated in the air and changed into larger solid pieces. More pieces emerged from the blood and covered his body. Soon his body was totally covered by these large solid pieces. In no time his body was covered from head to toe in this crimson-colored metallic armor.

The armor had sharp edges with spikes on almost every major piece of it. Spikes or claws were on the ends of every finger. The plate-mail armor was crimson all over and only offset by the eerie yellow glowing eyes under the helmet.

Katrina and Mike looked on with disbelief as he stood there looking at them. Katrina placed her hand on her hip and said, "Okay. Bullets didn't work, but I am not through yet. The only way you are getting the blood gem from me is by prying it out of the hand of my corpse," remarked Katrina.

James answered with a deeper voice, "That can be arranged."

Kescha appeared out of the shadows and surprised everyone. Her hair was down and she was wearing a nylon top and matching pants, a leather jacket with matching gloves and high-heel boots. The black nylon material fit her snug as a glove. It was a sleeveless top that showed off some cleavage and some of her midriff as it zipped up the middle. She had the collar sticking up, which created a wide V in the front down to her cleavage. Her gloves were fingerless and looped around her middle fingers as they went halfway up her forearm. The right glove had on the back of the hand a small red gem that was round, flat, and smooth. Around her waist was a black leather belt with a belt buckle in the shape of a skull. Skull earrings that matched her belt buckle decorated her ears along with a black leather chocker with the same skull on her neck. Her boots had zippers up the sides and went up to her knees.

Katrina and Mike looked at Kescha as she said, "He's mine."

Katrina inquired, "It's you again. What are you doing here?"

Kescha put her hands on her hips, smiled, and replied, "Katrina, I can't let you have all the fun. After all, you are not the only group that is determined to keep the blood gem safe."

James intervened, "This is becoming quite interesting. I wonder how many I will have to kill before you relinquish the blood gem."

Mike inquired, "What's her story?"

Katrina replied, "When I know, I'll tell you. As for now she is someone I ran into on a job."

"Run along, Katrina, I'll deal with him," offered Kescha.

Katrina responded, "That's fine by me, since I got what I came for. So are you going to tell me your name?"

"My name is Kescha, Katrina. I'll see you later," said Kescha.

They took off as Kescha held James at bay. She smiled, waved her right finger out, and said, "Uh uh uh. I'm your opponent now. If you want them, you will have to get through me."

James laughed at her remark.

"It's not every day I run into the accursed crimson armor. I wonder if you have mastered it," commented Kescha.

"Your knowledge of my armor is surprising," said James.

"You have no idea how far back my knowledge of the realm goes," said Kescha.

"I'm afraid the time to be nice is over as your life will be. Prepare to die, woman," stated James.

"Bear in mind your motivation to fight is for money, where mine is to protect this realm," stated Kescha.

Blood poured out of James' right hand and formed into a spiked ball, the size of a beach ball, and a very long chain.

Kescha smiled as the jewel on her glove glowed and a long two-bladed sword magically appeared in her hand. The blades were wide and curved. As she took hold of the black leather handle in the middle, the length of the weapon was almost as tall as her.

Blood poured out of James' left hand and formed into a foot-wide and ten-foot-long double-edged broadsword.

Kescha took off her jacket as she stood in a defensive stance and said, "Let's do it."

James raised his right arm and began to spin his ball and chain over his head. He swung the ball down as she dodged it. The ball hit a large stone statue of a wolf and crushed it. He followed up with striking down with the sword.

Kescha parried the sword as he picked up the ball and chain to spin it again. He swung horizontally with the ball and chain as she dropped below it, while going into a full split. As the ball missed her it hit the side of a bat stone statue behind her. Chunks of the stone broke off and fell to the floor. She rolled out of the way before the chunks hit her.

Again he followed up with a sword attack. Kescha parried and rolled out of the way as he continued to attack with the sword. As she got up he picked up the ball and chain and spun it, like before. This time he slashed with his sword first as she parried. He relentlessly attacked as Kescha successfully parried every attack.

Without warning Kescha parried one last time before his sword broke in half. She saw an opening and threw her sword, like a javelin straight at him. The sword hit him directly in the throat and caused him to fall backward.

Unfortunately, Kescha let her guard down and the ball was swung forward and struck her in the abdomen. The force sent her back flying, until she hit the giant bat statue behind her. She fell forward after the impact as the statue crumbled behind her. She was stunned as she lay on top of the ball with a couple of spikes sticking in her abdomen. The wind was knocked out of her to the point of almost knocking her out.

James was still alive as he let go of the ball and chain and the sword. The armor held on to the blade as it absorbed most of the impact and only a few inches of the blade penetrated his throat. He lay flat on his back as he took hold of her weapon and pulled it free from his throat. His throat made a nasty fleshy sound as the blade was pulled out. He sat up as he noticed she was stuck on the ball. His throat amazingly closed up and healed as the armor slowly mended itself where the blade cut it.

He stood up and walked over to her as her eyes opened. His massive hands grabbed her arms as he pulled her free from the spikes on the ball. As he lifted her up he noticed her wounds closed up almost instantly. She regained consciousness as he commented, "No normal person would have survived such an attack. What are you?"

Kescha smiled and said, "My bad. I guess my blade was not enough to stop you. If it wasn't for that accursed armor, you would be dead right now."

James replied, "No physical weapons can kill me in this armor." He squeezed her arms as he said, "With the strength the armor gives me I could easily crush your arms." Kescha gritted her teeth from the force of his squeeze as he continued, "Tell me what you are or I just might see how much pain you can take before finishing you."

She responded, "All right. I'll tell you." She frowned as she looked him in the eyes as she said, "The last thing you will see before your imminent death."

Her eyes began to glow an eerie yellow. Large black bat-like wings sprouted from her back and wrapped around him as curved foot-long horns grew out of her head. Her whole body caught on fire as her skin turned a crimson color and her clothes burned away like paper. Kescha's hair turned to a jet-black color, as did her razor-sharp fingernails, while they grew to a length of three inches.

Her body was burning red hot as the fire consumed the armor as well. Kescha said, "I am a succubus and I was only toying with you. Fire is one thing your armor has no defense against."

He screamed in agony, before his body was burned to a crisp. Fortunately, Kescha contained her fire and did not set fire to the whole place. His charred body turned to ashes as the armor had no inner frame and fell apart. She dropped to the ground gracefully and commented regretfully, "I had no choice but to kill him. The will of the armor consumed him totally."

Kescha stood there as she thought of what her master told her in the past. She was looking at her master as she was still in her demonic form.

He was standing in front of her as he remarked, "You cannot deny the darkness within you no matter how hard you try, Kescha."

Kescha looked at him and said, "There is still hope for mankind." Victor laughed as he walked away from her. She closed her eyes as her horns and wings turned to ashes and were whisked away by the wind. Her long black fingernails retracted to a shorter length as her skin returned to its golden brown color. The blackness of her hair disappeared as the shimmering white color took over, like white out covers a smudge on paper.

Kescha opened her eyes and was standing in the museum back to her human form naked. "Oh well, I have no important news for my master," remarked Kescha. She concentrated as her clothes magically formed on her body.

Her hair was tied back in a ponytail from the top part of the back of her head. She was wearing a long-sleeve top and a matching miniskirt, nylon gloves and matching high-heel boots. Big golden hoop earrings decorated her ears, while around her neck was a white nylon choker with a red heart charm. The white cotton material fit her body snug as a glove. Her top was collarless and accented her cleavage as it formed a V shape down past the top of it. It was more like a blazer with four golden buttons down the middle and stopped at her exposed midriff. On each sleeve at the end were three matching buttons like the front. Her fingerless gloves went up to her wrists. The right glove had on the back of the hand a small red gem that was round, flat, and smooth. Her miniskirt had slits up the sides for some apparent reason. The boots she wore had zippers up the sides and went up to her thighs.

Kescha held her right hand out as the gem on her glove glowed. Her weapon floated into the air and magically turned into smoke as it returned to the gem. She looked at the armor and said, "Well, I guess the museum is as good place as any for storage of an accursed armor with no wearer."

Katrina and Mike entered the lobby of the museum. The lobby was long, wide and full of statues of kings, queens, and other warlords. All of the walls were plain except for a few paintings of past events dating back 800 years ago. The floor was tiled like a checkerboard, while the ceiling was high with a few round lights lighting the dim area.

Katrina stopped as she saw Marcus and the others with him. She looked at Marcus and said, "Father, it's you, the one from my dream. What are you doing with Telka and Teresa?"

Marcus smiled and said, "It pleases me to see you again. Don't worry, daughter. She will be all right."

Teresa spoke up, "It's all right, Katrina. He saved us from Shawn."

Marcus knelt down and placed Telka on the floor gently.

Katrina was getting upset and asked, "Where is that coward? I'll deal with him myself."

Mike interrupted and asked, "This man is your father?"

Katrina looked at Mike and answered, "Yes, he is my real father."

A few feet away from them a large Plexiglas door stopped the hellhound from approaching. It growled as it breathed fire on the Plexiglas.

Teresa heard the hellhound's growl and inquired, "Katrina, what is making that sound?"

Katrina replied, "I don't want to stick around to find out."

Teresa noticed the hellhound burning its way through the Plexiglas, pointed at it, and said, "Well, it's burning through that glass over there."

Katrina and the others turned in its direction. Katrina responded by pulling her skirt up and drawing her gun. She aimed the gun at the beast as Marcus said, "I'll handle this, daughter."

"Whatever you say, Father," responded Katrina as she and the others got out of the way.

The fire was melting a hole through the glass, like a hot knife through butter. When the hole was big enough, the hellhound ran through it. As hellhound drew closer Marcus placed his palm in front of it. It lunged at Marcus as he commanded, "Stop." The hellhound was stopped in midair as Katrina and the others watched in amazement.

Teresa spoke up with surprise, "Wow! Your father is so cool, Katrina."

Marcus ordered, "Take your friends and get out of here. I will catch up with you later, Katrina. I promise. For now you must leave this place, before the police arrive in full force."

Katrina put her gun away as she inquired, "When will I see you again, Father?"

Marcus replied, "Soon. There is no more time for us to talk. Go!"

Katrina nodded as she picked up Telka and carried her away. Mike and Teresa followed her out.

With no one around Marcus lashed out a few wires from his sleeve. The hellhound was cut into pieces within seconds as it hit the floor after Marcus released it. It turned to ashes soon after.

Simone came on to the scene and saw Marcus. She drew her weapon, aimed it at Marcus, and said, "Hold it."

Marcus turned to her and looked into her eyes with his mesmerizing gaze. "Sleep," commanded Marcus. Simone fell under his control and fell on the floor asleep.

Back at the Delchor Corporate Building in the alchemist room the clock on the wall read 3:00 a.m. Carrie was watching the magical window as a look of shock appeared on her face. Carrie looked down with disappointment as she said, "My minions have failed."

"All is not lost, my dear," said Flusken as he entered the room. "We have all the time in the realm."

Carrie turned to Flusken and inquired, "Who is that vampire? He is very powerful."

Flusken looked upon the image in the cauldron and replied, "An old friend, one I have not seen in quite a long time."

Carrie inquired, "What about the woman who challenged the crimson armor?"

"Her name is Kescha. She is a servant of the dark priest. The real question I want answered is does the dark priest know the blood gem has been found?"

Chapter 12
The Purifying

The clock on the wall of Telka's shop read 4:00 a.m. as Katrina and the others returned. Katrina laid Telka on the couch of the front room, since she was still sleeping peacefully.

Teresa looked upon Katrina with concern and asked, "Is she going to be all right, Katrina?"

Katrina knelt down, looked at Telka's neck, and replied, "She'll be fine, but we have another problem."

Mike inquired, "What do you mean?"

Katrina looked at Mike and responded, "She's been marked by that vampire's bite."

Mike asked, "Could you explain?"

"Telka has a strong will, but she has been bitten and I can sense a blood link was established when he fed upon her. Once a vampire bites a human and establishes a blood link, the willpower of the victim begins to weaken," explained Katrina.

Teresa asked, "What do you mean, Katrina?"

"Well, if you compare it to a mirror, she has a fracture or crack in it. Shawn has an opening to her mind on a subconscious level and can now slowly work on weakening her will by invading her dreams," said Katrina.

Teresa inquired, "Can't you fix her, like me?"

Katrina shook her head and replied, "It's not that simple. Your will was not tainted and all I did was reinforce it. In her case the damage has already been done."

Mike asked, "Can you do anything to help her?"

"There is only one way to cleanse her of the mark," answered Katrina.

Teresa asked, "What?"

"I'll have to cleanse the bite marks with holy water," said Katrina.

Mike replied, "That doesn't seem too bad."

"You don't understand. When the holy water touches the bite marks, she will experience excruciating pain. It will purify it, but she will have to be conscious for the duration," explained Katrina.

Mike inquired, "Can't we just give her some painkillers beforehand?"

"No, drugs will only nullify the effects of the holy water," said Katrina.

Mike asked, "Do you know how to cleanse it?"

"Yes, but it is her choice to go through with it," answered Katrina.

Mike offered, "I have an idea."

Katrina inquired, "What did you have in mind?"

Mike asked, "What if we immerse her in a bathtub of warm water to relax her first?"

"That's not a bad idea. With her body relaxed, her body will release natural painkillers into her system and in turn help alleviate some of the pain," agreed Katrina.

Mike stated, "You are going to need help holding her down."

"You have a point there, Mike," said Katrina.

Mike offered, "I'll help. You can even blindfold me if you like."

Teresa smiled and said, "I like this guy, Katrina. Can I help too?"

Katrina replied, "No."

Teresa was shocked by her response and asked, "Why not?"

Katrina placed her hands on her shoulders and replied, "You have to realize this is going to cause her a lot of pain. If you happen to be around you might get overprotective and try to interfere. Do you understand?"

Teresa looked disappointed and said, "I guess."

Katrina smiled and said, "Good girl. Why don't you get the bath water ready, while we wake her up."

Teresa smiled and replied, "Okay," as she took off.

Telka woke up at that moment and said, "Where am I?"

Katrina placed her hand on her shoulder and said, “It’s all right, Telka. You’re safe with us back at the shop.”

Telka inquired, “What happened, Katrina?”

Katrina explained, “You were attacked by Shawn, and Marcus, my father, came to your rescue. He brought you to us and here we are.”

Telka noticed Mike sitting beside her on the couch as she asked, “Who’s this nice-looking guy?”

Katrina was flabbergasted by her question, since there wasn’t a proper introduction. She simply said, “Oh. Uh…”

Mike smiled and said, “My name is Mike. You’re Katrina, right?”

Katrina said, “Yes, and this damsel is Telka.”

Mike replied, “Nice to meet you, Telka.”

Telka asked, “Where is Nick?”

“We got separated. I hope he’s all right,” answered Katrina.

Telka smiled and said, “Oh, I’m sure he is. You really like him, Katrina. Don’t you?”

Katrina blushed as she replied, “Hey, let’s not get carried away.”

Telka asked, “Did you get it?”

“You bet. We’ve got those Drenkel Clan bastards right where we want them,” said Katrina. She pulled the blood gem out of her bag. Telka gazed at it with interest.

“I have to find out what they intend to use it for,” stated Katrina.

Telka said, “Katrina, I feel strange, like I just woke up from a bad dream.”

“You’ve been marked, Telka,” said Katrina.

Telka asked, “Am I going to become a vampire, Katrina?”

Katrina shook her head as she said, “No, but I must cleanse the bite marks on your neck.”

“If you must,” replied Telka.

Katrina explained, “I can, but it is going to hurt a lot. Otherwise, Shawn will come into your dreams and make you his slave.”

Telka touched Katrina’s hand and said, “I trust you, Katrina, so let’s do it.”

Katrina replied, “All right. Lucky for you Mike has agreed to help us.”

Telka was naked in the tub of the bathroom, waiting for Katrina to start the cleansing. The bathroom was laid out with a porcelain tub, commode, and a sink. A light shade of pink covered the plain walls, except for the many candles lit around the room. White covered the tiled floor and reflected the candlelight well as it matched the drop ceiling. Round lights were in the ceiling overhead, but they were off at this time. The tub was in the back left corner and had a shower wall and a pink curtain on a metal track. A couple feet to the right of the tub was the commode with a pink covering. Above the commode was a window with pink curtains. The sink was on the other side of the tub a couple feet away. On either side of the mirror above the sink were more round lights built into the wall, which were off.

Katrina had taken her coat off before going up to the bathroom. She was on her knees near Telka's head as her feet were facing the faucet of the tub. She asked, "What's with the candlelight?"

Telka replied, "They help me relax."

Katrina said, "Oh."

Telka turned to Katrina and commented, "This feels so kinky, Katrina."

Katrina assured her, "Don't worry, Mike will be blindfolded. Are you ready for him?"

"I think so," said Telka.

Katrina got up and opened the wooden door.

Katrina said, "She's ready, Mike."

Mike said, "Okay. Lead the way."

She led Mike into the bathroom blindfolded as she closed and locked the door. Katrina brought him over to Telka as she said, "Mike, I'll guide your hand."

"Okay," responded Mike.

Katrina stated, "And don't even think about trying something funny. I won't think twice about laying you out cold."

Mike replied, "I understand."

Katrina knelt down like before and Mike knelt down beside her. She placed Mike's left hand on Telka's left shoulder.

Mike offered, "If it will help you can hold my other hand if you like, Telka."

Telka agreed, "Okay," as she grabbed his right hand near the edge of the tub.

Katrina looked at Telka and asked, "Ready?"

Telka said, "Do it, Katrina."

Katrina opened a vial the size of a test tube. She gently turned Telka's head to expose the bite marks on her neck more. Katrina took hold of Telka's right hand as she poured the holy water on the bite marks. Telka closed her eyes as she screamed in agony. She squirmed a little as Mike held her in place with his strong masculine arm. The holy water touched the bite marks and felt like scalding hot war as it partially healed the bite marks. Katrina emptied the vial and asked, "Are you okay, Telka?"

"I'm all right," responded Telka as she opened her eyes.

Katrina stated, "We're only halfway done. Do you want to continue? We can stop, if you like."

"Keep going, Katrina," said Telka.

Katrina said, "Okay. Hold out for a little bit more." Katrina grabbed another vial from her pocket and pulled the cork off with her teeth. She poured the holy water on the bite marks again as Telka closed her eyes and screamed through the pain. She jumped again in reaction to the cleansing as Mike held her down a second time. At this point the bite marks fully healed and no trace of the bite marks remained.

Telka opened her eyes, turned to Katrina, and said, "Thanks, Katrina. I owe you one."

Katrina kissed her on the forehead and said, "I'll collect later." Telka felt relieved as she passed out from exhaustion.

Mike asked with concern, "Is she going to be all right?"

Katrina smiled and replied, "She'll be fine with some rest. Let's leave her alone." She led him outside of the bathroom and closed the door. She took off his blindfold and asked, "Could you go downstairs while I put Telka to bed, Mike?"

Mike said, "Sure."

"Thanks for your help," said Katrina.

"You're welcome," said Mike as he went down the stairs.

When Katrina was done with Telka she joined Mike downstairs in the front room. Mike handed her his card as he got off the couch and offered, "Let me know if I can help."

"I'll keep that in mind," said Katrina as she took the card.

Mike stated, "I should be on my way."

Before Mike could get out the door Katrina said, "Hey, Mike. Aren't you going to arrest me? I stole something. Didn't I?"

Mike turned around and said, "Forget about it. No one would ever believe my report. They would want to lock me up instead." Katrina smiled as he left.

Chapter 13
Recovery

In the meantime, Nick was staggering along on a ledge through the sewer tunnel below the Fright Club. The tunnel had a rounded ceiling and the walls were concrete. Ledges were on either side of the tunnel to allow workers to easily walk through the tunnel without treading in the water below. Water flowed at the bottom of the tunnel like a gentle stream. The water was murky and had an indescribable stench about it. Rats could be seen everywhere moving around in various numbers. Only moonlight from the drains cast indirect light in the dark sewers.

Nick managed to find his way back to the stone steps that secretly led up to the basement of the Fright Club.

Sheryl was looking around the main floor of the club as Michelle came down the stairs. Sheryl was wearing just a light blue tank top and matching panties. Michelle was wearing just a pink nightshirt and matching panties.

Michelle asked with concern, "What's wrong, Sheryl?"

Sheryl had her arms crossed as she looked at her mother with sad eyes and said, "Nicky isn't back yet and it's almost dawn."

Michelle gently placed her hands on Sheryl's shoulders and said, "He's a grown man. I'm sure he can take care of himself."

Sheryl sniffed the air as Michelle turned her head and heard noises from below. Sheryl stated, "I smell blood. It smells like Nicky's blood."

Michelle let go of her and said, "Go check it out, Sheryl. I'll catch up."

Sheryl magically transformed into a gray cat with green eyes and ran off.

Sheryl made it down to the sewer and found Nick trying to climb the steps below the club. She transformed back to her human form with her clothes on. Sheryl inquired, "Nicky, where have you been?"

Nick replied, "Oh, just fighting the bad guys as usual."

Sheryl saw his wound and said with surprise, "Oh, Nicky, you're hurt badly. I thought I smelled blood on the way down. Don't you die on me."

Nick smiled and replied, "I'll be all right. Just get your mother. She'll know what to do."

Michelle came down the steps and saw Nick wounded as Sheryl held him. Michelle inquired, "Nick, what in the realm happened to you?"

Nick said, "It's a long story."

Michelle turned to Sheryl and said, "Sheryl, help me get him upstairs."

Sheryl put his one arm over her shoulder as she asked, "Is he going to be all right, Mother?"

Michelle braced his other arm on her shoulder and replied, "He'll be fine after we nurse him a little bit. This is not the first time I have had to patch him up."

Michelle and Sheryl held on to Nick as they helped him up to the storage room.

The room was full of boxes with a few fold-up chairs on the one side. Brown-colored boxes were stacked neatly on a few metal shelves with a small metal folding ladder beside the one shelf. Panel lights from the white drop ceiling illuminated the room as the light reflected off the matching tile floor. Since decorating a storage room was not important, the walls were painted plain white.

They sat him down on one of the chairs as they prepared to help him.

Michelle asked, "Why didn't you pull the blade out?"

Nick replied, "The blade is silver. You know vampires can't touch silver blades."

Michelle ripped his bloody shirt off and threw it in a plastic bag. She picked up a pair of large pliers from a toolbox nearby as she said, "Sheryl, hold him steady as I pull it out."

"Okay," said Sheryl as she got behind Nick and placed her left arm around his neck, while placing her right arm over his chest.

Michelle grabbed the edge of the broken blade with the pliers and yanked it out. Nick was too weak to scream out from the pain of the silver being freed from his flesh. He was relieved as his wound closed up almost instantly.

Michelle stated, "You've lost a good bit of blood. How did you get back here?"

Nick replied, "I fed on the sewer rats to keep me going."

Sheryl said, "Yum."

Nick commented, "You know rat blood doesn't taste very good."

Sheryl laughed in response.

Michelle said, "Sheryl, help me get him to bed."

Sheryl agreed, "Okay," as she helped her mother take Nick to his bedroom.

His room was a modest size with dark wooden-paneled walls and green carpet. It consisted of a closet near the door, a bed, a nightstand, a dresser, and a TV on a small cabinet. The dark wooden nightstand had a clock radio on it with a shaded lamp. A matching wooden dresser was composed of four drawers. On top of the dresser was another shaded lamp. The ceiling was plain, except for a ceiling fan in the center with wooden blades. His bed was king size with a couple of pillows, sheets, and a spread in different shades of green. Under the one pillow was another desert eagle forty-four magnum, cocked and loaded. In the opposite corner of the room from the door was a door to a small bathroom. In front of the bed was a nineteen-inch-screen TV on a small wooden cabinet.

They sat him on the bed as he fell backward with no energy left and ready to fall asleep. Michelle took his pants off and threw them on the floor. Sheryl just watched as Michelle sat down beside him on the bed. Michelle offered, "Nick, the loss of blood has made you very weak. Take some of mine. You'll recover faster."

Nick refused, "No, you've done enough already."

Michelle said, "I'm not taking no for an answer." She removed her nightshirt, exposing her beautiful skin in order to prevent blood from getting on it. She dropped it on the floor as she approached Nick closer.

Sheryl was surprised and inquired, "Mother, why are you doing this?"

Michelle looked at her daughter and said, "Relax, Sheryl. It's not like I am going to have sex with him. You may give him some of your blood as well."

Sheryl smiled and said, "Okay."

Michelle sat him up and pulled him towards her. He opened his mouth as his fangs emerged. Nick could smell a sweet fragrance on her neck as he drew closer to it. The fragrance made her neck seem more inviting as he sunk his fangs into it. Michelle was in a state of ecstasy as Nick fed on her blood. She sensually ran her hands through his long hair as she enjoyed the moment. Sheryl blushed as she watched Nick suck her mother's blood. Nick finished and licked the wound. The bite marks disappeared almost instantly.

Michelle kissed Nick on the forehead and got off the bed. "Pleasant dreams, Nick," said Michelle as she grabbed her nightshirt and left the room.

Sheryl was excited by the fact that she and Nick were alone. Her heart raced as she took off her top and sat beside Nick on the bed. She placed her right hand along his strong chest and felt his heartbeat. Shivers went down her spine as her hand traveled down to his well-defined abdominal muscles.

Nick's eyes opened as he looked upon Sheryl's exposed flesh. He touched her right hand as she stroked his face with her left hand and traced it down to his neck. Nick licked the blood from his fangs as Sheryl caressed his neck and shoulder and offered, "Nicky, you can have more than just my blood, if you want."

Nick said nothing as she took his left hand with her right hand and placed it over her firm breast. Sheryl blushed as Nick slid his hand over to where her heart was and looked into her eyes.

He felt her heart beating fast and commented, "Your heart is beating so fast."

Sheryl said, "Take me, Nicky."

Nick placed his right finger on her lips as he placed his left hand on her shoulder. With his right hand he caressed her face as she closed her eyes. She said not a word as he drew closer and kissed her neck. He continued to travel down the side of her neck and kissed her sensuous shoulder. Her breathing began to become heavier as he sunk his fangs into her shoulder.

Sheryl jerked a little bit, but soon went into a trance like her mother. She embraced him and lovingly caressed his back as he fed.

When Nick was done he licked her bite marks and they disappeared. Nick fell backward on the bed and dozed off in no time.

Sheryl felt lightheaded and without thinking fell alongside Nick and went to sleep on the one side of him.

Chapter 14
Blood Sisters

It was 6:00 a.m. on the clock at Katrina's place as she returned from a long night of action. Dawn had approached as the sun rose, bringing with it a new day and repelling any creature of the night still lurking about to the shadows. Katrina had removed all of her weapons and her boots as she proceeded to the main bathroom.

The main bathroom was a deluxe bathroom for washing and bathing in a large tub. Peach covered the walls, while the drop ceiling was white and matched the tiled floor and any tiled walls. Tiled walls with non-see-through glass doors divided the room into three sections. Overhead panel lights in the ceiling illuminated the room, since there were no windows in it.

The first section had a porcelain sink and commode. It was located to the right of the door entering the main bathroom, while the commode was located in the corner to the right of the sink. Under the sink was a dark wooden cabinet for storage of cleaning supplies and other things. To the left of the door was a matching wooden cabinet built into the wall, which housed towels on some shelves.

The second section had a couple of faucets and stools. Two stainless-steel faucets faced the entering door with a few feet between them. They had detachable showerheads for rinsing off before entering the bath. Soap holders were near the faucets and attached to the tiled wall. In front of the faucets were very small white plastic stools, ideal for sitting down while washing.

The third section housed a large tub. It was a solid piece of custom-made porcelain and was inset into the tiled floor. The tub only came above the floor about a foot, while the rest of it was below the floor level. Since it was very large, it could easily hold six people with molded ledges inside to sit on.

Tula was soaking in the bathtub as Katrina came in the room.

Katrina said, "Is anyone in here?"

Tula answered, "Just me, Katrina. I'm in the tub."

Katrina asked, "May I join you?"

"Sure, let me wash your back," said Tula as she stepped out of the tub.

She took off her clothes and dropped them in a brown basket below the towel cabinet. Tula opened the glass door to the tub area, came out to the wash area, and waited for her. Katrina opened the cabinet and grabbed a yellow towel. She proceeded to open the glass door and entered the washing area. Tula stood there by a faucet and smiled as Katrina came over to the faucet beside her. She looked at Tula and said, "Hi, Tula."

"Hi, Katrina," said Tula.

Katrina asked, "Where's Emma?"

"She's sleeping right now," answered Tula.

"Oh," said Katrina.

Katrina grabbed the showerhead and rinsed herself down. She asked, "How are you doing, Tula?"

"I'm doing just fine," replied Tula.

Katrina sat down and began to lather herself up. Tula took the soap, sat behind her, and began to lather up her back.

Katrina said, "Thanks."

Tula smiled and said, "You're welcome. How was your date?"

Katrina blushed as she grabbed the showerhead to rinse off the soap. She said, "It was pretty good for a first date."

Tula looked at her and said, "You're blushing, Katrina. It must have been a really good date. Are you going to see him again?"

Katrina smiled and said, "I think so."

Tula hugged her from behind and pressed her breasts against her back.

Katrina was surprised and blushed again as she said, "Whoa, you are really stacked, Tula."

Tula replied, "Thanks, I am so glad to have met you, Katrina. I was so concerned that I was the only friend she had, when I left a while ago."

Katrina turned to her and said, "Could we continue this conversation in the bath?"

Tula smiled and said, "Sure."

Katrina and Tula hung their towels on a metal bar right before they got into the tub. They sat in the tub and enjoyed the steamy water as it relaxed them, like soaking in a natural hot spring.

Tula inquired, "So, how did you and Emma meet?"

"It's a long story, but I simply saved her from being attacked by a vampire," answered Katrina.

Tula said, "Oh, I just noticed you act more like sisters around each other than friends."

"In some ways we are sisters," responded Katrina as she looked at Tula and commented, "You have such lovely skin, Tula."

Tula replied, "Thanks. You are one of them. Aren't you?"

"No. I am only half vampire," answered Katrina.

Tula bluntly asked, "Do you drink blood?"

"Yes," said Katrina.

Tula was filled with curiosity and asked, "All the time?"

Katrina looked into her eyes and replied, "No. You sure are curious all of a sudden, Tula."

"Forgive me, I didn't mean to pry," stated Tula.

Katrina smiled and said, "I don't mind. What else would you like to know?"

Tula asked, "Have you ever tasted Emma's blood?"

"Yes," answered Katrina.

Tula inquired, "What's it like?"

Katrina asked, "What do you mean?"

Tula clarified, "To drink blood?"

Katrina stated, "It's like getting a rush of energy from the juice of a fruit."

"I've never had an experience like that from fruit," replied Tula.

"Well, it's not the easiest thing to explain. In some ways I connect with someone on a subconscious level," explained Katrina.

Tula said, "Katrina, I want to know what it is like."

Katrina was surprised by her request and said, "What?"

"I want to thank you for saving me that night and for helping my two sisters. The truth is I envy your closeness to Emma. Maybe I'll understand better if you feed on me too," stated Tula.

Katrina asked, "Are you sure about this?"

Tula nodded and said, "Yes, go ahead and drink some of my blood."

Katrina got behind her and began to massage her shoulders as she said, "Okay. Just relax. The prick of my fangs will only hurt for a second."

Tula closed her eyes as Katrina sunk her fangs into her neck. She only felt the pain for a second as Katrina began to suck her blood. Tula slowly began to feel pleasure and fell into a trance.

Tula was in a dream state and she could see into Katrina's past from the time she met Emma. It was nighttime in Vampiro City around 8:00 p.m. at a library four years in the past. The library was a rectangular-shaped building with two levels. There was a spacious green lawn with park benches and trees surrounding the building. A dark brick wall about five feet high made up the perimeter of the library and matched the brick on the building. On the front of the wall beside the entrance to the walkway leading up to the building was the library sign. The metal letters read: Vampiro City Main Library.

In the center of the building was the main entrance. Stone steps led up to two double glass doors under a pediment with dark round pillars. On the bottom part of the stone railings of the steps were stone statues of bats. Each railing had a three-foot-tall bat statue, standing with its wings wrapped around its body.

Emma was leaving the library as she passed Katrina on the sidewalk. She was wearing a long-sleeve blouse, vest, skirt and dress shoes. The white cotton blouse was buttoned all the way up to the collar. Her black polyester vest fit her snugly and had four golden buttons down the middle. The ends of her blouse overlapped her light blue cotton skirt, which went down to her knees. She wore a pair of brown panty hose and her shoes matched her vest.

Katrina was wearing a tank top, matching shorts, boots, gloves, and a cloak. The black nylon top and shorts hugged her body, like a glove. Her top was zipped up in the middle, while showing off some of her midriff. The leather gloves went up to her forearms and matched her black calf-length boots. Her cloak had a hood and she wore it over her head. A brown leather bag hung on her shoulder and crossed over her chest. In her one hand was a long cardboard box, holding her sword. Round red sunglasses covered her eyes.

She rounded a corner and ducked into an alley as Katrina noticed a man following her. Katrina followed them from a distance.

The vampire stood about five feet eight inches tall with a thin-type build. His looks were average with high cheekbones and a strong chin, clean-shaven, short-length blonde hair parted in the middle, and green eyes. His skin was pale. He was wearing a purple suit, and black dressy slip-on shoes.

Under his jacket he wore a blue shirt with a red-colored necktie. The necktie had a golden pin in the center, the size of a dime, with a fancy letter M in the middle. Judging from his looks, he looked about twenty-four years old. His name was Burton.

The scene flashed to a dark alley. The alley was long and very spacious. In the distance a large brown dumpster could be seen. The dark stone walls that made up the alley had no windows or doors, which made it feel even more enclosed. Light from the street lamps nearby was blocked and shadowed by the buildings around and added to the semidarkness.

The vampire cornered Emma as Katrina watched from a distance. He overpowered her and forced her to the ground. His hand covered her mouth as his fingernails became longer. She saw his eyes turn blood red as his fingernail cut her vest buttons off one by one.

Emma could do nothing as she watched him tear at her clothing. With her vest open he ripped her blouse open to expose her bra. His hand was tight as a vice over her mouth as she tried to squirm a little, while he continued. He traced his fingernail from her neck down to her bra and cut it apart.

The fear could be seen in her eyes as he pulled her bra open and fondled her firm breasts. He sensed her fear and it was intoxicating, like a drug and drove him to want more.

His lustful eyes gazed upon her exposed flesh as he continued to play with her nipples. Emma watched in horror as she noticed his fangs emerging from his mouth. He began to lick her chest all the way up to her neck as he prepared to bite her. Her heart was racing as he drew closer to her neck.

Katrina arrived near a dumpster and watched the scene without attracting attention. From there she put down her sword behind the dumpster. She took off her cloak and laid it alongside the sword. From her bag she took a wooden stake and held it behind her back. Katrina stepped out in the open and yelled, "Hey! Why mess with a young girl like that, when you can play with a woman like me?"

The vampire stopped before biting Emma and looked at Katrina as she lowered her glasses and exposed her vampiric eyes. He was drawn to her more for some reason as she smiled and showed her fangs, while slowly unzipping her top and exposing some of her cleavage.

He got up and came over to Katrina as she motioned him over with her finger. Burton noticed her red eyes and fangs as he commented, "You're right. I prefer vampires anyway." He took off his jacket and laid it on top of the dumpster.

Katrina commented, "She's not going anywhere, we can both snack on her later."

He began to kiss her as he fully unzipped her top and began to fondle her breasts.

She pretended to enjoy his caressing touch as she subtly prepared to stab him. Without warning she stabbed him in the heart from below. He went into shock as she shoved the stake in further, almost lifting him off the ground. His body began to combust and turned into ashes in seconds.

"Sorry, I don't share," said Katrina as she zipped her top up. She searched his jacket and found his wallet, looked through it, and said, "Ah, cool. This one was loaded." She put the wallet in her bag, picked up her sword and cloak, and went over to the girl still lying on the ground. Katrina offered her hand to her as she said, "Are you okay, kiddo?"

"Please, don't hurt me," said Emma as she grabbed Katrina's hand and got up.

Katrina looked into her eyes and said, "Trust me. I'm not going to hurt you. My name is Katrina. What's yours?"

Emma was still in shock, but managed to answer, "My name is Emma."

"It is nice to meet you, Emma," said Katrina as she placed the cloak around her as she offered, "Here, take this. You need it more than I do."

Emma began to cry as she buried her head in Katrina's chest. Emma hugged her and said, "Thank you so much. I was so scared. I don't know what would have happened if you didn't come along."

Katrina was a little surprised by her emotional outburst, but glad she was not hurt. She hugged her back as she responded, "It's all right. You're safe now. And you're quite welcome, Emma." Katrina let go of her and asked, "It's getting late. Is your place far from here?"

Emma let go of her and said, "I am not sure. I guess I got a little lost."

Katrina asked, "Are your parents home right now?"

"No. They are on vacation," said Emma

Katrina stated, "You can spend the night at my place if you like. It's not far from here."

The scene flashed to Katrina's living area at her place. Emma and Katrina were sitting on a couch and talking. Emma looked at her and asked, "What are you?"

Katrina answered, "My mother was human, but my real father was a vampire. Funny, I never met the guy. Ever since I was a teenager, I have had these eerie eyes and these funky-looking teeth."

"I think they're cool. You shouldn't describe yourself like that. It is so demeaning," commented Emma.

Katrina was surprised by her comment and asked, "Really? My appearance doesn't bother you?"

Emma assured her, "No, I think you are unique, Katrina. We all must be born for a reason, otherwise our life has no meaning."

Katrina hugged her in response and confessed, "It has been a long time since someone has treated me like a person instead of an outcast."

Emma hugged her back and smiled. Emma said, "Maybe fate brought us together this night?"

Katrina agreed, "Maybe." Katrina let go of her and offered, "Oh, I was going to take a bath. Want to join me?"

Emma accepted, "Okay."

The scene flashed to Katrina's main bathroom. Katrina and Emma were naked in the bathtub.

Emma looked at Katrina, touched her hands, and asked, "Katrina, is there something I can do for you now? I feel so indebted to you already."

"There is something, but I am afraid to ask," answered Katrina.

Emma answered unselfishly, "Anything. What is it?"

Katrina gently asked, "Could I have some of your blood?"

Emma nodded and said, "Go ahead."

Katrina asked, "Are you sure?"

There was sincerity in Emma's eyes as she answered, "It is the least I could do for you saving my life."

Katrina instructed, "Okay. Just relax and hold on to me. This will only hurt a little."

Emma nodded as Katrina pulled her wet hair back and exposed her sensual shoulder. Katrina's fangs came out as she drew closer to her delicate skin. Emma felt a sharp pain for a second as Katrina's fangs sunk into her flesh. The pain passed quickly as Katrina gently sucked her blood. Emma soon went into a trance as she dug her nails into Katrina's back. Emma was in a state of ecstasy as Katrina continued to feed and a small trickle of blood dripped down her back.

The scene flashed to Katrina's living area at her place around 4:00 p.m. Emma was wearing a new school outfit.

Emma smiled and said, "Thanks for the new outfit, Katrina."

Katrina smiled and said, "You're welcome."

Emma offered, "Now let me do something for you."

Katrina inquired, "What did you have in mind?"

Emma grabbed her hand and said, "Come with me."

"Okay," said Katrina as she followed her.

The scene flashed to Emma's bedroom in her house around 4:30 p.m. Her room was a modest size with pink-colored walls and raspberry-pink carpet. It consisted of a closet near the door, a bed, a nightstand, and a dresser. The wooden nightstand had a shaded lamp, a radio, and a phone on it. The phone was a plastic white duck Emma found in a catalog. When the phone rang, its bill would flap and it quacked like a duck. The wooden dresser was composed of four long drawers on either side of a desk with a wooden chair. On the desk part of the dresser was a large square mirror. A shaded lamp was on either side of the mirror. The ceiling was plain, except for a ceiling fan in the center with wooden blades. Her bed was round and double size with a couple of pillows, sheets, and a spread in different shades of pink. In the opposite corner of the room from the door was a door to a small bathroom.

Emma handed her a black leather coat and a matching pair of pants.

Katrina looked at the clothing and asked, "What is this?"

Emma smiled and explained, "Your new outfit for hunting. Do you like it?"

Katrina smiled and said, "I'll take it." Katrina hugged her and said, "Thanks, Emma."

Emma hugged her back and said, "You're welcome. My uncle is a weapons man, he could help you out too."

Katrina replied, "Let's go meet your uncle."

Emma suggested, "I think you should get your hair cut a little first."

Katrina asked, "What is wrong with my hair?"

Emma explained, "It's just too long for this kind of work and your hair could get in the way of things. I could style it for you."

Time elapsed and the scene flashed to Katrina in Emma's bathroom. The bathroom was very spacious and elegant with two sinks, a shower, and a commode. A white drop ceiling had overhead lights and matched the tiled floor. The walls were done in a canary yellow and matched the sink counter. Behind the marble like counter, which held the sinks was a very large mirror on the wall. Every faucet, lamp fixture, and towel bar was brass.

Emma was done cutting Katrina's hair and had her looking in the bathroom mirror. Emma asked, "Well, we are done. What do you think?"

Katrina opened her eyes and looked at her new hairstyle. She was pleasantly surprised and said, "I love it."

Emma asked out of concern, "Really?"

Katrina hugged her and said, "Thanks, Emma."

"You're welcome, Katrina," said Emma as she hugged her back.

The scene flashed to a building rooftop around 10:00 p.m. Katrina and Emma were enjoying the view of the city.

Katrina was wearing a light-colored blazer and a matching knee-length skirt. The blazer had three dark buttons down the middle and two on the sleeves. Under her blazer was a pink low-cut tank top. She was wearing high-heel dress shoes that also matched her suit. Under her arm was a matching purse that finished off the outfit. Around her neck was a small silver cross necklace and her ears were decorated by the same dangling earrings.

Emma was wearing her school uniform. Emma looked at Katrina and asked, "Katrina, can I ask you something personal?"

"Anything," remarked Katrina as she continued to look upon the city lights.

Emma inquired, "Why do you wear those broken earrings constantly?"

Katrina looked at Emma and confessed, "They are all I have left of my mother. She was wearing them before she died. I somehow feel closer to her when I wear them."

The scene flashed to Emma's house at her front door around 9:00 p.m. Katrina saw a note on Emma's door. She ripped it off the door. The note read: *If you ever want to see your friend again, come to a good view in the city by midnight or else she will suffer in your place.* Katrina's eyes glowed as she crumpled up the note. She stated, "If anyone harms Emma, I swear I will make them regret they ever existed."

The scene flashed to the same building rooftop as before around midnight. The roof was flat and made of concrete with only a few exhaust vents and an air-conditioning unit.

Katrina arrived on the scene with her Glocks in hand. She was wearing a long coat, a tank top, pants, boots, and gloves, all done in black. Her leather coat was full length, open, and the sleeves were cuffed up, exposing her forearms. The leather gloves covered half of her forearms. Her tank top hugged her torso like a glove and was tucked into her tight leather pants. Around her waist was a charcoal-gray leather belt with a steel round buckle. Below her belt was another charcoal-gray belt, with small containers, that held bullets. On the back of the ammo belt were two holsters that held her Glocks. A small charcoal-gray backpack was on her back and under her coat with a charcoal-gray sword sheath over it. A strap came around to her front and buckled above her waist. Her high-heel leather boots came up to her calves with zippers on the sides. Around her right boot was a small knife strapped to it. Around her left leg was a charcoal-gray two-strap knife sheath, which could hold a foot-long blade. Her ears were decorated with the same earrings and her hair draped over her shoulders. The hilt of her sword could be seen behind her left shoulder and pointed at an angle. All of her blades looked like oriental blades and had black hard molded plastic handles with grooves for easy gripping. Glasses with round red lenses covered her eyes.

Katrina saw Emma in a pink low-cut tank top and matching panties. The cotton tank top hugged her torso like a glove and showed off some of her cleavage. On her feet were matching slippers.

A female vampire was holding her from behind with her wrists tied together. The vampire stood about five feet eight inches tall with a slender-type build and petite-sized breasts. She was a pretty woman with pale skin, dark red hair, and blue eyes. Her dark-toned makeup and golden hoop earrings only enhanced her looks, while her age was about twenty-six years old. Her lovely hair parted in the middle and grew outward down to her neck. She was wearing a light-blue-colored blazer and a matching pair of pants. The blazer had three light buttons down the middle and two on the sleeves. Under her blazer was a green low-cut tank top. She was wearing high-heel dress shoes that also matched her suit. Beside her on the roof was an oriental sword in a black sheath. Her name was Beatrice.

Katrina yelled, "Emma!" Katrina froze as she watched the vampire carefully move. She aimed her Glocks right at her.

Beatrice had her right arm around Emma's waist and her left hand around her neck as she said, "Well, it is about time you got here. I was starting to wonder if you were coming." Emma was in a trance and didn't say a word.

Katrina's eyes glowed as she ordered, "Let her go, bitch."

Beatrice looked upon Katrina with her red eyes as her fingernails became longer and gently pressed against Emma's throat. She said, "Not so fast." She toyed with Katrina's concern for Emma as she remarked, "Now we wouldn't want something unfortunate to happen to your friend. Would we?"

Katrina calmly inquired, "What do you want?"

Beatrice instructed, "For starters get rid of the guns." Katrina hesitated as Beatrice took her right hand and sliced Emma's top down the middle of her breasts. Her fingernail cut the fabric open easily and didn't even break the skin as Emma's cleavage was now easily seen. Beatrice continued, "Otherwise, I'll find out how sharp my claws really are."

Katrina gave in, "Okay, I'll do it." She gritted her teeth as she threw down her Glocks on the roof. She did not break eye contact as she unbuckled her weapons belt and let it drop below her.

Beatrice smiled and ordered, "Now take off your coat."

Katrina refused, "You have got to be kidding."

Beatrice slipped her right hand in the cut she made on Emma's top and grabbed her breast. "I can see why my brother attacked your friend. She has a lot to offer," said Beatrice as she started to fondle Emma's firm breast. Emma said nothing, but blushed by Beatrice's erotic touch.

Katrina was furious and spouted, "You sick tramp!"

Beatrice smiled as Katrina took off her coat and threw it down behind her. Katrina was frustrated with being out of control and boldly asked, "Who are you? What are you talking about?"

Beatrice instructed, "Remove the backpack and I will tell you, slayer."

Katrina removed her backpack with little resistance and let it drop behind her.

She stated, "My name is Beatrice and you are the slayer who killed my brother."

Katrina replied, "He had it coming. One of your family killed my mother and that makes all of you my enemy."

Beatrice remarked, "So, this is blood for blood then? Care to settle this with swords?"

Katrina agreed, "That sounds fine with me," as she removed her glasses.

Beatrice threw Emma down and said, "Pick up your sword, slayer. When I am through with you, I'll deal with your friend. Maybe I'll keep her around and make her my plaything." Emma lay there and didn't move.

Katrina frowned as she picked up her sword and said, "Not while blood still flows in my veins, bitch."

Beatrice smiled fiendishly as she drew her sword from her sheath at the same time Katrina drew hers.

The two faced each other as they came within a few feet of one another. They both clashed swords and pushed each other away. Beatrice attacked first as Katrina blocked and countered. Beatrice backed away and attacked again. Katrina ducked below her attack and countered as she cut her face.

Beatrice felt her blood from her cut face. She frowned as she viciously attacked Katrina. Katrina blocked her attack, but still got her arm cut. She licked her arm as she attacked.

Beatrice blocked and countered as Katrina continued to slash and cut her abdomen. They clashed swords with no one gaining the advantage. Without warning she head-butted Beatrice in the nose. The shock drove Beatrice back as she was stunned.

Katrina moved in and kicked her straight in the gut. Katrina continued with her attack and went into a spin kick.

Beatrice side stepped her and countered with a kick to her back.

Katrina was stunned as Beatrice knocked her sword out of her hands. Katrina's sword rolled over halfway to where Emma was lying. Beatrice followed in and punched her in face. Katrina fell down on her back from the impact of her punch.

Emma got up and ran over to Katrina's sword. Beatrice got ready to strike Katrina with her sword as Emma took hold of Katrina's sword. Emma picked up the sword and rushed in to attack Beatrice.

Beatrice dodged Emma's attack and stabbed her in the gut. Emma dropped the sword as she went down to her knees. Beatrice stood over her and pulled the sword out. Emma collapsed below her.

Katrina drew her long knife from her thigh sheath. Satisfied with Emma being wounded, Beatrice went over to finish off Katrina. As Beatrice prepared to strike Katrina sat up and stabbed Beatrice up through the bottom of her chin. She went into shock, backed up and fell backward. She turned to ashes in seconds, leaving only the knife behind. Katrina rushed over to Emma. Katrina kneeled by her and hugged her.

Emma opened her eyes and asked, "Did you get her?"

Tears welled up in Katrina's eyes as she replied, "I got her, but why did you do that, Emma?"

Emma answered, "If I didn't distract her she might have killed us both. There is no greater love, than to give one's life for a friend. I love you, Katrina."

Katrina kissed her on the cheek and responded, "I love you too, Emma."

Emma stated, "Don't be sad, Katrina. I have no regrets. You gave me confidence I didn't have before and I feel better about myself. If I could choose to have a sister it would be you."

Katrina looked into her eyes and said, "Stay with me, Emma, you are the sister I never had."

Emma passed out as Katrina cried over her. Katrina held her as she looked up to the sky. Katrina prayed, "Please, God, don't take her away from me. I should have died, not her. She is the only friend I ever really got close to. Please, help me save her."

At that moment a man arrived on the roof from the stairs. The man stood about six feet one inch tall with a thin-type build. His looks were average with high cheekbones and a narrow chin, a thick mustache, short-length dark hair parted in the middle, and brown gentle eyes. His skin was fair. Judging from his looks, he appeared to be forty years old. He wore a dark suit with matching pants and shirt, and black dress shoes. His cotton shirt had a collar with no flaps and a white piece in front of the top button. Around his neck hung a large golden cross on a matching chain. He was the priest that Katrina met before.

Katrina recognized him and said, "Father," as he approached.

He placed his hand on her shoulder and said, "It is all right, my child. There is a chance you can save her."

Katrina looked up to him and asked, "There is, Father? What must I do?"

The priest instructed, "Drop some of your blood into her wound."

Katrina agreed, "I'll do anything you ask, Father," as she gently laid Emma down. Katrina removed her gloves and let them drop beside her. She took her knife from her boot and cut her wrist. As she put the knife down she let the blood from the cut drip into Emma's wound. Katrina let many drops of blood enter Emma's wound, before she looked at him and asked, "What now, Father?"

He replied, "Take my hand and hold one of hers. We will create a circle of energy." They both took one of Emma's hands. He continued as he held Katrina's free hand, "Now close your eyes. Concentrate on healing her. Believe it will happen and it will."

"Okay, Father," said Katrina as she closed her eyes. Katrina and the priest meditated in prayer for Emma to recover.

Within minutes Emma's wound stopped bleeding. A few seconds later Emma's wound began to close. Minutes later Emma's heart began to beat as her wound was closed. She began to gasp for air and sat straight up. Katrina opened her eyes in surprise and began to cry at the sight of Emma alive again.

Emma was disoriented and asked, "What happened? Why are you crying, Katrina?"

Katrina smiled and yelled, "You're back!" Katrina helped her up, hugged her, and kissed her cheek. She turned to the priest and said, "Thank you, Father," as she hugged him.

The priest smiled and said, "It is not I you should be thanking, my child."

Katrina held on to Emma, looked up to the sky and said, "Thank you, Lord! Thank you!"

The priest cleared his throat to get Katrina's attention. She looked at him as he gave her a silver cross with a black nylon choker. Katrina took hold of it as he explained, "Here, Katrina, take this. It will prove to be useful in the future. Let me know when you are ready to hunt again. I might be able to provide some guidance." Katrina kissed his hand and said, "Bless you, Father."

"I must be going now, Katrina. Take care of her. And when you are ready, Katrina, I will be waiting," remarked the priest.

Katrina inquired as he walked away, "Father, how did you know I was here?"

The priest turned around and replied, "The answer should be obvious, my child." With that said he turned back and walked away.

Katrina took her hand and said, "Let's go, Emma. We are blood sisters now."

Emma smiled with surprise and replied, "Really? Cool."

The scene flashed to Katrina's place at the front door around noon. Emma was ringing at the door. She was wearing a turquoise-colored sleeveless dress with matching sandals and a matching wide-brimmed hat. The straps on the cotton dress were wide and had a low U cut. It showed off some cleavage and went past her knees. Around her neck she wore a small golden chain and a small cross. Big hoop earrings decorated her ears, while her wrists had matching bracelets. Her hair glistened in the sunlight as her blue eye shadow and pink lipstick enhanced her natural beauty.

Katrina was still dressed in her nightshirt and panties as she answered the door. Katrina was half awake, when she saw her and said, "Emma, what are you doing here this early?"

Emma smiled and boldly stated, "Sisters like us should be together, Katrina, and so I have decided to move in with you."

Katrina scratched her head and responded, "Emma, this is a little sudden. Are you sure about this?"

"Yep, and I'm not taking no for an answer," replied Emma as she smiled.

Katrina smiled as she hugged her and said, "Cool."

The trance sequence was over and Katrina was behind Tula in the tub. She finished feeding and licked the bite marks on Tula. The marks instantly healed as Tula awoke from the trance.

Tula opened her eyes as Katrina asked, "How was it, Tula?"

She commented, "What a rush."

Katrina inquired, "You mean you liked it?"

Tula confessed, "Yeah, I liked it more than I thought I would. I just have one question."

Katrina asked, "What?"

Tula turned her head to look at Katrina's face, "Why are your hands on my breasts?"

Katrina blushed as she removed her hands and said, "Sorry, I don't remember."

Tula smiled and replied, "It's all right. My hands were holding yours. I didn't know this could get a little kinky."

Katrina explained, "It's different with every person, when they go into a trance."

Tula was amazed by her answer and said, "Wow. That's cool." She turned around to face Katrina, smiled, and gave her a hug. She said, "Thanks for sharing your memories with me, Katrina. Now I feel closer to you, almost like Emma."

Katrina blushed as she replied, "You're welcome."

Tula backed away and without warning kissed her on the lips.

Katrina's eyes got real big as she blushed and backed away from her. She looked at Tula and said, "What are you doing, Tula? I'm not into women."

Tula grinned and replied, "You're so cute when you blush, Katrina. I was just giving you some sweet payback for touching my breasts."

Katrina was trying to get mad at her, but couldn't. "Just don't do that again, Tula. I don't want to get the wrong idea about you."

Tula smiled and said, "Don't worry, Katrina. I would only do you if you were a guy."

Katrina stood up in the bathtub and said, "That's comforting I guess."

Tula started to feel dizzy and said, "What's going on? I feel so lightheaded all of a sudden." She drifted off as Katrina caught her under her arms.

Katrina held her up and commented, "Whoops. Maybe I took a little too much blood." She pulled Tula out of the tub and said, "Now this is a weird coincidence. First, I have to pull Telka out of the tub and now Tula. Well, at least I can't say it's been a dull night."

Chapter 15
The Reunion

It was 7:00 p.m. according to a clock on the street corner in the lower district or poor section of Vampiro City. This was the darkest area of the city, night or day, and most people who knew better did not come here. Of course this was the best area in the city to find black market items and weapons as well as information. Underground clubs and guilds were also found here, since police did not bother to patrol and enforce the law in such a small section of the city. For some this area was home to magic users and freaks as well as vampires not affiliated with a clan. Unofficially, the police made an arrangement with the inhabitants in which they would leave them be and not expose them to persecution as long as the inhabitants did not spill into the workingman section; of course this did not apply to bounty hunters and slayers. This area was known to have vampire whores who would satisfy any kind of fetish for the right price.

Near the border of the workingman sector was a weapon shop that Katrina did business with frequently. It was a two-story brown brick building with bars over the front of the widows. Above the steel door entrance was a sign that read: Mak's Weapons and Ammo.

Katrina's car pulled up to the curb, as the streets were very quiet, too quiet.

She turned the engine off and stepped out of the car.

She was wearing a pair of pants, a t-shirt, leather boots, and a coat. Her coat was the same leather one she wore at the museum heist. The pants were blue denim jeans and fit her snugly as they showed off her midriff. Her white t-shirt was tight fitting, low cut, and hung above her navel. Around her neck was a black leather choker with a metal skull on the front. Her high-heel boots were calf length with zippers up the sides and matched her coat. She wore dark eye shadow and lavender lipstick, which also matched her fingernails. Her trademark earrings were on as well, but her hair was styled differently and it hung over them and around her eyes. Glitter was sprinkled on her cheeks a little as well as around her neck and chest, which made her creamy pale skin more inviting in the moonlight.

Katrina walked past the neon sign in the window that read: OPEN. She opened the front door and walked in.

The front of the store had a counter with many guns nicely racked on the wall behind. The glass counter was long with a wooden mahogany cabinet on the end with a cash register on top. It was divided into two sections.

The first section encased several brands of handguns on the top level and other accessories, like sights, on the second. On the third shelf was a display of different kinds of ammunition for various types of guns.

The second section encased several brands of knives on the top level and other accessories, like sharpening stones, on the second. On the third shelf was a display of different kinds of equipment, like watches, compasses, and radios.

The wall behind the counter had a rack full of guns ranging from rifles to shotguns to submachine guns. On another wall was a display of different kinds of oriental swords. The other wall had a rack for displaying gun holsters.

Beside the cash register was a doorway that led to a back room. Mak was standing behind the counter as Katrina entered.

He was wearing a black tank top, black cargo pants and black combat boots. His tank top hugged his brawny chest and showed off his very muscular arms. Around his neck was a silver chain with a cross hanging from it.

Mak greeted her, "Hello, Katrina. You're looking lovely as always. What can I do for you today?"

Katrina replied, "Thanks, Mak, I look like a whore."

Mak inquired, "Why the look?"

Katrina explained, "You know, so the creeps in this area don't think I'm a bounty hunter or something."

Mak asked, "Are you on a job right now?"

Katrina said, "No. That's why I look like a vampire whore."

Mak stated, "You know, you will still attract some kind of attention."

Katrina answered, "I'm aware of that. Trust me. It's easier to fend of sleazy customers propositioning me than vampires trying to kill me."

Mak was concerned and asked, "Are you packing?"

"Always," said Katrina as she opened her coat and showed off her HK in a brown leather shoulder holster.

Mak approved, "That's my girl."

She smiled and covered her gun as she said, "I need some silver ammo."

Mak replied, "Okay," as he grabbed a couple of boxes of silver bullets from the counter and placed them on top.

Katrina continued, "And some information."

Mak inquired, "Do you need help with another job?"

She pulled the blood gem out of her coat pocket and placed it on the counter.

Mak looked at it closely and asked, "Oh, I see. This wouldn't be related to the incident at the museum would it?"

Katrina smiled and responded, "Now, Mak, you know me. I'm not into artifacts and other junk."

Mak agreed, "Yes, I know." He picked it up and took a closer look at it.

She said, "I know you are into relics and other stuff. It's called the blood gem. Do you know anything about it?"

Mak handed it back to her and replied, "Sorry, I have never heard of such a thing. My specialty is anything that blows up or burns fuel. I don't deal with that magical stuff."

Katrina placed the gem back in her pocket as she pulled some notes from her other pocket and handed them to him.

Mak took the money and offered, "Are you sure you don't need my help with something?"

Katrina smiled and said, "Maybe next time, Mak," as she picked up the boxes of ammo and placed them in her pocket.

She walked away from the counter as Mak said, "Be careful, Katrina."

She turned around and said, "I always am. Thanks, Mak."

"Anytime," said Mak.

Katrina left the shop and started walking over to her car. A white stretch limo pulled up on the other side of the street and stopped in front of her car. The back doors opened and a couple of twin vampires got out of the car. They walked across the street and approached her before she unlocked her door.

The twins stood about six feet seven inches tall and had solid-type builds. Both were dressed in very expensive silver silk suits. Their jackets crossed over with three dark buttons on the left side and three on the right. A black rose could be seen in their outside breast pockets. Under their jackets they wore midnight-blue cotton shirts with black neckties. Both had shaved heads with dark goatees on their rugged chins. Their skin was tan and square dark sunglasses covered their eyes.

The first one said, "Excuse us, miss, could we have a word with you?"

Katrina stopped and looked up to them, before unlocking her door. She turned to them and smiled.

The second one handed her twenty notes.

She took the wad of money and said, "Sure, I have a little free time."

The first one said, "Please, join us in the limo, where we can talk privately."

She replied, "Okay, just as long as you bring me back here," as she stuffed the notes in her pocket.

The first one answered, "That would be no trouble at all."

She nodded and entered the limo. The two entered the limo on either side of the back doors and shut them. The limo drove away as the conversation continued.

The interior of the limo was basically a couple of bench seats facing each other with a small island counter built into the floor. It had compartments for storing drinks and glasses. The top of the counter was brown and matched the cloth-covered seats. Light brown was the color of the carpet and the ceiling, which had a moon roof. The carpet was very clean and the seats were very comfortable.

Katrina sat down opposite to them and sensually crossed her legs as the first one offered, "Would you like a drink?"

She responded, "Sure. Do you have any blood wine?"

The first one said, "Of course," as he opened a bottle and poured it into a crystal goblet. He handed her the drink. She purposely leaned forward as she took the drink and said, "Thank you." The two men took the bait and subtly looked down her shirt and got a good view of her cleavage. She knew they were checking her out, even though they were wearing dark sunglasses.

The second one said, "Are you available for hire?"

Katrina couldn't believe the two men thought she was a whore. She thought it wouldn't hurt to play along just in case a connection of information could be established. Katrina took a sip and licked her lips as she responded,

"It depends. I don't just offer my services to just anyone."

The first one smiled and said, "I like this one. She has class, unlike the other whores in the lower district."

Katrina inquired, "What did you have in mind?"

The second one replied, "We work for the Daribus Corporation and our boss sent us here to hire some entertainment for a party next week." The first one handed her a couple of business cards.

She leaned over again, took them, and said, "I see. And your boss wants some private entertainment for his bedroom that night?"

The first one replied, "She is very smart and has good taste in apparel." Katrina smiled as she looked at one of the cards.

The second one agreed, "Yes, you are exactly right. Our boss would be thrilled with someone like you. You are just his type."

Katrina placed the cards in her pocket and inquired, "What do you mean?"

The two lowered their sunglasses and showed off their vampiric eyes. The second one clarified, "Our boss prefers to be entertained by vampires more than any other breed."

The twins were fresh vampires, a few days old from being embraced recently, and did not learn yet how to disguise their eyes that well. Katrina commented, "Oh, I see. Maybe we can do some business as long as the job does not require some really sick fetish or that bondage crap."

The first one stated, "I assure you our boss is very reserved and prefers just regular sex."

Katrina took another sip of the wine, licked her lips, and said, "It sounds tempting, but I may have other clients lined up by next week. I like to get my weeks booked in advance. A girl has got to pay the bills you know."

The first one said, "She sure knows how to deal."

The second one asked, "What is your rate for one night of entertainment?"

Katrina finished her drink, placed her right finger on her head, and replied, "Let's see. One whole night of entertainment will cost about six hundred notes."

The second one offered, "We'll double your rate and our boss will provide some others to feed on as well."

Katrina was making it difficult for them to hire her and she couldn't believe they were making the offer more attractive by the minute. This client was definitely an upscale customer. Of course Katrina was not into trading sex for information, but something told her to play along in case something could develop from it. She smiled and stated, "That sounds like an offer I can't refuse."

The first one said, "Excellent. How can we get in contact with you for the night, location, and time?"

Katrina placed the goblet on the counter, pulled a pen and one of the business cards out of her jacket, and wrote her name and number on it. She leaned over and handed it to the first one and said, "Here is my cell phone number. Leave me a message and I'll get back with you."

The second one asked, "What is your name, miss?"

Katrina said, "My name is Kat."

The first one said, "It was nice meeting you, Kat, we will be in touch."

The limo stopped and Katrina opened the door. She stepped out, turned around, and winked at them before she closed the door. She walked over to her car and said, "I don't believe it. They propositioned me as a whore." She unlocked her door as Marcus stepped out of the shadows and approached her.

He said, "Hello, Katrina. It is good to see you again."

Katrina drew her gun out of reflex, before she realized who it was. She lowered her gun as soon as she recognized him and said, "Father."

Marcus confessed, "It pleases me to hear you call me that, daughter."

Katrina put her gun away as she stated, "My mother never told me about you."

Marcus replied, "I don't expect you to understand, Katrina. I am not surprised if you hate me."

Katrina said, "I don't hate you, Father, but I have to know, why did you leave us?"

Marcus looked down and replied, "I couldn't live a normal life with your mother. When that night was over, I left. I didn't know that she had a child until she died." He looked into her eyes and said, "I regret now that I was not around to protect her. Can you find it in your heart to forgive me, daughter?"

Katrina replied, "I forgive you, Father," as she hugged him and continued, "I could never hold a grudge for the man who gave me life. But, I swear I will avenge her death."

Marcus let go of her and offered, "Let me help you, Katrina."

Katrina smiled and said, "Very well. Come with me. We have work to do, Father."

The two got in her car and drove off. As they were driving in the car they continued their conversation.

Marcus said, "I must apologize if I startled you."

Katrina explained, "It's all right. You can't be too careful in this day and age. The night is full of dark creatures."

Marcus replied, "Ah, yes, vampires are your enemy. Right?"

Katrina pointed at his ring and commented, "Mostly from the Drenkel Clan, the same family ring you wear."

Marcus inquired, "What about the one helping you last night?"

Katrina blushed and answered, "We have an agreement and a common enemy."

Marcus saw her blushing, grinned, and said, "Oh, I see."

Katrina focused on the subject at hand and asked, "Why is it that you belong to the Drenkel Clan?"

Marcus explained, "Because that is the clan that gave me my new life. The embrace only affiliates me. I do not engage in their activities anymore. One day you will realize that a family does not predestine one's path."

Katrina inquired, "Have you ever heard of a magical item called the blood gem?"

Marcus said, "No."

Katrina stated, "I read somewhere that it is used to cancel white magic. The Drenkel Clan in this area is up to something. I have to find out what that is, before it is too late."

Marcus replied, "There is a vampire who owns and runs the Grand Hotel in the wealthy sector of the city. His name is Charles. He has thrived in this area for a very long time. He has a lot of connections and might have the information you need."

Katrina commented, "I know where that is. I'll have to go pay him a visit."

Marcus stated, "Careful, Katrina, I know for a fact that he is very powerful and well guarded at all times."

Katrina proclaimed, "I can take care of myself, Father."

Marcus suggested, "I bet you can; however, I wouldn't go in that hotel alone, if I were you, daughter."

Katrina agreed, "Okay, Father, for your sake and mine I'll take some friends along just to be safe."

At that moment they arrived at Telka's shop around 9:00 p.m. They got out of the car and went in.

Teresa greeted them at the door, wearing the same fortune-telling outfit from before. Teresa smiled and said, "Hi, Katrina. I'm so glad you stopped by."

Katrina responded, "Hi, Teresa. I'm glad to see you too."

She commented, "You look so hot in that outfit."

Katrina said, "Thanks."

Without warning Teresa hugged Katrina as Marcus stood there. Katrina hugged her back and asked, "How's Telka doing?"

Teresa let go of her and said, "She's doing just fine, Katrina. I'll get her."

Katrina directed her attention to Marcus and said, "Before we do that, do you remember Marcus?"

She smiled and stated, "I couldn't forget such a cool guy like your father, Katrina." Teresa placed her hand out to shake his hand.

Marcus gently grabbed her hand and kissed it. He said, "Charmed to meet such loveliness."

Teresa blushed as she took in all of his charm. She smiled and said, "Follow me." They followed Teresa to the back room.

Teresa walked up to Telka and said, "Sis, we have guests. Katrina and her father stopped by."

Telka was pleased as she said, "Okay, Teresa, send them in and watch the front."

Teresa agreed, "Okay," and left the room. They entered the back room and greeted Telka where she was sitting at the table. Telka was wearing the same fortune-telling outfit from before.

Katrina said, "Hi, Telka. How are you?"

Telka said, "Hello, Katrina, I'm doing much better, thanks. And this is your father?"

Katrina explained, "Yes, he is my father, Marcus."

Marcus stepped closer to Telka as she placed her hand out to him. He kissed her hand and said, "Charmed to meet the loveliness of another sister."

Telka smiled and replied, "I'm honored to meet you, Marcus." She was curious as she asked, "This is your father, Katrina? He is such a gentleman."

Katrina answered, "Yes, he's the one that helped us in the museum the other night."

Marcus remarked, "We must learn the purpose of this blood gem. What's your plan, daughter?"

Katrina stated, "Telka and I are going to make an appointment to see Charles and find out what he knows."

Telka asked, "Are we going to sneak in?"

Katrina replied, "No, we are going to walk in the front door and ask him."

Telka was concerned and said, "You can't be serious, Katrina. That is a high-class place and regular people like us don't go there."

Katrina bent over next to her and said, "I will explain later. In the meantime we'll have some shopping to do."

Telka was puzzled and inquired, "What do you mean?"

Katrina looked at her and replied, "I'll call you tomorrow."

Telka gave up and said, "Okay."

Katrina said, "I'll see you tomorrow."

Meanwhile at the Delchor Corporate Building, the clock read 9:30 in the alchemist room. Carrie was standing by her cauldron and looking at her magical window.

Her lovely hair was tied back in a ponytail and hanging from the high part of the back of her head, instead of being braided, like before. She was wearing a sleeveless leather dress and matching high-heel shoes. The black dress was also strapless and showed off some cleavage as it accented her firm breasts. It had many folds and creases horizontally as it wrapped around and hugged her sexy body like a glove down to her knees. On her arms she wore a matching set of gloves that attached at the middle finger and thumb and went all the way up past her elbow. Around her neck was a black ribbon that accented her sensuous neck and shoulders. She wore dark eye shadow and matching lipstick. On her thumbs she wore silver rings and matching earrings as well as a matching anklet.

Carrie stated as Flusken entered, "They are up to something."

Flusken commented, "We should warn Charles. He will hold them for us and then we will be able to retrieve it."

Carrie smiled and said, "The fools won't know what hit them."

Chapter 16
The Informant

It was Thursday afternoon around 5:00 at Katrina's place. Katrina, Telka, and Teresa returned from shopping and entered the living area. Katrina and Telka were carrying shopping bags full of clothes.

Katrina was wearing a halter top, a matching pair of short shorts, and sandals. Her cotton blue halter top hugged her torso like a glove and showed off some of her midriff. The leather sandals were brown and showed off her red nail polish on her toes. Around her neck she wore a small silver chain with a cross on it. On her one shoulder hung a small leather purse that matched her sandals.

Telka was wearing a tank top, a matching pair of short shorts, white socks, and sneakers. Her cotton yellow tank top hugged her torso and had white buttons that started at the middle of her cleavage and went all the way down to the end. The only jewelry she wore was her golden hoop earrings and matching pentacle necklace. On her arm was a small brown leather purse.

Teresa was wearing a t-shirt, a pair of short shorts, white socks, and sneakers. Her green t-shirt was a little oversized and had a wide neckline. It drooped to one side and exposed one of her sensual shoulders, while a black fanny bag was strapped around her waist and prevented it from overlapping the ends of her shorts. The only jewelry she wore was her golden hoop earrings, bracelets on her wrists, and the rings on her fingers.

Telka commented, "Katrina, I can't believe you bought this expensive dress for me."

Katrina smiled and said, "Don't worry about paying me back for the dress. I have plenty of cash left over."

Emma was barefoot and wearing a t-shirt and a pair of short shorts. Her pink t-shirt overlapped her waist and had red hearts and lettering on it. The lettering read: I love hugs.

Emma was sitting on the couch and watching the TV, when she noticed them arriving. She got off the couch and said, "Hi, Katrina."

Katrina replied, "Hi, Emma. Where's Tula?"

"She's out job hunting," replied Emma.

Katrina set her bags down on the floor and said, "Oh well, I would like you to meet her older sister, Telka, and her younger sister, Teresa."

Telka put her bags down and responded, "Hello, Emma, It's nice to meet you."

Teresa went in front of Emma and said, "Hi, Emma."

Emma smiled and replied, "It is nice to meet both of you. Tula has told me so much about you two."

Without warning Teresa gave Emma a big hug and squeezed her a little too much. Teresa was only an inch taller than Emma and felt her large breasts mash against her own. Emma was a little surprised by her forwardness, but accepted her friendliness in stride. Teresa let go of her and commented, "My, Emma, you are really stacked."

Emma, a little embarrassed by her comment, blushed and said, "Thanks."

Telka giggled as Katrina cleared her throat and asked, "Emma, are you working tonight?"

Emma turned to Katrina and answered, "No, I'm actually off. I was hoping we could do something fun tonight."

Katrina placed her hands on Emma's shoulders and replied, "I'm sorry, Emma. I have a job to do tonight."

Emma looked at her and inquired, "You're not going to the hotel tonight are you?"

Katrina said, "I am and you are going to stay here where it is safe."

Emma understood and said, "Okay."

Katrina placed her arm around her and turned to Teresa. "Don't worry. Teresa will keep you company."

Teresa smiled and said, "Sounds like fun."

Katrina took Telka by the hand and instructed, "Come with me, Telka. It's time you paid me back."

"Okay," agreed Telka as they left the room.

Katrina led Telka to her bedroom down the hall.

As they entered Telka commented, "This is nice."

"Thanks," responded Katrina.

Telka noticed her stuffed cats in the corner and approved, "Ah, how cute. You do have a sensitive side after all."

She smiled and commented, "What can I say? They're my low-maintenance and worry-free pets."

Telka inquired as she sat on her bed, "What did you have in mind, Katrina?"

She sat on the bed near the phone and explained, "For this gig to work we need a chauffer that no one knows. I was thinking about someone human, like Mike perhaps."

Telka asked, "What does that have to do with me, Katrina?"

She handed her the phone receiver and instructed, "You are going to call him."

Telka was a little surprised by her comment and inquired, "Why me?"

She smiled and said, "Because he likes you. And if you ask him, he might be more inclined to do it."

Telka felt obligated and agreed, "Okay, I'll do it," as she took hold of the phone receiver.

Katrina handed her Mike's business card from the nightstand. She took the card and dialed the number. The phone rang a couple of times on the other end, before someone picked it up.

Mike answered, "Officer Mike Harrison speaking. May I help you?"

"Hi, Mike, this is Telka, the fortuneteller from the other night," answered Telka.

He was a little surprised by her call and said, "Hello, Telka. It's good to hear your voice. Is everything all right?"

"I'm better. Thanks," commented Telka as Katrina watched with anticipation.

Mike inquired, "What can I do for you?"

Telka explained, "Well, Katrina gave me your number and I was wondering if you are busy tonight?"

Mike answered, "No. Why?"

Telka explained further, "Katrina and I need to go to the Grand Hotel. But, we need a chauffer to drive us there. Otherwise, we won't blend in with the crowd. Could you help us out? I would be very grateful."

He asked, "You aren't going there to raise hell or something?"

Telka nervously looked at Katrina and said, "No. We are just going there to take care of some business, have fun, and maybe see a show. Can you help us?"

Mike responded, "Well, actually I don't have any plans. It's a date. Where should I meet you?"

She smiled and said, "Thank you, Mike. Meet us at Katrina's place at seven o'clock tonight. It's on the corner of Delos and Gryne."

Mike confirmed, "I know where that is. I'll see you then."

Katrina praised her, "Good job, Telka. I knew you could win him over."

Telka smiled as she hung up the phone and commented, "He said it's a date."

Katrina took hold of her hands and lifted her up. She commented, "It's time to make ourselves pretty for tonight."

Telka agreed, "Okay."

Moments later, Katrina and Telka were in the living area getting dressed.

Telka was taking off her top as she inquired, "So, how was your date with Nick, Katrina?"

Katrina was a little surprised by her question. She took off her top and replied, "Well, it was nice."

Telka had her shorts off as she asked, "That's it?"

Teresa handed Telka her dress as she said, "Please, don't tease us, Katrina. Tell us more."

Katrina had her shorts off as she replied, "Well, okay. We talked for a little while and it turns out we have more in common than I thought."

Telka slipped her legs into her dress and said, "Go on."

Katrina slipped her legs into her dress as she answered, "We danced for a while and we got closer as the time went on. Before I knew it, I was kissing him. I don't know what came over me."

Telka smiled as she slipped her arms into her dress and responded, "I do. You like him more than you are willing to admit, Katrina."

Katrina argued as she slipped her arms into her dress, "Okay, he's a nice guy and a gentleman, but I just met him."

Teresa zipped up Telka's back as she commented, "She has the hots for him, Telka."

Telka looked at her face and commented, "You're blushing, Katrina. Be honest."

Katrina answered as Emma fastened her back, "Okay, maybe I like him a little, but we were masquerading as a couple outside the van."

Telka smiled as she waved her index finger at her and said, "It didn't look that way to us."

Emma hugged Katrina and said, "I'm happy for you, Katrina. You haven't had a boyfriend in a while."

Katrina looked at Emma and responded, "Don't get carried away, Emma." Emma just smiled in response.

Moments later, Katrina and Telka were fully dressed in their evening gowns.

Katrina was wearing a strapless evening gown that went all the way down to her ankles. The dark silky material was thin and had a sparkling look to it as the light caught it from different angles. It hugged her torso snugly as it flowed out from the waist and hung like drapery. Up the left side of the dress was a slit that showed off her sexy legs when she walked. Her arms were covered in black silky gloves as her feet wore matching high-heel dress shoes. Around her neck was a black ribbon with the Drenkel Clan medallion hanging from it. It went well with the gown and accented her lovely neck and shoulders. For once she wore a set of golden hoop earrings, which matched the medallion. Dark shades of purple and lavender accented her eyes and lips as it made her creamy pale skin stand out. Her hair was pulled back and up with a golden comb to hold it together. On her shoulder hung a matching leather purse.

Telka was wearing a sleeveless evening gown that went all the way down to her ankles. The light silky material was thin and had a shimmering brightness to it that reflected the light. Its straps were wider than bra straps and flowed down into a low U-shaped cut. The dress accented her cleavage quite well as it hugged her torso snugly with a few folds that flowed under the U cut. Below her waist the material flowed out with many folds, like drapery. Up both sides of the dress were slits that showed off her sexy legs when she walked. Her arms were covered in white silky gloves as her feet wore matching high-heel dress shoes. Around her neck was a matching silky scarf. She wore a set of dangling diamond earrings, which sparkled against her tan skin. Her eyes and lips were done in a pinkish blend of makeup and went well with her luminescent gown and jewelry. Her hair was pulled back and up in a high ponytail with white ribbons to accent it. On her shoulder hung a matching leather purse.

Katrina stood by Telka and asked, “How do we look?”

Teresa stood by Emma and said, “You too look so beautiful. If I was a guy, I would date both of you.”

Katrina smiled as Telka asked, “What do you think, Emma?”

Emma replied, “I think you better take a bodyguard, like Nick, to keep the guys at bay.”

Katrina and Telka laughed at her response. Katrina winked and said, “Well, thanks to you we better have Nick around just in case.”

The sound of the buzzer at the front door rang, as they laughed some more. Katrina noticed the clock on the wall read 7:00 p.m. She turned to Emma and asked, “Emma, could you get the door, please?”

Emma spoke up, “Sure, I'll be right back.” She took off running and left the others in the room.

Telka turned to Katrina and asked, “Is Nick joining us on this caper, Katrina?”

Katrina smiled as she replied, “Oh, he will join us a little later.”

Emma led Mike up to the living area.

Mike was wearing a beige long-sleeve shirt, a pair of pants, and shoes. His sleeves were rolled up and his shirt was unbuttoned a little, showing off his hairy chest. The pants were brown and his shoes were black loafers.

Mike greeted them, “Hello, ladies,” as he looked at Katrina and paused, while looking at Telka. He looked into her eyes and commented, “You both look stunning tonight.”

Katrina smiled and replied, “Thanks, Mike.”

Telka blushed as she replied, “Thank you, Mike.”

Katrina commented, “It was nice of you to make it, Mike.”

Mike responded, “I'm glad I could help out. I just have one problem.”

Katrina inquired, “What's that?”

“I don't have a clean suit, since all of them are at the cleaners,” explained Mike.

Katrina said, “I have just the thing for you,” as she turned to Emma and asked, “Emma, could you get his uniform in the other room, please?”

“Okay,” said Emma as she left the room. She returned shortly with a chauffeur's uniform on a hanger.

Emma handed it to Mike as he inquired, “You want me to wear this? How do you know it will fit?”

Katrina smiled and said, “Trust me. It's just your size.”

Mike looked at it and asked, “How do you know my size?”

"I have my ways of gathering data like that," said Katrina as she smiled.

Emma led him and said, "Follow me, Mike. I'll show you where you can change.

It was 9:00 p.m. at the Grand Hotel as different limousines drove up to the main entrance. Outside the main entrance of the hotel, it was moderately quiet, except for the other limousines pulling up to the curb and the blend of chatter from people getting out of them. The night was warm with a calm wind blowing. Katrina's limousine came to a smooth halt as the driver's door opened. Mike stepped out of the car and closed the door.

Mike was dressed in a black suit and pants with matching loafers. Under his jacket he wore a white cotton shirt with a black necktie.

He walked around the car and stepped on to the curb beside it. He opened the back door and extended his hand as Katrina grabbed it and stepped out of the car.

Katrina smiled and said, "Thank you, Mike. You're such a gentleman."

"Don't mention it," said Mike as Katrina walked past him.

Telka took his hand next and said, "Thank you, Mike," as she stepped out of the car. Mike winked at her as she said, "We'll call you when we are ready to leave. When we're done here, would you like to go out later, just the two of us?"

"Sure, I'd like that," answered Mike.

Telka smiled as Katrina cleared her throat with her arms crossed. She turned to Katrina and said, "Sorry."

Katrina grabbed her hand and said, "Let's go. He's not going anywhere."

"I'll see you later," replied Telka as she turned to him and winked.

"Okay. I'll be waiting," said Mike as he closed the door.

The lobby of the main wing was full of all sorts of high-class people as Katrina and Telka stepped through the revolving doors of the main entrance. As they walked past the stone fountain in the center of the room, Telka noticed people in the crowd, mostly men, looking at them with interest.

Telka asked, "What are they looking at?"

Katrina replied, "Us, silly. We look good enough to stop traffic."

As they reached the reception desk on the far left, Katrina and Telka were met by the same cute female attendant from before. The attendant greeted with a smile and said, "May I help you?"

Katrina replied, "Yes, we are here to see Charles."

She asked, "Do you have an appointment?"

"No," answered Katrina.

She explained, "Without an appointment, I am afraid that is not possible. Charles is a very busy man."

Katrina placed her right index finger on the medallion hanging from her neck and replied, "Oh, I am sure he will work us into his busy schedule."

She noticed the medallion and responded, "One moment please."

The attendant walked away as Telka inquired, "What was that all about?"

Katrina explained, "I'm wearing a vampire medallion. I just hope it's enough for Charles to want to see us without just barging in. I am willing to bet he does some kind of business with the Drenkel Clan, whether he is affiliated or not."

Telka was still unsure of the plan and asked, "Do you think it will work?"

Katrina answered, "Sometimes you just have to take a chance. Charles would not be stupid enough to have vampires attack us on the main floor of the lobby."

"You have a point there," said Telka.

The attendant returned from the back and instructed, "Follow me."

She led them down a private staircase, which led to the basement level of the hotel. It had a main wing, right wing, and left wing, just like the other levels. The hallways were unexpectedly wide and tall for a basement level. Everything was gray but the floor, which was covered in black matting. The ceiling was covered with pipes and ducts going in every direction. Fluorescent lights were mounted to the walls and illuminated the otherwise dark level. Stone support columns could be seen every twenty feet, which broke up some of the light showing down on the floor and created some shadows.

Katrina inquired, "Are we almost there? This dungeon-like basement looks creepy."

She answered as they kept walking, "Yes, Charles's office is just around the corner." She led them to a room with large dark wooden doors. In front of the room were two vampires standing guard.

The two vampires stood about six feet tall with macho-type builds and wore dark suits and shoes. Under their jackets they wore white shirts with blue neckties. The first one had long brown hair in a ponytail with a goatee, while the second one had short black hair and a mustache. Both were wearing dark sunglasses as well.

They stopped in front of Charles's office as she explained, "He will see you, after you are checked."

Katrina noticed the attendant did not backtrack and inquired, "Wouldn't it be shorter to go back the same way?"

She replied, "It's a one-way door for security reasons."

"I see," said Katrina.

Telka inquired, "We have to be checked?"

The first guard explained, "You look harmless, but Charles is very strict about concealed weapons."

The second guard added, "The frisking will only take a minute."

The first guard stood behind Katrina and checked her back. He continued by feeling her sides as he slid his hands in front and squeezed her firm breasts. He could tell she wasn't wearing a bra. Katrina was furious as she channeled her emotions into her hands and clenched her fists. He continued by sliding his hands down to her waist and gently patted her crotch. As his hands kept traveling he squeezed her toned butt. Katrina gritted her teeth in response, even though she wanted to ram his face into the wall. He squatted down as he felt her muscular legs under the gown. He was done as he stood up and smiled at her. Katrina held her frustration back as she smiled in response.

The first guard looked at Telka, since it was her turn now to be frisked.

The second guard stood behind Telka and checked her back. He continued by feeling her sides as he slid his hands in front and caressed her firm breasts. He liked the feel of her firm breasts, since only the light fabric separated her skin from his hands. Telka was a little surprised and blushed as a shiver went down her spine. She met Katrina's eyes and remained calm. He continued by sliding his hands down to her waist and gently felt her crotch. As his hands kept traveling he groped her curvy butt. Telka's heart rate began pick up as she stood still, while trying not to look embarrassed in front of the other guard. He squatted down as he felt her shapely legs under the gown. He was done as he stood up and smiled at her. Telka smiled in response as Katrina held her cool beside the other guard.

Katrina crossed her arms and asked, "Did you get a good feel?"

The first guard smiled and said, "Yes I did," as he looked at her purse.

Telka joined in, "Was that fun?"

The second guard replied, "Yes it was," as he looked at Telka's purse.

Katrina took her purse back and said, "I like a man with strong hands. What do you say we take care of these boys later?"

"Sounds like fun," said Telka as she took back her purse.

Katrina offered, "We'll let you have it later. Are you game?"

"Oh, yes, we both get off at midnight," responded the first guard with a smile.

"Yes indeed," agreed the second guard.

The first guard opened the door and said, "You may enter now."

The women walked past him and entered the room. It was 9:30 p.m. by the time Katrina and Telka entered Charles's office. The doors were closed behind them.

It was a very spacious office with a couch, coffee table, a couple of chairs, a deluxe bar, a fireplace, and a desk with chair. On either side of the doors were giant green plants that were eight feet high and just two feet shy from touching the ceiling. Panel lights in the blue drop ceiling illuminated the room quite well and matched the blue carpet. The walls were covered in a dark brown paneling. A dark brown wooden desk faced the door with two chairs in front of it. On top of the desk a white computer monitor could be seen as well as other office things, like a matching phone and neatly arranged papers. To the left of the desk and chairs was the deluxe bar. The bar counter was glossy dark brown, like the desk, and the under part was black. Four round stools with seats matching the color of the chairs were neatly spaced out in front of the bar. Behind the counter was a series of dark brown wooden cabinets. In front of the desk and chairs was a very long and comfortable couch with a glass coffee table in front of it. The couch was dark brown leather, and matched the chairs in front of the desk. Behind the desk was a matching color swivel chair. On the right side of the desk was the fireplace. The fireplace was done in dark brick with a very large painting above it.

The painting was a portrait of a young woman with long fiery red hair and creamy pale skin. She had jagged bangs in the front combed to the one side. The rest of it was pulled back into a high ponytail and tied off with a purple ribbon. In the portrait she was sitting in a large comfortable chair with her hands on her lap holding a bouquet of red roses. She was wearing a purple colored dress with no sleeves. The straps were wide with folds as they hugged the sides of her sensual shoulders. The neckline was a low-cut V, showing some cleavage. Around her neck was a sparkly diamond necklace. Her ears were decorated by matching dangling diamond earrings. The silky dress was close fighting and complemented her figure, while accenting her firm, larger-than-average-sized breasts. Its bottom was shaped like a bell with many folds and hid her feet. Her lips were a luscious red and her blue eyes were mesmerizing. The expression on her face was a simple smile of her lips, while hiding her teeth.

To the left side of her on the arm of the chair sat a young teenage girl with a slender-type build and petite breasts. Her left arm was leaning on the back of the chair to steady her as her legs were facing out to the side and crossed.

In her right hand she held a white and a black rose. She was wearing a fancy pink dress. Her dark hair went down to her shoulders with saw-tooth bangs and went well with her brown eyes. The silky dress had no sleeves with thin shoulder straps and went down to her knees. Its neckline was conservative and showed off her delicate pale neck. Around her neck was a golden chain with a heart-shaped locket. Her cute face was innocent with a lovely smile.

As they entered Katrina whispered to Telka, "I am ready for a barf bag now."

Telka giggled as they saw Charles from behind his desk. Charles was wearing the same suit as last time.

Charles got up from his desk and greeted them, "Good evening, ladies. I understand you needed to see me."

"Yes, we need your help," responded Katrina.

Charles confirmed, "You need my help with the blood gem, right?"

Katrina was caught off guard by his question and inquired, "How did you know?"

Charles smugly replied, "I know many things, Katrina."

Worry was in Telka's voice as she said, "He's on to us, Katrina."

Charles smiled, crossed his arms, and stated, "There is no escape. The walls are thick, soundproof, and the doors are reinforced. Even if you manage to get out of this office alive, the basement is covered from every corridor by my guards. They will not let you reach the surface without my authorization. I'll let you beg for mercy."

Katrina frowned and said, "You arrogant toad. You are going to tell us what we need to know."

Charles was enjoying listening to her boldness and inquired, "Oh, really? Why is that?"

A card flew from Telka's purse and into her hand. She held up the card as she commanded, "Light, come…"

A plant close by to her lashed its vines out and interrupted her card command as they ensnared her. She dropped her card as the plant lifted her off the floor.

Charles mentally picked up the card from the floor, looked at it, and commented, "A sunlight card. I haven't seen a card wielder in ages."

Katrina yelled in concern, "Telka!"

"I have been around for a long time and have seen many tricks," stated Charles as he threw down the card.

Katrina's eyes glowed as she proclaimed, "I am going to wipe that grin right off your face."

"Go ahead," responded Charles.

Katrina leaped into the air and went into a kick. Charles dodged as she spun around and attempted a kick to the head. Charles grabbed her leg and flung her across the room. She flipped around and landed on her feet.

He asked arrogantly, "Is that all you got?" Katrina ran at him and went into a spin kick to the head. Charles dodged again as she spun into a kick to the gut. Charles was measuring her kicks as he effectively dodged them. She finally spun into a leg sweep and knocked him off his feet.

Charles flipped up and commented, "Not bad. Play time is over." He rushed towards her and attempted a kick to the head. She smoothly dodged it as he punched her in the gut. The impact lifted her a couple inches off the floor as she bent over. For that brief second of being defenseless Charles followed up with an elbow to her spine. Katrina was stunned as she fell unconscious.

Telka screamed in despair, "Katrina!"

Charles looked at her motionless body as he commented, "You fight well for a vampeel, but you are still an amateur." He left her on the floor as he walked over to Telka. Charles could sense her fear as he said, "I think I'll have a little snack."

The strong vines trapped Telka as he held her neck. Telka screamed as his fangs drew near, "Katrina! Help me!"

"Your fear is whetting my appetite. No one can help you now," stated Charles.

As his fangs were about to touch her Katrina woke up. "Leave her alone, leech," said Katrina as she grabbed her purse on the floor.

Charles let go of Telka and turned around. He responded, "So, you still have some fight in you. It won't matter. I have injured your spine and it will take a while for your injury to heal."

Katrina refused to listen as she tried to get up and failed. Charles watched her as he commented, "You can't even walk."

Katrina yelled as she looked at him, "I'm not done until my heart stops beating!" Charles went over to Katrina and picked her up by the throat. He smiled as he said, "That can be arranged. I must admire your determination, though." Charles noticed a small perfume bottle in her hand. He grabbed it, looked at it, and asked, "What is this? Holy water?"

"Never leave home without it," answered Katrina.

Charles threw her on the sofa as he commented, "I think I'll have some fun with you, before I deal with your friend."

“I’ll get you, you filthy slime,” stated Katrina.

He threw the bottle at the fireplace and watched it shatter on the floor. Mist came from the bottle as Charles turned away. “So much for that. By the time you can get up it will be too late,” commented Charles as he sat down beside her motionless body.

Her arms felt numb and were not strong enough now to fight him off. She said, “Wait.”

He inquired, “What is it?”

She inquired, “Before you have your way with me, could you tell me what the blood gem is for?”

Charles was curious by her inquiry and said, “Why should I tell you? You won’t live long anyway.”

“Before I die, I would like to know why I risked my life for it,” answered Katrina.

He felt no harm could be done now if she knew and answered, “All right, I will tell you.”

She smiled and thought to herself, “You arrogant pig.”

Charles explained, “The blood gem has magical properties, as you may already know. It is called the blood gem because of its crimson color and was discovered five hundred years ago. At that time there was a conflict between good and evil and the gem was lost. For centuries we have been searching for the blood gem and at last we have found it, thanks to you. Once we have it, we will free our blood queen from her prison.”

Katrina was curious and inquired, “What is so special about this blood queen?”

Charles continued, “She is a hybrid of half vampire and half demon. Her blood will spark the dawn of a new age for vampires and it will liberate us from the clutches of darkness.”

She inquired more, “What do you mean liberate?”

Charles was on a roll and went on, “With her blood we will be able to walk in the daylight forever.”

“Humanity will have nowhere to hide,” commented Katrina.

“You catch on quick, my dear,” commented Charles as he was finished with his talk and smiled lustfully at her.

She stated, “I will stop you even if it costs me my life.”

Charles laughed as he remarked, “Okay, stop me,” as he licked her face from her chin to her cheek.

Katrina turned her head in response as he taunted, “I’m waiting.” She tried to move as he started to fondle her breasts and almost pulled the fabric down.

"I know you can feel this," remarked Charles as he moved his hand up her dress. He taunted her some more, "Come on. Beat me to a pulp."

Nick appeared behind Charles and tapped him on the shoulder. Charles stopped and unwisely turned around as he replied, "What the…?"

Nick punched Charles in the face and sent him flying across the room. Nick looked at Katrina in his bounty hunter outfit and asked, "Are you all right, Katrina?"

Katrina smiled as she responded, "It's only a broken spine. I'll be fine."

"Wait here," said Nick as he leaped off the couch.

Charles quickly got up as he said, "Who the hell are you?"

Nick replied, "My name does not matter. You hurt Katrina and now I'm gonna hurt you."

Katrina smiled at Nick's reply.

Charles had a look of disgust on his face as he commented, "You filthy rat. You will pay for this intrusion."

Nick extended his hand toward him and said, "I'm waiting."

Charles gritted his teeth as he lunged straight at Nick. Nick dodged his attack and kicked him in the gut. Charles quickly got up and threw some punches as Nick blocked them all. On the last punch thrown Nick spun around and hit him with a back fist.

Charles jerked back as he remarked, "Not bad, boy."

Nick attempted a kick to the head as Charles ducked and countered with an uppercut to his chin. The force of the uppercut flung Nick a few feet as he landed on his feet. Nick regained his ground as he said, "Not bad, old fart."

Charles charged at Nick. Nick defensively grabbed his arm and flipped him to the floor. As Nick moved in to attack Charles, he retaliated with a kick to his head.

Nick fell backward as Charles pounced on him. He grabbed Charles by his arms and monkey-flipped him over his head. Charles flew through the air and hit the wall. As they both got up Charles grabbed a sword near the fireplace. Nick grabbed a couple of daggers from his coat.

Charles arrogantly stated, "Your daggers are no match for my sword. I will cut your head off."

"It's not the size. It's how you use it, Chucky," remarked Nick.

He came at Nick with a down-striking motion as Nick did a cross block with his daggers. Before he could react Nick kicked him in the groin. Charles instantly dropped his sword as he crunched over. Without hesitation Nick spun into a kick and hit him in the gut. The force of the kick knocked Charles back against the wall.

Before he could recover, Nick threw his daggers across the room. The daggers pinned Charles's shoulders to the wall as he squirmed and yelled, "You will pay dearly for this!"

"Shut up and stick around," replied Nick as he took his hat off. He threw the hat across the room and it landed on Charles's face. Nick ran over to Katrina on the couch and sat down beside her. He took off his mask as he looked into her eyes and asked, "Katrina, can you walk?"

"Like I said, my spine is broken. If I was a normal human, the paralysis would be permanent," answered Katrina.

Nick asked, "You need blood, right?"

"Yes, it will accelerate my healing," confirmed Katrina.

Nick offered, "Well, carrying you out of here will only make us vulnerable. Take some of mine."

Katrina was a little surprised by his offer and asked, "Are you sure you want to do this?"

"Yes," replied Nick.

Nick held her close to him as she opened her mouth. She drew closer to his neck and sunk her fangs into his thick neck. Katrina closed her eyes as she sucked his blood. Within minutes her bones in her back snapped back into place and her spine mended. For that brief moment in time she experienced closeness she never felt before.

She opened her eyes and found herself naked in a hot spring surrounded by forest trees. The moon was full as it shone through holes in the eerie fog. She turned around and saw Nick in the spring with her. The water level covered half of her breasts as she looked at him and felt no embarrassment. She gazed upon his mesmerizing eyes and kissed him.

A moment later her eyes opened and her sensual experience was over. She felt her heart racing as she said, "What a rush!" Katrina finished and licked the blood from her lips. She looked into his beautiful blue eyes and kissed him.

Nick was a little surprised by her kissing him as she pulled away. He asked, "What was that for?"

Katrina smiled and replied, "Thanks, silly. Besides, you earned that one."

Nick commented, "I'm glad you brought me along."

Katrina placed her finger on his lips and said, "We'll talk later. Free Telka, while I deal with Charles."

He grabbed her hands and helped her off the couch. Nick put his mask back on and inquired, "What did you have in mind?"

"I'm going to interrogate him," explained Katrina.

Nick handed her some daggers and said, "Here, these should come in handy."

Katrina took them and winked at him. She took two of the daggers and threw them across the room. Both of the daggers hit Charles and pinned his hands to the wall. Katrina walked over to Charles and took the hat off of his head.

Charles looked at her as his eyes glowed and said, "I will drain your body dry for this."

Katrina smiled as she grabbed his jaw and asked, "Where is your office safe and what is the combination, Chucky?"

"I will tell you nothing, bitch," replied Charles.

"Apparently, I haven't made myself clear," remarked Katrina as she grabbed the last dagger. She aimed it at his crotch and said, "There are far worse things than death. For example, have you ever felt a silver blade on your skin?"

Sweat ran down his face as he said, "You wouldn't."

"I will do whatever is necessary to take from your family what you took from me," stated Katrina.

Charles inquired, "What are you talking about?"

Katrina explained, "It is a matter of blood. The Drenkel family made me the scornful woman I am, when they killed my mother. The members of that clan will pay one way or another."

Charles admitted, "I am not a part of the Drenkel family. I belong to the Catholom family."

Katrina rolled her eyes as she replied, "Oh, sorry to hear you are in league with them. You must pay the penalty of association."

"You're not human," remarked Charles.

Katrina pressed the dagger against his pants as she said, "You're right. Now talk! It's not like I receive government funding."

Charles gave in and confessed, "All right. It's behind the counter of the bar and the combination is 34R – 26L – 36R."

Katrina smiled as she slapped his cheek and remarked, "That's a good boy."

Nick came over, looked at Katrina, and said, "Nice dress."

Katrina placed her hands on her hips as she looked back at Nick and inquired, "What?"

"I was just wondering about those numbers," remarked Nick.

She smiled as she said, "Yes, by chance they happen to be my measurements."

Nick gave her a thumbs-up and said, "Cool."

Katrina waved her index finger at him and remarked, "Keep your mind on the job, bud."

"Okay," replied Nick.

Telka was now free and laughed at the whole measurement dialog. She looked at Nick and said, "Thanks, Nick, you will have plenty of time to flirt with her later." Telka walked over to behind the bar and found the gray metal safe.

Nick picked up a suitcase and a wardrobe bag near the fireplace, where he materialized, and carried them over to Telka.

Charles inquired, "What do you hope to gain by hunting and robbing us?"

"Payback with interest," replied Katrina.

Nick placed the brown suitcase on the counter and opened it. Telka squatted down to the safe and opened it, using the combination. With the safe open she took the notes of money from it and placed them all in the empty suitcase. She turned to Katrina and said, "Katrina, I have the money."

Katrina looked in her direction and replied, "Cool."

Nick closed the suitcase of money, grabbed it by the handle, and walked over to Katrina. He placed it beside her and inquired, "What are we going to do with him?"

Katrina commented as she handed him his dagger, "Killing him would be too good for him. I will let him live with the humiliation instead."

Telka joined Katrina and asked, "Katrina, shouldn't we get out of here?"

She said, "Yes. Let's get changed and get out of here. Nick, cover his head and face."

Nick replaced his hat over Charles's face and replied, "Yes, my queen."

Katrina remarked, "Oh please," as she unzipped the brown wardrobe bag and took out her slayer outfit, including her weapons. Telka took out her change of clothing from underneath Katrina's. They quickly kicked off their shoes and slipped out of their gowns as they helped each other unzip their backs.

Nick was a perfect gentleman, as he dared not turn around while they were half naked. All Nick could hear was the buckling of belts and zippers as clothing came together. As Katrina finished he could hear her slide her sword in its sheath on her back. Telka was fully dressed as she let her hair down and placed the other clothing in the wardrobe bag.

She was wearing a strapless pink dress and a matching pair of high-heel dress shoes. Her cotton dress was conservatively low cut and accented her cleavage, while it complemented her lovely figure and hung below her knees. Around her waist she wore a silver chain with round links. Around her neck was a pink scarf, which accented her sensuous neck and shoulders. The only jewelry she wore was a set of wide hoop silver earrings and a ring on her finger. On her right middle finger was a golden ring with a round smooth gem, a shade of green, in the center of it.

When Telka was finished, she zipped up the wardrobe bag and placed it on her shoulder. Katrina let her hair down as she put on her red glasses. She said, "You can turn around now, Nick."

Nick turned around and saw Katrina and Telka in their outfits. "What a babe," responded Nick.

Telka grinned as Katrina said, "I'll take that as a compliment I guess."

He inquired, "What's the plan?"

Katrina said, "I'll tell you on the way out of here."

Charles stated as Nick took back his hat, "I swear you will not leave this hotel alive."

Katrina sarcastically replied, "I am shaking in my panties, Chucky. Let's go."

Chapter 17
The Escape

Telka picked up the suitcase full of money and followed Katrina and Nick as they headed for the exit from Charles's office.

As the double doors opened, the guards turned around. Katrina quickly threw a couple of syringes at them. They hit them square in the chests. The guards were in agony as the liquid was directly absorbed into their bodies. Within seconds their bodies dissolved away, leaving behind only their clothing.

Nick looked at them and inquired, "What was in those syringes?"

"Holy water," answered Katrina as she shut the doors.

Nick remarked, "I won't ever ask you for a shot."

Telka said, "I hope we can get out before he gets free."

Katrina commented, "He's not going anywhere fast. Those silver daggers will keep him at bay, until someone frees him." Katrina explained, "We are going to split up. Telka is going to join Mike and we are going to leave through the sewers."

"I like that plan," responded Nick.

Katrina asked, "Telka, do think you can handle any guards that come your way?"

"Sure, as long as nothing grabs me," replied Telka.

"Oh, and one more thing. We'll meet back at my place in a few hours. Go ahead and have your date with Mike, Telka. Just don't make a mess in the limo," said Katrina.

Telka blushed as Nick laughed.

Katrina said, "You will have to go back to the stairwell, Telka, and backtrack to the main lobby."

"I'll see you later," replied Telka as she walked away from them.

Katrina and Nick walked in the opposite direction. After walking about ten feet Nick asked, "Where is the sewer entrance?"

Katrina replied, "I forgot you were in a bottle the whole time we were down here. It's just up ahead."

They stopped in front of a large rusted metal door. The door was locked with a padlock and chains.

Nick commented, "The door is locked."

Katrina inquired, "Why would they need to lock a door to the sewers?"

Nick replied, "Maybe to keep the rats out?"

"I wonder," said Katrina as she grabbed the chain, broke it, and opened the door.

The door led to a dark flight of stone steps leading down. Katrina led the way as Nick followed behind her.

Meanwhile, Telka made it across the basement level and could see the lit up staircase before getting to the Y junction. Guards approached from both wings and stopped in front of the junction.

Their faces were covered in a dark material with red glowing eyes. All of them wore charcoal-gray trench coats. Under the trench coats they wore black pants and turtleneck shirts. Black leather gloves covered their hands and matching leather boots covered their feet. Across their chests was a black nylon strap connected to a HK MP5K4A submachine gun.

Ten of them stood between Telka and her path.

Telka put down her stuff and said, "Could you help me? I'm lost."

The guards raised their weapons and opened fire. Telka activated her ring, which created an invisible barrier around her. The bullets bounced off the barrier as they emptied their clips.

Telka smiled and said, "You will have to do better than that."

They dropped their clips and reloaded as a tarot card flipped into Telka's hand. Telka threw the card out on the floor and commanded, "I summon the black knight!"

A seven-foot-tall figure in black plate-mail armor magically appeared in front of her. The figure was massive with spikes on its shoulders, arms, hands, and legs. Its helmet had small spikes on the sides and two large horn-like spikes curving slightly downward from the top. The ends of its hands had spike-like claws and it held a spiked ball and chain, the size of a basketball, in its left hand. Between its shoulders hung a green leather cape. It was practically a black silhouette except for the cape and its eerie glowing yellow eyes.

The guards aimed their weapons at it as Telka ordered, "Take out the guards."

The black knight approached the guards as they opened fire. The bullets bounced off his armor as it raised its ball and chain. Since they emptied their clips and were out of ammo, they let go of their weapons and drew their stun rods.

The black knight swung its ball and chain over its head as it moved forward. They all charged at it in turn. The black knight swung its ball and chain and knocked the first two out of the way. They were sent flying to the left corridor.

One got under its ball and chain and hit it with his stun rod. The stun rod had no effect as it grabbed him and threw him at two others. The black knight did a crisscross pattern and knocked down two more guards as it moved forward.

One of the guards pulled out a bowie knife and threw it at its face. The knife hit it between the eyes. It let go of its ball and chain and sent it flying at one of the guards. One of the guards was hit in the head as the force of the impact knocked his head off. His headless body soon fell down on the floor.

The black knight went down to one knee as the last two guards charged in with stun rods. It grabbed the one guard by the throat and lifted him off the floor. The other guard got careless and rushed in as the black knight speared him with his fingers in the chest. The black knight broke the guard's neck with his hand and dropped his lifeless body. It took hold of the knife, pulled it out of its face, and dropped it. The other guard died instantly, as it slid off its other hand and fell on the floor.

Telka remarked, "Good boy." The black knight disappeared as Telka walked around the dead bodies and headed for the stairwell.

Moments later Telka left the main entrance with a man dressed in a black suit carrying her bags. She led the way as she headed towards the limousine.

Mike was standing by the limousine, while Telka approached him. Mike commented, "You changed your clothes."

"I know," responded Telka.

Mike looked at the man dressed in a black suit and asked, "Who's he?"

Telka explained, "Our limo driver. Since our work here is done, why don't we start our date?"

Mike opened the trunk as the driver placed the luggage inside. Mike was a little surprised and said, "Okay."

The driver closed the trunk and walked over to back door. He opened it and Telka smiled as she climbed in. Mike gave him a friendly nod and followed Telka in the back. The driver soon started the car and drove off.

The interior of the limo was basically a couple of bench seats facing each other with a small island counter built into the floor. It had compartments for storing drinks and glasses. The top of the wooden counter was dark brown and matched the leather seats. Brown was the color of the carpet and the ceiling, which had a moon roof. The carpet was very clean and the seats were very comfortable.

Mike sat beside her and inquired, "How did your party go?"

Telka replied, "It was a little rowdy at first, but Katrina took care of it and it went smoothly after that. We got the information we needed as well as some additional funding."

Mike asked, "She didn't steal it? Did she?"

Telka answered, "Last time she checked, it wasn't a crime to rob a vampire."

Mike was a little surprised by her answer and said, "A vampire? Oh forget it."

Telka curled up beside Mike, which surprised him a little. Mike inquired, "Where's Katrina?"

Telka explained, "Oh, I forgot to tell you. She left with Nick."

Mike confirmed, "The guy from the museum?"

Telka agreed, "Bingo."

Mike looked at her and inquired, "So, how come the clothes you are wearing are different?"

Telka asked, "Don't you like what I'm wearing?"

Mike replied, "I do. But…"

Telka shushed him by placing her finger on his lips.

Telka said, "Too many questions can spoil the mood. Thanks for helping me out the other night and joining me tonight, Mike."

Before he could respond she kissed him. Mike smiled and responded, "You're welcome."

Telka suggested, "Let's go see a movie."

Mike said, "Okay."

As the limousine drove off Telka said, "Now that you don't have to worry about kissing me, would you like to have your palm read?"

"Sure," replied Mike.

Katrina and Nick reached the bottom of the steps and entered a large sewer tunnel. The stone tunnel had ledges on either side with water flowing in the middle, like a stream. Its ceiling was arched and very dim with a lot of shadows.

Katrina closed her eyes and switched her vision to aura vision.

Nick asked, "So where are we going?"

Katrina replied, "I had my car parked a few blocks away from the hotel, so we wouldn't draw attention to ourselves."

Nick commented, "Good thinking. My outfit would stick out like a sore thumb and yours would be the nice one in a ritzy place like that."

Katrina said, "We are almost there, just a block and a half to go."

As they continued through the dark spacious corridor, Katrina noticed something and stopped in her tracks. She drew her Glocks as Nick asked, "What's wrong?"

Katrina answered, "I can see why the access door was locked. We're in were-rat territory."

Nick said, "I don't see them."

Katrina informed, "They're up ahead in the crossover junction."

The crossover junction was a spacious area where one tunnel crossed over another tunnel and the water in the upper tunnel spilled into the tunnel below. Katrina and Nick were in the upper tunnel.

The were-rats were climbing the walls effortlessly, as they waited for Katrina and Nick to get closer.

Nick inquired, "Is there any way to avoid them?"

Katrina remarked, "No, our way out is past the crossover junction. Besides, if they haven't smelled us, they have at least heard us by now."

Nick pulled out a couple of Uzi nine-millimeter submachine guns as Katrina asked, "Are you packing silver?"

Nick said, "Yes."

Katrina commented, "Good, silver works on them just like werewolves."

Nick inquired, "How are they different?"

Katrina explained, "Aside from their obvious rat-like appearance, they climb walls extremely well and their very quick. Careful of their teeth, they can gnaw through almost anything. Most of them hate vampires."

Nick commented, "If they want a fight, we'll give them one."

Were-rats were on the stone ceiling squirming around as they approached. They varied in colored fur, from black to brown to gray. Their red eyes glowed in the dark. Fur covered all of their bodies except for their forearms, lower legs and their four-foot-long tails.

Katrina instructed, "I'll lure them out. You cover my rear."

Nick agreed, "Okay."

Katrina closed her eyes and reset her vision to night vision. She concentrated and allowed her perception to dilate, so things in motion would appear slower to her, a gift her father apparently passed on to her.

The were-rats attacked as Katrina approached the junction. Two on either side leaped at her. She aimed upward and shot both of them in the heart simultaneously. They fell down in the tunnel below.

One ran along the wall to her left as she shot it in the head. It dropped like a stone, while another came from the right and she shot it in the head. It too dropped like a heavy stone.

Several climbed the tunnel wall from below. Katrina picked them off one by one, before they got too close to her.

As she nailed the last one, both of her guns were out of ammo. Katrina stopped for a second and realized her guns were cocked open. She commented, "Oh no. I'm out."

Nick grabbed her from behind at the waist and said, "My turn." Katrina was surprised by his grabbing as he leaped in the air to cross the junction. In midair he fired his Uzi at them as they entered the junction and squealed in response.

Nick made it across with Katrina as he emptied his one clip. He said, "Head for the ladder. I'll hold them off."

Katrina agreed, "Okay." She ran towards the ladder and scaled it in no time. Nick followed closely behind her and aimed his other Uzi in his hand at the junction.

The were-rats were relentless as they climbed up to the junction and followed them. As Nick climbed the ladder, he mowed them down with a continuous spray of silver. Katrina effortlessly lifted the manhole cover with one hand as she slid it away and climbed out. Nick was right behind her as he climbed out and replaced the manhole cover.

Katrina commented, "Don't worry. They won't follow us."

Nick asked, "Are you sure?"

Katrina explained, "Were-rats are subterranean monsters. They don't even like street lights."

Chapter 18
Loss and Gain

The clock on the wall of the boardroom in the Delchor Corporate Building read 11:00 p.m. Flusken and the other vampires were gathered around the table. Flusken announced, "Gentlemen, we have the blood gem."

Morgan commented, "That vampeel is becoming a real nuisance."

Larrin added, "She knows its purpose."

Curton spoke up, "She could interfere with our plans."

Flusken agreed, "You have a point there. Now that we have the blood gem, action should be taken to get rid of her."

Morgan inquired, "How are we going to capture her?"

Larrin commented, "She is very cunning."

Curton stated, "Breaking into her dwelling and attacking her is out of the question."

Flusken stated, "I am well aware of our restrictions to dwellings."

At that moment Carrie entered the room. She was wearing a long-sleeve blouse with no collar and a matching skirt. The white cotton blouse had a U-cut down to the top of her cleavage. Her sleeves hugged her upper arms and exposed her sensual shoulders as they widened out more down to her wrists. From the bottom of the U-cut down the front was a crisscross stitching, which showed off her cleavage. Her midriff could be seen as her skirt was worn below her waist a little. It had a slit up the one side and went down to her calves. Her top and skirt hugged her sexy body like a glove, while her feet wore matching sandals. Her hair was done in the usual braiding with rings as her other usual jewelry of earrings and bracelets were also worn.

Carrie suggested, "There is another way. We will let her come to us."

Flusken inquired, "What do you mean?"

Carrie replied, "I have a plan."

It was Friday around 3:00 a.m. when Katrina and Telka returned to the firehouse. Katrina was in the living area, when she noticed Teresa was lying unconscious on the floor and said, "What the hell?" At that instant she rushed over to her and looked at her. She took off her gloves and checked her neck for any injuries. Katrina placed her right index and middle finger on her neck and checked for a pulse. She was relieved to feel a pulse and said, "Thank God."

Telka entered the room and saw Katrina tending to Teresa. Telka reacted, "Teresa!" as she rushed over to her.

Katrina looked at Telka and said, "She's all right, Telka. She's just unconscious."

Katrina picked her up from the floor and gently placed her on the couch.

Telka inquired, "What happened here, Katrina?"

Katrina answered, "I don't know. I have a bad feeling about this, and Emma usually greets me when I return." Katrina instructed, "You check the kitchen and the main bathroom. I'll check the bedrooms and we'll meet back here."

Telka agreed, "Okay."

Moments later, Katrina and Telka returned to the living area.

Katrina asked, "Did you find anyone else?"

Telka replied, "I found no one, Katrina."

Katrina responded, "Oh, no. All I found was Tula sleeping in her bed."

Telka asked, "Emma's missing?"

Katrina suggested, "Emma knows better not to go out on her own."

Teresa woke up and said, "They took her."

Katrina kneeled down to Teresa, placed her left hand at the side of her face, and asked, "Who took her, Teresa?"

Teresa answered, "I don't know what they were, Katrina. It happened so fast."

Telka said, "Take your time, Teresa."

Teresa continued, "They were some kind of monsters, Katrina. They grabbed her and knocked me out with some kind of spray."

Telka stated, "They couldn't have been vampires, since vampires have to be invited by the owner in order to enter a dwelling. They could have possibly been minions of an alchemist."

Katrina confirmed, "Like the ones we ran into at the museum."

Telka agreed, "It's possible. You don't think they came for the blood gem as well?"

Katrina said, "I left it on the kitchen table. Please, tell me you saw it there, when you checked earlier."

Telka looked down and said, "Katrina, it's gone."

Katrina was shocked and responded, "What?"

Telka remarked, "Someone must have taken it when we were at the hotel."

Katrina was furious as she yelled, "Damn it!"

Telka looked at Katrina with sad eyes and said, "We've lost, Katrina. We don't even know where they are."

Katrina stood up, placed her hands on Telka's shoulders and replied, "Don't say that, Telka. It is not over yet. Not by a long shot."

Telka smiled and said, "You're right, Katrina. We can't give up yet, otherwise they win."

Katrina crossed her arms and inquired, "How did they know where we were and what we were doing?"

Telka suggested, "It must be an alchemist at work. This one is very skilled and I bet he or she has been spying on us. They've been watching us from the start and managed to be one step ahead of us."

Katrina asked, "How?"

Telka explained, "An alchemist can spy on anyone that possesses a certain object with their spell on it."

Katrina reached into her pocket and pulled out the medallion. She looked at it and said, "Why didn't I think about it before? It's the medallion I have."

Telka agreed, "That makes perfect sense."

Katrina asked, "How do we cancel the spell?"

Telka replied, "Pouring holy water on it should do the trick."

Katrina opened a vial of holy water and poured the liquid on the medallion. A chemical reaction took place with a small puff of smoke rising from it.

Telka inquired, "What are we going to do, Katrina?"

Katrina answered, "I'm not sure just yet. I'll get in contact with my father and see if he knows anything. For now let's get some rest."

Meanwhile at the Delchor Corporate Building, Carrie was observing the magical window from her cauldron. She was wearing the same white outfit, but her hair was unbraided and she had taken off all of her jewelry. The magical window vanished before her eyes. Carrie was surprised as she remarked, "Oh no. I must tell Flusken."

Carrie found Flusken in the lounge with Evelyn and Claudia. The lounge was a spacious room with a couch, a couple of chairs, a deluxe bar, an entertainment center, and a bed. Small circular lights in the blue drop ceiling illuminated the room quite well and matched the blue carpet. At this time only half of them were on so the room was somewhat dim. The walls were plain and covered only in a purple color. In the center of the room was a long black leather couch, which faced the entertainment center. The black wooden entertainment center was decked out with a fifty-inch-screen TV, a DVD player, and a sound system, complete with surround sound. To the left and right of the couch were matching chairs with no arms and an angled back. Behind the couch was the bed. It was a king-size waterbed with burgundy satin sheets and a raspberry velvet spread. On the right side of the bed was the deluxe bar. The bar counter was glossy black and the under part was blue. Four round stools with seats matching the color of the couch were neatly spaced out in front of the bar. Behind the counter was a series of black wooden cabinets.

Flusken was sitting on one of the chairs wearing only a cyan-colored satin robe.

Evelyn was standing behind him, wearing only a violet-colored satin robe, while massaging his shoulders. Her fingernails, eye shadow, and lipstick matched the color of her robe.

Claudia was on her knees, wearing only a magenta-colored satin robe, while massaging his feet. Her fingernails, eye shadow, and lipstick matched the color of her robe as well.

She stood about five feet eight inches tall with a slender-type build and petite-sized breasts. She was a pretty woman with pale skin, dark blonde hair, and green eyes. Her makeup and jewelry only enhanced her looks, while her age appeared to be twenty-seven years old. She had saw-tooth bangs, which covered her forehead, and the back of her hair went down to her shoulders.

Carrie entered the room and walked towards the other chair and sat down. She had a concerned look on her face as she said, "Flusken, I need to talk to you."

Flusken looked up to her as he said, "This had better be good, my dear. I am very tired."

"My window has vanished," stated Carrie.

Flusken was not surprised a bit as he replied, "Is that all? It doesn't matter now."

Carrie argued, "But we cannot spy on them anymore."

Flusken arrogantly stated, "We have the blood gem. They are helpless to stop us."

Carrie responded, "Flusken, you know our enemy is very resourceful. Don't dismiss them so quickly. It is better to err on the side of caution, than on the side of carelessness."

Flusken replied, "Carrie, you have served me well and your efforts have not been overlooked, my dear. Let me handle the vampeel and her friends. If we stick to the plan our ultimate dream will be a reality."

Carrie agreed, "Yes, you're right as always, Flusken. You have protected me for this long. I should not doubt your abilities now."

Flusken inquired, "Carrie, is that all that is troubling you?"

Carrie replied, "Yes, Flusken."

Flusken said, "Good, I am glad that is settled."

Carrie got up and said, "I should be going now, Flusken."

Flusken ordered, "Wait. Stay awhile."

Carrie argued, "I wouldn't want to intrude."

Flusken objected, "I insist."

She sat down on the chair and relaxed as Flusken ordered.

Flusken instructed, "Eva, Claudia, give her a vampiric sensual massage."

Both of them got up and smiled lustfully as they walked over to Carrie. Carrie was concerned and objected, "Flusken, I'm fine, really. This is not necessary."

Flusken got up and assured her, "It will help you relax and fall asleep soundly. I assure you, they will not harm you. You have my word on that. Think of this as a reward." He got up and walked off as Carrie asked, "You are leaving me alone with them?"

Flusken stated, "They have already fed tonight, my dear." He continued to walk out as he said, "Even if they did bite you, they wouldn't take much blood."

Evelyn got behind her and started to massage her temples. She said, "Just relax, Carrie, and let yourself enjoy it."

Claudia got on her knees at the foot of the chair and removed Carrie's sandals. She said, "Flusken loves our massages so much. You should feel privileged that he offered this to you." She took one of her feet and began to massage it.

Carrie didn't say a word as she watched them closely.

Evelyn commented, "You're so tense. Are you afraid of us, Carrie?"

Carrie answered, "Would it make you feel empowered if I said yes?"

Both of them smiled as Claudia commented, "Don't worry, Carrie. You don't need to fear what we are going to do to you. It won't be fatal."

Evelyn stated, "We'll make you feel so good, Carrie, that you will sleep like the dead, when we are through."

Carrie felt trapped, since she did not trust the two vampire women. However, if she made a run for it, she knew it would be a violation of trust towards Flusken. Shivers went down her spine as they continued to touch her.

Evelyn slid her hands down to Carrie's neck and felt her pulse rise. She remarked, "You have lovely skin for a human, Carrie."

Carrie did not know how to take that comment. She thought about being polite and said, "Thanks."

Claudia continued to massage Carrie's feet as she looked at her in the eyes and smiled. She asked, "Does that feel good?"

Carrie responded, "Yes."

Claudia looked at her as she started to lick her toes.

Carrie objected, "Stop that."

Evelyn gently rubbed her neck in small circular motions and said, "Don't knock it till you try it. I don't see you jerking your foot away."

Carrie could feel Evelyn breathing down her neck as she began to gently nibble on her ear. She objected, "Stop that."

Evelyn stopped and responded, "What's the matter? You never had your ear nibbled on before?"

Carrie replied, "No."

Evelyn said softly in her ear, "I didn't feel you jerk your head away." Carrie blushed as she remarked, "You ignorance about this is so cute." Evelyn continued to nibble on her other ear as she slid her hands down to Carrie's shoulders.

Carrie was starting to feel more relaxed as she closed her eyes. Evelyn began to massage her shoulders firmly as the tension in them began to fade away.

Claudia pulled the tie loose on her robe. She opened her robe and let the ends fall past her shoulders, while exposing her firm perky breasts. She took one of Carrie's feet and started to massage her foot between her breasts.

Carrie never felt such a sensation like that before and began to let it relax her even more.

Claudia worked her way up to her calves and massaged them firmly with her hands. While she was kneading her calves, Claudia raised Carrie's knees up to bend them. Claudia rubbed her breasts against Carrie's knees and shins and enjoyed the sensation as her nipples became erect.

While massaging her shoulders, Evelyn began to kiss Carrie's neck softly. Carrie was so relaxed that she was almost asleep. Evelyn gently raised Carrie's toned arms up and began to rub her upper arms. She worked her way down to her wrists with gentle rubbing motions.

Evelyn let her arms bend at the elbows and rest as she pulled the tie on her robe loose. She opened her robe and let the ends fall past her shoulders, while exposing her very large firm breasts. She took one of Carrie's hands and gently sucked every finger in turn, while rolling her tongue. When she was done, she took the hand and placed it between her breasts and massaged it. Evelyn repeated the technique with Carrie's other hand and enjoyed the sensation as her nipples became erect.

Claudia worked her way up to Carrie's thighs and extended her legs as she straddled her. She undid Carrie's skirt and fully exposed her sexy toned legs and her white panties underneath. Claudia bent down and massaged her legs with her breasts in an up and down motion.

Carrie was drifting off to sleep as Evelyn put her arms down by her sides. She pulled on Carrie's sleeves and exposed her shoulders more. Evelyn began rubbing her lips on her shoulders in a caressing motion. The pulling put more tension on Carrie's blouse as Claudia started to untie the string, holding Carrie's top together. She could see Carrie's erect nipples protruding through the cotton fabric. Claudia came closer and slowly pulled the string all the way out, causing Carrie's breasts to burst out.

Carrie opened her eyes and said, "No." Carrie couldn't move with Claudia almost sitting on her thighs and Evelyn holding her shoulders to the chair.

Claudia replied, "Oh, yes." Claudia began to suck on Carrie's nipples back and forth, while fondling them.

Evelyn commented, "Don't worry. We are not going to violate you, Carrie, just pleasure you a bit."

The sensual pleasure she felt was arousing her more and distracting her from protesting. Carrie softly stated, "I don't play that side."

Claudia smiled as she continued to rub her breasts against Carrie's. Carrie finally relaxed again, closed her eyes, and the tension in her body lowered.

Carrie would not admit it, but she was enjoying the erotic massage to a certain extent.

Claudia got off of her and moved her legs to touch the floor. She got behind her and supported her back with her breasts against her back as she sat up. Evelyn got close to Carrie and rubbed her breasts against hers. Carrie was almost moaning to the soft sensation of their flesh meshing together.

Evelyn began to caress Carrie's breasts as Claudia pulled her long hair away from her neck. Without warning Claudia bit Carrie on the neck and started to suck her blood. Carrie soon went into a trance as Evelyn ran her tongue from Carrie's breasts all the way up to her neck. She lowered her head and began to suck Carries nipples as Claudia continued to feed.

In a short moment Claudia was done and licked the bite marks on Carrie's neck. Within seconds the bite marks disappeared. At the same time Evelyn and Claudia got up from Carrie and left her lying on the chair. Carrie had passed out and was in a deep sleep. Evelyn came over to Claudia and licked the remaining blood off of her lips. Evelyn kissed Claudia on the lips as they embraced each other.

Chapter 19
The Trap

Katrina was sitting outside at a round wooden table with matching chairs in front of a coffee shop. All of the tables had a green umbrella in the center. The sign on the coffee shop read: Mary's Café. It was a cute establishment surrounded by other restaurants on the same street. A street clock on the corner read 3:00 p.m. as the sunlight peeked between the tall buildings in the workingman district. Katrina was drinking a tall glass of iced tea with a lemon slice stuck on the top of it. The area was full of people walking on the sidewalk as cars were filling the streets for the beginning of rush-hour traffic.

Katrina was wearing a tube top, a matching knee-length skirt, and sandals. Her cotton blue tube top hugged her torso like a glove and showed off some of her midriff. The leather sandals were brown and showed off her blue nail polish on her toes. Around her neck she wore a small silver chain with a cross on it. On her one shoulder hung a small matching leather purse. Red sunglasses covered her eyes as her hair was pulled back in a ponytail, showing off her dangling earrings.

Katrina was looking at the back of a business card from the café. It read: *Meet me at Mary's Café by 3:00 p.m. alone or you will never hear from Emma again.* The note was signed: *Carrie*.

At that moment a blue limousine pulled up to the curb. The door opened and Carrie stepped out of it. She walked up to Katrina and removed her dark sunglasses.

Carrie was wearing a blazer with a matching skirt and high-heel boots. The outfit complemented her sexy figure and was close fitting. Her blazer was colored in a pine green, which fastened on the left side with two silver buttons and had two other buttons on the right side forming a square pattern. The skirt came down to her knees and had a few folds in it. Her leather boots went halfway up her shins with a silver ankle bracelet on her left boot. Under the blazer was a turquoise-colored cotton tank top. The tank top was low cut and showed off some of her cleavage. Around her neck was a ribbon that matched the color of her tank top as well as her eye shadow, lipstick and fingernails. Her hair was pulled back into a ponytail, while she wore her usual silver earrings, and thumb rings.

Carrie commented, "So, vampeels can be out in the daylight after all," as she sat down across from her.

Katrina looked up to her and inquired, "You must be Carrie?"

Carrie replied, "Yes, your reputation precedes you, Katrina. I see you found the note on your bed."

Katrina kept her cool as she replied, "Get to the point."

Carrie pulled a picture out of her breast pocket and slid it across the table. Katrina caught it and looked at it. It was a picture of Emma tied up in a chair. She stood up and looked at Carrie. If looks could kill, Carrie would have been a pile of ashes by Katrina's glare.

Katrina inquired, "Where is she? If you have harmed her, you will suffer my wrath."

Carrie sat there with her arms crossed as she said, "She is safe for now, but that entirely depends on you."

"You cowardly witch," remarked Katrina.

Carrie replied, "Hurting me will accomplish nothing."

As she sat back down Katrina asked, "What do you want?"

Carrie stated, "Come alone to the Delchor Corporate Building at 6:30 tonight. That is if you ever want to see Emma again." Carrie got up and walked away from the table. She reentered the limousine and closed the door. Katrina gritted her teeth and crumpled the picture in her hand as the limousine drove away.

It was 5:00 p.m. according to the clock on the wall of Katrina's bedroom. Katrina had just taken a shower and was drying her naked body with a pink towel. She placed the towel on a rack to dry and stepped into her bedroom. Katrina pulled a pair of blue panties out of her drawer and slipped them on.

Tula knocked on the door as she asked, "Katrina, may I come in?"

Katrina said, "Yes," as she slipped into a blue tank top.

Tula was wearing a blue bikini top and a matching pair of short shorts. Her hair was pulled back in a ponytail. As always she was wearing golden hoop earrings, bracelets and a chain around her neck.

Tula entered the room as she saw Katrina putting on her black leather pants. Tula inquired, "Katrina, where are you going?"

Katrina answered, "Isn't it obvious?" as she zipped up her boots and continued, "The Drenkel family has Emma and are using her as bait."

Tula asked, "Katrina, if it is a trap, then why are you going?"

Katrina buckled on her weapons belt and replied, "Trap or no trap I have to save her. Those arrogant bastards revealed their lair to me." She put an Uzi nine-millimeter with strap across her chest and on her shoulder.

Tula grabbed her arms and objected, "Katrina, you can't go there alone."

Katrina gently took Tula's hands away from her as she fastened her cross chocker to her neck. She smiled and said, "I don't plan to," as she put on her leather coat and gloves. Katrina picked up a note from her dresser, handed it to Tula, and instructed, "Call your sister, Telka, she will know what to do."

Tula took the note and hugged her as she said, "Be careful, Katrina. Bring her back to us."

Katrina smiled and said, "I will." She immediately went out to the area where the poles were and quickly wrapped her arms and legs around the closest two-inch-diameter pole as she gracefully slid down to the garage. As she reached the floor of the garage she said, "Hold on, Emma. I'm on my way."

The clock of the lobby read 6:00 p.m. as Katrina entered the main entrance of the Delchor Corporate Building. Katrina looked around the empty lobby as she drew her Glocks. She noticed a couple of guards at the information counter were lying on the floor and knocked out. She moved past the counter and saw two more guards lying around. As she walked past them, she said to herself, "What is going on here? All of the guards are knocked out. This is strange, even for a trap setup."

Katrina closed her eyes and had her aura vision take over. She walked further back and saw an envelope, marked Katrina, stuck on a wall next to the elevators. Katrina took the envelope from the wall and opened it. She pulled out a note that read: *Take the elevator to the top floor.* Katrina pushed the up arrow and entered the first elevator as the doors opened.

Since she was still in aura vision, she saw everything in the elevator as shades of blue and gray. No auras of any kind were visible in the area. She pressed the top floor button and the doors of the elevator closed.

Katrina said, "Emma, I'm coming," as the elevator ascended. Without warning the elevator filled up with gas. She scrambled to stop the elevator as she stumbled and chocked on the gas.

Moments later, the elevator stopped and the doors opened on the top floor. Katrina was groggy and slow to react from the effects of the gas. She was lying on the floor of the elevator with her eyes halfway open.

Shawn picked her up by the throat and said, "Welcome to your own hell," as he threw her against a wall. Katrina was stunned as she tried to quickly get up. Her Glocks were dropped on the floor as Claudia kicked them away from her reach.

Claudia was dressed in a black leather outfit. She wore a strapless top that zipped down the middle. Below her midriff was a pair of tight leather shorts. A pair of high-heel boots that went all the way up to her thighs covered her legs. On her head she wore a cap with a visor. Gloves that went past her elbows covered her arms. She wore dark eye shadow and lipstick as well as black hoop earrings.

Claudia commented, "She's early. I like that in a woman." Claudia got behind her and pulled her sword out of her coat as she stood up. Katrina turned in her direction as Claudia punched her.

Katrina almost stumbled as Shawn grabbed her and pulled her coat off. Claudia spun around and kicked Katrina on the side of the face. Katrina fell down from the blow in front of Shawn. She refused to give up and grabbed the long blade strapped to her leg. Katrina got up as she faced Claudia.

Claudia stabbed her with her own sword in the gut, before she could even attack with her blade. She agonized in pain as she dropped her long blade. Katrina dropped to her knees as Claudia pulled the blade out. Claudia commented, "It's a very nice silver blade, too bad it won't hurt you like it hurts us."

Shawn picked her up and locked her arms behind her back. Claudia dropped the sword as she spun around and kicked her in the face again. Blood flew from her mouth, as she felt woozy from all the abuse. Shawn held her up again as Claudia spun around and kicked her in the face again. Blood flew out of her mouth and ran down her neck as she could barely stand.

At that moment Emma entered the hallway. Emma was wearing a sleeveless dress with matching high-heel dress shoes. The white silky dress had straps that fastened behind her neck and formed a diamond cut down to her cleavage. It was tight fitting around the torso as it accented her firm breasts and showed off a generous amount of cleavage. The length of the dress went all the way down to her ankles with a slit on both sides up to her thighs. Around her neck was a golden chain with a Drenkel Clan medallion hanging from it. Her hair was pulled back slightly and tied off with a ribbon. With her hair pulled away from her ears a set of golden dangling earrings could be seen. Emma's eyes were decorated in pink and lavender and her lips were colored in a lavender lipstick.

Katrina's head was facing downward as she felt weak as a kitten. Claudia smiled as she saw Emma approach. Claudia grabbed her hair on the top of her head and pulled her head up so that she could see Emma and remarked, "Look who has come to join the party."

Katrina's vision was blurred as Emma came closer. Her vision then focused, she saw her, and said, "Emma, what have they done to you?"

Emma was a partly turned vampire and had the characteristic vampiric eyes and fangs. She came closer and removed Katrina's cross choker from her neck. Emma responded, "It's not so bad, Katrina."

Katrina's eyes glowed as she said, "You...bastards..."

Shawn pulled her hair back and bit her in the neck as Emma backed away. In no time Katrina fell unconscious from the shock as Shawn sucked her blood. Claudia licked the blood that ran down Katrina's neck and chin.

Emma pleaded, "Please, don't kill her."

Claudia turned to Emma and placed her hands on her shoulders. She stated, "This bitch deserves to die for what she has done to us."

Emma offered, "I'll do anything. Please, don't kill her."

Claudia inquired, "Why do you care so much for her? You are one of us now."

Emma explained, "We are blood sisters."

Claudia smiled fiendishly and said, "How sweet. Hmm. Maybe we can use her for some amusement after all."

Emma repeated, "Please, don't."

Claudia placed her hands on Emma's face as she kissed her. Emma did not fight her advances as Claudia rolled her tongue in her mouth. She turned to Shawn and ordered, "Shawn, don't drain her completely."

Shawn stopped feeding and inquired, "Why? She deserves to die after all."

Claudia placed her hand on his face and said, "It will make Emma very sad if you kill her right now. Besides, we can keep her around for a bit and play with her." She grabbed Katrina's top and tore it open. Claudia started to fondle Katrina's breasts as she said, "She has so much to offer. It would be such a waste, don't you think?"

Shawn agreed, "You have a point there. We could always torture her some more and dispose of her later."

Claudia suggested, "And Emma could join in on the fun," as she licked the blood running down his chin.

Shawn looked at Emma and smiled fiendishly.

Chapter 20
The Message

It was 8:00 p.m. by the time Tula arrived at Telka's shop. She walked in the front room and saw Teresa behind the counter.

Tula was wearing a white tube top, a leather vest, a velvet miniskirt, and leather boots. The cotton tube top hugged her firm breasts like a glove, while accenting her cleavage. Her vest had about four buttons and was worn open. The miniskirt had a black leather belt around it and fastened below her naval. Her boots were high heel and came up to the middle of her thighs. She wore a golden cross and chain around her neck with matching hoop earrings.

Teresa was wearing her fortuneteller's outfit. She said, "It's about time you stopped at the shop, Tula. Sis has missed you."

Tula responded, "I know. I'll make it up to her."

Teresa came around the counter and gave her a hug. She stated, "I'm just glad you are all right, Tula."

Tula agreed, "I'm relieved you are too, Teresa."

Telka walked in from the middle room. She was wearing her fortuneteller's outfit. Telka had a serious look on her face with her hands on her hips. She said, "Tula, when did you get into town?"

Tula turned to her and replied, "A few days ago."

Telka scolded her, "I'm hurt, Tula. You have been in town for a few days and haven't stopped to see me."

Tula had a guilty look on her face as she said, "Sorry, Sis. There is no time."

Telka opened her arms and stated, "There is always time for a hug. Now come here."

Tula listened and hugged Telka as she explained, "I called for a reason, Sis."

Telka let go of her and asked, "What is it, Tula?"

Tula pulled a note out of her pocket as she said, "Katrina told me to deliver this," as she handed it to her.

Telka took the note and remarked, "You are off the hook for now, little sister."

"I'll make it up to you later, Telka," replied Tula.

Telka read the note. It read: *The vampires have Emma. I have gone to save her. I don't have time to explain. Don't try to stop me. You will find me at the Delchor Corporate Building downtown. I have to go this alone. If you don't here from me by the time you read this, call Mike and the others.*

Telka dropped the note in response.

Chapter 21
Bound

A clock on the wall of the torture room read 10:00 p.m. at the Delchor Corporate Building. The torture room was a small room with chains, a sink, and a table. It had one window that could show light in, if the black blinds were open. The white drop ceiling matched the tiled floor and reflected the panel lights in the ceiling. Gray covered the plain cement walls except for a metal rack holding various tools for torturing. In the corner near the door was an electric hoist with a chain fed through a bracket on the ceiling. At the end of the chain was a set of shackles. In another corner was a long metal table. Next to the table was a large metal sink.

Katrina was being held up by chains that were shackled to her wrists. She woke up as she noticed her hands were bound and she was hanging from the ceiling. Her feet dangled at least a foot off the floor as she noticed her body had been stripped down to her panties. All of her clothes and weapons were laid out on the metal table.

Shawn approached her as he said, "Awake are we? Good. The only reason you are still alive is because Claudia persuaded me to stop and the fact Emma practically begged me to."

Katrina remarked, "Lucky for me someone likes me around here." She noticed his scarring on his face and remarked, "The last time I saw you, your face matched. How does it feel to be splashed with holy water?"

Shawn smiled fiendishly as he grabbed her jaw and said, "Of course killing you would be too easy. Too quick. There are far worse things I can do to you than kill you."

Katrina replied, "That's one of my favorite lines and you don't frighten me, Shawn. I have seen better bad-guy intimidation routines in movies."

He punched her in the jaw as he said, "That was for Basil."

She licked the blood from her lip and asked, "What's the matter, coward? Can't beat me unless I'm tied up?"

Anger could be seen in his eyes as he punched her in the gut.

The chains rattled as she swung a few feet away from him by the force of his punch. Katrina swung back and forth until the momentum dissipated and she hung there almost motionless. Blood dripped from her nose as she responded, "How could you? You blood-curdling scumbag."

He grabbed her by the back of her hair and pulled her head back as he inquired, "What are you talking about, bitch?"

Katrina was about to cry when she said, "How could you use such an innocent girl?"

Shawn smirked and answered, "Oh that. Very easily. She will soon be one of us."

Katrina frowned as her arms tensed up in her shackles.

Shawn grabbed her chin and licked the blood off her mouth.

Katrina proclaimed, "Before this night is over you will die by my hand."

He was amused by her bold statement and said, "Is that so? In your weakened state? I figure I drained about half of your blood from your body. Those shackles and chains will hold you no problem." Shawn looked at her body and commented, "Your bite marks, cuts and scratches haven't even healed yet."

Katrina replied, "It doesn't matter. My friends will stop you even if you killed me."

Shawn replied, "Let them try."

She inquired, "You have what you want. What do you want from me?"

Shawn looked at her lustfully and said, "I'm going to make you my pet."

Katrina retorted, "I'll bust your balls first."

Shawn grabbed her neck and said, "Oh, I am going to love breaking you. And so you don't feel so alone, Emma will get to join in. Oh and let's not forget about Teresa. I have plans for her as well."

Katrina gave him a nasty glare as he released his hold on her neck and asked, "What do you mean?"

Shawn explained, "You see, Teresa is going to pay for scarring my face. I thought what better way than to embrace her and keep her around."

Katrina replied, "You're sick."

He continued, "Maybe, but Emma and Teresa will be responsible for keeping you alive. They won't try to escape, but I know you will. You see, if you try to escape, I will kill both of them right in front of you."

Katrina was now afraid, not for herself but for her friends. She replied, "They will never go for that arrangement."

Shawn retorted, "Didn't you know? The will of the master is imprinted on the newly embraced. And it is rare for a new vampire to defy his master, let alone turn on him. Emma must have an exceptionally strong bond with you. That was unexpected. It takes a long time for a new vampire to regain his free will." Shawn placed his hands on her face and said, "I know you care for them both. And you have a lot of spirit, much like your mother."

Katrina inquired, "How do you know my mother?"

He explained, "I know you have been searching for the vampire that killed your mother ever since you were a child." Shawn drew closer to her ear and whispered, "I know, because I killed her."

Katrina jerked on her chains as Shawn said, "So much for avenging your mother's death." Shawn backed up and turned away as the door opened and Claudia entered the room. He stated, "Claudia, she is ready for you."

Claudia walked over to Katrina as Shawn said, "You may play with her now. I must join the others."

He left the room as Claudia smiled at Katrina. She looked at her naked flesh and began fondling her breasts.

Claudia commented, "They are very nice and firm."

Katrina glared at her and spat on her face. Claudia licked the spit off her cheek as she smiled. She slapped Katrina across the face.

Claudia grabbed a black leather whip from the rack and commented, "You are a frisky one. I like that." Claudia rubbed the whip along Katrina's body and remarked, "I will teach you pain and pleasure, slave."

She began to whip Katrina. Katrina's body jerked at the sting of the whip and began to bleed.

She whipped her some more as she said, "Your blood looks so luscious." Claudia whipped her again as Katrina jerked in response to the whip lashing her naked flesh. Claudia came closer to her and licked the blood off her chest.

Evelyn entered the room as Claudia turned in her direction. She was wearing a long-sleeve dress with a matching pair of high-heel shoes. Her hair was let down and flowed when the air caught it. The silky dress was black with puffy shoulders and close-fitting wrists. On the outer part of the wrists was an open crisscross pattern of fabric from the wrists to the forearms. The dress had a low-cut square neckline, revealing the top of her cleavage up to her collarbone. Below the cut of her dress in the center was another pattern of crisscrossing lines of fabric, which showed off more of her accented cleavage and matched the pattern on her sleeves. The dress hugged her torso closely and complemented her figure as it flowed out more below the waist. Around her neck was a wide silky black collar with an oval-cut emerald in the center. It had a smooth finish and went well with her eyes. Golden dangling earrings with round-cut matching emeralds decorated her ears.

Claudia was surprised and asked, "Eva, what are you doing here? I thought you were joining the others."

Evelyn replied, "I came to check on you, lover."

Claudia smiled and said, "How sweet." She went over to Evelyn and kissed her.

Evelyn asked, "What are you doing?"

Claudia answered, "Just having a little fun with our new pet."

Evelyn noticed Katrina's stuff on the table and walked over to it. She picked up Katrina's long blade and looked at it. Evelyn commented, "This blade is finely crafted. Did Shawn leave you behind to watch her?"

Claudia replied, "Yes, she is going to make a fine pet."

Evelyn walked over to Claudia and smiled as she said, "Not if she bleeds you first." Without warning Evelyn stabbed Claudia in the gut. Claudia was stunned by the silver blade as the blood dripped from her wound.

Claudia was shocked and asked, "Why, Eva?"

Evelyn responded, "You bore me, Claudia. It was fun while it lasted, but I was just using you." Evelyn fiendishly smiled as she pushed Claudia into Katrina.

Fangs emerged from Katrina's mouth. She sunk them into Claudia's shoulder. Claudia tried to pull away, but she was too weak, due to the silver blade still in her. Katrina was slowly regaining her strength as she lifted her legs and wrapped them around Claudia's abdomen.

Claudia was trapped as she reached out to air with nothing to grab on to in hopes to pull herself free. Katrina put her into a painful trance as she continued to feed on her. Evelyn crossed her arms and watched her lover suffer in knowing she was being betrayed and being drained by the one she was causing pain to at first.

Katrina finished and let go of her. Claudia fell to the floor, almost lifeless as if all of the life was sucked out of her. Katrina broke her chains as she landed on the floor. She licked her lips, as she felt refreshed. The bite marks on her neck, the lash marks, and the stab wound healed instantly with no scarring. She looked at Evelyn and inquired, "Who are you?"

Evelyn replied, "I am Evelyn, one of the three vampire originals."

Katrina asked, "Why are you helping me?"

Evelyn explained, "The Drenkel Clan seeks to tip the natural balance in this realm. I can't have that."

Katrina was surprised by her answer, "I don't believe this. A vampire elder seeks to keep balance in the realm?"

Evelyn further explained, "You must understand, Katrina, the balance of the realm must be maintained by the ones strong enough to do so." Before Katrina could say any more Evelyn vanished into mist.

Katrina remarked, "Whoa, that's deep." She rolled Claudia over, unzipped her top, and removed it as Claudia asked, "What are you doing?"

Katrina replied, "You owe me a shirt, bitch." She put the top on and zipped it up. It fit her a little tighter as she filled it out more than Claudia.

Claudia stated, "It doesn't matter. Your friend will be one of us soon and the blood queen will be free."

Katrina put on her pants and zipped them up as she said, "That's what you think."

Claudia inquired, "What are you going to do? You don't have a chance against all of us," as Katrina zipped up her boots.

Katrina put on her weapons belt. She pulled the long blade out of Claudia's abdomen and said, "Who said I was going to do it alone? I do have one question though."

Claudia snarled, "I will tell you nothing."

Katrina said, "Oh, this is an easy one. Can a drained vampire fly?" Claudia had a look of horror on her face as Katrina grabbed her by the back of her neck. A few seconds later a window shattered as Claudia was thrown out of it. She fell helplessly below and crashed on the roof of a parked car.

Chapter 22
The Ceremony

It was 10:30 p.m. at Telka's shop where all of Katrina's friends gathered to discuss Katrina's predicament. Nick and Marcus joined Telka in the front room of her shop.

Telka stated, "She can't go this alone. We have to go after her."

Nick was wearing his bounty hunter outfit. He remarked, "If she knew it was a trap, why would she do such a thing?"

Marcus explained, "She has an emotional attachment to the girl. It is her weakness."

Telka commented, "She is half human after all, but why would she leave a note for me?"

"She knows where the vampire lair is," answered Marcus.

Nick confirmed, "It makes sense now. She had to go alone so she wouldn't endanger her friend's life."

Telka stated, "We can follow her directions to the lair."

"They won't be expecting us," remarked Marcus.

Nick agreed, "Let's do it."

Meanwhile, at the Delchor Corporate Building, the preparations were at hand to begin the ceremony. It was 11:00 p.m. and Flusken and the others were assembling on the roof.

The Delchor Corporate Building was a conglomerate made up of four office towers arranged in a square pattern. It was located in the wealthy sector of Vampiro City. The towers were connected by several walkways that joined in the middle of the square, every five floors. On the roofs of the towers was a central walkway platform that connected all four roofs together. At the base of the towers two streets intersected between the buildings. Around each tower was a very wide sidewalk. The whole Delchor Corporate Building was surrounded by other commercial entities as well.

Flusken was dressed in a black silk cloak with a hood over his head. The underlining was red as it draped over his black robe. The sleeves were long and became wider at the ends, compared to the shoulders. Around his neck hung a steel chain with a steel pentagram symbol on it, the size of the bottom of a coffee mug. Wrapped around his waist was a purple sash tied off. Under his cloak was a matching scarf that hung with horizontal folds as it draped across his chest. He wore dark dress pants under the robe with dark slip-on dress shoes.

"It is time," stated Flusken as he led Emma to the center of the platform. Behind Flusken was Carrie carrying the blood gem.

Carrie was wearing a strapless dress, cloak, and boots. The dark green nylon dress was close fitting and complemented her sexy figure, while accenting her firm breasts and cleavage. An upside-down triangle was cut into the center of the front and showed off more of her cleavage. Her arms were covered by sleeves that attached to her arms and spread out more at the wrists. The front of the dress came down to her thighs and spread out longer in the back down to her knees. Her black leather boots were high heel with zippers up the sides and went up to her thighs. The cloak was black nylon and had a hood over her head. It was held together with a small round golden broach, the size of a fifty-cent piece. She wore her silver round flat earrings, a bracelet on her left wrist, a bracelet on her right upper arm, rings on her thumbs, and an anklet on her left boot. Her hair was braided as before with rings in the middle of the braids.

Following Carrie up the metal steps was Morgan, Larrin, Curton, and Shawn, all wearing similar cloaks as Flusken without the purple material.

At the center of the dark metal platform was a large pentagram symbol, cut into it about an inch deep. The symbol was large enough for two people to stand in it with plenty of room in the center.

Flusken stopped and faced Emma in the center of the pentagram. He turned and nodded to Carrie. Carrie knelt down and placed the blood gem in the center of the pentagram between Flusken and Emma. Carrie stood up and back away from them and as she stepped outside the lines of the pentagram.

Flusken commanded, "Now, Emma, activate the blood gem," as he handed her a steel dagger.

The dagger had a double-edged six-inch blade with a black leather-wrapped handle. On the end of the handle was a molded skull with fangs.

Emma took the dagger from him as she knelt down and cut her wrist with the dagger. She held her wrist a few inches over the blood gem as her blood dripped from the cut on to it.

Flusken said, "Only an incomplete vampire or possibly a vampeel can activate the blood gem."

Within seconds it began to glow a bright pink color as it absorbed the blood dripping on it.

Flusken instructed, "That should be enough, Emma. You may stop bleeding now."

"Yes, master," said Emma as she stood up and looked at him. She brought her wrist to her mouth and licked the blood from her wound. The wound healed almost instantly as she licked her lips and enjoyed the taste of her blood. Emma inquired, "Master, when will I be able to feed? I'm so thirsty."

Flusken grinned as he said, "Soon, my dear, soon." He stroked the side of her face as she smiled in agreement. Flusken took the dagger from her, turned to the others and ordered, "It is time, everyone, complete the pentagram and the ceremony will be complete." Morgan, Larrin, and Curton took out daggers from underneath their cloaks. Carrie stood and watched as Flusken and the other vampires cut their palms and allowed their blood to drip into the grooves of the symbol. Their blood flowed from their palms like a gentle pouring of water from a pitcher. As their blood followed the tracks in the platform and completed the symbol, the mixture of blood began to glow. It shimmered in the moonlight like a glow in the dark toy. Everyone stopped dripping blood into the pentagram, stood back, and waited.

Meanwhile, many floors down, Katrina was in a hallway headed towards a square walkway. The hallway was dark and lit partially by some round lights in the brown drop ceiling. Light brown wooden doors were on either side of the dark brown walls. The tiled floor matched the ceiling with a dull look to it.

Her vision was in aura mode as she headed forward. Katrina had her Glocks drawn as she saw a human aura in the walkway. Since she detected no other aura around the human, she lowered her guns as she reset her vision to normal. She recognized it was Mike as she approached him. Mike was dressed in his police uniform.

Katrina inquired, "Mike, what in the realm are you doing here?"

Mike explained, "I got a call from Telka. I just happened to be in the area, so I found my way here."

Katrina inquired, "Where's your partner?"

"She went home, since my shift was over," answered Mike.

Katrina asked, "If you came in from a different tower, how did you get by security?"

"I have my ways," answered Mike.

Katrina remarked, "Well, I only came alone, so that my friend would be safe."

Mike asked, "Is she?"

"There isn't much time. I'll explain on the way to the roof," stated Katrina.

One section of the square donut-like walkway was two street lanes long and a street lane wide. The entire thing was a metal frame with Plexiglas on the two sides and the roof. One could see the city streets from both sides as well as the sky. The walking surface was filled in with wooden boards and covered with flat brown carpet.

They made it across the walkway and headed down another hallway in the other tower. The hallway was semi dark and lit partially by some yellow round lights in the white drop ceiling. Brown wooden doors were on either side of the gray walls. The tiled floor matched the ceiling with a glossy look to it.

Mike inquired, "So what's going to happen on the roof?"

Katrina replied, "A resurrection ceremony of some kind."

Mike asked, "Who are they trying to resurrect?"

"The blood queen," answered Katrina.

Mike had a puzzled look on his face as he said, "Blood queen?"

She explained, "It is a little complicated to explain. All I am going to say is that if we don't stop them, a new terror will be unleashed on humans. It will give vampires the ability to move freely in the daylight."

Mike agreed, "That would be catastrophic. They seem to be a menace in the nighttime as things are now."

Katrina commented, "They would be virtually unstoppable, not to mention a royal pain in the neck."

"I guess we have our work cut out for us," commented Mike.

"I just hope I'm in time to save Emma," said Katrina.

Mike inquired, "What do you mean?"

As they came to a T-junction they turned left, after seeing a sign marked: Elevators. The sign pointed to the left.

Katrina replied, "She's been embraced by one of them."

Mike confirmed, "She's a vampire now?"

Katrina explained, "From what I could sense, she's not a full vampire yet."

"I don't understand," remarked Mike.

"Vampirism is not an infectious disease or curse contracted by a single vampire bite. It is a more involved process than that. First, the vampire drains about three quarters of the victim's blood. Second, the victim drinks about half of the vampire's blood. Finally, the ingested vampire blood mixes with the victim's blood and transforms him into a half vampire," explained Katrina.

Mike asked, "So if your friend is a half vampire, what's the difference?"

She informed, "Half vampires have the strength and sight of a vampire, but they cannot morph. Like full vampires, they have the thirst for blood. They are very dependent on their master, since their own free will is gone. Their free will slowly returns, once they fully change. The funny thing is Emma pleaded for my life, I guess my bond with her was not totally broken."

Katrina found the elevator that appeared to be on line and said, "Here's one we can use." She pressed the up arrow button and waited for the doors to open. As the doors opened Mike replied, "After you."

She smiled and said, "Thank you, Mike."

The elevator was somewhat fancy with brown metal doors, light wallpapered walls, a white-marble-tiled floor, and a light-colored ceiling with an overhead light and an access hatch. To the right of the doors was the control panel with round numbered buttons for every floor. Below the panel was a portable phone in case of an emergency. As the elevator began to ascend Katrina and Mike continued their little discussion.

Mike asked, "So how do they go full circle?"

"They have to drink live human blood to replenish the other quarter of blood they are lacking. They must be keeping her like that for a reason," replied Katrina.

Mike inquired, "Can she be saved?"

"Yes, if she hasn't drunk any blood and I kill her master by dawn, she will change back," answered Katrina.

Mike asked, "Why are vampires in small groups or sometimes alone?"

Katrina explained, "Vampires are very selective with whom they bring into their clan. If someone is not worthy, then they are turned into ghouls instead or killed."

Mike asked, "What's a ghoul?"

Katrina informed, "A ghoul is a vampire's slave. A human that ingests a vampire's blood becomes a ghoul."

Mike inquired, "What's the difference between a ghoul and a half vampire?"

She explained, "Ghouls have the strength of a vampire and can extend their fingernails into claws. They crave blood, but only their master's blood will sustain them. As long as their master sustains them they will never age. Otherwise, they will revert to their true human age and possibly die."

"Oh," responded Mike.

The elevator abruptly stopped as if something was blocking it. Katrina closed her eyes and changed her vision to aura vision. She looked up and saw beyond the elevator ceiling and into the shaft above. All she saw were giant cobwebs and faint auras of something crawling within the shaft.

Mike was concerned and asked, "What is it?"

Katrina answered, "You are not going to believe this."

Mike responded, "Try me."

Katrina replied, "I think we have a pest problem on our hands, like giant spiders."

Mike asked, "Okay, what do you want to do?"

A few spider beasts landed on top of the elevator. The thud was felt by both of them as Katrina suggested, "Let's get out of here."

Mike agreed, "Okay."

Just then the power to the elevator shut down and the lights went out. An emergency power light came on and lit the elevator in a rich orange color. Katrina reset her vision back to normal night vision and said, "Whatever is up there is too big to fit through the access panel."

Mike drew his gun as he commented, "No offense, but somehow that doesn't sound reassuring."

Katrina looked at the doors and remarked; "Don't worry. I'll get the doors open."

Mike asked, "Do you know how hard it is to open a set of elevator doors manually?"

Katrina smiled and replied as she looked at him, "I must have neglected to tell you about my vampiric side."

She pulled out her long blade and placed it between her teeth. Katrina got on her knees and placed her fingertips inside the groove between the doors.

Mike watched as she spread the doors apart effortlessly. The elevator was halfway between floors with the doors open above the current floor. They had two feet of clearance to drop down to the current floor. Mike looked on with amazement as she said, "Hey, take the blade."

Mike took the blade out of her mouth and placed it between the doors. He noticed her fangs as well as the view down her top.

Katrina caught his eye, smiled, and said, "Quit looking at my perky breasts and give me some room."

Mike backed up and replied, "Sorry, I just happened to notice you have fangs."

This hallway looked similar to the hallway many floors below, except at this height of the building nothing could be heard. The place was deserted at this time of night and not even sounds from the streets below could be heard. It was too quiet as if death was present and suffocating the life out of the air.

Katrina bent down to look for any enemies below as Mike inquired, "What are you?"

She answered, "I'm a vampeel. Now let's get out of here, since the hallway is clear." Katrina took her sheathed sword out from her backpack and threw it down to the floor below. She then took off her coat and threw it down to the floor below. Katrina turned around, faced Mike, and said, "Ladies first."

Mike nodded as she lay on her belly and stuck her feet out of the opening. She pushed backward and quickly slid out of the elevator and dropped to the floor below. Katrina landed gracefully on her feet as she stood up and said, "Your turn, Mike."

The elevator began to violently shake as Katrina said, "Come on." Katrina picked up her coat, as Mike was getting ready to come out.

A spider warrior monster drew closer from another hallway. It was a humanoid creature that appeared to be half human and half spider. Its face had the fangs and mandibles of a spider with four round red eyes, two on each side. The rest of its head was still human shaped. Its skin was dark and leathery, almost black with a dim shininess to it. Behind its back were four large spider legs, which sprouted out like an X pattern. It walked on its human legs with the knees slightly bent. The limbs were transformed with claws on every finger and toe. Its clothes were partly shredded as it still wore a pair of pants and shirt of a security guard uniform.

In an instant Mike spotted the spider humanoid monster sneaking up on Katrina from behind and yelled, "Katrina, look out!"

The spider warrior spewed a web line from its mouth at Katrina. Katrina dodged it as she threw her coat at it.

The elevator shook some more as the long blade popped out from between the elevator doors and fell to the floor. Katrina caught the blade as it fell. The elevator doors slammed shut as she yelled, "Mike!"

The spider warrior ripped through her coat and came running towards her. It attacked downward with its two upper spider legs. Katrina dodged both of them as she attacked upward with her long blade. The long blade went under its chin and through the back of its skull. She gritted her teeth as she twisted the blade and pulled it out. The spider warrior ceased to move and fell dead on the floor below. Blood began to spill out of it and covered the floor red.

Mike yelled through the elevator doors, "Don't worry about me, Katrina. I'll be all right. One of us has to get to the roof. Good luck."

Katrina looked at the creature in front of her and commented, "I really did like that coat." She noticed the shredded security guard uniform and pondered, "Why in the realm is this security guard a monster? Vampires usually don't rely on monster creations like this." She picked up her sword and sheathed it as she said, "I don't have time to worry about their origin now. I guess I'll take the stairs." Katrina headed for the staircase and left the floor.

The stairwell was simple with white walls, no windows, dark metal railings, and gray-tiled steps. Katrina wasted no time as she began running up the stairs.

Above the elevator in the tall dark elevator shaft, three spider beasts crawled off of the elevator and scaled the shaft walls. The elevator stopped shaking as Mike thought of what to do next.

Spider beasts were monster spiders, about the size of a bull. They were dark skinned like the spider warriors with larger eyes and fangs. They had four red eyes in the front of the head and two larger ones spaced out more behind them.

Mike commented, "Giant spiders or not I have to get out of here. I guess I better climb out of here and up to an accessible floor." Mike opened a false panel in the elevator and found a portable metal ladder to use. He set it up and stuck it under the access hatch. Mike climbed up and unlocked the hatch. He opened the hatch slightly as he used his flashlight to scan the area. Mike saw a lot of spider webbing blocking the elevator as he scanned around. He saw nothing else around as he fully opened the hatch and looked upward. With the light shining upward he saw three of the spider beasts heading right for him.

"Uh-oh," said Mike as he quickly dropped down and locked the hatch. The spider beasts squealed as two of them dropped on to the top of the elevator. Mike felt the thud of the two as he jumped down from the ladder.

One of the spider beasts clawed at the access hatch, grabbed hold of it and ripped it off its hinges. Mike drew his gun as he aimed at the opening. The one spider beast looked in and saw Mike as it spewed a web line at him. Mike dodged the web line, fired his weapon, and unloaded his clip into its face. Blood dripped into the elevator, as the spider beast appeared to be dead and didn't move.

He reloaded his gun as the other spider beast clawed at the elevator and tried to rip the roof apart. Its claws were slowly ripping the roof apart as if it was made of thin tin foil. Mike was trapped, since the other spider was lying over the access hole.

He holstered his gun and commented, "I guess I am going to have to light things up a bit around here." Mike concentrated as a flame appeared in his hand. He directed it upward and blew apart the dead body of the spider beast blocking the hole. Mike quickly climbed out of the elevator and blasted the other spider beast on top of the elevator. The spider beast caught on fire and fell off of the elevator and down the shaft. As it fell it let out a painful shriek on the way down. He quickly fire blasted the webbing holding the elevator. As the last bit of webbing was burned off the elevator shook free and the tension on the cable tightened. Three more spider beasts crawled down the shaft as they shot web lines at him. Mike carefully dodged them as he fire blasted every one of them. They all fell past the elevator and down the shaft below.

It was 11:30 p.m. by the time Telka, Nick, and Marcus arrived outside of the Delchor Corporate Building. They all got out of her van that was parked in front of the building across the street. They quickly crossed the street and met outside the main entrance. Telka closed her eyes and concentrated as she touched the note that Katrina wrote earlier.

Telka opened her eyes and said, "She is above us."

Nick asked, "Where?"

"She is on the roof. We must hurry," commented Marcus.

Nick stated, "That's one hundred stories up."

Telka interrupted, "I won't slow you down. Go ahead."

Marcus inquired, "You are staying here?"

Telka explained, "I have a feeling that I will be more helpful down here for the time being."

Nick said, "Take care then. I guess we will meet up later. Okay, Marcus, let's go bust some heads."

Marcus nodded as the two took off and flew straight up.

Meanwhile, Telka made it up to the second floor by using the stairs nearby. She followed her instincts and found the elevator shaft that Mike was in.

At the same time Mike had killed the last of the spider beasts in the elevator shaft. The elevator was making a strange creaking noise as Mike noticed the cable on the elevator was breaking. Mike responded, "Uh-oh," as he was about to leap for the ladder on to the elevator shaft, when the cable snapped and the elevator dropped with him still on it.

A tarot card flew into Telka's hand as she commanded, "Whirlwind, come to my aid!" A whirlwind appeared from the card and went in between the elevator doors and straight up the shaft. Within seconds the whirlwind slowed down the elevator in the shaft as Mike was still on top of it.

Mike responded, "What the…?" The elevator was lowered to the second floor as Mike dropped into it.

Another card flew into Telka's hand as she commanded, "I summon Berserker!"

A seven-foot-tall goblin with a solid-type build appeared magically from the card. He had green skin with droopy pointed ears. His eyes were yellow with a strong chin and a dark goatee. He was bald and had golden hoop earrings in both ears. Black leather bands were on his forearms and matched the loose-fitting trousers he wore. Dark brown leather boots that went up to his calves with wide cuffs covered his feet. Around his waist was a dark brown leather belt with a golden buckle.

Telka looked at him and ordered, "Pull the doors open." Without hesitation the goblin pried the doors open effortlessly as Telka said, "You can come out now, Mike."

Mike stepped out under the goblin and said, "How did you know I was in there?"

Telka placed her hands on her hips and replied with a smile, "Mike, I'm a very powerful fortuneteller. I know these things."

Mike came over to her and said, "And beautiful too."

Telka blushed as he embraced her and said, "I owe you one." Before she could say anything else, he kissed her. Telka grinned and stated, "You can pay me back later. How about a bath when we are done here? You look tired."

At that moment his cell phone rang off. Mike backed up and said, "Hold that thought." He grabbed his cell phone and answered it. "Yes," said Mike.

He nodded a couple of times and replied, "I'll be right there." Mike hung up the phone and looked at Telka. Mike said, "I'm sorry, Telka. I really have to go. Could I take a rain check on the bath?"

Telka was disappointed and remarked, "Okay, there's always a next time. Call me."

"Absolutely," replied Mike. As he held her hands and started to walk away he asked, "What was that thing holding the doors open?"

As the elevator crashed to the bottom Telka said, "What thing?"

Mike turned back and saw it was gone.

Telka grinned and said, "He's one of my servants."

The glow of the blood gem intensified as the group on top of the roof watched with anticipation. Everyone was standing outside of the pentagram waiting for the emergence of their blood queen.

Flusken grinned as he said, "Excellent, soon she will be free."

Katrina arrived at the roof from the staircase and quietly ducked behind a large air conditioning unit. She took hold of her Uzi and switched off the safety. With all of their backs facing her, Katrina fired the weapon. Morgan, Larrin, and Curton were in her line of fire and were shot several times, before she emptied her clip.

Flusken noticed the bullets coming and placed an invisible barrier around him. The bullets exploded with fire as they hit his barrier and dissipated in the air.

Carrie reacted soon after Flusken and mentally placed a similar force field around herself. Her force field protected her as well as Flusken's did as she waited for the spray of bullets to stop.

Shawn ducked behind Flusken and was unscathed by the phosphorus bullets.

The bodies of the three combusted immediately as Katrina dropped the clip and reloaded. They shrieked in terror as they were reduced to ashes in a matter of seconds. Flusken and Carrie faced Katrina standing in plain sight.

Carrie crossed her arms and commented, "Phosphorous bullets. Crude but effective."

Flusken turned to Shawn and commented, "What a surprise. It was foolish for me to think you had her under control."

Shawn was in shock as he said, "It can't be. She was weak as a kitten when I left her with Claudia."

"Fool. You underestimated her," remarked Flusken.

Shawn was filled with regret as he looked down and said, "I should have taken care of her when I had the chance."

Flusken waved his hand at her and said, "Go ahead. Take care of her now."

Shawn walked in her direction as he gritted his teeth and noticed the top she was wearing. He asked, "How did you get her top?"

Katrina placed her hands on her hips as she said, "Claudia let me have it, before I tossed her out the window."

Shawn's body grew larger as his clothes disappeared. The color of his skin changed to a light gray as his hands and feet became longer. His head became bald, as his ears grew long and pointy. The nails on his hands and feet became black, longer, and razor sharp. His monster form was complete.

Shawn's eyes glowed red as he replied, "You bitch! I'm going to kill you!"

Katrina smirked and replied, "Promises, promises."

He lunged at Katrina as she fired her Uzi at him. Rage consumed him as he managed to dodge the bullets.

Katrina backed up as he got closer. She emptied the clip as he knocked the gun out of her hand. He struck downward as Katrina leaped above him and dodged his attack. Shawn hit the surface of the roof.

Katrina landed a few feet back from him as she drew her sword. Shawn charged in as Katrina faced him head-on. She sidestepped him and stabbed him right in the heart.

Shawn was stunned as Katrina looked at him and said, "You let your anger get the best of you, Shawn." She twisted the blade as she yanked it out. "Now die like the monster you really are," spouted Katrina.

Shawn was in agony as he burned from the inside out and turned to ashes.

Katrina said, "Now my mother can finally rest in peace."

Flusken clapped his hands as Katrina looked at him. He crossed his arms and stated, "Very good. You have saved me the trouble of disposing of him myself. However, you cannot take us all on. What will you do now, Katrina?"

Katrina grinned and replied, "Who said I was alone?"

Nick and Marcus appeared behind Katrina, where she stood. She looked at them and said, "It's about time you two got here."

Nick commented, "I'm glad to see you're okay, Katrina."

Marcus said, "It pleases me as well to see you alive, daughter."

Katrina smiled as Nick noticed her top and commented, "I like that top. It's sexy."

Katrina smiled and asked, "Really?"

Nick confirmed, "Really."

Flusken inquired, "Marcus, it has been a long time. Are you still sore at me for what happened in the past?"

Marcus stated, "I have severed my ties with you, Flusken, and the clan. Since you are fighting my daughter and her friend, this makes you my enemy."

Flusken asked, "Do you plan on fighting me too, old friend?"

"No, old friend, this one has a bigger bone to pick with you than I do. I just came to watch," answered Marcus.

Flusken agreed, "Fair enough, I'll deal with the young one then." Flusken turned to Emma and ordered, "Emma, kill Katrina."

Emma objected, "But, master."

Flusken yelled as his eyes glowed red, "I said do it! Your will belongs to me."

Emma's eyes glowed red as she replied, "Yes, master."

Carrie grabbed an oriental-looking sword from under her cloak and handed it to Emma. She took hold of it and walked over to Katrina.

Emma clashed swords with Katrina as she said, "Emma, stop this." Emma ignored her as she attacked continuously. Katrina ducked down and foot-swept her. She got up and said, "Emma, I don't want to kill you."

Emma flipped up and replied, "I must kill you, Katrina. My master demands it." Emma slashed at Katrina as she countered and tripped her.

Emma fell backwards as Katrina said, "Emma, we're blood sisters."

"I have a new family now and I cannot defy my master," remarked Emma as she got up. Emma faked an attack and ducked into a foot sweep. Katrina fell down as Emma slashed at her. She rolled out of the way and kicked Emma in the gut. Katrina got up as Emma flew backward from the kick.

She recovered as she slashed downward at Katrina. Katrina sidestepped her and knocked her blade out of her hands. The blade flew over the side of the building. Katrina dropped her sword and said, "Emma, you're not one of them yet. Fight it, Emma. Let me help you."

Emma ducked down and grabbed Katrina's sword and slashed at Katrina with it.

Katrina was furious and said, "Why, you little brat! That's it! This is for your own good!" Katrina dodged her attacks back and forth. Emma slashed at Katrina as she dodged and punched her in the face. She fell unconscious on the roof as Katrina knelt by her and held her. Katrina said, "Sorry, Emma."

Nick and Flusken faced each other. Flusken commented, "This night has been anything but boring. Prepare to be sacrificed to the blood queen."

Nike looked at Flusken and said, "Not without a fight, you demented parasite."

Flusken asked, "Do I know you from somewhere in the past?"

Nick explained, "You were the one who killed my lover right in front me a long time ago."

Flusken inquired, "So, you have been searching for me all this time just to avenge the death of your frail lover? Why would you do such a foolish thing?"

Nick said, "I was offered a chance to transcend death in order to face you again. It became an obsession to become strong enough to face you once again."

Flusken asked, "You wanted to fight me evenly matched. Hmm. Could you be the bounty hunter that I left for dead two centuries ago?"

Nick pulled his mask off. As it dropped to the roof he said, "Let's finish this. You killed my lover long ago. I have come back to settle the score."

Flusken finally recognized him and said, "Ah, yes, it is you after all. You did this all for love. How pathetic. Love makes humans weak and it has made you weak."

Nick replied, "You're wrong. Love makes us strong. I have nothing else to live for."

Flusken stated, "Then you will die foolishly, bounty hunter. For the only way to defeat me is if you have mastered all the gifts of a vampire and your hatred for me consumes you."

Nick said, "We shall see."

Flusken asked, "Who is your master?"

Nick replied, "Brandilla Catholom."

Flusken was surprised and said, "Interesting, she has turned against me and made you a tool of vengeance."

Nick said, "Leave her out of this. I am what I am by my own accord."

Flusken replied, "It doesn't matter. I will not be denied what I have worked so hard for."

Nick proclaimed, "Brandy is the one I can thank for this moment tonight. She won't be disappointed."

Flusken stated, "Well then, prepare to defend yourself, bounty hunter. For our battle will not be done with swords, fists, or guns. We shall fight as real vampires do, with our powers." Flusken leaped into the air and flew over to a building construction site nearby. Nick leaped in the air and followed him.

The construction site was a tall steel-girder building with no walls, but plenty of steel, concrete, pipes and bricks lying around.

Flusken mentally lifted a wooden water tower and threw it at Nick. Nick was at least twenty feet away from him as he saw the water tower approaching. He spun vertically as the water tower came closer. Nick burrowed through the water tower as if he were a drill. The water tower blew apart as pieces of wood and metal fell on the ground below.

Flusken commented, "Not bad."

Nick responded, "That was nothing."

Flusken mentally lifted a section of a brick wall. He broke the wall down into smaller pieces and bricks as he hurled the wall fragments at Nick. Nick dodged the bricks and pounded the larger chunks into dust.

As the bricks tumbled on the ground below Nick asked, "Is that all you got?"

Flusken said, "Try this."

Flusken mentally picked up a couple of steel girders and hurled them at Nick like giant steel arrows. Nick turned into mist as the girders passed through. Nick reformed when it was clear.

Flusken commented, "You are stronger than I thought."

Nick remarked, "You are overconfident."

Flusken pulled out a dagger from his cloak and said, "Let's see how you deal with this." Flusken threw the dagger directly at Carrie. Carrie watched the battle intently as she saw something coming her way. Her eyes got big as she realized too late the object was aimed at her. The dagger hit her in the abdomen as she hunched over.

Carrie said in disbelief, "Why, Flusken? Why? I thought you loved me," as she fell off the platform to her death below.

Nick frowned as he said, "You coward. She had nothing to do with this."

Flusken stated, "She refused my gift of immortality. At that moment my love or compassion for her died within me. She marked herself as expendable."

Nick remarked, "You are sick. You cannot turn off feelings like that."

Flusken commented, "And you do not possess the ability to use the last vampiric gift." Flusken looked over at Katrina and Emma and said, "Whom should I kill next to prove my point of how you can't defeat me?" He mentally pulled on the platform over the towers. As the supports began to twist and break apart Nick looked on in horror as the platform was separating, like a jigsaw puzzle in the air.

Katrina and Emma were still on the tower as they began to slip on one side of it. Nick threw a few daggers at Flusken as he quickly raced in the air to save Katrina. Flusken blocked the daggers mentally as the platform began to break apart and fall off the one side.

Katrina grabbed Emma as they fell off the platform. Nick said, "Katrina!"

as he flew back to her as fast as he could.

Katrina grabbed on to the ledge of the building, while she had an arm around Emma's waist.

Nick descended and landed on the ledge above Katrina. He grabbed her hand and pulled them both up effortlessly.

As they stood up Nick looked at her with concern and asked, "Katrina, are you all right?"

Katrina replied, "I'm fine. Get that coward before I do."

Nick said, "Okay."

Flusken mentally picked up a bunch of metal pipes with a diameter of about two inches. He hurled the pipes at Nick like a volley of arrows.

Katrina saw the pipes, before Nick did, and yelled, "Look out!"

Nick was surprised as he faced the incoming pipes. He extended his right hand as his eyes glowed red. The incoming pipes were stopped in midair, within a foot of touching him. Katrina looked on with amazement. Without warning a dagger flew past the pipes and hit Nick in the chest. He was stunned as he lost concentration and the pipes fell on the roof. Nick fell backward as if he was dead.

Nick lay on his back as Katrina had a look of horror on her face. Katrina knelt down over Nick and said, "No!"

Flusken remarked, "Fool. You only learn when it is too late. A vampire can only focus on one kind of object at a time when using telekinesis."

Katrina pulled the dagger out of him. She lightly pounded on his chest and said, "You big dummy! You didn't have to help me!" She began to cry as she looked at his face and confessed, "You can't die on me, Nick! I need you."

Flusken laughed as he remarked, "Parting is such sweet sorrow. Soon the blood queen will be free and the realm will be ours. Your compassion for this half breed has made you weak and cost you everything." Flusken was still too far away to notice any movement from Nick, while Katrina was blocking his view.

Katrina looked up at Flusken and glared at him. Her eyes glowed red as she grabbed for her gun.

Nick grabbed her arm, as he said, "Don't get mushy on me now, Katrina."

Katrina was surprised as she looked back at him and said, "Nick?"

Nick stated, "We'll talk later. I have a new reason to live now. It's time to swat this bothersome fly," said Nick as he winked at her. Nick stood up as Flusken watched in disbelief.

Flusken yelled, "It can't be! I killed you!"

Nick explained, "You missed my heart by two inches, you old fossil. Your arrogance has made you sloppy." He mentally picked up the pipes and hurled them back at Flusken. Flusken prepared to block the incoming pipes as Nick quickly grabbed Katrina's Uzi.

"Time to fry, scumbag!" said Nick as he fired at Flusken. The phosphorus bullets zoomed past the pipes as Flusken focused on the pipes instead. Nick emptied the clip as the bullets penetrated Flusken's body. Flusken was consumed by the phosphorus and burned uncontrollably.

All this time the blood gem was still on a piece of the platform that didn't fall off. Blood flowed out of the blood gem and poured on one of the other roofs below. As the blood continued to flow it started to take shape, instead of becoming a puddle. By the time blood had stopped flowing a crimson silhouette of a female was formed and lay on the roof.

She opened her eyes, which had an eerie yellow glow to them, as she sat up and looked around. The blood on her naked flesh flowed off of her body and into her mouth. Her lovely golden-brown skin was revealed as her jet-black hair instantly grew out of her bald head. Her lovely hair parted in the middle and grew outward down to her neck with jagged ends. She got to her feet as she looked at her body and smiled.

The female figure stood about five feet eleven inches tall with a toned-type build and larger-than-average-sized breasts. A white-colored dress with a matching cape magically appeared on her body. The silky dress had sleeves with slits up the sides that went down to her elbows. A slit went down either side of the bottom of the dress and touched her ankles. Her fingernails and toenails became a crimson color and matched her luscious lips. On her wrists and ankles golden bans with various jewels appeared. Her ears were magically decorated with dangling earrings that matched her bans. The dress fit her loosely and flowed in the wind with many vertical folds and wrinkles. Around the waist her dress fit closely with a cloth belt tied off. Her cape was attached to her shoulders with a very high collar that stood up on its own. The front of the dress was open like a V and flowed down to her waist. Her firm breasts could be partially seen in the middle unsupported.

Flusken saw her and remarked, "It is too late. I may die, but the blood queen lives." Flusken's body totally burned up and became scattered ashes.

Katrina noticed the female figure rising in the air and said, "What the...?"

Marcus commented, "We're too late. She is here."

Chapter 23
The Blood Queen

The blood queen was free as she floated in midair with her cape waving behind her. She was excited as she remarked, "Free at last!"

At that moment Emma woke up. Emma turned to Katrina and asked, "Katrina, what's going on?"

Katrina helped her stand up and inquired, "Emma, is that really you?"

Emma confirmed, "Of course it's me, Katrina."

Katrina smiled, placed her hands on Emma's shoulders, and stated, "We'll talk later. We have to take care of her first."

The blood queen looked around at the city and was amazed at what she saw. She commented, "The realm has changed dramatically since I have been imprisoned. A realm with a new face to conquer as I see fit."

Katrina put her hands on her hips and spoke up, "Not if I have anything to say about it."

Nick inquired, "Who are you, anyway?"

She turned to them and said, "Very well. I will tell you, before I annihilate you all. For centuries vampires have been searching for a way to protect themselves from sunlight. Centuries ago, a dark priest made a deal with a certain vampire. The dark priest then summoned a particular demon. That demon mated with the vampire and she bore a child. I was that child born from that demon. I am half vampire and half demon and I have the best of both realms. I possess the powers of a demon and the skills of a vampire. My blood will free the vampiric kind from their restriction to the night."

Katrina remarked, "If vampires could walk in the daylight, no human would be safe."

She agreed, "You are correct. Before I could do such a task, the high priests trapped me in a magical prison. I have been waiting there ever since. Now I will have my revenge. I am Cassandra, the blood queen!"

Nick sarcastically commented, "I hope she is finished. My ear is ready to fall off."

Cassandra fired a lightning bolt at the party. Telka came on the scene and created a force field with her ring.

Nick remarked, "I thought you weren't coming."

Telka said, "Mike was in trouble and I saved him, before he had an urgent call and had to leave. I felt you might still need my help."

Katrina said, "Well, thanks for coming, Telka."

Telka asked, "What are we going to do, Katrina? I can't hold back her attacks forever."

Katrina stated, "She can't attack us all at once. Nick, Father, could you attack her from opposite sides?"

Nick said, "That might work."

Marcus agreed, "Yes, it is worth a try."

Nick and Marcus flew at her from opposite sides. She noticed their approach and remarked, "Your tactics are flawed." Cassandra flung huge fireballs at Nick and Marcus. Nick was knocked back into a building behind him. Marcus was knocked back as he deflected the fire with a force field.

Telka had a card in her hand and commanded, "I summon Ice fairies!"

Three ice fairies magically emerged from the card. They were all about three feet high with slender builds and petite breasts. Their skin was pale with a bluish tint, while their eyes were clear blue, like an icy lake in the winter. Ocean blue was the color their long hair. Their ears were slightly pointed, like elves. Light blue was the color of their lips and nails. Their bodies were covered in a sleeveless dress that went down to their thighs. The silky white dresses were quite conservative with a U-cut neckline and shoulder straps. They complemented their figures with a loose-fitting look and a few folds as their bottoms fluttered in the wind. On their backs were butterfly-like wings that were transparent and almost as big as they were.

They quickly flew up to the blood queen and encircled her. Before she could react the ice fairies breathed their frosty breath on her. Within seconds they encased her in a huge block of ice. Gravity pulled on the huge block of ice as it fell to the roof of the tower everyone was on.

Without warning the block of ice shattered and the shards went in every direction. The ice fairies flew in to attack her again. Cassandra cast a wall of flame at them and they disappeared in the fire as it dispersed.

Nick grabbed the back of her and snapped her neck. She was stunned for a second as Marcus appeared in front of her and stabbed her in the chest with a sword.

Cassandra asked, "Is that all you got?" Marcus and Nick were surprised as she grabbed Nick by the arm and flung him away from her. She mentally repelled Marcus as he was sent flying backward. Cassandra placed her hands on her head and cracked her neck back into place. She looked at Katrina and Telka as she pulled the sword out of her.

Cassandra commented, "Fools, he stabbed me an inch below my heart."

Katrina had her Glocks drawn as she fired silver bullets from them. Cassandra became mist as the bullets passed right through her. Katrina was a little surprised as both of her Glocks were out of ammo and with the barrels slid open.

Cassandra crossed her arms and said, "Amateurs. I am having fun toying with you."

Katrina was beside Telka as she inquired, "Telka, do you have a monster that you can summon that is impervious to her attacks?"

Telka replied, "I'm not sure."

Katrina said, "It doesn't have to kill her. We just need something to delay her so we can regroup, otherwise Marcus and Nick are going to be caught out in the open as the sun rises."

Telka thought as a card flew into her hand. She said, "I have just the thing." Telka held the card out in front of her and commanded, "I summon Golem!"

Before their eyes an eight-foot-tall rock golem magically emerged from the card. It had yellow glowing eyes and was colored a sandy brown.

Telka ordered, "Get her." The golem acknowledged her order with a nod and headed in Cassandra's direction.

Cassandra commented as the golem approached, "What do we have here? Another monster summoned by the fortuneteller?" She noticed the others were fleeing to a maintenance shed on the roof. Cassandra said, "Come back here and quit delaying the inevitable."

As the golem approached she flung two huge fireballs at it. The fireballs dispersed as soon as they hit it. It kept her attention as she tried to use more of her fire attacks on it. The battle between Cassandra and the golem had carried over into Saturday as the sun began to rise off the distant horizon.

Nick looked at his watch as it read 6:00 a.m. While the blood queen was still distracted, the whole group assembled in a shed on the roof.

Marcus closed the door of the shed as they gathered around. Marcus commented, "This doesn't look good. The sun will be up soon."

Nick asked, "Telka, can't you use your sunlight card to blind her temporarily?"

Telka replied, "No, it won't work now. It is one in a group of cards that can't be used during the daytime."

Katrina had an idea and said, "That's it."

Telka asked, "What do you mean?"

Katrina explained, "She has been in that prison for so long in darkness. The sunlight will be too much for her to adjust to and may blind her. That will be our opening to strike."

Telka said, "Katrina, Marcus and Nick will be vulnerable."

Katrina stated, "I know, but we don't have much choice."

Marcus asked, "How are we going to kill her?"

Telka replied, "A silver blade will kill a demon as effectively as a vampire."

Katrina remarked, "Then we have a chance."

Cassandra blasted a hole in the wall of the shed. The group was stunned by the blast.

Cassandra stated, "Fun time is over. Accept your fate. Serve me or die!"

Marcus charged at Cassandra and said, "Never!" Cassandra blocked his attack and speared him with her claws.

Katrina was surprised and yelled, "Father!"

Marcus held on to her throat as he said, "Forget about me. Use your sword and kill her!"

Cassandra remarked, "You have made your last mistake. Your efforts will be in vain."

Marcus retorted, "That's what you think," as he mentally caused the wall behind him to crumble. The rays of the sunlight showed through the hole. Nick ducked out of the way into a corner from the rays of sunlight showing through.

Cassandra was stunned by the brightness of the sunlight as she dropped Marcus.

Marcus fell and said, "I will always love you, Katrina."

Katrina screamed, "Father! No!" as she watched him burn to ashes.

Cassandra covered her eyes and turned around. She said, "That accursed light is unbearable!"

Katrina drew her sword as Cassandra spun around and broke through the floor. She descended a few floors below as Katrina proclaimed, "Oh no you don't! You're not getting away from me ever!" She jumped down the hole after her.

A few floors below Katrina landed into an empty room. The room had a white drop ceiling with a white-tiled floor to match it. Gray was the color of the plain drywall as it looked like the room was still under construction. Panel lights partly lit the room, since only half of them were on and the rest were missing fluorescent bulbs.

Cassandra surprised her from behind and knocked her over. Katrina was stunned as she dropped her sword and hit the floor hard. Cassandra kicked her in the gut and watched her roll away from her. Katrina tried to gain some ground as Cassandra picked her up by the throat with her left hand. She stated, "You have caused me a lot of trouble. It is too bad that we are not on the same side. I admire your determination though, so I will give you a quick death."

Katrina looked her in the eyes and remarked, "You're forgetting one thing."

She grabbed a needle from her belt as Cassandra asked, "What is that?"

Katrina stuck the needle into her chest and said, "Demons are affected by holy water also, bitch!"

Cassandra dropped her as she quickly pulled the needle out, before it could inject her with it. Katrina quickly grabbed her long blade and stabbed her in the heart. Cassandra backed up as she shrieked in pain. Katrina watched as Cassandra's body disintegrated and left nothing behind, but her long blade.

At this time everyone left the shed and were making their way down the building. Inside the shed Marcus's body miraculously reformed. He was naked as Kescha appeared from the shadows.

She was wearing a sleeveless dress with matching high-heel boots. Her lavender nylon dress had a short collar that stuck straight up as it opened into a wide V down to her belt. The dress went down to her ankles with slits up both sides to her thighs. Her firm breasts were unsupported as the material clung to them. The open V of the front showed off her cleavage and the centerline of her torso. On her hands were matching gloves that looped on her middle fingers and thumbs, while going up to her upper arms. Her boots were calf length and had zippers that went up the sides. Around the waist of her close-fitting dress was a raspberry-pink nylon belt with a red heart in the center. The red heart matched the color of her lips, fingernails, and her small round earrings. Her hair was down and free-flowing.

Kescha effortlessly picked him up and commented, "You have had a busy night, Marcus. It was entertaining to watch. I guess it wasn't necessary for me to intervene after all. Oh well, no news to report to the master. The dark priest gave up on searching for the blood gem a while ago. All is not lost, except for a few more members of the Drenkel family."

Chapter 24
Loved Ones

It was Sunday around 4:00 p.m. at Catholom Gardens, the largest cemetery in Vampiro City. It was the oldest cemetery in the city that existed even before the city was established. Located in the workingman sector of the city, it stretched for miles to the edge of town. A gray stone wall about four feet high surrounded the cemetery with a sign to the right of the main gate. The sign was made from a dark marble plaque and read: Catholom Gardens.

Katrina's car pulled up to the cemetery and parked on the street in front of the cemetery. She stepped out of the car and entered the cemetery.

Katrina was wearing a black dressy outfit, consisting of a blazer, a skirt, and a pair of high-heel dress shoes. The polyester blazer was close fitting with three golden buttons in the middle, while the skirt was knee length with a slit up the one side for easier movement. Under the blazer she wore a black tank top. Around her neck she wore a silver chain with a small silver cross that hung down to her cleavage. She was wearing her same dangling silver earrings as before. Dark sunglasses covered her eyes, as her hair was loose and draped over her shoulders. A matching leather purse hung over her shoulder and completed the outfit. In her one hand she was carrying a red rose.

As she entered the cemetery the pathway was wide enough to drive a car and was made of stones, pieced together like a puzzle. The cemetery had many other pathways with various tombstones of sizes and shapes, surrounded by green grass. In some areas there were stone monuments with doors leading underground, dating back to the age of monarchy. Only the wealthy had the privilege of having a private underground room to store their coffin.

Katrina walked for at least a quarter of a mile before she stopped at a particular grave. She pulled a white handkerchief from her purse and placed it in front of the tombstone. As she knelt down on the handkerchief she placed the red rose on the ground in front of the tombstone. She looked at the tombstone as she removed her sunglasses.

The tombstone was about two feet high with a rounded top. The engraving read: *Here lies Rachael Herrick. Loving mother and wife.*

Her eyes were sad, but she did not cry as she touched the tombstone with the palm of her hand.

Katrina said, "I miss you, Mother. I should be angry with you for not telling me about him. I'm sure you had your reasons, but I forgive you. He is probably with you right now, but for some strange reason I can still feel his presence. At least now your spirit can finally be at peace. Someday you and I will be reunited. Until that day comes, my battle with the forces of darkness will not end."

At that point Katrina got up and took the handkerchief. She placed it in her purse as she started to walk away. Katrina paused and remembered something as she turned around. She smiled as she faced the grave again.

Katrina said, "By the way, I have a new man in my life." She put her sunglasses back on and left.

Printed in the United States
92271LV00005B/97-111/A